FIRES

SIMON AND SCHUSTER
NEW YORK

This book is a work of fiction. Any resemblance to actual people or events is coincidental.

Copyright © 1980 by Robert Reiss
All rights reserved
including the right of reproduction
in whole or in part in any form
Published by Simon and Schuster
A Division of Gulf & Western Corporation
Simon & Schuster Building
Rockefeller Center
1230 Avenue of the Americas
New York, New York 10020

Designed by Irving Perkins
Manufactured in the United States of America
1 2 3 4 5 6 7 8 9 10

Library of Congress Cataloging in Publication Data

Reiss, Bob.
    Summer fires.

    I.   Title.
PZ4.R377Su [PS3568.E517]   813'.5'4   79-17642

ISBN 0-671-24655-0

*A very special thanks to Jonathan Coleman,
Deborah Katsh, Esther Newberg,
Ruth Ravenel and Curt Suplee.*

To my parents, with love and gratitude

ONE

THE SMALL boy raced across the darkened construction lot, one hundred yards past the barbed wire and "KEEP OUT" sign, thirty from the door to the building, the Doberman pinscher in his wake—a big dog, all muscle and jaw. There was no way to get back to the gate.

The tower ahead was high, fifteen stories, with scattered construction debris, a concrete mixer, and a small empty trailer at its base. The rising silver moon was pierced by TV aerials. The street outside was black and deserted. Not even a car had gone by in twenty minutes. There was the snap of jaws behind. The building was getting closer and he reached out and, amazingly, *the door opened* and he was inside, bolting it, and even as he leaned, heaving, against the barrier, listening to the insane howling on the other side and the animal hurling itself against the wood, which shuddered but held, he knew that he'd never get out of here tonight—that the workmen would find him in the morning. From now on he'd leave stealing plumbing to the pros, but at least he'd escaped the dog.

He began to shake. It was going to be a long night.

Carlos Perez turned and looked up.

What he saw was awesome, and he went white with fear.

TWO

THE MAN in the dark suit said, "I see the ship." He turned to the pilot and pointed, squinting. They had been flying east since dawn, into the rising sun and along the coastal ranges of the Mediterranean. Below, anchored lazily in a sun-drenched cove and surrounded on three sides by steeply tiered cliffs, was a large yacht. The pilot saw it and nodded. The little plane dipped effortlessly to begin a circular glide toward the unruffled sea.

They had seen no sign of life for the past twenty minutes. The face of the man in the dark suit was an expressionless oval, as undisturbed as the expanse of cobalt-blue sea and sky sandwiching the little aircraft. He was Oriental, maybe forty-five, clean-shaven, with a pinched mouth

11

slightly depressed at the edges, as if its owner spent a great deal of time in corporate boardrooms. His thick hairline was moist with sweat he seemed not to notice, the intelligent almond eyes concentrating on the scrubby hills sweeping past. The suit was expensive, conservative and crisply pressed, the tie knotted even in the Eurasian heat. The fingers were manicured, tapping every few moments on an attaché case wedged between his leg and the door, away from the pilot. His eyes scanned the countryside carefully, suddenly focusing on something that startled him.

The pilot said, "I saw it too. A flash. Probably nothing but I'll check." He spoke into the radio, then said, "Could have been mica in the sun. There's a lot of that here."

The passenger remained silent and turned his attention back to the yacht, where the deck, which moments before had been placid, was now the scene of frantic activity. The plane had been spotted. Men in white were rushing to the bow and lowering a small speedboat to the water. Seeing this, the Oriental gave a slight sound of approval, reached down and put the attaché case in his lap, fingers drumming on it to reassure him it was there.

"Forty seconds," the pilot said. The plane circled for the final time and began racing along several feet above the sea. A dolphin broke the surface ahead, then plunged out of sight as the pontoons hit the water, sending up a dazzling spray which was instantly left behind. The speedboat had detached itself from the ship and, nose in the air, was racing toward them. The man with the attaché case watched the diamond hue of its wake and said, "Fifty minutes until the planes arrive. I have time for a swim."

He waited calmly as the launch approached, slowed and drifted toward his door. A sandy-haired sailor waved and reached to help him out of the plane but, frowning, the man in the dark suit instantly realized he did not recognize the second man in the speedboat, a clean-cut, swarthy sailor, young, maybe Italian. Lebanese? There was a deference in the sailor's posture, but his eyes were flecked with nervousness. They cleared. The man in the dark suit opened the door himself as the sandy-haired man started singing. " *'New York, New York, it's a wonderful town.'* Have a nice trip, Mr. Trench?" He had a cockney accent and he was a big, taut man, tan and muscular.

Trench nodded and smiled, then moved with surprising grace from the plane to the boat, clutching the attaché case all the while. When the transfer was completed he stood up, put one hand on a railing to steady himself, looked the Englishman full in the face and said, *"How is he?"*

The Englishman waved to the pilot, who was steering the plane toward the shore. "Fine, sir. Drinking a bit the last few days but we've been keeping him sober. Even took a swim yesterday . . . *don't get mad* . . . I went with him. No danger there. We saw a shark, bloody fucker. Saroyan shot it." The Englishman indicated the new crew member standing nearby. "We needed a replacement because Woods got sick. It was a damn good shot."

Trench turned to scrutinize the new man. "Excellent marksman, eh?" His voice was soft but not gentle and he kept his eyes on the man's hands.

"Yes, sir," the sailor replied.

"Drive the boat."

"Yes, sir."

The yacht grew larger as they approached. Soon it dwarfed the speedboat. "Welcome back, Mr. Trench," a deckhand called, throwing a ladder over the side. The two sailors waited for the Oriental to precede them onto the deck but he said to the new one, "You go first." After the swarthy sailor had done so, Trench hefted himself with quick, easy pulls onto the ship. From where he now stood the nearby hills seemed steeper. Shading his eyes, he caught sight of the search party the pilot had dispatched, picking its way along the rocky cliffs. With short, powerful strides he crossed the deck and entered the main cabin, a huge, bright, comfortable room filled with glass cases of tiny sea artifacts: shells, coral, doubloons. Everything sparkled. A black butler stood by the doorway and extended his hand for the attaché case. Politely but firmly, Trench shook his head.

"Lunch will be ready in thirty-five minutes," the butler said. "We couldn't get fresh lobster so cook decided on crab. Is that satisfactory? Hearts of palm and strawberry shortcake. Seven places. Would you like a drink?"

"No thank you." Trench continued past, glancing into the dining room as he did so. Sun flooded in through portholes to dance on the wineglasses and well-polished brass, creating a midday pattern of shadows on the teak floor. A portrait of an Oriental woman in a rice field hung above the head of the table. He nodded at a waiter setting places, then continued along various lengthy hallways which brought him, finally, to a shuttered door, his own cabin. He locked the door behind him and crossed a dense carpet to a painting of a factory. Sliding the painting aside, he turned the dial of a safe several times until the bolts clicked. The compartment inside was filled with securities he didn't examine at all. Instead he turned away from the safe, still holding the attaché case, and moved behind a large mahogany desk. He reached beneath the desk, twisted the handle of a drawer to a vertical position, then returned to the safe. Grasping the sides of the safe, he pulled the entire box from the wall, revealing another, deeper compartment behind. He pushed the attaché case into this space, replaced the safe, closed it and covered it again with the painting.

14

Trench then changed into a bathing suit and white terry-cloth robe, checked his watch and left the cabin, retracing his steps toward the deck. When he neared the dining area, however, he turned into a conference room, again locking himself in. The room was expensive, a lengthy rectangular table at its center and large crystal chandelier overhead. The walls were soundproofed with Russian oak, the ridge-backed chairs well cushioned. Normally he would complete the upcoming task with the help of the Englishman, but Trench was suspicious of the way the sailor had greeted the plane. He began in one corner, systematically running his hands under the table and chairs, the cushions, the portholes. His eyes surveyed the walls. He stood on a chair to reach the light fixture, then peered intently at each of the prisms. He ran his hand along the glass. Five minutes passed. When he was satisfied, he pressed an intercom switch and said, "Mr. Ravenel to the conference room." Moments later there was a polite knock and the English sailor entered, wearing a white tee shirt which bulged and tapered from the shoulders to the waist. Trench's voice was cold, suspicious and disapproving. "Why did you bring the new man to the plane? Had you checked him out *that carefully?*"

The color drained from the sailor's face. His body went rigid and his breathing quickened. Trench's stare bore into the terrified man for a full thirty seconds before he said, "Don't do it again. You will not be paid for a month and someone else will swim with me. I think it was a mistake." He paused. "Stay here until the guests arrive. No one comes in before." He turned, never quite taking his eyes from the drooping, relieved figure behind him, and left.

Emerging into the light on deck, he checked the time again. A hundred yards off the port bow the search party was rowing back, empty-handed. So, there had probably been no one there. He shrugged, shed his robe, beckoned

15

a sailor to swim with him and dived into the water, cutting the surface as precisely as he dressed, taking pleasure in the perfection of the dive, in the angle, in the speed, in the coolness and clarity of the water. A blue damselfish drifted by into the boat's shadow, and he cooed with delight. Under the water it sounded like a gurgle. He loved pretty things.

Twenty minutes later the other planes began arriving, swooping down along the cliffs for landings. Clad in a fresh dark suit, Trench watched from the railing as the launch picked up the first passenger and conveyed him back to the yacht. He too was dressed conservatively and his mouth had the same humorless expression as his host's. He shook Trench's hand briskly and said, "Where is he?"

Trench spread his hands and allowed a slight smile to play on his lips. "Lunch first," he said. "Did you have a nice trip?"

The guest looked preoccupied, doubtful. "I don't know," he said. "I have to be in Athens by eight." He looked at his watch, then gazed out at the passenger getting out of the second plane. His tone changed, becoming more pleasant. "My, my," he said. "Is that who I think it is? You must have something very sweet indeed."

The launch brought back more visitors. Some knew each other by name, others only by reputation. A servant guided them to the dining room. Finally the launch arrived with the last of the guests, a man and a woman. The man was burly, well dressed, the sun glinting off rings on his fingers, the hair thick, curly and red. His companion was a tan, leggy blonde with cascading hair and high cheekbones who looked wide-eyed at Trench as they pulled up. Trench gazed down at them, particularly at the woman, angrily. The redhead did not seem to catch his mood.

"Hello, you damn gook," he called, and gave the hearty laugh of a big American. "Long time no see, eh? Not since Seoul." He turned to his companion. "Honey, say hello to Wot Chow Trench, richest Korean in the world. A *billionaire!* Trench, this is Candy, mainstay of my domestic tranquility! Ha! Candy!" He pinched her and she squealed, then pretended to threaten him with the big bag on her arm.

Trench watched the playfulness without changing expression. He said, "Welcome, Congressman," then bowed to the girl after helping her on deck. His smile didn't extend beyond his mouth. "You are probably tired and thirsty," he said. "Some refreshment after a hot ride? My mate will show you where you can wash."

"Are you really a billionaire?" the girl ogled.

The congressman howled. "Honey, would I *lie* to you? Would I tell you a story? Get along. We got some talking to do." He slapped her butt. Then, to Trench, as the girl wriggled away, "Long way from Benson, South Carolina! What a piece! I found her in Istanbul." He pumped Trench's hand. "How ya' been?"

Trench seemed unaffected by the congressman's good spirits. He waited until the girl was out of sight, then asked quietly, "Why did you bring her?"

The congressman waved the question away. "Oh, hell. She's just a little honey secretary I met in Istanbul. Harmless enough. No brains, but what an ass."

"I told you to come alone," the Korean said.

"Oh, I just thought I'd show her a good time on the plane. Don't you worry now. Just give her a big ole lounge chair in the sun and she'll forget we're alive."

"But," repeated Trench, "*you were told to come alone.*"

This time the congressman realized his indiscretion. There was a pause, and his face colored. "Well, golly, Trench, I guess I didn't understand how important it was."

17

"No," said Trench icily, "perhaps you didn't." He glanced thoughtfully at a doorway through which the blonde had disappeared. "Anyway, we have things to talk about. You like seafood?"

The congressman seemed relieved at the change in subject. "Love it," he drawled.

"Good. I think you'll like my other guests. They're already waiting for us." Turning, Trench moved across the deck, leading rather than accompanying the congressman through the hatch, along the hallway and into the dining room. The others were already seated.

The congressman said, "Sorry I'm late, gentlemen. Peter Macklinburg from South Carolina." He shook hands all around, then Trench sat and signaled the waiter. The glasses were filled with wine and the meal commenced, marked by general ease and light conversation, although one of the guests kept glancing at his watch. After a while, looking up at the painting on the wall, the congressman said, "Who's the lady, Trench?"

"My mother."

"Hmmmmm. Attractive. And what's that behind her, a field? I didn't know you were a farm boy, too. Bet you got her in some goddamn palace now in Switzerland. Huh? With servants."

"No, not really."

"You don't mean she still lives *there?*"

"No," said Trench. "She was killed during the war. By the Communists."

The congressman looked at his plate. When everyone had finished eating, cigars were passed around and, although the men continued to joke and chat, all but the host seemed to grow markedly restless. Finally Trench rose as the waiters were clearing the table, and as if that move were a signal, the others pulled back their chairs too.

"Now," Trench said, "I have something I believe you

would all like to see. Please come with me." He led them to the conference room, where the Englishman was still on duty, motioned the guests to their seats and told the sailor to watch the door outside. He signaled the guests to remain where they were and left the room, returning several minutes later with the attaché case.

"I returned from New York this morning," he said. "I'd like to show you what I brought back with me."

He opened the case and extracted six identical, thin files which he distributed around the table. There was a brief silence as the men concentrated on the material, as if it were a diamond to be examined for flaws. Then one of them gave a low, long whistle. Another murmured, "This is incredible. I can't believe it," but he kept reading. Others scrutinized the material before them with varying degrees of awe, doubt or eagerness. Footsteps echoed faintly overhead. The guest who had been the most impatient during lunch was the first to raise his head from his file. "I can promise you categorically that we're prepared to back you with unlimited resources, under an arrangement I'm sure we can work out, but I have one question."

"Which," Trench said, rising, "I think I have anticipated. Please come with me." He beckoned to all of them and they rose again to move through the ship, this time to a lower level and an oak door guarded by a sailor leaning against the wall. When the sailor saw Trench he straightened, extracted a key from his pocket and opened the door.

Immediately there was a grunt of surprise from within. Inside sat a middle-aged, white-bearded, florid-faced man in a tee shirt who stared out at them, his expression changing from fearful to curious to eager. Lean, gnarled, aging prematurely, with yellowish skin and thin, weak-looking arms, he smiled and bowed theatrically, his hand sweeping down along the floor. "Gentlemen," he said, "how kind of

19

you to visit." The room behind him was small but comfortable, furnished with a rumpled, unmade bed, a small night table, an ashtray crammed with butts. *Scientific Americans* lay strewn about the floor. A porthole was open. A light breeze ruffled the thinning hair. "Are you reporters?" the man asked. "Gentlemen of the press? No. You're too well dressed. Colleagues! Yes, I can see you're educated. How I've waited for this day. I suggest we open a bottle of rosé in celebration. Good drink makes for good conversation. Men such as ourselves enjoy the finer things in life. I can tell."

In disgust the impatient guest said, "He's a drunk."

Trench shrugged. "Yes, but remember the file." To the bearded man he said, "A small bottle of rosé would be nice, Dr. Ciccone. Very chilled and very delicious."

The man looked slavish.

"And afterward," Trench said, signaling the sailor, "we can talk about New York and your overthrust belt, then, tonight, you and I and Mr. Ravenel will take a trip in the plane."

In response the drunk's eyes grew sly. "Only a *small* bottle?" he asked.

Unperturbed, Trench nodded. "Very small."

Dr. Ciccone pouted. His posture became more stooped. He scratched his head and looked over the men before him, one by one. Gone were the pretenses of a moment before. He turned and went to the porthole. He started to whine. "At least tell me where we are. No one tells me anything."

Half an hour later the men left the room, satisfied expressions on their faces. One by one they left the yacht during the afternoon until only the congressman remained. Standing by the aft railing, watching a seaplane lift into the dusk, he felt the boat begin to rock. The afternoon breeze had turned to a chilly wind and the first early stars were silver in the velvet sky. The cliffs had faded into silhouettes. The congressman looked out beyond the water. "Incredible news," he murmured. "Imagine what will happen to the man who breaks it."

There was a light tug at his sleeve. Trench was smiling up at him, the Korean's even teeth very white under the rising moon as he held out an envelope. "You came from far away and I appreciate it. Just a token."

The congressman waved away the gift but kept looking at it. "I couldn't."

"Please. I'd be offended." Trench pressed the envelope into Macklinburg's thick fingers, which seemed to take it by themselves. Without looking at it, Macklinburg put it in his pocket. "Oh, hell," he said. "Next time you get to Washington I'll show you the best goddamn time *you* ever saw."

Trench nodded. He had not taken his eyes off the congressman's face and he said, "Of course I'm embarrassed to ask this, but I must request a very slight favor."

"Name it."

Trench did, and the congressman grew rigid. "Oh, hell," he said. "I couldn't do *that.*"

"Such a small request."

"You call that *small?*"

Trench extracted another envelope from his pocket, but this time the congressman waved it away angrily. "No," he said firmly. "Not that. You never said anything about that."

"Correct," said Trench. "I never said anything. They were just gifts, tokens of friendship. Every month, but I never said anything."

The congressman stared at him, licked his lips. Before he could say anything Trench held up a hand. "The matter of the girl is still not settled," he said. He beckoned, and the Englishman emerged from the shadows several yards away, startling the congressman, who had not known he was there. Trench said to the sailor, "Has the congressman's friend been comfortable this afternoon?"

The sailor grinned. "Sure. Margaritas on the rocks all day. Pretty bird."

For the first time the congressman noticed the Englishman's powerful biceps and long, curling hands. His mouth dry, he said, "Oh, come on, Trench. I just picked her up a couple of days ago." He moved toward the Korean to make a point but stopped when he saw Ravenel's stance, tense, like a drawn bow.

Trench turned to the sailor. "Bring her here," he said, and as the sailor padded off Macklinburg said lamely, "She's just a piece of ass."

Trench did not answer. At length there were footsteps in the darkness and the Englishman returned with the girl, who was now wearing a handsome pair of white culottes and a low-cut blouse. She swayed slightly, moving as if she knew the effect she had on men, her eyes wide and expectant, like a child expecting a present. "I had such a good time today and Mr. Ravenel is very nice. Do we have to go now?" She giggled. "I hope not. Can't we stay a little longer?"

"We, uh, do have to go," the congressman said, watching the sailor behind the girl. Trench addressed her in his flat, even voice. "You can go below deck, please. The congressman will be leaving alone."

At once the girl's posture became more erect, a look of bored amusement entering her eyes. She nodded, her lips curling upward, eased forward and planted a kiss on the congressman's cheek. "Well, Pooky," she said, "it was nice while it lasted." Without waiting for a reply she turned and walked off.

The congressman stared after her with a mixture of amazement and incomprehension which abruptly turned to fear. He turned back to Trench and said weakly, "I met her in the hotel lounge . . ." His voice trailed away. "Jesus," he whispered. "She works for *you?*"

Ravenel came up behind him. "The launch is ready," he said.

Out beyond the boat, the red and green lights of a seaplane blinked and the engine revved up. Trench said, "So sorry you have to go," steering his guest to the ladder. "Of course you'll do me that little favor. I appreciate it. Please say hello to your wife."

The congressman, looking as if he were in shock, started to climb over the side, turned to Trench and shook his head. "All that time," he said. The Korean, expressionless, walked away into the darkness. Ravenel looked down and waved as the congressman climbed into the launch.

" 'Bye, mate," he called. "When you want to play, you got to pay."

Thousands of miles away, in New York, twelve-year-old Carlos Perez stood by the door of the high rise and looked up, gaped, way up, into the ceilingless building for what must have been thirteen, fourteen stories, where rising, reaching for the skylight, was this . . . thing. Metal and monstrous, a squat huge platform and a high tower. The moon, coming through the windows, played dully on its sides. He'd never seen anything like it but was reminded, staring at it, of a ride at Coney Island. But a ride? In a building? And anyway, there was no time to wonder and guess because two men were emerging from behind the platform; and there was nowhere to run because the dog was still outside, barking viciously, and the men were very fast so they caught him quickly. He struggled as he felt himself being lifted, a hand pressed against his mouth. One of the men yelled at the Doberman, "Be quiet!" and the roaring ceased. A low snarling replaced it.

He couldn't see the man who was holding him but the other one was short and pleasant-faced, dark but not a black. They opened the door and hustled him past the now obedient dog, across the yard, through a gate and toward a black Ford. Looking back, he saw the sign on the high slat fence—"LOW-INCOME HOUSING. TO BE COMPLETED IN . . ."—followed by a series of progressive dates, all crossed out, and finally a white spray-painted "NEVER."

They reached the Ford. He was shoved onto the floor in back. The pleasant-faced man got in with him and the other started the car. They lurched off, traveled a few minutes and then stopped. He was dragged out of the car into a street he recognized, where a series of gutted and abandoned buildings terminated in a vacant lot. Terrified, he tried to cry out but they stuffed a rag in his mouth.

There was no one in sight. The men carried him across the lot to one of the gutted buildings which they entered by ripping protecting boards from a doorway. Inside, bulging shapes skittered away at their approach, melting into the walls. Rats. The boy squirmed, whimpered, and kicked, but to no avail. They reached a stairway and, picking their way around the bottles and boards, began to climb. At the top they entered an apartment without a front door.

A voice in the dark said, "It's about time," and the thin, probing beam of a flashlight stabbed out into the blackness, coming to rest on Carlos' face. He squinted into it, and from across the room, the voice said, "Who's that?"

The man holding him ignored the question, although the other one said, "Get on with it." The beam still shone in the boy's eyes, blinding him, then moved off, crisscrossed the floor, and traveled along a dark line in the dust where someone had spread liquid. An unlit candle sat in the middle of the dark area. Carlos smelled gasoline.

"This place'll go up like the goddamn Fourth of July," said the first man. The boy again began to whimper and twist, and was slapped.

"Where should I put the kid?" said the man who was holding him.

"You said no one would be here," the voice responded.

"So? We were surprised."

There was a pause, then the pleasant-faced one said, "Put him over there, near the candle."

"No." The first voice was reluctant. "Not near the candle. Put him in the corner, on the rags. Tie him. The rope'll burn."

At the word "burn," the boy began struggling again, screaming through the rag in his mouth, but the sound was muffled. He kicked out, felt his feet strike something soft, heard an "Oooof." The hands that held him let go and he fell to the floor, hitting his head, crying out. He thought he was going to be sick. One of the men, he couldn't see which one, picked him up again, carried him to the corner and laid him gently on the pile of rags. Dust rose around him, clogging his nose. He screamed again through the rag.

When the man was finished emptying the can he stood back—the boy's eyes were adjusting to the darkness—and sighed. The boy couldn't move his feet now. Maybe if he had time he could get loose. "Listen, kid," the man said, "I'm really sorry. No one asked you to go in there."

And then from across the room, he heard a scratching sound and saw the quick glow of a match.

THREE

It was a very hot summer and there were fires every night. The man in the window waited for them. They lit up the sky above the gutted rooftops, reflecting off the broken panes and flickering in his face. Below or in neighboring streets, small armies of firemen fought to cool the ashes of one building before the next alarm, and at times, when the actual flames were not visible, he could see the lights of distant Manhattan through a rusty glow he had come to associate with the sound of sirens. The newspapers, when they bothered to mention the blazes at all, said youth gangs were responsible.

He was a man who several months before would have been called young, a man who had graduated ninetieth in his class from a generally respected law school, who had once been mentioned on the thirty-second page of *The Wall Street Journal* and had then enjoyed a brief period of notoriety among friends. He could lunch at the good mid-town restaurants and call the waiters by their names, although they did not remember his, could offer an unspectacular squash game, but had not done so in weeks. Or was it months? He didn't think about it anymore. Now he was a man who worked in a slum poverty office and climbed to a sixth-floor walk-up at night. When the fires started, the lines around his eyes did not exactly soften, but his face assumed an expression of anesthetized pain.

He kept no television in his apartment nor any books. The previous tenant had left behind a radio he had switched on once only to shut it off when the news came on. The only sounds in the studio were of his own footsteps or of the Puerto Rican couple next door. They fought in Spanish and occasionally threw things at each other. The wife wanted to move away from the Bronx. During lulls in their battles he often heard classical music —Debussy or Ravel—coming through the other wall. He didn't know who lived in that apartment and he didn't care. When he was finished with each night's vigil by the window, he slept on a single mattress on the floor, the unwashed sheets yellowing under the single light bulb. The walls were veined with cracks made more prominent by the fact that there was nothing to distract attention from them. He had had a wife and daughter until ten months ago but had smoked in bed, started a fire and killed them. When he couldn't shut out the memory, the image that haunted him most was that of his twelve-year-old's nightgown bursting into flames like a torch while he was pulled out of the bathroom window. Now he was a man who considered himself dead but who fed himself anyway.

Miles Bradshaw was the name that had burned up on his Park Avenue business cards, but these days few people asked what he was called and that was the way he wanted it. He moved the pencil over the papers on his desk, keeping his thoughts off his family. He was in his office.

"I asked you a question. What are you going to do about it?"

The speaker was a handsome, angry black, maybe thirty, silver-haired and dressed in work overalls, with a thick Jamaican accent and a steel lunch box on his thigh. One powerful hand rubbed against the other in agitation. The black eyes were intelligent and accusing. Both men were sweating from the heat.

Miles, writing rapidly, said, "First we have to fill out the complaint form."

"Complaint form! I'm losing half a day in this stinking legal-action office and I still can't get anything done! The elevator has no door, do you hear? An empty shaft! My kids could fall in! The neighbor! It almost happened last week!"

The windows vibrated from a passing elevated train and the steam laundry downstairs. Miles didn't have to look out the streaked window to know that the few pedestrians visible would be accompanied by dogs. A bank on the corner was vacant, the clock stopped. The rest of the block was spotted with gutted stores.

He said, "I'll *call* the landlord but let me fill out the form first."

With that, the muscular visitor sat back a bit, although he still looked ready to break something. Miles asked for and recorded the vital information. Like many of the people who came to see Miles, this man was a tenant of Lester Barrett, one of the last big absentee landlords in the South Bronx. Across the room, the window stopped rattling for a moment, then started again from the trains.

Miles Bradshaw was of slightly taller than average

height, brown-haired, with a mouth that could accommodate a lopsided grin, which never showed itself anymore. At one time he had been the kind of person strangers nodded hello to on the street. His eyes were slate gray, his shoulders slightly stooped, his overall appearance mussed without being sloppy. Completing the form, Miles heard the voice of the office manager, Marcus, through his thin partition.

"Name please."

A flat voice, a voice for taking names, which was what Marcus was forever doing. Miles completed his own form and looked up at the face of the man opposite him, a face that reflected unspoken challenge as well as a glint of hope. Miles reached for the phone, dialed Barrett's number, and looked away from the complainant, knowing full well what was about to happen. A woman with a heavy Irish brogue answered. "Barrett City Co-Ops."

He asked for Mr. Barrett and the woman had him identify himself, spelled his name, even though they'd spoken before, made him hold the line and returned to tell him the landlord was "on vacation," of course a lie, but Miles explained about the elevator and asked if someone could help. He gave her the address when she asked but wouldn't tell her the name of the complainant. Her voice grew colder. She sounded as if she did this twenty times a day.

"Mr. Barrett likes to personally handle complaints. Perhaps he can call you when he gets home next week."

Miles exhaled. "Then what do you need the complainant's name for if Mr. Barrett isn't in the office?"

"Excuse me?"

Maintaining the facade of politeness from the dismal hope that someday he might receive cooperation, Miles said "Nothing" and "Thank you" and heard the click before he was finished. Trying to keep the frustration from his voice, he told the visitor, "I can send your complaint to the Buildings Department with a priority stamp. They could have an inspector at your building within a week."

"Then what?"

"He'll send a report to the Legal Department and—"

The man stiffened. "Is that you? The Legal Department?"

Miles shifted uncomfortably. "Uh, not me. We don't have enough people here to handle litigation so—"

"What's *litigation?*" The man's eyes looked at him accusingly. Another runaround, they seemed to say. Another lie.

Miles said, "Litigation is trial work but we're so snowed under here that the only lawyer, uh, me, hasn't time to go to court."

The man's anger rippled across his face. He rose and said, "Send the form." He muttered something else Miles didn't catch and didn't want to, shook hands coldly, obviously disgusted with himself, and left.

Miles rose, walked to the window and watched the man emerge angrily from the steam laundry downstairs, hands in his pockets, as Marcus' voice came from the other side of the partition. "What was the *date* you first discovered this problem with the plumbing?"

Miles sighed.

Marcus was a sallow-faced man who wore green and brown polyester leisure suits and hats one size too small. He always carried an umbrella and rubbers in case it rained. "Welcome to the outpost," he had greeted Miles wryly on his first day. "Last vestige of the Lindsay years. Used to be a few dozen of these offices around the city. Local headquarters, the liberal dream. Now we're the last ones left. City Hall doesn't want to close us because someone'll start screaming about abandonment, but no one really cares about us being here. Try to get something done and watch what happens.

"Used to be two lawyers here. A good one named Tesser actually beat Barrett in court one year." He pointed to two huge posters depicting slum dwellers on a cleanup campaign: "IF YOU'RE NOT WITH IT, *GET* WITH IT!" and "CLEAN A STREET TODAY."

"They're sort of a shrine to the only effective thing we ever accomplished here. No one touches the posters. Tesser's an assistant DA in Nassau County now. More money there. Politics." The little man shrugged. "Anyway, Barrett's been taking it out on the tenants ever since."

He stopped and looked Miles over, as if seeing him for the first time. "Hey, you're a little old for this. What are you, thirty-five? Generally we get them out of law school. When Bluestein called from City Hall and said an old friend needed a job, I still figured a kid. Why would anyone with experience want to come here?" Marcus eyed him with a glimmer of interest. "Don't want to say, huh? Okay. Let me introduce you to the secretary. This is Samantha. She thinks I don't give a shit about anyone who comes in here, right, Samantha?"

She was sullen, monosyllabic but efficient, Miles would later find out. "Yeah."

Miles was amazed at how Marcus could change when he had a visitor, becoming officious, distant, his voice calm and machinelike. Still, the administrator was capable of delivering surprises. Once, when Miles had been working late, Marcus had appeared in the doorway, looking terribly distraught. Startled, Miles wondered whether something had happened to Marcus' family, but the little man had said, speaking almost as much to himself as to Miles, "These people think I hate them. It's not true. I don't *see* them. Just the paper work. It's better that way."

He never brought up the subject again and, anyway,

Marcus' lapses into rebellion or creativity were rare, brief disturbances on an otherwise bland and apparently uncaring surface.

At four forty-five the air outside was stagnant. The sun moved across the rooftops, garish, like a strutting pimp, blinding him when he looked up. Across the street emaciated dogs were loping across an empty lot. They stopped to watch him. Four black men in old army fatigues approached from the other side of the street, walking German shepherds on leashes. Their laughter was rich and warm in the heavy dusk. The dogs were only slightly fatter than the wild ones in the lot. The sidewalk was littered with broken bottles, crushed pie plates, a Nestea can, and torn newspapers. All the summer odors of putrefying rubbish reached him, smelling like the alley behind a Chinese restaurant in Harlem in August, following him on his walk down the street and around a corner. The next block was the same, as was the next. He came to a block encircled entirely by a green slat fence with a barbed-wire gate. On the fence a sign proclaimed "LOW-INCOME HOUSING. TO BE COMPLETED IN . . ." A series of crossed-out dates followed. Several workmen moved in and out of the building, a couple of them casting Miles idle glances, and a bulldozer roared across the lot. From a black Ford parked nearby, an Oriental watched the work through the rear window.

Miles moved on, unaware of the eyes on his back. Two corners later he paused at a pet store, closed for the day, where a lone cocker spaniel pup moved back and forth in a cramped cage in the front window, searching for a way out. The window was protected by heavy wire mesh. Miles put his hand against the glass but the dog ignored it in its despair.

Finally he reached his own block, which was slightly more populated than the others in the neighborhood because it housed a police station. The station was called Fort Apache because a gang had attacked it one night with crossbows and arrows, the arrows screaming through the windows and impaling two officers. Fort Apache glowed brightly at night as if to ward off another attack, and the bottom windows were boarded now, painted police green. Nearby stoops were filled with Puerto Rican men in undershirts, drinking beer. The sound of a crying baby and tinny Latin music came from a first-floor tenement window, barred, like most of them, against intruders. A child riding by on a bicycle fell over. Miles picked up the boy, brushed him off and put him back on the seat. The boy smiled and said, "*Gracias.*"

Miles' building was the last on the block, no different from the rest except for the unusual fact that it was still totally occupied. The lock on the front door was broken so he had only to push to enter. Two teenagers were kissing on the landing under a crayoned figure on the wall labeled "LITTLE HENRY." The boy had both hands under the girl's blouse. Miles didn't bother to check the mailbox, but passed the couple and mounted the stairs. Five flights. At the top he was home. As he approached his door he heard the soft strains of a Bach cantata from the next apartment. As usual, the door, which had no name on it, was closed, but as he turned the key he heard footsteps on the stairs and watched a delivery boy appear in the hall with a very small bag, not at all heavy-looking, and knock. The music stopped. Miles turned away, pushing open the door to his own apartment.

Inside, the shadows were evening deep and a cockroach skittered under the stove in fright. The screaming began next door.

"*I afraid to walk on the street. Let's get out now!*"

"Will you shut up. I work all day in the cab!"

He took off his shoes, lining them up by the mattress. The faucet made a low moan when he turned it on, and the water ran slightly red at first. He rolled up his sleeves and soaped his hands, washed the sweat off his face and dried himself with paper towels.

He heated some canned ravioli and ate it standing up at the sink, washing it down with cool water and grapes. When he was finished he put the trash in a plastic bag and went to the incinerator. The screaming had stopped but the classical music had started again. He retraced his steps, closed the door of the apartment behind him and went to the window. Outside, the sky was vivid in its gaseous splendor, making silhouettes of a flock of pigeons circling a rooftop several blocks away. The moon was rising, full. He sat in his rocking chair by the window, and all expression went out of his face.

The light faded swiftly. Soon he was alone in the dark. The stoops cleared along the street, and the police cars, which patrolled the area like skulking wary cats, began leaving Fort Apache. The screaming started again next door. After a while the stars came out. From somewhere down the block came noises of a party, of television, of babies crying, a dog, cars that needed mufflers, but at length even they died away, and Miles sat and watched the night sky, rocking.

Then it happened.

Later, trying to reconstruct the scene, he could not be sure whether he had been looking directly at the window when he saw the flash or whether his eyes had been attracted by the brightness. Where there had been only darkness a moment before, there was now an explosion of light from an abandoned boarded-up building across an empty lot. For an instant the brilliance confined itself to an upstairs window. In the glare, writhing frantically in a strange stooped position, like a question mark, illuminated only as a silhouette, was the form of a child—too small to be more than a teenager, slender, with wide boy shoulders —wrapped in flames. Miles rose to his feet. Within moments the silhouette disappeared and soon the entire structure was a sheet of yellow and orange flames. Even a block away Miles could hear the popping wood and see the glowing cinders sailing over the gutted rooftops. Footsteps sounded in the hall. Below, people were streaming out of the building to watch the blaze.

But the figure, the silhouette, that was what stayed in his mind, and although part of him was urging that he join the crowd, go to the building, tell the firemen what he had seen, even though he knew rescue was hopeless, his body wasn't responding. It was reacting instead to a memory, another fire and another burning child. His fist began clenching and unclenching. His face filled with a deepening horror, eyes wide, remembering. There were sirens in the night, growing louder. The screaming began next door and he joined it. He clutched his head, tried to shut out the scenes by closing his eyes, but they only grew more vivid. After a while his actions became less violent, his breathing heavier. The last things he heard before crumpling on the mattress were the sirens and the low, wistful classical melodies from the apartment next door.

That night the dream came to him with particular sharpness. He was in his old bedroom, the lights off, watching Johnny Carson. Paula was asleep next to him in their warm, comfortable bed. Carson told a joke and the room filled with muted laughter. In his dream, Miles felt a tug at his bladder but decided to wait until the show was over before attending to himself. He fell asleep. The glowing cigarette tip wavered and tumbled to the mattress, where it started to smolder.

Music from the television woke him. Senses dulled by

35

exhaustion, he did not smell the smoking mattress and rolled out of bed, turned off the TV and went into the bathroom to relieve himself. He decided to shave. Paula hated his bristles on her face so he generally shaved at night instead of in the morning. The room filled with steam. Smoke began seeping under the door, and although he thought he smelled something odd, he did not become alarmed. He finished shaving, brushed his teeth, shut off the light and opened the bathroom door.

The bedroom was ablaze. Even as he stood paralyzed, the fire shot across the bed and leaped from the blazing quilt to the carpet. A bottle of perfume on the dressing table exploded. Paula was a blackened lump on the bed. Miles was sick with shock and terror. The smell of burning flesh permeated the bedroom. He saw his daughter Louise at the door, screamed at her to leave, but a spark must have touched her nightgown and she became a torch. Miles leaped forward to reach her as the curtains toppled over her body, muffling her screams. Intense heat engulfed him then, scorching his hands and legs, driving him back. Flames were racing up his pajamas. Choking, he tried to douse them by rolling against the wall, unable to see his daughter anymore.

But then, in the dream, a different thing happened. In the spot where he had seen Louise, he *saw the boy!* Same height as Louise, writhing in the same agonized way. But there was something else. *The boy had no arms.* No, that wasn't it, because the shoulders were too bulky, as if the hands were pinned to the sides or clasped behind the back. The image grew larger, filling his vision with his daughter's face. Then it was gone, and the boy twisted before him, imploringly . . .

A boy with his hands clasped behind his back.
A boy stumbling around a room on fire, twisting as if . . .
As if what?

36

As if to free himself!

A boy who had been *tied up!*

Tied up! No! He tried to reach the boy, failed, turned back, groping along the wall to the bathroom, the smoke blinding him, the window . . . crashing in. A ladder burst through the glass . . . hands reached for him, pulled him out, the smoke pursued him into the frosty night as if angry that he had escaped. And Miles was screaming at the lights and faces below, "My daughter's in there! My wife! *I did it!*"

The sun was pouring through the window when he opened his eyes. He was sprawled on the mattress, fully dressed, one hand in his hair as though he had been pulling it. His forehead was laved with sweat, the sheet soaked and his head stuffed.

At first his terror was undiminished by the daylight. The dream had been so vivid that now his apartment, unlike the images of the night before, seemed unreal. Lying there trembling, he experienced the same fright and nausea, the weakness in his legs, the same horrible accusations he had suffered the night of the fire. Couldn't he have tried one more time to save his daughter? How had he known without checking that his wife was dead on the burning bed? Why did he *dream* about smoke coming under the bathroom door if he hadn't really noticed it? The sun, pouring through the window, was like an interrogator's lamp. And what about the boy last night? All that remained to make the awful emotional tableau complete would be to have that arson inspector, Lieutenant Goldstein, standing over him as he had in the hospital, chewing gum, asking over and over, "*What* time did you go to the bathroom, *Counselor?* Mighty interesting fire insurance policy you have, *Counselor.* You *forgot* that the cigarette was on the bed?

37

How long have you been married? You a gambler, *Counselor*? No? Ladies' man? Attractive secretary you have, don't you think?"

He showered and left the apartment. For once, the hallway was quiet. Outside, steam rose from the pavement and the heat puddles promised a scorcher of a day. His Hush Puppies sounded rubbery on the sidewalk. When he arrived at the office Marcus was clearly agitated but said nothing.

The little bell above the door rang and the business day commenced. Marcus' mood improved after he actually stopped an eviction with a phone call. Miles met with three or four complainants, filled out forms but didn't feel as if he were accomplishing anything. Then, around noontime, several visitors began discussing the fire of the previous night.

"It was still smoking this morning. They pulled a boy from the wreck."

"*Qué mal!* Who was he?"

"I don't know. The PO-lice say he started the fire."

"He was in a gang, they said. What this city does to children."

Miles was rocked by a distress which frightened and amazed him in its powerfulness. How could the police blame the boy? The boy had done nothing. The longer Miles sat there the angrier he became. If Miles had questioned himself he might have decided he was reacting like a protective father, but he wasn't thinking at all. Instead he left his desk on an impulse and did something which would have been unimaginable an hour before—he walked across the street to a phone booth and dialed the police, not wanting Marcus, Samantha, or the whole waiting room, for that matter, to hear what he was going to say.

"Forty-First Precinct." Miles envisioned various policemen he saw each day outside Fort Apache and tried to match the brusque, deep voice to a face. He felt strangely vulnerable, as if the officer on the other end might figure out who he was. He said, speaking rapidly, "The building that burned down last night? On Clancey Street? I heard you blamed the boy for the fire, but he couldn't have started it because he was tied up."

There was a pause. *"What do you mean, tied up?"* the voice on the other end demanded. Miles imagined the cop leaning into the phone, as if trying to see the person on the other end.

"I was sitting in my room. I saw it."

"Who is this?"

Miles felt panic. "I just want to tell you what I saw."

There was a brief silence, during which he heard himself breathing into the receiver, then the policeman's voice became strangely friendly. "Well, okay then." Miles heard the sound of paper being rolled into a typewriter. "Who are you?"

"I saw a flash of light and he was silhouetted against it."

"Silhouetted? Silhouetted against the light, eh? What did you say your name was?"

"Listen," Miles said, afraid he was staying on the line too long, "I'm not going to tell you my name. I just want to let you know what I saw. Someone tied the boy up and set the fire."

The voice said, "Do you know who the boy was?"

"No, I just saw him for a second."

"Then how do you know he was tied up?"

"I could tell."

"You could tell." Miles now imagined the policeman nodding to himself, sitting back in his chair, perhaps looking at the ceiling, perhaps beckoning someone else to listen at an extension. "Maybe you should come in and tell us exactly what you saw," he said.

"I *am* telling you, I . . ." There was the faint sound of a receiver being lifted. "Who's on the line?" he demanded, hearing the strident tone of his own voice. The damn police blamed you for everything, just like after his own fire. He could never go through that again.

"No one," the voice said, soothing now. "You saw a boy tied up. You were in your apartment. You saw a silhouette. You didn't see the boy's face."

Miles hung up, sweating, feeling ridiculous for his own fear. He hadn't done anything wrong but he didn't want them to know who he was. He just wanted to ease his conscience.

Marcus was inquisitive when he returned to the office. "Did I see you leave to make a call?" He winked. "Very suspicious. A woman?" He paused. "Hey, what's the matter? You look terrible."

Marcus' concern was so genuine that for an instant Miles was tempted to tell him everything, not only about last night but about the other fire too. He stopped himself. What was the point?

Instead he returned to his desk, but today the work failed to distract him as it usually did. Was there something else he could do for the boy? Call the police again? Write an anonymous letter? He couldn't be certain they'd respond to either. Find the boy's parents and let them know their son was innocent?

Samantha always kept a *Daily News* on her desk and Miles flipped through it, looking for any reference to the fire. There was none. Maybe the authorities had not yet identified the boy. Miles decided to call the Fire Department and check, so for the second time that day he crossed the street to the phone booth.

"You a relative?" the spokesman at the Fire Department asked.

"A neighbor."

40

"Not a relative? Not press? Sorry."

He hung up, dejected, then called back. He disguised his voice, said he was from the *News* and asked the same question.

The voice said, "You have to get that information from press relations. I'll give you the number."

Five minutes later Miles reached someone who gave him the information he wanted. "The boy's name? Carlos Perez, age twelve. Want the address?"

"Uh, please."

He got it and hung up. *Twelve!* Marcus was waiting when he returned. "Three more calls! Something's happening and you won't tell me what. You need money? No? I could tell from the beginning there was something. You were like a dead man, but today you're different. Your eyes . . ."

Miles tried to avoid him, but Marcus grabbed his wrist. "It's three o'clock. Go home early today. Whatever's bothering you, I hope it gets better. You need anything . . ."

Twelve years old, he thought, walking past the construction site as usual on his way home. Who would tie up Carlos Perez and start a fire? A gang? Had Perez been a member? The police said so. Still, what could the boy have done to deserve that awful, fiery punishment?

The hallway of his building smelled odd, but he was too preoccupied to place the odor; however, as he reached his landing, he saw immediately that smoke was coming from under his neighbor's door.

Miles hurled himself at the door, pounding. There was no response. He moved back, lifted a foot, kicked open the cheap pine, then stopped short. The sight that met his eyes stupefied him.

The smoke was coming from an oven beside which stood one of the most beautiful women he had ever seen. She had whirled at the sound of the door, frightened, but now rapidly composed herself, rested one elegant hand on a slim curved hip, and reached with the other for a pack of cigarettes on the counter. She tossed her head so that her hair flowed about her face and, giving him a glance of intelligent appraisal, said in a low, throaty voice, "I didn't think it was the delivery boy. He knocks." She turned and began working at the oven, coughing while removing a roast.

Miles said, "I saw the smoke . . ." and broke off lamely. Her air of poise and control heightened the sense of absurdity he felt for having broken in.

"And thought you'd rescue me." She had a small, inviting mouth, a dark little O which stretched, as it did now, into a slight upward curve when something amused it. Her eyes were deep brown, her hair curled in a fashion which reminded him of 1940 or 1977, he couldn't decide which. Her dress was mid-calf length, sheer and clinging in a way which left only minor details to the imagination. He was strongly and instantly attracted to her and that in itself was unexpected. This was the second time today he'd been buffeted by forgotten emotions, and he felt totally off balance. She moved from the stove to the window, her face partially obscured now by hanging plants which steamed the panes. The apartment was comfortably cool, he realized, then heard the soft hum of the air conditioner. The overall effect was strangely ephemeral but at the same time complete, total; time seemed suspended in the room. The lace curtains, plush carpet, flowers on the table, and big cushiony chairs made him feel as if he had stepped into an old photograph in a cameo. Then he noticed the stereo and the television. Too much money for this part of the world. There was a sense of completion, almost revelation, to the apartment. He felt embarrassed by his intrusion, as if he had stumbled upon someone naked.

The girl seemed oblivious to his discomfort, interested

yet uninterested at the same time. Her accent was slightly Hispanic. "Who are you?"

"I live next door."

"Really?" The voice was dry and she licked her lips. "Which side, the quiz-show side or the footsteps side?" She looked him up and down slowly. "You don't look like the quiz-show type. You must be the footsteps. Every night. Footsteps and silence. A man of mystery."

She fell into a chair, crossed her long legs and began moving one up and down casually. "Or maybe that's how you get your exercise. Twenty miles a day in the apartment. You're home early this afternoon. I generally don't hear you for another two hours. What do you say to that? Nothing? Strong, silent type. Door-kicking type."

Miles blushed. "Listen, there was *smoke* coming under the door . . ."

"And what were you going to do if there was a fire?" she asked. "Run through the flames and rescue me? How sweet." She stopped when she saw his face. "It's all in fun, door kicker. You have a name?"

"Miles."

"Miles. Miles and miles." Her eyes misted over with some private vision, then looked at him as if she had momentarily forgotten he was there. "I'm Elena," she said.

"I have to go."

"So soon? Late for your pacing?"

He clenched his fists. "I don't need this," he said. "Next time I see smoke I'll put a goddamn rug in the crack to make sure you get to enjoy all of it. *You know what a fire can do?* Last night I saw . . ."

He stopped, not wanting to talk about the boy, and although Elena had watched him with a sort of interest during the beginning of his tirade, all the color had drained out of her face when he mentioned last night. Now she stared at him with a twisted, pained expression.

"You saw what?" she demanded.

"Nothing."

"No, not nothing. What did you see? *Tell me!*"

They watched each other, Miles realizing that their faces held the same look. She said, "I was at my window last night, ten or ten-thirty. I saw a fire start beyond the vacant lot. In a window, in the fire I saw a . . . boy and . . ." She seemed about to say more but stopped abruptly and turned away.

Miles said, "What did you do?"

"I wasn't sure I saw him."

"Did you call the police?"

"I don't have a phone," she said.

Miles thought it a stupid response. He said, "There are phones outside."

"What did you see, Miles? The same thing?"

He looked at the ground, knowing he was answering her question by doing so, and then he was amazed to hear her voice return to its carefree tone.

"Such is life in the big city. People witness horrible things and then do nothing, *comprende?*" She sounded almost relieved. "You know what else people do, or rather, what they think? They think a person who runs away from something runs *far* away, but that's silly, don't you think? Why go someplace romantic when you're really trying to hurt yourself? Why go someplace nice when there's much greater retribution close to home? Were you born here? Do you agree? *I* agree. I always agree with myself." She sounded like someone who spent a lot of time alone and she watched him carefully.

He said, "I don't know what you're talking about."

"Really?"

"Yes, really."

"Do you like my music?"

Again he was thrown off balance, perplexed and irritated by her changes. He nodded in confusion, and she said, "It's Debussy. Impressionist. Classical. He was . . ."

44

"I know who Debussy was," he said coldly, realizing that he had not lost his temper in months.

Her eyes brightened a little, appraising him, then seemed to lose interest again. She yawned. "I think I'm going to eat now," she said. She paused, her expression becoming slightly vulnerable. "Want to join me?" But he was angry and he walked to the doorway. She frosted over. "Good. There wasn't enough for two. But you'll come again, won't you? I want you to. I'll knock on the wall when I want you."

Who is she? he thought, back in his own apartment, rocking furiously in the chair. And why is she living here? She obviously had the money and the education to go elsewhere. He'd heard the unmistakable bitterness in her voice. He was powerfully attracted to her, even now imagined her moving around on the other side of the wall. The music switched to a piece by Ravel. After a while the moon came out. He envisioned her long legs. Her waist was so slender he felt certain he could completely encircle it with his fingers. *"I'll knock on the wall when I want you,"* she had said, and he felt the anger rise in him at the memory. Tonight his apartment seemed cold and sterile, almost pathetic in its unfriendliness. His anger became worse. His mind was racing, unstoppable, wondering about the boy and the woman.

The boy was dead.

And the woman was on the other side of the wall.

Was she telling the truth about seeing the fire? Why had she been so terrified when talking about it? And why the stupid excuse about no telephone?

He shook his head. What was the point of doing anything about either of them? He crisscrossed the room, conscious of the fact that she could hear his footsteps in the other apartment. He stopped and looked out the window. Forget about them, he told himself. Carlos is dead and Elena's trouble. I can feel it. Lots of trouble.

45

But he couldn't forget. That night he stayed up a long time, thinking about both of them, and when he woke the next morning he had a feeling that somehow, for him, everything had changed.

FOUR

HE'D BEEN knocking a long time, and although there was no response from inside the apartment, Miles had the feeling it was occupied. Carlos Perez, the boy who had died in the fire, had lived in a building not unlike his own. The graffiti on the old walls was growing faint under scrub marks, and he heard the sound of a broadcast baseball game tinny and muffled in the narrow passage, which smelled of cabbage and disinfectant.

He knocked one more time and was about to give up when the door jerked open and a woman snarled at him through the crack. "*What do you want?*"

"I . . . I was hoping to t-talk to you about Carlos."

"*Jesucristo!* I told the sergeant everything *three times*. What do you want from me now?"

A voice came from the dark behind her, quiet and controlled. "Cops again, Maria?" Miles wondered who was there but couldn't see past the mottled, swollen face of Perez' mother. Her mouth was twisted, her jowls streaked, her hair piled impeccably in vast bushy coils which seemed ready to spring.

Miles said, "I'm not a policeman."

The face seemed to leap out at him like an attacking bird. "Then who are you? An arson inspector? You gonna tell me my kid started the fire? *Leave him alone!* He's dead and he didn't . . ." She stopped, blood, hate and grief effusing her face.

Miles involuntarily stepped back. He said, "I *know* he didn't start the fire."

Again the voice from inside. "You want him to leave, Maria?" The woman didn't answer. Her expression, which had frozen at Miles's words, now wavered between anger, suspicion and disbelief. "You're not an arson inspector?"

"No."

"Then who are you?"

"I . . . uh . . . live a block away from the fire."

"*And?*"

"I saw it. He didn't start it."

She was confused. She considered a moment, then opened the door, revealing her thick, heavy body, cheap, well-pressed dress and the rickety polished furniture inside. She stepped back from the entrance and Miles moved into the apartment. Portraits of John F. Kennedy and Pope Paul hung on the wall above a kitchen table, where a man sat in an undershirt, watching him. Six inches from his right hand lay a large kitchen knife. He didn't glance at it or touch it, but it was there all the same. Miles only reluctantly moved his eyes away when he heard the door shut. The woman had her big fists on her hips and eyed him as if, now that he had gotten into the apartment, she was waiting for him to change his story. She said, "*Well?*"

Miles didn't know how to start. "I was sitting at my window two nights ago and I saw the fire start. Carlos was inside the building but I think he was, well, tied up."

The man said, "What's he talking about?" He didn't look at Miles and he didn't move.

"I only saw him for a second, but that's what I thought. The police said he started it . . . that he was in a gang and . . ."

The woman screamed at him. "Carlos weren't in no gang! I'd kill him if he was in a gang! He hung out with nice people! No gang!" Her fists started clenching and unclenching, and the man at the table shifted his head around and picked at his teeth with a matchbook, watching her like a dog ready to protect its master.

Miles said, "I didn't say he was in a gang. I just . . ."

"You *are* a cop, aren't you? The sergeant didn't believe nothing I said so he sent someone else." She stepped toward him, shaking with rage.

The man said, "He's a cop."

Miles shook his head. "No. *I told you.* I just live nearby. I called the police but I don't think they believed me."

The woman turned to her companion. "Those bastards don't believe anything they don't want to. They say Carlos was in a gang so they'll do anything to prove it." Then, to Miles, "Even send people to pretend they're neighbors."

"I'm *not* a policeman!"

"Then what are you here for? What do you want?" Perez' mother looked about to cry but then pushed it all back inside her. Her eyes bulged.

Miles shook his head, wondering how to explain. "I thought I . . . should tell you because I wanted to . . . help and . . ."

"*Why would you want to do that anyway? What do you care?*"

She was watching him carefully now. The man at the table still looked disinterested in what Miles was saying. Miles decided there was really only one way to reach them,

49

but the thought of telling the truth scared him and his emotion must have appeared in his face because her expression changed to one of guarded concern. Miles said, "My daughter died in a fire. I saw it."

For the first time Mrs. Perez didn't challenge him. She sat down, looked at the man at the table as if trying to make up her mind about something. She seemed to sense Miles's anguish and knew enough not to ask any questions. She said, "What do you want to know?"

Miles sighed. "I was hoping you could give me the names of some of Carlos' friends to talk to."

He couldn't tell if she smiled or grimaced. "Some *friends*? Some *gang* friends? Okay, Mr. Good Neighbor. I already told the sergeant who some friends are, so I might as well tell you. If you're a cop, that will waste your time, getting the same as the sergeant. The story is the same now as before. It will always be the same. If you're not a cop, like you say, good luck. Carlos didn't start any fire." The man moved his fingers several inches toward the knife. The woman cried out, "*Did you hear me? He didn't do it! Ask* his friends! Ask Eduardo! They did everything together. They were in the same class in school! Eduardo Morales! He's a good boy. Just like Carlos was." Her voice cracked and she made a little strangled meowing sound. Her shoulders started to heave up and down.

"He's upset you," said the man at the table, rising. He was much thinner than she was. He touched her shoulder, but her head was in her hands and she didn't look up.

Miles wanted to ask which school Carlos had attended but the man had an odd look in his eyes. "Thank you," Miles said. "I have to go."

Mrs. Perez didn't look up.

He waited several seconds but there was no response. The man glared at him. Miles backed to the door and he said, "I'm sorry about your son." The man stiffened. As

Miles closed the door behind him he heard the woman's muffled cry from within. *"Carlitos!"*

He was glad to be out of the apartment. There had been a time, he realized, when interviewing two people would have been as simple as crossing a street. He was troubled by the degree of difficulty he had had talking to them.

The sun was at its zenith above the buildings. Perez' block was not as dilapidated as some neighboring areas. Which school had the boy attended? he wondered, and went into a candy store looking for a Yellow Pages. The phone booth was empty, but the counterman produced a book from under a shelf, explaining, "Kids rip 'em up."

Miles located the only junior high school in the vicinity, eight blocks away. He took a bus. The principal had a dazzling smile and the air of a gossip. Miles wondered if he was gay. They sat in a small office while an air conditioner clacked noisily, throwing cold air on Miles. After he explained why he was there, the principal said, "We really aren't supposed to let anyone wander off the streets and talk to students. The boy died in a fire, you say?"

Miles nodded.

"And you *saw* him burn?"

"Yes."

The principal shuddered. "How awful," he said. He drummed his fingers on the glass covering of his desk. "I imagine if I denied you permission to speak to the boy, you would just wait outside until school let out and talk to him then, wouldn't you?"

The principal obviously wanted him to say yes and he wasn't sure why but he nodded.

The principal glanced at the clock. "All right, but just for ten minutes. I'll have to be present during the interview. We *are* legally responsible."

The principal dispatched a messenger, then "Would you like some tea? I always have a cup at one-

51

thirty. It makes the day go faster. I used to work in Queens. Junior high. The children were so much more motivated there. Here all we can do is keep them occupied. So sad. And to die in a fire."

There was a knock and the boy who entered was Hispanic, with hair to his shoulders, a denim shirt and old jeans. His look was calm and slightly curious. He seated himself when motioned to do so and said, "What?"

The principal explained the situation while Eduardo examined Miles. He seemed quite intelligent and nodded periodically. When the principal was finished the boy said, "How do I know he isn't a policeman?"

Miles frowned. "What can I say? I'm not."

The boy pursed his lips and glanced at the principal, who looked like a movie fan waiting for the curtain to rise. Then he nodded. "Okay," he said. "I don't think you're a cop. But you ask the questions."

Again, Miles wasn't sure how to begin. "The police say Carlos was a member of a gang."

"I wouldn't exactly say he was *in* a gang, but he hung out with the Kings a lot."

"The Kings?"

"The Latin Kings. You never heard of them?"

Miles shook his head, trying to recall if he'd heard the name before.

"Jesus," Eduardo said disdainfully. "He never heard of the Latin Kings. Where you been? They're the biggest Spanish gang in the city, the guys with the blue jackets with the crown. They're all over the place."

Miles said, remembering, "I've seen the jackets."

"Okay. That's the Kings. Carlos' mother would have killed him if he joined, so he was just friendly with some of the guys. Carlos' mother is a real terror. Once I saw her break a table. Anyway, I wouldn't talk to the Kings if I were you."

"Why not?"

52

The principal leaned forward, watching them both.

"They're unpredictable," Eduardo said. "You know Freddy Seller, the half-wit? One time he's walking on Willis Avenue and he sees this King, his name is Happy, grab an old lady's purse. The lady tells the cops Freddy saw the snatch and the cops browbeat him into picking Happy from a lineup. But Happy gets off anyway. The cops didn't tell him his rights and, besides, he's only fifteen. The judge can't see his record. Everything goes back to normal, only one day eight months later Freddy doesn't get home one night. His father calls the cops. A week later they find him in an empty building, tied up, spread-eagled on the floor. The Kings told him there was a party. He was dumb and he believed them. They tortured him bad. They burned his back with a hot iron, punched and kicked him in the face, and then Maybug, who's real good with a knife, bled him all over the floor. Maybug got sent up. Freddy's body was rotting when they found it. Everybody knows the story." He looked at the expression of fascinated horror on the principal's face and shrugged.

Sickened and disbelieving, Miles said, "But Carlos was a friend of theirs. You don't think they'd hurt *him?*"

Eduardo shrugged. "He wasn't a *member.* And anyway, maybe they were mad at him for something. The police say Carlos started that fire but I don't believe it. The Kings might do something like that, but mostly they just steal plumbing from empty buildings and sell it to the junk dealer on King Street, Goralski. A Polack. Maybe he can help you. But . . . uh . . . you ain't gonna tell no one you talked to me, right?"

"Sure," Miles said. "Where can I find the Kings?"

The boy shook his head. "I wouldn't go there if I were you. Why not tell the cops?"

"I *told* the cops," Miles said, ashamed that he was not being entirely truthful. "And they didn't do anything."

53

The boy nodded. "Bastards." Then, "It's your life. You can mostly find the Kings around the pinball place on King Street. Get it? Latin Kings? King Street? Anyway, they're across the street from the junk dealer and the president is named Rodriguez. If he's not there, he's probably at the meth clinic two blocks away. Good luck, man. I know Carlos didn't burn no building, but you're crazy. If the Kings had anything to do with it, you'll end up like Freddy on the floor."

The principal stood up. "I'm afraid Edward has to return to class now," he said. He had a faraway look in his eyes, as if he were fantasizing about what he had just heard. "And I'm sure Miles won't tell anyone he spoke to you today. What amazing stories you tell. If only we could teach the students to *write*. Goodbye, Edward." When the door closed he said to Miles, "Are you sure you wouldn't like some tea? No? Nice meeting you."

Miles didn't plan to talk to the gang, not at first. Eduardo's warning had had the desired effect. The junk dealer, however, was another matter.

The bus let Miles off by an abandoned lot piled high with bulldozed rubble. Two hundred yards ahead the junkyard looked right at home. "CASIMIR GORALSKI, METALS" read the sign. "SALE TODAY! PLUMBING!" The lot was filled with unrecognizable metals, car parts, dented refrigerators, old stoves. A German shepherd, flanks lean and matted, eyed him sullenly as he passed. He found Goralski in an indescribably filthy shack on the edge of the yard, balancing an unlit cigar between his teeth. One ear was cauliflowered, the blond hair crew-cut. He looked like the sixth-grade bully who had grown fatter and older, and he was poring over a ledger. A calendar of nudes hung on the wall behind him. He looked up, moved the cigar to the side of his mouth and said, "Yeah. What can I do for you?"

"I wanted to talk."

"Talk?" Goralski stared at him as if he were crazy. "Whaddaya mean 'talk'? You want some plumbing? Car parts? What? I got things to do. You wanna see some plumbing?"

Miles said, "The other night a boy was killed in a fire."

Goralski tilted his head and his eyes became hooded. "You a cop? I'm surprised. I always know a cop."

"No."

"Then whaddaya want?"

Outside, the dog started barking. Goralski looked Miles in the eye and said, "I don't know no kid."

"His name was Carlos Perez."

"Perez. Perez. So what? I'm sad. Whaddaya want with me?"

"He was tied up."

The junk dealer leaned forward. "*Who* was tied up?"

"Carlos Perez," said Miles.

Goralski got out of his chair with surprising agility. He was much bigger when he stood up and his arms were tattooed with more nudes. He seemed irritated and nervous.

"Look, I don't know what you're talking about and I don't know why you came here. You're not a cop? Fine. I ain't talkin' to you. Who told you to come here?"

"No one."

"No one, huh? You just wandered off the street, right? Saw a junk shop and figured you'd come in and talk about a kid getting burned. Who told you to come here?"

Miles said, swallowing, "I just heard that you knew him."

Goralski paused and looked outside as if he were trying to see if someone was there. The dog started scratching at the screen door as the junk dealer closed the distance between himself and Miles until their faces were inches apart. The cigar smelled forty years old.

"I been here eighteen years," Goralski said. "I know everybody in this neighborhood and I don't know you. What's your name?"

"Miles."

"Faggot name. Miles what?"

"Bradshaw."

"Well, get the fuck off my place, Miles, and don't come back. I don't know who you are but I don't like you. And I'll tell you something else. Yeah, I heard of Carlos Perez. The cops say he burned down that building and he probably did. He's done it before. Everybody thinks the landlords around here are rich, but they're not. They're pathetic suckers. The rich ones got out years ago after milking the shines, and now only the jerks are left. And what are they left *with?* Nuthin'. So they pay a kid ten dollars to burn down the building and then they collect fire insurance. Understand? And they hold the land and don't pay taxes. A little math. Get out."

Miles turned to leave, then had another thought.

"How do you *know* he's burned down buildings?" he asked.

"I know." Goralski's face was coloring.

"How well did you know Carlos?"

The junk dealer screamed, "Get the hell out of here!"

Goralski watched Miles leave, mopped his brow, then reached for the phone.

"I don't know what's going on over *there,*" he said, "but I think you oughta know what just happened."

Out on the street, Miles felt frustrated. Why had Goralski ordered him away, then volunteered a lecture on landlords? Why had he told two different stories about Carlos? *Had* Carlos burned buildings down? And why had Goralski seemed so upset? Across the street, several teenagers were lounging against a storefront beneath a neon sign that read "PINBALL PALACE." Latin Kings. One sat on the curb, looking bored. All of them appeared too young to be dangerous, so on an impulse Miles crossed the street and approached the tallest boy, a lean Hispanic with a pimply face.

"Hi," said Miles.

"Hi," said the boy, his voice friendly.

Miles relaxed, decided to try some small talk. He asked about the games at the pinball parlor and the boy asked if he played. The other Kings paid little attention, concentrating instead on some girls coming up the block in halter tops. Each boy tried to outdo the others at wolf whistles.

"Is someone named Rodriguez here?" Miles asked.

The tall boy looked at him with some wariness. "Why?" A pause. "Do you know him?"

"No."

"You a cop?"

Miles shook his head. Several feet away, the girls came up to the Kings, who began flirting with them. One boy put his arm around a girl's waist. They bumped hips and laughed, and the boy Miles was talking to looked jealous. He said to Miles, "Tell me what you want to talk to Rodriguez about and I could give him a message."

Surprisingly, Miles felt much more at ease with the gang member than he had with the junkman. "I wanted to talk to him about Carlos Perez," he said.

"I know Carlos," the boy said. "He died in a fire."

They looked at each other a moment, then Miles said, "I saw it."

The boy's eyes widened. "Yeah?" he said. "That's what you want to talk to Rodriguez about? Rodriguez and Carlos were friends." The boy considered a moment. "I can get Rodriguez. You wanna wait here?"

"Sure."

The boy pushed himself off the wall with his elbows, approached his companions and spoke to them in a low voice. They glanced back at Miles, nodding and smiling. "I'll be back in ten or fifteen minutes," the spokesman said. "Wait."

He walked off, boots clicking on the pavement. Miles looked for an awning or anything that would provide some relief from the sun, without any luck. His shirt clung to his back, and he was very thirsty, he realized. The other Kings ignored him, seemingly cool even in boots and jackets. Ten minutes passed, but the boy did not return. The Kings continued to flirt with the girls and, aside from glancing at Miles periodically, ignored his presence. Fifteen minutes passed and Miles became fidgety. He searched the street for the boy, who finally reappeared with an apologetic grin.

"Sorry, man, but Rodriguez is a little busy. He wants to talk to you though. He says maybe you could come to see *him.* He's real close, only a couple of blocks away."

As he spoke the other boys drifted over to listen and watch. Miles grew uncomfortable, wondering what a gang leader did when he was a "little busy." He realized with a sinking feeling that he was surrounded. "I don't know . . ." he began, but the tall boy smiled and said, "Oh, it's very close."

The ring of bodies seemed to move at the same time, propelling him lightly up the block. The boys talked to one another in Spanish, laughing and gesturing, almost ignoring him yet moving him along. One wore a knife at his belt. Miles remembered the story of the half-wit and surreptitiously searched the street for passersby who might help him. No one was there. They stopped in front of a large building which Miles guessed was an old factory or warehouse.

"Meth clinic," the spokesman said.

Miles relaxed a little, chiding himself for having felt so threatened. The clinic would be filled with doctors and patients.

But his feeling of security disappeared as soon as the Kings pushed open a heavy metal door and entered the building. As the signs indicated, the structure did house a meth clinic, but it was also apparent that the medical area occupied a very small space. Miles didn't see *any* doctors, only a battered-looking sign, "CLINIC," and an arrow pointing down a stairwell. A line of bleary-eyed, drooping teenagers, one of whom was twitching uncontrollably, lounged on the stairs. A black woman moved up and down the line, recording information on a pad.

The Kings led Miles away from the clinic entrance and up several flights of deserted stairs, the translucent windows atop each flight enclosing wire-meshed grids. Heels echoing sharply on the tile, they moved down a hallway so narrow that only one person could pass at a time, toward a room from which a light gleamed faintly. Three boys, whom Miles took to be members of the gang, stood by the door. Inside, an ancient fan turned slowly on the ceiling. The walls were paneled with some kind of smoky wood and the floor was thickly carpeted. The overall effect of a comfortable office was jarringly incongruous.

A stocky, muscular boy seated on the edge of a desk said, "I'm Rodriguez." He looked about fifteen, but his voice had the authority of a much older person. "Have a seat," he said, pointing to a stuffed leather chair. The Kings ringed Miles in a semicircle, looking down at him, their hands in their pockets or flat at their sides, their eyes filmed over. Miles guessed that some of them found the location of the clinic downstairs a great convenience.

Rodriguez' voice was surprisingly raspy. "What did you come here for?"

59

Miles groped for an answer. "I'm . . . well . . . I wanted to find out about him."

"And?"

Miles looked at the unsmiling faces. The boys who had brought him clustered around the door as he thought again of what they had done to the half-wit and cursed himself for coming to this building.

Rodriguez said, "Talk to me."

"I heard you were friends."

"Yeah."

"I saw the fire."

Rodriguez leaned toward him. "So?"

Miles frowned. He had expected more of a response. "I *saw* it."

Rodriguez looked impassive. "What's it to you?"

"He shouldn't have been there. Someone tied him up."

Silence.

Rodriguez looked away slowly, exhaled and turned back. He said, "Where'd you get those shoes?"

Miles said, "What?" He wasn't sure he had heard correctly. Everyone was staring at him, at his shoes. "I just got them downtown somewhere," he said.

"Downtown."

"Yes."

"Those shoes."

Miles shivered, the perspiration icy on his back. He shuffled his feet under the chair.

Rodriguez jabbed a finger at him. "What do you mean, he was tied up?"

"I don't know. I'm not sure. I . . . I couldn't see his arms."

"So who tied him up?"

"I don't know."

"You think *we* tied him up?"

"No, no," Miles said quickly.

"Then why'd you come here?"

Miles searched his mind desperately. He had come to see if the Kings were connected with Carlos' death, but it would be sheer idiocy to *say* that. He cursed again the impulse which had brought him here, then said, "I was hoping you might tell me . . . if he was supposed to be . . . maybe you would know because you were friends . . . supposed to be around the building."

"What do you mean, *be around?* Let me see your wallet."

Miles fumbled for the wallet, brought it out. What now, a robbery? One of the two Kings flanking Rodriguez held out his hand and Miles gave him the billfold. The boy searched it thoroughly, shook his head at Rodriguez and handed it back. He said, "No cop."

The ceiling fan revolved soundlessly. Rodriguez looked up at a lock on the wall and scratched his wrist. His left boot rubbed at the calf of his other leg. There was a light sheen breaking out on his upper lip. Miles sensed he was tired of talking.

"Someone told me landlords burn down their own buildings," Miles said to break the silence.

Rodriguez looked at the clock again and nodded impatiently. "Yeah, yeah. Landlords. You know who owns that building? A guy named Scowcroft who works at the zoo. Absentee. An asshole."

He scratched up and down the length of his arm and stood up. The Kings at the door immediately came to attention. "Carlos was my friend," he said. Rodriguez turned and left the room, the two boys following like lieutenants. Miles was unsure whether he was free to stand up now, but after a moment the tall boy who had escorted him to the building said, "You wanna go back?"

Miles tried not to show his relief. As he left the building, he saw Rodriguez in the clinic line, arguing with the black woman with the pad, the other two boys at his side like bodyguards. The heavy metal door shut behind Miles; one of the Kings dug a dime out of his jeans and went to a pay phone in the hallway.

"Rodriguez says there's a problem," he said.

Miles sat in the rear corner of the bus all the way home, relieved, humiliated, angry at himself. His thoughts rambled back to the interviews he had conducted when he was on Park Avenue; the polite questioning of well-dressed clients, the mannered taking of depositions. That was the world he had left behind, but this was a game with altogether different rules. Or did it have any rules at all? The boys in that abandoned factory were a bunch of glassy-eyed teenagers who knew more about the street than he ever would and who could easily have killed him this afternoon. Carlos' mother had loathed him. The principal had only wanted to hear stories. The junk dealer had hated him for a reason he couldn't fathom.

Worst of all, he really hadn't learned anything useful. He still didn't know anything about Carlos Perez. Maybe the boy *had* burned down the building. What did it matter anyway? Why had he started asking questions? Because of a tenuous and ridiculous connection between his dead daughter and a boy he had never even met?

He climbed the stairs to his apartment and, as usual, was greeted by the classical music from next door. As soon as he was inside, the girl started knocking on the wall. How did she know he was home? Footsteps, maybe. He ignored her and poured a glass of milk, brooding, trying to understand the strange and upsetting emotions washing through him. *Tomorrow I'll go back to the office,* he promised himself, sitting by the window. The knocking on the wall began again. The Spanish couple started screaming at each other. Slowly the light faded in the apartment. He thought of the blazing silhouette and tried to make it go away.

The pleasant-faced man sat by the telephone, listening.
"Miles Bradshaw," he said. His voice was tinged with a slight foreign accent and he wrote the name on a pad, drew little swirls around the M. *"Did he tell you where he lived? No? Did you ask him?"*
He gazed out of the trailer and across the construction site.
Men in hard hats moved in and out of the low-income housing project. The earth started to vibrate.
"Find him."

FIVE

MILES FOUND himself in unexpectedly good spirits the next morning, looking forward for the first time in several weeks to going to work. It had rained during the night and the air smelled cleaner, sweeter; the inquiries of the day before were far away. The impenetrable question of what had happened to Carlos Perez seemed to have nothing to do with him. Youth gangs or greedy landlords—whoever was in the business of burning down buildings—that was the domain of the police, not this poverty lawyer, he told himself.

He entered the office jauntily and grinned at Samantha. "Go-od morning!" His voice was light, surprising them both. "Every client scores today," he said. "To hell with the

City. Today I accomplish a lot." She looked at him as if he were crazy.

He felt like the old Miles this morning, the cheerful Miles people had taken to so easily when he worked on Park Avenue. The feeling was strong, welcome, and unexpected. A young woman in a tight skirt, with bare attractive legs, was already seated in his office. She was Hispanic, reminded him of the girl from next door. He sat on the edge of the desk and decided that whatever her problem, he would do his damndest to solve it.

"My name is Miles Bradshaw," he said. "I'm the attorney here. What can I do for you?"

Her name was Marta and her problem was rats from a neighboring building. "*My* building is clean," she said, wringing her hands in distress. "My landlord a good man. He lives in New Jersey but takes care of the building; paints, exterminates, gives heat in the winter. But next door . . ." Her face twisted in anger and disgust. "The landlord he not care. He don't talk to tenants before he let them move in and he no take care of garbage. His basement is filled with big rats. Lots of them." She held up her hands to indicate an eighteen-inch length.

"Last night I wake up about two or three and I hear this scraping noise in the kitchen." She shuddered. "Like fingernails, scratching. I get out of bed and turn on the light. A rat! I tried to hit it with a broom but it ran under the sink. I don't know where it is now. It could still be there. I no wanna go back today. I'm going to my sister."

It was a familiar story. The good buildings were always the first to be abandoned. Tenants there had the money and inclination to move. And no matter how clean a building was kept, if there was an empty lot next door, or an abandoned structure, the rats needed only a one- or two-inch opening to get inside, where they would crisscross the pipes and chew through walls to reach food.

Normally Miles wouldn't have bothered to follow through on a case like this, but today, feeling lucky, he dialed the Buildings Department.

A gruff voice answered. "Inspectors." Miles identified himself and explained the situation. "Would it be possible to get an inspector over there today?" he said. "It's an emergency."

The voice sounded weary and almost disdainful. "Come on, Mr. Bradshaw. You know the score. We got budget cutbacks. You got a signed complaint from someone in the building?"

"No, but this is special."

"Of course it's special. They're all special. What's the story over there? The girl in your office now? Sitting there? Every inspector we got is out on a signed complaint. City Hall wants proof we ain't goofin' off. Maybe if someone from the building calls, we can work something out, *maybe*, in a couple of weeks."

Miles thanked him and hung up. The girl watched him hopefully. "We need a signed complaint from a resident of the bad building," he said.

The hands started moving on her lap. "Eempossible," she said. "They're afraid the landlord will kick them out. *I'll* sign the complaint."

Miles let out his breath. "It isn't the same," he said, spreading his hands and then pulling them back suddenly when he realized that was what Marcus did when he couldn't help someone.

"*Why* isn't it the same? The rats will be there no matter who complains."

How do you explain bureaucratic rules to people who don't want to hear about them? Miles's good mood began to dissipate. He moved behind the desk to the chair and sat down. "We only have a limited number of inspectors," he said, "only enough to work on an emergency basis. We need written complaints."

The woman seemed to slide down in her chair. Then she shot up again and jabbed an angry finger at him. "What good are *you*, then?" she said. "Why not fire everyone in this office and replace them with inspectors? What good is a lawyer if there's no inspector?" She made a disgusted sound. "I afraid to go back to the apartment tonight. When I think of rats coming in the bedroom when I'm asleep . . ." She shuddered, looked at him imploringly. "There's got to be a way."

They were interrupted suddenly by shouts from Marcus' side of the partition. "WHAT DO YOU MEAN YOU CAN'T DO ANYTHING! THE BUILDING BURNED DOWN! THE LANDLORD DID IT! I SAW A BOY RUNNING AWAY WITH A GASOLINE CAN! STOP WRITING AND LISTEN TO ME!"

Miles went into the reception area where the visitors had stopped talking. Samantha was leaning forward at her desk, watching Marcus and his visitor, a man in a doorman's uniform who had probably gotten up early to come here before work. She kept one hand on the telephone should a call to the police seem necessary.

"I SAW IT!" he screamed.

Marcus, cool as usual, said, "We're a legal office, not arson investigators. The Fire Department—"

"DON'T TELL ME ABOUT THE FIRE DEPARTMENT! I BEEN THERE AND THEY TELL ME THEY CAN BARELY PUT OUT ALL THE FIRES. HOW THEY GONNA INVESTIGATE THEM! YOU'RE THE CITY! WHAT ARE YOU GOING TO DO WITH THAT PAPER, EAT IT?"

"*I saw a boy,*" the man had said. Miles felt the perspiration break out on his back. No one else in the waiting room appeared concerned. They were just glad to have a break in the monotony. Marcus said something in his official tone, which set off a fresh round of abuse.

"YOU KNOW WHAT YOU DO IN THIS OFFICE?

NUTHIN'! AND MORE NUTHIN'! YOU SIT HERE
AND TAKE NAMES AND FILE PAPERS! MY HOUSE
BURNED DOWN! I HAD ALL MY MONEY IN A
CLOSET! DO YOU CARE? YOU'RE JUST SITTIN'
HERE WAITIN' FOR QUITTIN' TIME! YOU'RE A
FRAUD! A WASTE! A SHIT!"

Each barb pierced Miles. Wasn't there a landlord *he*
should be talking to? What was he accomplishing in the
office today? He certainly hadn't been any help to the
Hispanic woman, who was even now storming out of the
place. The doorman went next, slamming the door behind
him, his heavy footsteps receding down the stairs. An old
woman whose eyes reflected bewilderment and anger said,
"Am I next?" Marcus was already reading the file on his
next complainant. The old woman said, "I haven't gotten
my Social Security check in two months."

"Come into my office," Miles said, knowing full well that
he could do nothing legal for her, that she, like many
others who came here to rant about potholes, or the Vet-
erans Administration, or even a runaway child, was seeking out the only visible government representative she
could find.

He gave her forty dollars of his own money and told her
that it was a loan from the City, although he knew he'd
never get it back. Then, at lunchtime, he told Samantha
he was quitting for the day, and he left for the zoo.

The bus took him out of the slums into a more prosper-
ous section of the Bronx, where there were newer projects,
small homes and well-kept stores. People looked better-
dressed and for the first time in months he was conscious
of his own shabby appearance.

He felt impelled to resume his quest not so much expecting to learn anything more about Carlos as simply

wanting to talk to the landlord and ease his nagging sense of disquiet. The day was unusually hot and sultry, and the open windows provided a refreshing breeze.

The zoo itself was moderately busy for a July weekday, filled with children from City day camps who moved in lines of two, holding hands, along the meandering pathways. Lunch bags and soda cans spilled over the tops of trash cans. Khaki-uniformed park attendants swept orange-drink containers into hand-held bins, and the air was thick in places with the musty odor of animals or hot dogs. The last time Miles had come to the zoo had been with his own daughter. The memory was painful and he was tempted to leave. From somewhere behind him came the howl of monkeys. A parent was haranguing a child for wandering off. Brightly colored stuffed tigers were clutched in tiny fists.

Miles located the Administration Building, a two-story neatly maintained brick structure on the main plaza. The office of the landlord, Paul Scowcroft, was in a second-floor alcove. His secretary, a sour-faced woman in a frilly pink dress which did not suit her fifty-odd years, pursed her lips when Miles entered. Did Mr. Scowcroft expect him? Miles said no and she looked disapproving. The secretary disappeared into a back room to return a moment later with the landlord. Miles instantly decided they were a matched set. The same picky look was at the corners of the mouth, the same condescension in their eyes.

Scowcroft said, "I'm very, very busy this afternoon." He ran his hands through his hair, which was black and combed straight back, giving him a weasellike appearance. "We've got a Tasmanian wolf shipping in at Kennedy tomorrow. On loan from Auckland. What do you want?"

Miles had the feeling the man was going to turn away momentarily. Shifting his stance, he said, "I was hoping

69

to talk to you about a building you own that burned down."

Instantly, Scowcroft was transformed from a sour-faced bureaucrat to an ingratiating host. He pumped Miles's hand as though greeting a long-lost brother. The secretary's expression had changed as well and she was bobbing pleasantly and smiling. The two faces mirrored each other. It occurred to Miles that they were lovers. Boss and secretary, in the zoo.

Scowcroft grasped Miles's arm and pulled him into his office. "Sit down. Would you like some coffee? A soft drink? It's certainly hot out there, isn't it, Mr. . . . ."

"Bradshaw," Miles said.

"Fine. You have a card?"

An odd question, Miles thought, and shook his head, but Scowcroft didn't seem to mind, settling back expectantly behind his cluttered desk. When Miles said nothing, Scowcroft offered, "I bought that building to renovate it, and the fire wiped me out. Those bastard kids." He paused, shook his head vindictively. "If that boy hadn't died . . ." His voice trailed off to imply the terrible retribution he envisioned, then he bent over and opened a bottom drawer. When he straightened up he held a piece of paper in his hand. Miles suspected that Scowcroft had been working on this paper when he had interrupted him, not on the Tasmanian wolf, whatever that was.

"I've itemized my losses," Scowcroft said, "from the plaster to the woodwork. I'd put in the woodwork only several days before the fire and, of course, the tools burned too. The building was basically very sturdy. Losses come to about . . . sixty-two thousand dollars." He chuckled, and Miles was afraid for a moment that he was going to get up and wrap his arms around him. "Maybe I overestimated a *little*," Scowcroft said, "but the building had sentimental value. I'd never been a landlord before."

Miles said, "I'm afraid I'm not following you. Why are you telling me this?"

The smile faltered, was replaced by a look of uncertainty. "You're from Aetna, aren't you?" Scowcroft asked. "The insurance investigator who called a while ago?"

"Oh, no, no," Miles said quickly, spreading his hands to emphasize the point. The landlord's facial muscles shifted again. He had an incredibly mobile face, and Miles, watching it, said, "I live across the street from that building."

Scowcroft stiffened. "And?"

"And I saw the fire start." Miles was baffled by what he read as terror in the landlord's eyes.

Scowcroft swallowed, laughed nervously, shoved the paper back into the drawer, and looked anxiously at the clock, seemingly involved in a series of rapid calculations. Then abruptly, like a summer storm, the darkness left his face and the smile was back. "Have you ever seen a Tasmanian wolf?" he asked.

Miles shook his head.

"Very beautiful animal. Almost extinct. Very vicious." Scowcroft glanced back at the clock. "I want very much to talk to you about the building and what you saw. I'm sure it will help the insurance investigator. But my problem right now is that I've got to finish some paper work. Could you possibly come back at four-thirty? I'll have more time to talk. Would that be okay?"

Miles agreed, vaguely disturbed by a feeling that something was going on here that he didn't understand. Still, why not wait? He had nowhere else to go, even if the zoo stirred up memories he would rather forget. Scowcroft steered him to the door and the secretary started to smile when they appeared in the outer office, but then saw something in her boss's face and stopped. Miles thanked her. As he was leaving he noticed Scowcroft through the glass door on the phone, gesturing rapidly. Downstairs he passed a man in a gray suit entering the building, attaché case in hand. The Aetna representative.

The zoo turned out to be even more depressing than Miles had anticipated. The World of Birds was near the Administration Building and he wandered there first. His daughter had particularly liked the South American toucan. "Funny nose, Daddy," she had said with a giggle. He left there quickly.

Strolling leisurely, he bought a hot dog with lots of mustard and sauerkraut from one of the stands, some of the red tangy onion sauce dripping on his thumb and napkin. Sparrows perched on the railing as he passed, dropping to the ground when a morsel of food fell, snatching it, swallowing it back on the railing. A large crowd of school-age children stood at the rhino pit, watching one of the animals slumbering in the dust while birds perched on its gently rising flanks. A camp counselor lectured about the beast.

". . . very dangerous when aroused. It eats plants and is called the tank of the plains. Also, rhinos are very stupid, capable of charging someone, forgetting what they're doing in the middle of the charge and stopping. Very dangerous. Generally, they're in the Asia part of the zoo but they've been moved here today."

He moved out of earshot, remembering cute comments his daughter had made about the animals, the terrible clarity of his vision weighing him down. Several laughing children ran in the direction of the monkey house and he proceeded in that direction himself, remembering the little hand folded in his own. "Daddy, can we watch them feed the seals?"

Losing himself in the luxury of an imaginary daughter, he agreed and headed for the seals, his steps shorter now as he made allowance for a small presence. And now his wife was with him also, her arm tucked through his. For an instant he felt complete again.

People were gathered about the seal pool, watching an attendant with a great handlebar mustache throwing chunks of raw fish from a pail which swung at his side. The seals barked and raced around the pool, occasionally catching a morsel in midair and earning an ovation from the youngsters. The crowd intruded upon his daydreams, and the image of wife and daughter faded, leaving him with an aching sadness. He checked his watch, hoping it was time for his meeting with Scowcroft, wishing, in fact, that the meeting were over and he on his way home, the dusk acting as a balm for his troubled soul. And so, in this intensely personal mood, he was puzzled abruptly by a sense of warning, of instinct. A peculiar sensation seized him, the sort of feeling one has upon accidentally meeting another's eyes. Perhaps he had already unconsciously spotted the man moving toward him through the crowd and had not processed the sight, but now he looked up, met the Oriental's eyes and held them. A short man, maybe a Filipino, with a very pleasant face, was approaching him. The intensity of the stranger's look startled him, and he tilted his head at the man in an unspoken question, pointed at himself as if to say "Me?" and waited for a response. When none was forthcoming he stepped toward the man to see what he wanted, but detected something in the eyes, a stiffening, which stopped him, and he became irrationally nervous. Turning his head he caught a glimpse of a second man coming at him from the opposite direction, also staring at him. There was purpose in the look.

Confused, Miles hoped that the men were looking for each other, and he moved aside, but they changed direction to match his own. A roar from the crowd made him jump as a big seal caught a fish in midair. He backed into the open and began walking away quickly.

He glanced back. Both men broke from the periphery of the crowd at the same moment, matching his pace with theirs so that the distance separating them remained the same. Miles took a sudden turn and headed for the bear house. He left the path, strolled past a "KEEP OFF THE GRASS" sign and turned to see them still following, their resolute stride filling him with a sense of terrifying unreality, as if they were actually stalking him. He wanted to believe he was imagining the entire episode, but each time he changed direction they stayed with him.

It was time to turn back if he wanted to get to the Administration Building by four-thirty, and he would have to pass the two men to get there. For a moment he wondered whether they had been summoned by Scowcroft, but the idea struck him as ludicrous. Ahead, a policeman lounged against the red brick side of a public lavatory. Approaching him, Miles saw the bored expression turn to one of concern. The policeman was young, in his mid-twenties. He pushed himself off the wall and asked, "Are you all right? You look sick."

What could he tell the cop? Two men were after him? "I'm being followed," he said, aware, even as he said it, of how ridiculous he sounded. The policeman looked skeptically amused and Miles turned to point them out.

They were gone.

He experienced a horrible sinking feeling and turned back to the policeman. "I know it sounds crazy," he said. "I was watching the seals at feeding time. Two men . . ." He stopped, began again. "It's *true!*" But he thought, *Is it* true? Maybe it was a coincidence. Were the men really there, following me at all? To the officer, who had an innocent, wary face, he said, "Maybe I imagined it," although that didn't seem right either.

The cop accepted the explanation. "Hot day," he said, and troubled, Miles repeated the word. "Hot." What should he do now? Turn around? Walk back to the Administration Building? Leave the zoo? He had to decide quickly.

Miles gave a nervous laugh of embarrassment and headed back toward the Administration Building. His watch told him he was five minutes late.

Quickening his steps, he moved around the penguin house and out of sight of the policeman, past a refreshment booth, a zoo attendant sweeping the path, the reptiles, and briskly approached the cafeteria.

The two men came around the corner of the building.

Miles panicked. There was no one else on the path. The grounds were emptying rapidly. The men fixed their eyes on his face, as if trying to mesmerize him, their hands flat at their sides with a tension and suppressed violence that made him shudder. The pleasant-faced man abruptly smiled.

This is crazy, Miles thought, backing away. He walked hurriedly in the opposite direction, thinking, *Scowcroft will wonder what happened to me.* The men quickened their pace so that they were advancing on him and he resisted the temptation to run, feeling like a man walking away from a dangerous animal. If you ran it would charge. He had to get out of the zoo.

But the twisting paths which had earlier diverted him now confronted him like a labyrinth. Which way was out? At a crossroads where a young couple lounged on a bench he paused for an instant to try to read a posted map, aware that his delay was allowing the men to gain on him.

The arrows and numbers on the map seemed to merge, sending him in opposite directions, making no sense either because of an idiot cartographer or his own mounting fear. To the couple on the bench he said, "Uh . . . excuse me." They had the open amiable faces of young lovers. "Do you see those two men back there?"

The men had stopped by a tree and appeared to be deep in conversation.

How could he explain without sounding absurd? "Forget it," he muttered, and moved away, hearing their puzzled laughter behind him. A policeman strolled by. "Closing time," he called. It was the same officer Miles had spoken to before, and he watched the cop pass the two men and nod a greeting as he would to anyone.

Miles plunged ahead, oblivious to where the twisting paths were leading him, catching snatches of conversation or blurred faces, until he found himself back by the lovers on the bench. With a horrified groan he changed direction, passing the zoo bar and the Children's Zoo. The path ended ahead in an abrupt T at the fence encircling the rhino pit. A turn and an eighty-foot walk were necessary to skirt the area where the big animal was still asleep, the sparrows hopping about in the dust around it. Miles backed against the fence, a wave of fear and nausea striking him, and saw one of the men advancing on him, diagonally, from the left, blocking his escape both in that direction and from where he had come. The Filipino emerged from the right, trapping him against the fence.

The two men rushed at him. The steel guardrail was at his back, warm from the sun, and a heavy animal smell came from the pit. The Filipino flicked a knife out of his pocket. In that frozen instant, some instinct of self-preservation cleared Miles' mind and he realized he had only two choices: either yell for help or jump the fence. Several campers came into view about a hundred yards away, but they were too young and too far away to aid him. No one was close enough to stop the attack.

So he jumped the fence.

Immediately a child's voice cried out, "Ma! A man just

jumped into a cage!" Miles was seized with a sense of the absurd, the impossible. The two attackers were ten feet from the fence and the space in front of them began filling rapidly with curious onlookers. Miles stood about twenty feet from the sleeping animal, which looked a great deal bigger up close than it had appeared from the outside. Its flanks rippled and a tiny eye twitched. Miles froze. He heard cries behind him.

"GET OUTTA THERE, YOU JERK!"

"IT'S GONNA WAKE UP!"

"HEY! WAKE UP! DINNUHTIMMMMMME!"

An empty Coke can came flying out of the crowd and fell short of the sleeping animal. The kid who had tossed it was pouring the contents of another can on the ground, obviously getting ready to throw that too. Miles looked for a policeman in the crowd but saw none. Fifty yards separated him from the far side of the enclosure, with only a tree behind which to seek protection. In order to reach the far side safely he would have to walk directly past the sleeping rhino.

He didn't think he could do it, but perhaps the gathering crowd would protect him from attack if he went back over the fence the way he had come.

Miles inched toward the fence, saw the pleasant-faced man move toward him, and stopped. Behind him, some distance away, the door to the rhino cage loomed, black, and he wished the animal were inside, behind a locked gate, instead of being here while he stood paralyzed beside it, afraid it would wake up and gore him to death. Should he go across the pit or over the fence? *Decide,* he ordered himself. *Quickly!*

He began to cross the pit but was startled by a movement just inside the door of the cage. A huge form loomed out of the shadows and a gasp went up from the audience.

Another rhino lumbered into the pit.

The crowd was screaming. Policemen shoved their way to the rail. The animal saw him and charged, head lowered, tiny feet pounding with incredible speed. Miles twisted away and fell. The rhino tore past, turned and stopped, observing him. Remembering what the camp counselor had said about the stupidity of the beasts, he looked into the squinty bloodshot eyes. The long tusk shook back and forth.

The first rhino snorted and, waking, rose.

Miles backed toward the tree. He would never have time to get over the fence. Climb the tree? The branches were too high.

One of the rhinos came after him. He felt the breath on his arm, and panting, saw the other one circling. He heard gunfire—the police were firing into the air to distract the animals, who looked away for an instant. One trotted off to investigate. If only they were in that cage, the door closed.

That gave him a desperate idea. When the rhino near the tree turned its head, he decided to take a chance and ran for the cage, praying the animal wouldn't start immediately after him. He didn't know anything about zoo cages but figured there had to be a way to close them. If he could shut the door before the rhino reached him he might save himself.

The distance between Miles and the yawning door seemed to stretch. There came a roar from the crowd behind him, which meant the rhino had started after him. He could feel the ground trembling under his feet. At the door he almost tripped, but he looked around wildly for a lever and saw that there was a sliding door, on a track. Turning and throwing his weight against the steel, he saw the rhino barreling toward him, and then the gate was moving, and it clanged shut. There came the crash and reverberation of the rhino hitting the door. He heard it wheezing on the other side.

Heaving from the effort and shock, Miles slumped to the floor of the cement enclosure, which extended some thirty feet ahead to steel bars and reeked of rotten food and huge chunks of manure which lay on the floor. Beyond the cage were a tile hallway, where several tittering couples stared at him, and the glass doors which led to the outside. The doors were flung open and three policemen rushed in, followed by zoo attendants and Scowcroft, his face red with fury. The attendants opened the cage and the police rushed in, grabbed him and, pinning his arms behind him, propelled him into the hallway.

"Hey!" Miles said. "HEY!"

One of the policemen said, "You could have been killed out there."

A second one, whom Miles recognized as the officer whose aid he had solicited earlier in the afternoon, indicated Miles with his head. "That's the guy," he said.

Miles said to Scowcroft, "Tell them to let me go. After I left your office I was on the way back and . . ."

The weasellike official peered into his face, then turned to the sergeant. He said, "This guy's a nut. I never saw him. Get him out of the zoo."

Miles struggled against tightening grips. "What do you mean! I was in your office! You *told* me to come back. YOU CALLED THOSE MEN!"

The sergeant ignored him. "Ya wanna press charges?"

Scowcroft shook his head. "We'd both be up all night with paper work. Just get him out of here."

"We could drive him over to Bellevue," the young cop suggested, twirling his finger at his forehead.

The sergeant poked Miles in the chest. "Listen, Buster. You're a lucky guy after what you did. You coulda been killed. And you could still go to the slammer. Want to go to jail? Keep shouting. Want to go home? Shut up."

Miles quieted, white with fury, and the hands holding him relaxed, then let him go. Scowcroft left the building.

Miles wanted to call after him but decided he had better not.

One of the policemen steered him by the arm toward the exit. Miles experienced a stab of fear when he saw the pleasant-faced man watching him from the ranks, then realized the man was angry. Miles had escaped. Back in the pit, both rhinos were rolling blissfully in the dust.

At the zoo entrance Miles began to alternately shiver and sweat—a delayed reaction of shock.

The cop said, "What's the matter?"

"Nothing."

"Roll up your sleeves."

"Huh?"

"Do it!" Miles complied. The cop studied his arm and said, "No drugs?"

Offended, Miles said, "What do you think I am?"

"Aaaaah," the cop said, pushing him toward the subway. "Go home. And don't come back."

There was no sign of the two men as Miles hurried to the tracks. The ride home seemed to take forever. The boy had been murdered, he now knew, and the two men from the zoo were probably looking for him. He needed to talk to someone right away and was amazed when he realized whom he had in mind.

SIX

Standing in the doorway in her already familiar pose, hands on hips, head inclined in amusement, Elena took his breath away. Her slender wrists were circled by bracelets, her dress sheer and clinging, the slightly mocking smile ever present. "Well," she said. "A neighborly visit. I didn't even knock." She started to say something else but stepped back, tilted her head. "Something's wrong."

He was glad she had said it. He moved into her apartment, again experiencing that sense of vivid unreality which permeated even his fear. He was unclear about what he wanted to say, knowing that he needed to talk. For the last twenty minutes he had been pacing back and forth in his apartment, glancing out the window every few moments as if expecting to see the pleasant-faced man and his glaze-eyed companion below.

Who were they? Would they find him? They knew his name but not where he lived or where he worked. They didn't even know he was a lawyer. On the other hand, the fact that he had seen the fire was good evidence that he lived in this neighborhood. Should he call the police? They hadn't believed him at the zoo and he had nightmarish memories of the way they had treated him after his own fire. And what of the boy he'd seen killed?

Suddenly he missed his wife very much.

Elena was eyeing him with a look that told him sarcasm was just around the corner. She said, "Lose the rent? Get fired? I love riddles." Then, raising an eyebrow, "Sit down. I'll make coffee. No. Maybe Scotch would be better." She moved with a sinewy leanness to a hutch and poured, and he watched her over the rim of the glass as he drank. The liquor seared his throat, making him feel better.

She retreated to the armchair opposite, dangling a shoe up and down on one foot. Obviously she didn't think whatever was bothering Miles was too serious.

He said, "Someone tried to kill me this afternoon." He stopped, stunned by the raspiness of his voice.

Across the room the shoe stopped moving and her brows caved inward. She opened her mouth but no sound came out.

Miles said, "In the zoo. The landlord. They killed the boy too."

There was a sharp intake of breath and her eyes grew wide; she dropped both feet to the carpet and leaned forward. Somewhere in the back of his mind he was surprised that she had not shown more shock but now was not the time to dwell on that.

And anyway, how to proceed? Miles was painfully aware

of how absurd his story might seem, particularly to someone like Elena, who treated everything as a sarcastic joke.
He shrugged. The simplest way was probably the best.
Haltingly, he told Elena of the trip to Carlos' mother, to
the junior-high-school friend and to the junk dealer. He
told her about the landlord and the pleasant-faced man,
about the horrible chase in the zoo. In his memory it
seemed like one of those bad dreams where your feet don't
move fast enough to carry you from danger.

The light faded and her cigarette glowed in the dark.
When the butt went out she lit another, the match flaring
to reveal her face. She looked pale and frightened.

He concluded with a shudder. "They know my name."
The room filled with laughter from another apartment,
raw and sexual. Miles envisioned a couple embracing.
There was a burst of heat lightning outside that signaled
an approaching summer storm. Elena switched on a lamp,
her perfume suddenly more powerful in the light, and
Miles braced for her attack, glad nonetheless that he had
unburdened himself.

But if he expected her to laugh he was mistaken. Her
face was blank, unfocused. He had the impression that he
had triggered some bad memory. After a moment she
trembled, shook herself and was back, horrified. "You're
going to call the police?"

Hesitantly, Miles nodded, afraid to explain his reluc-
tance and bitterly recalling the arson investigator, Goldstein, who had dogged his steps after his own blaze; at his
office, friends' apartments, the funeral home, restaurants;
a lean, tubercular shadow, persecutor, the very presence a
chilling accusation which could not be ignored. On top of
the awful fire dreams each night, Goldstein had been unbearable.

How can I tell her? Miles asked himself, knowing he
wouldn't be able to bear it if she were to start giving him

that post-Goldstein look. He felt bad enough when he saw doubt in his own eyes in the mirror.

He knew he was procrastinating, but he said, "At the zoo the police laughed at me."

"So?"

"So whoever I call will *check* with the zoo."

She considered that. "I see." Then, "Don't tell them about the zoo. Just the boy."

The answer, of course, had been obvious, but Miles hadn't permitted himself to see it. Now there was no excuse. After several moments he made a rumble of acceptance in his throat. He forced himself to rise and she smiled as if to spur him on. He was surprised to see a look approaching sympathy on her generally unemotional face and was, in fact, more touched by it than he would have cared to admit. Squaring his shoulders, he left the apartment.

The evening was strangely quiet. A lightning storm raged overhead and couples clung to fire escapes, wide-eyed. The rooftops were illuminated as during a night bombing raid. A patrol car rolled by, its occupants dark shadows through the window.

Miles wrestled with himself over whether to call the police or the Fire Department. Since he had already called the police anonymously and suspected that he might be remembered for hanging up on them, he decided on the firemen. Let *them* notify the police.

The phone booth had been spray-painted and the directory savaged, but at least the receiver emitted a dial tone when he picked it up. The voice on the other end was polite—Irish. "Fire Marshals. McGrory," it said.

Miles envisioned white hair and a florid, intelligent face. He fought off the urge to hang up. "My name is Miles Bradshaw. I'm an attorney for the City and I want to report an arson. A boy died in the fire."

The voice became concerned. McGrory wanted details and Miles supplied them, omitting any reference to the zoo or his own investigations. When Miles finished, McGrory said, "We'll send a man out. Have you called the police?"

Miles said, "I thought the Fire Department handled arson."

"Of course." A pause. "Could I have the spelling of your name please?"

Miles gave it.

"And your address?"

Gritting his teeth, Miles supplied that too.

"Most people call the police first," McGrory said, waiting to see if Miles would respond. "You have a phone number, Mr. Bradshaw?"

"No. No phone."

Another pause. "You don't have a phone. You're an attorney. You don't have a phone." The officer seemed to be wrestling with the facts. "Why are you calling now if the fire occurred three days ago?"

Stay calm, Miles ordered himself, panicking and desperately trying to think of a way to dispel the marshal's suspicion. He glanced up toward Elena's apartment. Framed by the window, holding a curtain with one hand and shading her eyes with the other, she was looking down into the street. He felt better seeing her there and a solution occurred to him. In a suitably embarrassed voice he said, "I didn't want to get involved."

The line worked, of course. The fireman had probably heard it hundreds of times before. The sigh on the other end was one of acceptance and Miles sagged with relief. The officer thanked him for calling, said an inspector would be dispatched, and hung up.

Miles was heady with elation. He had done it! He slapped the booth in joy. There was the distant rumble of

85

thunder, and when he stepped into the street a slight breeze tousled his hair. The storm was moving in. Elena's curtain had fallen back into place. He wanted to share his triumph with her. A burst of laughter came from a fire escape. Bongo drums beat out a Latin tempo and the street resounded with the noise.

He took the steps two at a time, panting by the time he reached the sixth floor. There was a pause of several seconds after he knocked, then her voice called to him, curiously numb, "Come in."

He sensed a change in mood immediately.

The lights had been dimmed and she was facing him in the armchair, legs crossed, blue cigarette haze around her head. The posture was stiff, haughty, distant. He wished he could see her face better.

"You called the police," she said, voice strangely emotionless.

"Yes."

"And they're coming."

"Yes. I feel better."

He tried to understand what could have happened while he was downstairs. Had he offended her in some way? Was she upset that he had called the arson people? Nonsense. She had *wanted* him to call. Her damn personality changes were driving him crazy, and although earlier he might have simply left to puzzle over her in the privacy of his own apartment, tonight he was feeling strong. Trying to mask the frustration in his voice, he said, "I don't understand you. One minute you're friendly, the next it's like we've never met."

She waved the smoke from her face. "I'm changeable, am I?"

"Yes."

"And you don't like that. Poor Miles. Miles doesn't like that, does he?"

86

"He damn well doesn't," snapped Miles, feeling his resolution to remain calm disappearing.

She sighed, went to the stereo, pulled a record from its jacket. The soothing melodies of Schubert filled the room. She took several deep breaths, as if to compose herself, and he was startled to see pain in her eyes. He had the impression that she was struggling with something inside, but had no idea what.

When she got very close he looked into her pupils and saw himself reflected there; tiny Miles Bradshaw in deep, dark pools. Her lips parted softly and she wet them with her tongue. "It's hard to break habits, isn't it?" she said. "To do something you're afraid of."

He was angry that his good spirits had dissolved, angry at her moods, angry at himself for liking her. "Riddles," he said. "If you want to say something, say it."

"Say it," she repeated.

"That's right."

But she didn't say it. Anger, despair and bitterness washed across her face. "I've been talking to myself so long everything I say sounds like a riddle," she said, but she was talking to herself *again,* Miles saw, and he didn't answer.

Still, there was an imploring look in her eyes which softened him enough to try a reconciliation. He had never liked the apartment and now he said, "Let's go somewhere. Call a cab. Anywhere. We'll talk, get coffee."

"No."

He was taken aback. "What do you mean, no?"

"I can't."

"What do you mean, you can't? What are you talking about?"

She said nothing, looking at the floor, miserable, and as he turned, furious, she cried out, *"Everyone has something she's ashamed of! Don't you?"*

He turned back. There was the vicious sound of rain on

the window. If there had been one argument in the world that would have made him stay, that was it.

She said boldly, "I can't go out because I'm . . ." but then faltered. Her voice dropped. "Because I'm afraid."

The words hung there. Miles said, "Afraid? Of what? A cab? Me? What?"

She swallowed. "Of space. I get dizzy, nauseous. I feel weak . . . I get frightened, can't breathe. Do you understand?"

"You're afraid of space," Miles repeated dumbly, his anger gone and replaced by bafflement.

She took a deep breath and said in level tones, "I'm afraid to go outside."

Miles recoiled. He had heard of people like Elena, who were afraid of elevators or heights or dark rooms, but he had never actually met one. From the look on her face she was obviously telling the truth, but to think that Elena was *afraid* . . . she seemed so *strong* . . . was astounding. Dumfounded, he turned her words over in his mind as if to impart some logic to them.

That was why he had never felt comfortable in her apartment. It was not merely a home, but a prison. The silence hung between them like some great black cloud of disbelief, and she said, still looking away, "I didn't want to tell you. I thought you'd leave."

Miles waited for more. She formed her lips into a thin line and sighed. "I guess you can't hide things forever, can you?" She was about to tell a story; he saw she was casting about in her mind for a beginning that she seemed abruptly to find in something she saw on the floor.

She said, "Look," pointing into the kitchen. He followed the line of her finger, saw a movement by the baseboard. "Cockroach," she said. It disappeared into the wall. "Nothing unusual about a cockroach, is there? Not here. Not in New York. But when I was a girl you know what my

88

mother would have done had she found a cockroach . . . a *single cockroach* . . . running along her fine marble halls? Or near the pool? Or on the patio? She would have fired the gardener, the grounds keeper . . . even the maid. She would have called an army of exterminators. My mother couldn't stand dirt, insects, strangers. I don't know why. I think she was a little sick."

She shrugged. "I asked her once. I was twelve or thirteen at the time. She had just told me not to go to some store, or movie, or neighborhood . . . whatever it was that day . . . by myself. Going places by yourself was dangerous, she said. I was very protected. I said to her, 'Why are you afraid of everything?' She started to yell. She didn't make sense. I think something happened to her once."

She looked up as if daring him to question any part of the story and he remained silent.

"But I'm getting ahead of myself, aren't I?" she said. "All this happened in Puerto Rico, where I grew up. Best private schools, tutors, riding lessons. I was a champion, with trophies. And a shooting champion as well. Me. Then." Her expression became wry. "Oh, yes," she said, and wove around the furniture into the bedroom, hips swinging. There came the sound of a drawer being opened and then she appeared again holding a pistol. She pointed it at him and Miles felt a stab of fear. "Bang," she said. "That's one dead Miles." The corner of her lips rose a fraction. "Or maybe I could slice off the tip of your earlobe. You have a very attractive earlobe. Or maybe you'd like to put a cigarette in your mouth . . . like in the movie . . . so I can shoot it in two." She rotated slowly on one heel, sighting various objects around the room. "My husband gave me this," she said, ignoring Miles's surprise. "He insisted I keep it in the apartment. He worked nights sometimes. A mechanic."

"Your husband?"

"He's dead."

He didn't say anything. Her tone became aggressive, caustic. "A mechanic. Surprised a girl like me would marry a mechanic? A lower-class mechanic? A filthy mechanic, who works with his *hands*? Not a surgeon? Not a businessman, like my father? That's what my mother said. She hated him, wouldn't allow him in the house after that first time, but he wasn't comfortable there anyway." She smiled to herself. "He said it was like a museum, not a home."

She sat down, put the pistol on the coffee table so that it faced Miles. "I'm boring you, aren't I?" she said, but she didn't seem to care whether she was boring him or not. She seemed to need to talk, and Miles found that he was forgetting his own concerns listening to her.

He said, "No, no. Please go on." He didn't know whether she'd heard him or not. She sniffed the air, momentarily distracted.

"Someone's cooking cabbage again," she said, and, agitated, moved to the window, her face partially in shadow now, the smoke from the cigarette curling softly by the glass, moist from the hanging plants. She rested one arm akimbo on the other, her now familiar pose, body slightly curled, beautiful, and she began again.

"Do you know how I met him? I was on the beach, our private beach, with Miguel, the bodyguard." She was amused at the memory. "Can you believe I had a bodyguard? Miguel was . . . well . . . friendly but . . . stupid. A great big man. I couldn't really talk to him, and the beach was very white, beautiful, long. So different from anything here. It lay at the bottom of a hill below our house, along a winding path through tall grass. My father was away on business. He brought cars from the States, furniture, anything that cost a lot of money for wealthy people on the island. A genius. I didn't see him too much." She swept her hand to indicate what lay outside the window as if to compare her childhood beach to the street below.

"That day something strange happened. A man came wading ashore. He must have swum over from the hotel beach two miles off. I was surprised. It was far and he didn't seem particularly athletic. He was built rather like you. Average. But shorter. Had a scar on his face which the sun had turned red. I could see it as he came out of the water, waving, and when he got close there was another one, here." She looked down and pointed to the upper torso, near the heart. Gently, as if tracing the jagged line across her husband's chest, she indicated its length and direction as Miles found himself growing irritated. Jealousy? Ridiculous, but he was grateful when she put her hand back at her side and resumed the story.

"I was glad to see someone new and I liked him right away, I think because of the scars. They gave him character, you know. Made him look vulnerable." She laughed. "Mysterious. The only strangers I ever met were those my mother arranged to come to the house.

"Anyway, he came right up. He was admiring me on that blanket. I looked pretty good in a bathing suit. Haven't worn one in a while but probably still do. He wanted to know my name. Did I live near the beach? Why weren't there any other people here? He was from New York, he said. The Bronx. On vacation, back to see his family. He was nice. I liked him. I was disappointed when Miguel got up . . . He had his orders . . . and told him he would have to leave. The beach was private.

"Well, he *started* to leave, but he must have seen that I didn't want him to, so he turned and asked Miguel who *he* was. My father? That was pretty funny and I started to laugh, told him no. Miguel was a bodyguard. Then *he* laughed. A bodyguard? Why did I need a bodyguard? And anyway, no bodyguard was going to make him leave if I wanted him to stay.

"Next thing I knew Miguel was on the ground, moaning." She laughed joyfully, lost in admiration. "What a

91

punch. A right hook. I don't think Miguel had ever been knocked down in his life. For the next few hours he just sat there and watched until it began to get dark. I invited Esteban up to the house. When my mother saw him she was suspicious, then unfriendly." She shook her head, then lapsed into a ruminating silence, composing the scene in her mind before continuing. "Dinner was on the table so he stayed," she said. "We got him some clothes and went into the dining room. Esteban came from a poor family in San Juan . . . lots of brothers and sisters . . . three in a bed . . . father gone. He'd gotten his scars in an accident in the Navy. The shrapnel was still in his chest." She sighed. "With each story he told, my mother's face got darker and after he left she ordered me not to see him again." A shrug. "Three weeks later I married him."

She lapsed into a reflective silence and Miles watched her, not wanting to disturb her mood. In a way he was glad he could stare unabashedly as she wasn't seeing him or anything else in the room. Her expression was distant, peaceful, but when she spoke again her voice was tinged with sadness.

"I came back here with him. My mother cut me off." She held up a hand as if to stop an ugly thought. "Don't worry. He told me what to expect, so I wasn't surprised. You probably think a rich girl like me hated it, but I didn't. I was in love.

"I didn't really meet any friends here, but I was used to spending time by myself and when Esteban wasn't working we went everywhere; Manhattan mostly, to the discos—he loved to dance. To museums, the waterfront. He liked to go to the yacht clubs. He wanted a boat and was saving for one. Then one day I got a call from the gas station where he worked. He was tuning up a car, nothing dangerous, and the shrapnel just shifted in his chest. The doctors had always said that could happen.

"I stayed here. Twenty-two years old. The check started coming every month from the Navy. My mother wouldn't write me back. I never could understand her. And then one day I . . . I . . ." She looked up suddenly, as if she had forgotten he was there and had almost allowed the momentum of the story to carry her into a forbidden area. She seemed to fumble for something to say but was obviously still thinking about the next part of her story. Her cigarette shook. She returned to the chair, sat down, leaned forward and placed her hands in her lap.

"And then I became afraid of going outside."

Miles waited for more. "I don't understand," he said. "You were afraid because your husband died?"

"Yes."

"No. You were going to say something else. What was it?"

"Nothing. You're mistaken."

"I don't understand."

"Of course not. There's nothing logical about this."

"No, you were going to tell me something else. You were going to tell me why you became afraid."

Her silence acknowledged the truth of his statement, but he didn't push. She was watching him, deeply embarrassed. What had begun as an answer had only led to more questions. Although he knew more about her now, it seemed as if he knew *less*. He said, "We can talk about it later," but she seemed not to have heard.

Still, he was grateful that she had made an effort to explain herself. And suddenly he was very tired, wanting to be alone and think. He thanked her for the Scotch and left.

Miles lay on the mattress and closed his eyes, but sleep eluded him. The music had stopped next door. It was still early, only nine o'clock, and he propped himself up on one elbow and looked around the apartment. *How bare it is,* he thought. *I should get some furniture.* He imagined tables and chairs, a couch, paintings on the walls. A vision of the living room in his old apartment—before the fire—flashed into his mind. He considered going to the chair by the window but decided against it. Not tonight—no fires.

Then he thought about the pleasant-faced man in the zoo and shuddered. Would the man come looking for him? After the conversation with Elena this evening, the events of the afternoon seemed more distant, and Miles was no longer gripped with the earlier sense of urgency which had driven him to call the Fire Department. The lone wail of a siren broke the night as if to remind him of his own vulnerability, then it faded.

He thought about Elena. Was she sleeping? Too early. Watching television? He didn't hear anything and the walls were thin. The image of her by the window lulled him.

At that moment there was a knock on the door.

Because he was thinking of Elena at the time, because he would have liked her to be the one in the hallway, he rose automatically to the door, anticipating her lovely face.

But it wasn't Elena who appeared before him.

Miles' smile died. Goldstein stood in the doorway: tall, stooped, tubercular, the same black raincoat crumpled about the lanky frame, the same shuffling suspicion in the movements. He looked as if he lived at Nedick's. Hands in his pockets, eyes accusing, certain and triumphant, as if he had ferreted out a dangerous criminal, the arson investigator didn't smile or even blink, but looked past Miles into the apartment. The gaze was deliberate, measuring. Miles grew dizzy watching him there, all the fear and guilt flooding back into him. Goldstein, who had hounded him, accused him, made the nightmare aftermath of his own fire worse. Goldstein was back.

"We generally come with a policeman when a death is involved but in your case I made an exception, *Counselor*," said Goldstein. "Didn't leave any forwarding address when you left Manhattan, did you? Mail's piling up in the post office. I can't tell you how pleased I was when you called." The marshal trudged into the apartment without waiting for an invitation and began moving along the walls like a dog staking out territory.

He said, "We always check our files when there's a death, just in case, and, of course, you were there. And I was there with you. Two deaths in ten months. Two twelve-year-olds. Two calls from Miles Bradshaw. We watch for repeaters, know what I mean? Once isn't enough for some people. I didn't think you were that type, but even *I'm* wrong sometimes." He revealed a set of yellowed teeth in what Miles imagined was supposed to be a smile. "Surprised to see me?"

Miles merely stared at the sneering countenance across the room. Goldstein's cheekbones were prominent, the nose thin, aquiline, the forehead high, the eyes gray as the complexion.

"Haven't had much time to fix the place up, have you? Or are you planning on moving again now that there's been a fire nearby? By the way. Whatever happened to that insurance money you got?"

"Nothing," Miles said, throat dry, constricted.

"I can check that, you know. It's easy."

"So check it," Miles snapped.

Goldstein shrugged, turned away and spoke with his back. "And even if you haven't touched it, so what? Some people wait for years before spending insurance money. They think they're the first ones to think up things."

"What do you mean, *'to think up things'*?"

Another shrug. "What do you think I mean?" He droned on, but Miles stopped listening, trying to fight his way out of shock and compose himself. The marshal was leaning against the peeling plaster, eyes hooded with a deceptive lazy look which Miles imagined had deceived plenty of guilty people over the years. They stared at each other as Miles silently cursed the arson bureau, Goldstein and especially himself for calling the authorities. The initial shock was wearing off and his inclination was to throw Goldstein out of the apartment. Screw him.

But even now the logical part of his mind was struggling furiously to keep himself under control, to prevent a recurrence of what had happened between him and Goldstein last time and to remember that a boy toward whom he felt a responsibility had been murdered. Since Goldstein would be the only arson investigator to work on this case, if Miles really wanted to help Carlos Perez he was going to have to convince the inspector that he was telling the truth. Kicking Goldstein out of the apartment wouldn't accomplish anything, and besides, with the murderers aware of who he was, he desperately needed an ally, not another enemy.

As an attorney Miles had been trained to ignore his emotions in touchy situations, to overcome doubt with logic, to construct chains of convincing argument. Still, it was harder to maintain calm now because he wasn't operating on behalf of a client but for himself. He was sweating with effort.

And Goldstein, meanwhile, sighing, as if about to enter into a game with an inevitable outcome, said, "Let's hear it." He pulled a pad out of his pocket.

Miles warned himself not to speak of the zoo. Goldstein would try to twist his statements to incriminate him. He chose his words carefully.

"I was sitting at my window three nights ago, just looking out . . ."

"Just looking out," Goldstein repeated casually, writing. His tone said, *You're a liar, Bradshaw.*

Miles felt an urge to justify his presence at the window but said instead, "I saw a fire start down the street. Across an empty lot. There was an explosion in a window."

The pen moved up and down.

"And in the flames I saw the silhouette of a boy."

Goldstein asked, without looking up, "How did you know it was a *boy*, Counselor, if it was only a silhouette."

"I . . . uh . . . later heard it was a boy."

"Of course. But why did you say it was a boy just now?"

"I just said it, that's all."

"For no reason."

"No."

"I see," Goldstein said. He put the end of the pen in his mouth. "Go on."

"Next day I heard that the police were blaming the boy for the fire, but that was impossible . . ."

"Of course it was. *You* knew who started the fire."

Ignore him, Miles told himself, gritting his teeth. *It's important to convince him.* "It was impossible because he had been tied up. I was upset that the boy was being blamed."

Goldstein stopped writing. "Why was that?" The raincoat rustled as he settled himself into the chair.

Miles said, trying to control his anger, "Wouldn't *you* have been upset?"

"You're suggesting that you and I get upset over the same things?"

Miles didn't give him the satisfaction of an answer. He began pacing, working off the urge to smash Goldstein in the face. He was conscious of the sound of his own footsteps, and also of the fact that Elena could hear them.

But could she hear the conversation too? He stopped, his face draining of color, and Goldstein said, "You're worried about something."

Miles nodded coldly, realizing that the less he seemed openly intimidated, the calmer Goldstein became. He wondered for an instant if Goldstein's inferences weren't simply part of an investigative strategy, but his glimmer of hope was destroyed with the marshal's next words.

"You've got to fabricate your story *faster*, Counselor. All these pauses are boring me. I would have thought you'd have figured it all out by now. After all, you've had three days to rehearse. It isn't like you to let things go until the last minute. And by the way," Goldstein said, "as long as you're stuck on the next point, I need some information. Where do you work now?"

Miles felt the old sick feeling gathering at the pit of his stomach, remembering his last meeting with the partners at the Park Avenue law firm where he had worked; the muted tones, the skyline of Manhattan brilliant in the sunshine outside, and the partners, inside, looking not at him during the meeting but at their fingers, their files, the table. The senior partner had done the talking.

"Miles, you've done superb work for us up until your . . . ahhh . . . tragedy. And it's only natural that your work might slacken up in times of . . . ahhh . . . mourning." A pause. "We know what you're going through. We've all lost loved ones here." The heads along the table bobbed up and down but the eyes remained lowered. The senior partner continued. "The difference in your case, frankly, is that we've all had visits from this Mr. . . . ahhh . . . Goldstein . . . who, silly as it seems, believes you responsible for the fire at your apartment." He raised his hand in a gesture of corporate sympathy.

"As *friends*, Miles, we deplore Mr. Goldstein's implications. I've complained to his office. Need we even explain how we have tried to make him understand how mistaken he is?"

The senior partner shrugged helplessly. "But he persists. He thinks we're trying to protect you. As *business partners*, you must understand that we have to look out for the interests of the firm." One associate dared a glance at Miles but quickly lowered his eyes when their gazes met. The senior partner said, "While we know, without a doubt, that you will be cleared in this investigation, our *clients* are not going to look favorably upon your presence here, at least not at the moment. A brief leave of absence might be a good idea, don't you think? Perhaps in six months, when Mr. Goldstein is as satisfied as we are of your innocence, we can resume our relationship."

That was it. They were kicking him out. As far as he was concerned at the time, six months could have been six years, or sixty years, for that matter. They believed Goldstein, not him. He had been living in a hotel at the time, his own apartment a blackened wreck, and had returned to the sterile room more depressed than he had ever been in his life. After the fire, the guilt, and Goldstein, now this; abandoned and betrayed.

Still, he had always been interested in public-interest law, had only started working on Park Avenue because he had been offered one of those $150 a week summer jobs while he was struggling through law school at the State University of New York in Buffalo and had stayed on with the firm when he graduated. He needed money then to support his family. Now he didn't. When he heard on the radio a week later that the mayor had put out a call for professionals to work for the City at low pay, for the community interest, he volunteered. They had placed him in the South Bronx and he had commuted back and forth from the hotel for a week, then moved to the Bronx. There was nothing for him anymore in Manhattan and the pulse and excitement served only to accentuate his depression.

Goldstein was watching him like a hawk eyeing a sparrow. Miles said, "I work for the City now. In a Street Action office."

"The address?"

Miles gave it. "You going to talk to them?"

"Any reason why I shouldn't?"

"None, except that I lost my last job because of you."

"Because of *me?*" Goldstein said. "*I* made you lose the job? Aren't you forgetting something? Like who started that fire?" he hissed. "You know who I hate? Sure, I hate 'em all, the guys who start fires, but most of them are stupid, not like you. Even if they get away with it, what do they get? A couple hundred bucks? Nothing! You catch 'em eventually. It's a sick life. But what about you? You had a lot of money to start with. A wife and a kid. A smart guy like you, who sits back and makes preparations and then thinks he's outsmarted us, that's who I hate the most. *I* didn't lose you your job, *Counselor. You* lost it."

Spent, Goldstein fell back into the chair, breathing heavily, and caught his breath.

"Take you. A criminal lawyer. I'm sure you know that a forensic unit could normally establish easily whether or not someone was tied up in a fire. By rope marks. Indentations on the wrists. Position of the arms. But in this case the fire was too intense and the building partially collapsed. You know that too. Maybe that's why you waited three days to call. You wanted to see whether or not we could tell about the body. You figured this was the one in twenty cases where testing would be useless."

Miles gaped. "I never thought . . ."

"How about it, *Counselor? You* tied the boy up and you get your jollies from watching us try to catch you. You burned down your old apartment and killed your wife and kid. You did it for insurance but found out you liked it . . . it's happened before . . . something perverted about fooling the arson inspector appealed to you. You decided to try again."

Goldstein's voice fell almost to a whisper. "Before I came

here tonight I phoned the local precinct to tell them that I'd be in the area, that I knew you and I wanted to question you alone. They told *me* that two days ago some guy called and told them the same story that *you* just told me, that he was sitting by his window and he saw a fire start and a boy tied up. Everyone thinks cops are stupid and they forget anonymous calls. Well, they don't. That was you who called, wasn't it?"

Miles nodded, feeling as if Goldstein were backing him into a corner. Goldstein pressed on. "Why," the investigator demanded, "did you call two days ago and hang up on the officer who answered?"

"Because . . ." Miles said, groping for words through the terror haze, but then his mind cleared and the anger was there, cold, and he saw the fire marshal across the room, and he knew that he had done nothing wrong, and he began to shout. "Because of people like you! Because I was afraid they'd take it the wrong way! I didn't start the other fire, but you hounded me! Made me lose my job! My friends! *You did it!* I have to live with what happened and that's bad enough without having people like you make it unbearable! *That's* why I hung up! I should have hung up tonight! Get out of here!"

Goldstein half rose in the chair, pointed a long finger at Miles and raised his voice. "You were *afraid?* That's why you hung up? And you're not lying? *Then what happened in the last three days to change your mind? Why'd you call again?*"

There was pounding on the wall. So Elena had heard! So what! It would have come out anyway! He turned back to Goldstein and stopped dead, the impact of the marshal's question hitting him like a blow in the stomach. His surge of anger subsided and there remained only the awful demoralizing realization that Goldstein had, as always, twisted facts and driven him into some predetermined corner; now he would have to tell the fire marshal what had happened at the zoo this afternoon. And of course Goldstein would call the zoo to check. And of course the police there would tell him Miles was a liar.

He struggled to find another avenue of escape but there was none. Goldstein was glaring at him, and Miles, breathing deeply, like a man about to take a very long dive, said, "You probably won't believe me. Someone tried to kill me this afternoon."

For a moment Goldstein did nothing, then he inclined his head, as if to inquire what new diversion Miles was indulging in, and slowly raised an eyebrow, waiting for elaboration. Miles began the story of the afternoon.

Twenty minutes later, when he had finished telling Goldstein all the things he had sworn to keep secret an hour before, the marshal surprised him by remaining silent for a long time, lost in thought. When he finally spoke it was with measured dislike. "Let's assume for the moment that your story is true."

"You believe me?"

"No, but in a few days you're going to *think* I do. Last time I investigated a fire you were involved in I tried to fight you. It didn't work. Why do it again?" He paused, let his breath out slowly. "This time I'm going to play along. You say someone tried to kill you? In the zoo?" He shook his head. "What a file this'll make. You say you want to find the men who killed Carlos? Fine. You and I will look for them together. You can lead me around, show me what you saw, who you talked to. After a while you'll even start to like me. You don't think you will, but you will. And then you'll make a mistake. And then I'm going to get you."

"But if you don't believe what I told you—"

"Don't worry. You'll get a *real thorough investigation.*"

Goldstein's eyes held challenge. Miles said, "I don't care why you undertake the investigation as long as you do. Frankly, I'll feel safer."

"That's how I want you to feel," Goldstein said.

"I know. But I *didn't* kill the boy. You'll see."

Goldstein shrugged, yawned, looked at his watch. "Okay then. We have to do some interviews, check your story, records. When are you free, counselor?"

"I have vacation time coming. I'll take a few days off."

"Good. I'll be here tomorrow at"—he checked his watch again—"nine o'clock. Early start. Oh, one other thing. What was that knocking I heard on the wall when we were talking?"

"Knocking?"

"Yeah, knocking. Eleven-thirty is a little late to be hanging pictures, don't you think? There was something about the way you looked when it started."

Knowing he wasn't going to be able to lie to Goldstein, Miles said, "I guess."

"It's a friend of yours who lives next door?"

Miles nodded, face taut, knowing what was coming next.

"A woman?"

"Yes."

"And you've discussed the fire with her?"

"Yes."

"As well as the fire which took place in your own apartment?"

"No!" This vehemently, but Goldstein ignored the tone.

"Guess it wouldn't do any harm to talk to her. She's still awake, obviously. Want to come?"

Now that Miles had calmed down he cared very much what Elena knew about him, and Goldstein was the last person he would have chosen to tell her about the other fire. "No."

"I'll see her myself then," Goldstein said, watching him.

Rigid with anger, Miles said, "Get out."

He watched Goldstein go and then fell, dejected, onto the mattress, heard the investigator's footsteps in the hall and retreated into a fleeting fantasy of himself strangling

103

Goldstein. He heard the knock and imagined her opening the door. There was the murmur of conversation, then Elena's voice, lifted in rage. "You're lying! Get out!" The door slammed. Rapid footsteps in the hall were followed by an incredible pounding on his wall. He was up in an instant, running for her door.

SEVEN

THE MAN with the pleasant face, whose name was Lai, was at that moment driving south along Manhattan's Riverside Drive, terrified he might be late for his appointment. His black Torino rattled as it hurtled over bumps and past slower-moving vehicles, and he checked the rearview mirror for police.

The night was vivid and still, the great black towers of Harlem hulking in the east like thugs in greatcoats. The George Washington Bridge stretched like a garrote across the river's neck, and sporadic colored lights indicated the presence of small craft on the Hudson.

It was a night similar to the one on which he had met the Korean, a night of brooding expectation turned suddenly violent. Even in retrospect it filled him with a primal fear he associated with Trench, a feeling which had been reinforced many times over since that first shocking encounter, six hours before Lai's scheduled execution, after an explosion had blown the bars off his Manila jail cell.

Prior to that he'd been a strong-arm man in a waterfront union, enforcing unpopular edicts on shipowners, rising in the ranks through a combination of savagery and intelligence. He had come to Trench's attention after pulling off a particularly complicated piece of violence against a reform politician. The resulting hue and cry had convinced his boss that his own safety lay in Lai's arrest, so the little assassin had been betrayed and sentenced. His reprieve had been engineered by the Korean.

He had been hustled along an extremely circuitous route to one of Trench's yachts, already bound from Manila when he boarded it, and then, later, on the open sea, offered a choice: work for the Korean or . . . well . . . Trench didn't explain the alternative but it seemed pretty clear. Lai was wanted for murder in the Philippines and Trench offered good money. He joined.

There followed a period of instruction at a Corsican villa which refined his skills with a knife, a two-year internship on the boat, then special jobs in Vienna, Saigon and Lisbon, assignments for an American businessman in Venezuela and Texas, and finally, for the last three months, the filthy slums of the Bronx.

He wished he were back there now instead of on his way to the yacht. Trench, who had flown in today with Ravenel, was like the Manila union, Lai had long ago learned, in the sense that once you went to work for him there was only one way to stop. Lai's failure to kill Miles Bradshaw in the zoo had constituted a major blunder and he considered omitting the incident from his report tonight. Then he could find Bradshaw on his own, deal with him, and report a success instead of a failure.

But it wasn't easy to hide things from Trench. If the Korean suspected treachery he could be quite deadly, but he did not take kindly to slipups either. Lai, not normally a nervous man, was sweating despite the air conditioning. He whipped the Torino past a sluggish Volkswagen in the left lane, its driver hugging the steering wheel and squinting over the dashboard. Night-blind. The idiot.

At a sign that said "79TH STREET BOAT BASIN" Lai swung the car onto a narrow exit, up to the street and immediately back down into an underground parking lot which reeked of rust and sewers. Despite the late hour, it was filled with cars. "BOAT OWNERS," proclaimed notices on girders, "YOUR CAR WILL BE TOWED AWAY UNLESS YOU DISPLAY A PARKING STICKER. AVOID MISTAKES."

He locked the car, instinctively checking to see if anyone was lurking in the shadows, strode across the lot along a funnel-shaped sidewalk and then through a doorway to the waterfront.

Lai ignored the meandering walkway, the quaint soft lamps, the moon reflected on the calm water. Ahead, barred by a wire fence to uninvited visitors, lay the marina, berths filled with big Chris-Crafts, houseboats and ketches. Fifteen feet of water separated the first row of boats from the granite-lined shore, and a bearded teenager wearing a tennis hat sat on a stool by the gate, his shoulders twisting to the rhythm of the Bee Gees on the radio. "Can I help you?" he asked.

"My name is Lai and I'm here to see Mr. Trench."

The boy's voice became more respectful. "Oh. You're expected." He pushed open the gate. "Mr. Trench's boat is the big one all the way in the back."

Lai picked his way past the boats. Water lapped against freshly painted hulls and sea gulls squawked overhead.

The air smelled of salt and charcoal. Someone must have had a cookout. The window of a small ketch framed a miniature TV and two pairs of feet. The pop of a cork echoed along the docks.

When he reached the Trench boat he saw colored lights looped across the masts, and shimmering blondes in evening gowns mingled on deck with silver-haired men in tuxedoes. Young girls. Money and beauty.

Ravenel guarded the ramp. "Been murderin' niggers up in the slums, Chinko?" he said.

Lai bared his teeth. "Fuck you." He pushed past the catlike sailor. Two minutes to meeting time. Sailors circulated among guests with trays of drinks and hors d'oeuvres. A woman blocked his path and ran her hands over her lean hips. "My, my," she said, "you have such a nice face."

He brushed by her and hurried into the main passageway, the party sounds growing muffled behind him. Giggling and moaning came from behind one of the closed doors. From another, a man's voice was raised in protest. "But Congressman!" A stairway took Lai past guards to a lower level where he could no longer hear the party. Chest constricted in fear, he knocked at a mahogany door.

"Come in, Mr. Lai." Trench spoke perfect English but liked to practice the Filipino Tagalog language. He was seated behind his antique oak desk, back ramrod straight, manicured hands folded neatly before him.

Lai started. Something new had been added to the cabin. Occupying an entire corner was a huge and meticulously crafted reproduction of a city; tiny buildings, trees, even rubble lots and street signs. Lai realized in amazement that it was the South Bronx!

Sure! The construction site where he worked sat at the center of the table, surrounded by red or black buildings. Black was the predominant hue, with red moving like an arrow into the dark rectangle. Lai realized that each red building was a structure he had burned.

Behind him, Trench cleared his throat to draw attention, indicated that the Filipino should sit and said, "Mr. Lai?"

The Filipino took a moment to marshal his thoughts, then began his report. He told Trench that in the past month he had supervised the burning of thirteen buildings. In each case the police had suspected arson but had proved nothing. A boy had managed to penetrate the construction site but had been caught and killed in a fire. Lai had increased security measures after that.

Trench nodded in approval. Lai said five more buildings would be burned within the next few days. Three were still occupied by tenants. Trench waved an impatient hand. Tenants were unimportant. Lai explained that work at the construction site was going well.

Trench interrupted. "When do you think we'll have the test results?"

As a margin for errors, Lai gave a generous estimate. "A week."

"Ah. Good." Trench rocked back and forth approvingly. He peered into one of his glass cabinets, at a display of bright seashells, slid open the case and removed a small conch. He held it up to the light, admiring the flaring colors. He said casually, not fooling Lai with his attitude, "Anything else?"

In the fraction of a second it took Lai to decide whether or not to tell the truth about Bradshaw, he remembered an incident he had witnessed years ago in Lisbon. A Trench lieutenant had come on board to report on a campaign of factory acquisitions, but the man had been ill at ease, and Lai, watching in fascination from behind a two-way mirror, had realized that the man was a thief. So had Trench, but the Korean had offered the offender a second chance. Admit that money had been taken and no punishment would be meted out. The grateful Portuguese had immediately confessed.

Lai would always remember the sound of the man's screams which had risen even as the body thrust upward in the seat. Blood spilled from the mouth and the head jerked toward the ceiling. Later Lai learned of the four-inch blade hidden in the chair. Everyone had a weakness and Trench's was that he liked messy death. On the boat he could afford to indulge himself. The room was a chamber of concealed devices.

Lai decided to tell the truth.

Hesitatingly he said, "There *is* one more thing; there was a witness to one of the fires. He saw the boy die. We're trying to find him."

Trench didn't look up. "Ah, yes," he said. "Miles Bradshaw."

The air seemed to drain out of the cabin. Lai's relief was so profound that he almost collapsed in the chair, but he forced himself to continue the conversation so that Trench would not know he had almost lied. "We're trying to locate Bradshaw now, but he's not in the phone book and no one in the neighborhood remembers him. He's average-looking and there's nothing unusual in the way he dresses. Maybe his name isn't even Bradshaw. If he were smart he would have changed it. Maybe he's working for someone."

Trench's irritated expression indicated that he had had the same thought. Lai pleaded, "How did I know he would jump into the animal cage?"

Trench's pupils were tiny. "You're supposed to plan for all contingencies."

Lai had the urge to bolt for the door, but the only way to deal with Trench was to show no fear. He said, "We're paying some of the policemen in the local precinct, some

110

firemen, store owners, a journalist. If he goes to the police there's a good chance we'll get him."

Trench glanced up at the ceiling as if contemplating returning to the party, and yawned. The effect was that of someone releasing air from a dangerously inflated balloon. Lai was safe for the moment. The Korean smiled at him.

"You'll report here daily."

"So this is Fort Apache," Goldstein said.

They stood outside the police station and the sun was relentless, heat puddles shimmering on the street even though it was only nine-thirty. True to his word, Goldstein had appeared at Miles's door at nine, wearing the black raincoat despite the heat. Leaning against the doorframe and picking at his teeth, he had said, "Before we go anywhere else we have to check with the local precinct. Professional courtesy."

Miles had been in too good a mood to mind. His initial resolve to slam the door in the marshal's face had changed after Elena had kicked Goldstein out of her apartment last night. He replayed the highlights of that sweet memory in his mind now: Elena's voice raised in fury at Goldstein, the pounding on the wall to summon Miles to her apartment, her face twisted in fury of which he had never suspected her capable. At first he had thought it was directed at him, but then she had demanded, *Did you do what he said?*

"No," he had answered, and then the best part: Elena had calmed slowly, the look he dreaded failing to appear in her eyes. She had touched him lightly on the wrist and said, to reassure him, "Don't worry. He's just an angry cop." Even in retrospect he was dazed. He was sure no one had ever disbelieved Goldstein so completely.

With her gentle encouragement he had finally told the

111

real story of the fire. He saw her face, horrified, sympathetic, compassionate. They passed a long time in silence, and after a while stood very close to each other, hands touching, eyes locked.

But then a strange glaze had come over Elena's face, as if she had touched some private nightmare, and she had gently disengaged her hand to back away, mystifying him. Still, after he had left, there had been a gentle buoyancy to the night, and he had felt as if he had assumed some subtle edge over the fire marshal. For the first time in a long while the world had seemed manageable. When he awoke this morning he had almost been happy.

Maybe Goldstein had sensed his mood or maybe he had decided, as he had promised the previous night, that he would try to get close to Miles as an investigative strategy.

In any event, there was a complete and surprising lack of antagonism this morning. The sneering *"counselor"* had been dropped from the end of every sentence and Goldstein had modified his tone of voice while explaining why they were visiting the police.

For some reason, perhaps because of his new attitude, Miles had believed him.

They looked up at the precinct house, which was wedged into the block as if hiding there, a sooty granite facade with no decorative adornments to be stolen or vandalized, no stairs to impede speed of entry, no quaint electric globes saying "41st Precinct" to be shot away in the night. The feeling of safety radiated from the building for at least five feet before it disappeared. Outside, two bearded whites, obviously plainclothesmen, huddled, conferring. A squad car drove up and collected them. Even in the daylight they seemed alien here. Miles was amazed they would come back day after day.

Miles had often wondered what the building looked like inside and took it all in at a glance. It reminded him of an

112

empty union hall: the huge expanse of green linoleum, the phones ringing, the ammonia smell. Cops sat behind strips of railing, taking down complaints, and on an endless drab wall were tiny plaques, memorials to dead officers.

Goldstein got directions from a bored-looking policeman behind the watch desk. A flight of marble stairs led to a door marked "DETECTIVES." The office inside, small without being cramped, was lined with desks manned by a dozen plainclothespersons who looked up when they entered. At the rear of the room, a prisoner paced in a wire-mesh cage. A fan rotated slowly on the ceiling.

A thin, balding cop in faded Levi jacket, jeans and boots ambled over. He was sipping coffee from a steaming Styrofoam cup and licked the tips of his fingers as if he'd been eating something sugary. He said, "Can I help you?"

Goldstein introduced himself and Miles, and the cop led Miles into one of the little cubicles which lined the office like mouseholes. "Have a seat," he said, indicating a cramped metal desk in a corner. He left, closing the door behind him.

The walls, intimidating in their bareness, were painted an institutional green. A huge window provided an excellent view of a brick wall ten feet across an alley. The far wall, which was buckling, seemed to be supported by the row of high file cabinets pushed against it, on top of which sat a lone transistor radio.

For the first time today Miles felt the beginnings of nervousness. Goldstein was obviously talking to the cops outside and he wondered what the marshal was telling them. He considered distracting himself with the radio, but at that moment the door opened to admit the most monstrous black policeman he had ever seen. The cannonball head rested atop a thick, knotted neck, and the shoulders

113

were as wide as the surprising grin. He stretched forth a mammoth hand and said, "Lieutenant Dewlen." His voice sounded like a diesel truck at 3 A.M. Adjusting himself to a chair which accentuated his size, he hit the desk as if he'd just heard a funny story and said, "Three winos decide to start a fire last night in an abandoned building. They start at the front door with a can of gasoline and *back up the stairs!* Then they light a match. Can you believe it? How dumb can you get, torching a building after backing into it!"

He winked at Miles. "Arson," he said. "It's a booming business, a big goddamn rip-off. Know how many fires there were last year in New York? Fifty-four thousand. Know how many arsons? *Twenty-seven* thousand. Half! National average is eight percent, and it's getting worse. Around here it's mostly a clique of guys who do it. They all know one another. Last week one of 'em got mad at a friend who set off a fire and burned his niece. Made her a cripple. The uncle started yelling and we made four arrests."

The lieutenant paused. He sounded as if he were giving a speech in an elementary school.

"Oh, there's lots of reasons for arson," Dewlen said, leaning forward with an air of conspiracy. "A guy's on welfare and he wants to move to a new apartment, but the welfare people won't let him. What does he do? First he takes all his furniture out of his apartment and stores it with a friend. Then he finds some junked furniture on the street . . . old stuff . . . people throw it out . . . and fills his crib with *that.* No one will know the difference after it's burned. Then he starts a fire. The welfare people put him in a relocation home and give him a couple thousand dollars for new furniture." Dewlen unwrapped a cigar and stuck it in his mouth. "He gets to move. He gets the money. What a racket. Goldstein says you started that fire."

Miles felt as if someone had snuck up from behind him and grabbed him around the chest. Despite his best intentions his defenses had been lowered by the lieutenant and it was several flustered moments before he could say hoarsely, "Goldstein is wrong."

The cop nodded sympathetically. "Maybe he is, but Goldstein has a reputation. He's a pretty tough son of a bitch, I hear. Always wants maximum penalties. Me, I understand circumstances. Circumstances can force a guy to do things he never even imagined considering. Understand what I'm driving at?"

"I think so but I'm not sure."

Dewlen put his hands on the desk; his voice was low, reasonable. "I'm saying that if you were to tell *me* that you started that fire I might make a deal . . . maybe manslaughter two. Goldstein would want . . . well . . . you know." He seemed sorry even to have had to bring up the subject.

"But I didn't *do* anything," Miles insisted.

The big cop was up in an instant, apology all over his gigantic face. "Okay, okay. But if you ever change your mind . . . you know. We all have our jobs to do. No hard feelings."

"No, of course not." Dewlen looked so troubled that Miles had the urge to pat his shoulder and tell him everything was all right. He smiled. "Hey," he said, "what is this, the tough cop and the good cop? Goldstein and you?"

Dewlen seemed taken aback for an instant, but then he laughed boisterously, hitting his thigh over and over again. When he calmed down he said, "Funny idea. We all work different ways. Some try to intimidate and some to be nice. Sometimes *I* get mean and sometimes *Goldstein* probably acts friendly. At bottom we're all just trying to find out the truth. I wonder which way is best. Catch more flies with honey, my daddy used to say. You ever want to discuss that fire of yours, come back. We'll talk. Here's my card. But right now," he said, dipping into a drawer for a form, "I need some information." He showed his teeth in a smile.

"What's your address?" he said.

Goldstein's Chevy Nova was double-parked at the end of a line of policemen's family cars, looking as if it needed six months' worth of cleaning. The floor was covered with dust, jumper cables, which the marshal tossed in back, old *Daily News*, McDonald's wrappers and a can of compressed air for flat tires. A plastic hula dancer hung from the rearview mirror. It looked dead. When Goldstein turned on the ignition the radio blared out news. He switched it off. The glove compartment fell open. Old road maps spilled out onto Miles's knees. Goldstein's investigations were the only meticulous thing about him.

The inspector said, "Didn't tell Dewlen anything, huh? I didn't think you would." It was the first time he'd spoken since they had left the station. For Goldstein, that was nice. "Where did you say Carlos lived?" he asked.

Mrs. Perez gave them about ten seconds before slamming the door in their faces. "*Policia!* I *tol'* you not to come here again! Bastards!" Goldstein pressed hard at the bell. There were screams and the sound of something shattering against the door. Goldstein tried again. More screaming. The investigator touched Miles on the shoulder to indicate that they should go. At the staircase Miles turned back. The mother's skinny companion was looking out at him, butcher knife in his hand.

The effeminate principal became excited when he was introduced to Goldstein. "An *arson* investigator! How *thrilling!* What *stories* you must tell. And you want to talk to Edward again?" A frown crossed the dainty features. "I don't want to make a habit of taking the boy from class, but, well . . . I suppose this one time . . . I'll have to be present, of course."

The boy was clearly unnerved by the inspector but seemed to understand that Goldstein's involvement was necessary. He repeated the story he had told Miles two days before, then said, "Remember. Not to tell anyone."

He seemed sorry they had met in the first place. He said to the principal, rising, "Can I go back to class now?" Then, at the door, "Just remember what happened to Freddy the half-wit." He looked at the floor. "And maybe to Carlos."

The junk dealer was in his yard, sorting through piles of rusty auto parts. Hand-painted signs on the nearby shack said, "TV SALE TODAY! LIKE NEW! BEST PRICES IN TOWN!"

When Goralski saw them outside the fence he kicked his way over and snarled through the wire, lips curled back over his bad teeth, "Take one fuckin' step in this yard and the dog'll tear you to pieces. No warrant! I'll sue if you come in!" The animal began to howl. "Shut up, you fuckin' bitch!" The shepherd tucked its tail between its legs and retreated a step but kept up the din. Goldstein pulled out the notebook and the junk dealer started screaming. *"What are you writing? I don't give you permission. DON'T take anything down or I'll sue you."*

Minutes later they watched him from their car, framed in his window, gesturing frantically into his phone.

"Probably calling a truck to haul away stolen merchandise," Goldstein said.

The street in front of the meth clinic looked like a setting for a game of glass jacks. Thousands of shards littered the length of the block. "Gang fight," Goldstein said matter-of-factly as he pulled into a parking space which had a lesser concentration of pieces. The usual line of glaze-eyed teens awaited treatment inside. They could have been the exact same patients Miles had seen on the previous visit, the same drooped posture, emaciated chests and faces, same dreamy sluggishness in their movements.

Rodriguez totally ignored their arrival. His head was buried in a *Hulk* comic, his booted feet on his desk in the office. After almost a minute, his glance drifted away from the page and settled on the visitors. Miles waited for a sign of recognition and was disappointed. He said, "Remember me?"

"You?" Rodriguez seemed to search his memory. "No."

"Sure you do," Miles smiled, confused. "I was here a couple days ago. I came here with some of the Kings."

The eyes showed disbelief. "Here? To my office?" Rodriguez glanced sharply at Goldstein, as if he were afraid of offending the marshal, and his next words indicated why. "It's not *really* my office," he said. "The social worker lets us hang out here if we don't make trouble. We never *bring* anyone here."

Rodriguez craned his neck to see what Goldstein was scribbling on the pad. Miles' voice rose slightly. "What are you talking about? First I spoke to some Kings at the pinball place . . . across the street from the junkman's."

Rodriguez said, "Goralski."

"Yes. Goralski. They told me you wanted to see me, brought me here. You and I discussed Carlos Perez."

"Sorry, man. I know who the junkman is, but I never spoke to you. You are making a fa-bri-ca-tion." He seemed pleased at the big word. His eyes gleamed for a moment, then faded and drifted back to the comic.

Goldstein made a bored sound, but Miles felt a streak of angry stubbornness take hold. Moving closer, he saw the little acne sores on Rodriguez' face. He had forgotten that the kid was only fifteen. There was the faint outline of a scar extending from the lower lip. Miles had to keep from shouting. "You told me about the landlord. We talked about the fire and about Carlos. *Why are you lying?*"

Rodriguez drew his feet off the desk slowly, cords on his neck taut. "I don't lie."

They glowered at each other. Miles said, "Bullshit."

Rodriguez dropped his hand to his pocket, looked at Goldstein, and stopped. "My gang is everywhere," he said, like a fifteen-year-old uttering childish threats, but Miles was haunted by the story of the half-wit. Rodriguez' pale-blue eyes bored into him. Miles felt like a dog on a leash.

Goldstein said, "Let's go."

"*But he's lying,*" Miles spat when they reached the car. By now his fury, refueled by Rodriguez' amused look when Goldstein pulled him out, was redirected at the fire marshal. "'What kind of investigation is this anyway? You don't ask questions and if people ask you to leave, you go! Why'd you take me out of there? What the hell are you doing?"

Goldstein unlocked the door, gestured Miles inside. "You think if you'd stayed there he would have changed his story? At all? You think he would have told us anything new?"

"No. But he was still lying. How are you going to find out anything if you don't press people?"

"Oh, I'll talk to him again. Alone. I can't watch you both at the same time. You could be giving each other signals. Right now I want to see how these people react when you show up. Maybe Rodriguez was lying and maybe he wasn't. I'm not finished with him."

Goldstein checked his watch. "You hungry?" he said.

His tone was a peace offering, and somewhat mollified, Miles realized he hadn't eaten yet today.

"You like deli?" Goldstein asked.

Grudgingly, "Yes."

"Good." Goldstein put the car in gear and made a U-turn. "There's only one really good deli left in the Bronx. Near the Throgs Neck Bridge. Immobilizes you with the smell . . ."

They lapsed into silence, driving past boarded-up Latino social clubs and men selling colored ices from pushcarts, then under the El tracks, the steel latticework creating a midday shadow mosaic on the hot street below. The sidewalks were strangely underpopulated. Miles could think of no better term to describe them than "bombed out."

Goldstein pulled onto the Cross Bronx Expressway, a pulsating ribbon of exhaust packed with chugging diesels and overheated cars. Traffic stalled. Goldstein turned on the radio and switched stations, then shut it off in disgust. "Rock crap," he shouted over the trucks on either side of them. "No one plays good music anymore."

After a while he ran his eyes over the abandoned buildings on both sides of the expressway.

"New York," he said. "What happened to it? You grow up here?"

"Queens," Miles said. "Whitestone."

"Brooklyn," said Goldstein. "Brownsville. My father was a fireman—a lieutenant. He used to take me on the trucks with my sister. What a kid, my sister. Always getting in trouble."

Miles had never thought of Goldstein as a person who had an existence outside of the sleazy investigations, and his irritation drained away, to be replaced with curiosity.

Goldstein said, "I don't know why I'm thinking of this now, but there was a synagogue at the end of the street

120

where I grew up. My uncle was the rabbi. He used to give me lima beans to plant in his back yard. Ha! Lima beans! Me and my sister. They burned the synagogue down four or five years ago. Changing neighborhood." He shook his head. "What happens?"

Goldstein ruminated a moment. "We were really close, my sister and I . . . still are. She lives in Brooklyn. Married a flake. An accountant. He left her, went west. Sends her money sometimes. No return address. No kids. She's a teacher. Oh, hell, tell me about yourself. You always wanted to be a lawyer?"

Miles shrugged. "I guess. I was the first one in my family to go to college. My father was a baker. I won a state scholarship to Buffalo. It's not hard to do. I don't know. Somewhere along the line law started to seem like a good idea. Security. Also, I wanted to help people."

He broke off abruptly, remembering that Goldstein didn't exactly consider him a man who "helped" people. The ensuing silence was awkward. The conversation had gotten too personal and Goldstein backpedaled.

"Arson's a disease," he said. He pointed to the side of the road. "See those buildings? Landlords can buy the worst ones for as little as ten thousand dollars, then buy one hundred thousand dollars' worth of insurance and pay a kid a couple hundred to burn out the top floor. Always the top. That wrecks the roof and then the building when it rains. Ninety thousand profit, not bad, huh?" He stopped, eyes on the rearview mirror. "You see that car behind us?"

"Which one? The station wagon?"

"No. In the left lane. A black car. Ford."

"What? The Torino?"

"It's been behind us since the methadone clinic," Goldstein said.

It took a moment for the inspector's implication to sink

in, but when it did Miles whirled in horror and stared back into traffic. The black Torino idled forty feet back, windows tinted so that its occupants were invisible. He sucked in his breath. He had no doubts as to who was in that car.

"It's following us," he said.

Goldstein didn't seem particularly concerned. "I didn't say it was *following* us. I just noticed it, that's all. Maybe we're both headed in the same direction. Remember, the meth clinic was our last stop."

Miles rocked in agitation, thinking only of that long, glinting blade at the zoo, like an ice pick or a stiletto. What would it feel like to be stabbed? A punch and a slither in his chest? Incredible pain? The leering face above him, terrible in its pleasantness? Bitterly he said, "Yeah, the same direction. We're both going to the deli."

Goldstein's voice took on a note of reassurance. "They won't try anything in traffic."

"That's what I thought at the zoo," Miles retorted, thinking, Who would stop them if they *did* come over? Goldstein? The inspector wasn't even armed. Other drivers? Forget it. This was New York. People got killed in subway cars and nobody bothered to help. Miles made sure his door was locked, but that only made him feel worse, as if by checking he had confirmed the possibility of attack.

Goldstein said, "Relax, Counselor. It's probably nothing. Maybe I shouldn't have mentioned the car. I just wanted to see how you'd react. Look, a lot of cops eat at this deli. No one will bother us there. We'll see what happens."

Miles kept his eyes on the mirror. Whoever was in that Torino, he felt, was returning his look. A space opened up directly behind them, the Ford slid into it, and Miles was seized with the urge to bolt from the car. He controlled it. Alone on the side of this hot and hostile highway, how much better off would he be? And suppose the men in the Torino decided to come after him? What then? He didn't know where the subway was around here; there weren't any cabs. And he wasn't exactly a four-minute miler. Without Goldstein he was helpless. There had to be a way to convince the arson inspector of the danger they were in.

Goldstein sighed next to him. "Tell you about a case I had maybe five years ago," he said. "A doctor, wealthy guy like you, decided to kill his wife, collect some insurance, run away with the nurse."

Miles stared at him in amazement.

Goldstein said, "What a nurse. Bluest eyes I've ever seen. French name. She and the doctor'd been making it in the office. Couldn't keep their hands off each other. The wife probably would have divorced him, but he couldn't afford the alimony. Nurse liked the good life, know what I mean?"

Miles didn't care what he meant. He said, pointing at the two-way radio, "Why don't you use *that?* Call for help?"

"Relax. There's nothing to call about yet. I'll finish the story."

"What the hell does this story have to do with that car?"

Goldstein said, "You'll see. Anyway, one day there's a three-alarmer at the doctor's house. Whole top floor's on fire within minutes. Very suspicious when that happens. The wife's asleep. Burned to a crisp."

Miles whirled on him, but Goldstein didn't seem to be baiting him. Miles, thinking of his own wife, momentarily forgot the Torino.

Goldstein said, "The jewelry was gone. Looked like burglary and arson. The pattern of the fire indicated that an incendiary material had been spread throughout the top floor, especially the bedroom, and there was a gasoline odor.

"At first the doctor had what looked like an airtight alibi; three witnesses placing him elsewhere. But in arson that's not too unusual. A guy spreads gasoline and then lights a

123

candle. Takes the candle half an hour to burn down to where the fire starts. By that time the guy's been in Clancy's Bar for twenty minutes making sure everyone notices he's there.

"I talked to the witnesses separately. One, it turned out, owed the doctor money. Another was a relative. The third hated policemen." He paused. "Oh, the doctor started that fire all right.

"But arson's one of the hardest crimes to prove. Know how we eventually got him? You'll never guess. He confessed!" Goldstein shook his head. "Hard to believe, isn't it? You know why? The goddamn nurse, *that's* why. When she saw I was making him nervous, she actually put the moves on me. I guess she figured she could get anyone to do anything. Incredible.

"He walked in when she was taking her blouse off, went to pieces when he saw that, started crying."

At any other time Miles probably would have been fascinated but now he only demanded, in fear and vexation, "Why are you telling me this?"

"I'm trying to show you that people go through an awful lot of trouble to try to fool an investigator. After all, the alternative's jail."

The words sank in slowly, and when Miles understood them, he could scarcely believe what he was hearing. "Wait a minute," he said. "Are you telling me you think that *I* arranged for that car to be there?"

"No. What I'm saying is that it's conceivable that you *might* have arranged for the car. And if something's conceivable to me, I check it out. If I can think of things, so can other people."

Miles squirmed with anger and frustration. There was no way to reach Goldstein. For an instant they broke free of traffic and accelerated into a clear lane. Seconds later the Torino was behind them again, having fallen back to a discreet distance, matching speed in a bizarre stalking ritual.

The Torino drove past them and turned a corner when they parked, and Goldstein said, "See? It's gone." Miles refused to believe him.

The restaurant was packed with a lunch-hour crowd that included cops at an adjacent table who laughed regularly and raucously at what were probably dirty jokes. The voice of the counterman cut through the din, haranguing a steady line of customers.

"Hurry up, think I got all day? What is this, a quiz show? Of course the corned beef is lean. Make up your mind, lady. A *quarter pound* of lox? Whaddaya havin', a party?"

The glass case displayed shanks of pastrami and hot dogs tied together as well as fat bottles of red pickled peppers. Cans of Heinz beans and plastic containers of mustard were stacked on the shelves. The air was spicy with the aroma of smoked meats and knishes.

Goldstein was wolfing down a corned beef and tongue combination and slurping an orange soda from a glass. He said jovially, lost in culinary heaven, "What's the matter? You're not eating."

Miles looked down at his untouched salami sandwich, picked up half of it and put it down. He kept glancing at the door, expecting the pleasant-faced man to appear. He said, "How can you eat?"

Goldstein grinned. "Like this." He pushed the rest of the sandwich into his mouth so that his cheeks bulged.

Miles wasn't amused. "Ha, ha. Big joke."

Goldstein finished the soda and sucked at the ice at the bottom of the glass. The cops at the next table got up to leave.

125

"Listen," Miles said, "you said that if something was conceivable to you then you check it out, right?"

Goldstein nodded, leaned back in his chair and put his hand on his belt. He looked interested.

"And isn't it *conceivable* to you that that car is following us?"

Goldstein conceded the point with a nod of his head.

"Then what's wrong with using the car radio to see who they are? Call for help. You don't have to approach them yourself."

Dryly, Goldstein replied, "I'm not afraid of them." In his own quiet way he seemed offended.

Miles made an effort to erase the mistake. "I didn't mean to imply that you were afraid," he said. "But isn't it better to have several people confront them? Suppose they're armed?" He paused. "You're the one who said it, Goldstein. The alternative is jail. Don't arsonists ever get rough with the inspectors?"

Appeased, Goldstein nodded matter-of-factly, as if the conversation were purely academic. "Sure they do. There was a marshal in Queens, Rego Park. Name of Calabrise. Italian. Someone actually ambushed him one night. He was working on an arson in a Klein's. Turned out to be a stock boy who'd been fired, but he got Calabrise first."

Miles pushed the salami sandwich away. "Okay, you admit it," he said. "Now what about the Torino?"

Goldstein shrugged as if he saw no connection. "It's a moot point. I'll lay ten to one it's not there when we leave."

"Suppose it is?"

Goldstein seemed to be wrestling with a decision. He let out his breath and adjusted his tie. "Listen, counselor," he said, "do you realize what you've been asking me to believe? Let's look at your story logically. First you tell me a boy got *tied up* and murdered in a fire. By whom, I wonder? There's the landlord of the building, you say, *plus* a

126

street gang. Then all of a sudden two *more* men are involved, and not only in the killing of the boy but in an attempt on *your* life. And we're *still* not finished. Suddenly you and I are being followed by this *car*. You're relating a classic paranoid fantasy. Don't look so surprised. I read psychology."

He spread his hands and kept his voice logical, persuasive. "This is a horrible thing to say but arson fires happen every day in New York, and what's so important about this one fire and this one boy that all these people are involved?"

Miles, following the thread of his reasoning, saw the next point clearly and completed it. "It's more logical that someone who was 'involved' in a fire ten months ago would be involved again, isn't it?"

Goldstein seemed uncomfortable. "I said it last night; I said I'd stick with you and complete the investigation. I didn't say I was going to change my mind about what happened, certainly not right away."

He fumbled with his wallet to pay the bill and Miles said bitterly, "Of course not. How much do I owe?"

"Forget it."

"Five bucks? Here's five bucks."

Goldstein didn't refuse the money. He probably figured it would have worsened the mood. They shouldered their way through the line and went outside, where the hot, crowded avenue pulsated with activity. This was the North Bronx and it was alive; buses, cars, pedestrians all moved by in urban profusion. Miles scanned the boulevard for the Torino but it wasn't there.

They got into Goldstein's car.

Then a bus across the street pulled away and Miles saw the Ford parked behind it, maybe a hundred yards off.

He pointed. Goldstein followed the line of his finger, started, put his hands on his hips, looked at Miles and

127

shook his head. Then, watching the sideview mirror, he started the car and pulled into traffic. A puff of exhaust rose from the Torino and it left its parking space, keeping a distance between them but following close behind. Goldstein went for the radio.

"Goldstein to desk," he said.

He removed his thumb from the microphone button and static filled the car, then an aggravated male voice. "C54545," it said. "For Christ sake, Goldstein, use the *number,* not your name. We got in trouble last month with the FCC."

Goldstein said, "Stand by." He turned to Miles. There was command in his voice. He said, "Find the Bronx map in the glove compartment."

Miles yanked it open eagerly and the maps began to slide over his knees again. "Christ, Goldstein, you're a slob." He pawed through the mess; maps of Brooklyn, Queens, Westchester, more Brooklyn. He had the feeling Goldstein had been driving around adding to his collection at gas stations for years, too lazy to sift through the glove compartment each time he needed a map.

"Nassau County, Jersey, Manhattan, *Bronx!*" Miles cried triumphantly, unfolding it. "What now?"

Goldstein was concentrating on the rearview mirror, turning down side streets to convince himself that the Torino was really following them. The black car trailed doggedly behind. "Find the zoo."

"Got it."

"If I'm not mistaken there's a way to reach one of the parking lots directly from the highway. See it?"

They shot around a corner and up a ramp to the Cross Bronx Expressway. Seconds later the Torino materialized, matching their speed.

Miles said, "I found the lot. There's an exit off the Bronx River Parkway that takes you directly into the zoo."

128

"Which lot?"

"Only zoo exit on the parkway."

Goldstein picked up the microphone again. "Goldstein to desk."

"C54545. GOLDSTEIN!"

Goldstein acted as if he hadn't heard. "I'm being followed," he said, "on the Cross Bronx Expressway. There's a black Ford, a Torino, I think, behind me. New York plates, license 33YSE. I'm in the gold Nova. License TI854. I'll reach the zoo in about ten minutes. When the car follows me in, I want it intercepted. Driver may be armed."

The voice said, "Got it. Good luck."

They looked at each other with the satisfied expressions of conspirators. Ten minutes later, they passed a sign, "BRONX ZOO ¼ MILE." Goldstein signaled a turn and the exit came up on them, a white lane curving away from the road and into the lot, where police were waiting. The fire marshal eased the Nova into the turn and Miles swung around, watched the Torino slow, approach the exit . . .

And speed away.

Miles exploded. "Dammit! They're driving off!" He smashed his fist into the dashboard as the Torino hurtled over a hill and disappeared. "Someone warned them!"

Moments later the radio crackled to life. "We checked the license you gave us," the voice said. "There's no such number registered in New York."

EIGHT

"AND THEN what happened?" Elena said.

Her face was cupped in candlelight, soft in the honey glow. A violin concerto played on the stereo. Miles's throat was dry. He kept wetting it. They were on their second bottle of wine.

After all the unnerving experiences of the day, the car chase this morning, the visit to the zoo and the late-afternoon trip with Goldstein to the gloomy basement of an old hotel, Elena's unexpected dinner was a surprise in more ways than one. There was an odd and subtle anticipation to her mood this evening which wove an electric suggestiveness about the room. Her eyes seemed bolder, almost seductive, and yet somehow demure. When Miles had

130

knocked at her door an hour ago it was obvious that he
had been expected. The table had been set, the lights
dimmed.

He refilled their glasses. Her chin was cradled in her
palms and she tickled the candle's flame with a soft out-
pouring of breath. "When you got to the zoo, then what?"

He lifted his goblet, excited by the thought of delaying
the outcome of the evening, forced his thoughts back to
the afternoon, to Goldstein and the zoo. The bottle was
empty. He reached for another even as he began to speak.

Miles had suspected how Scowcroft would react when
Goldstein showed up at the zoo and he had been right.
After making them wait for ten minutes the little bureau-
crat had hurried from his office, phony grin and out-
stretched hand for Goldstein, single cutting glance for
Miles.

The next half hour had been a circus of fabrications in
answer to Goldstein's questions. Had Miles ever visited
Scowcroft's office? Of course not! The only time the landlord had ever seen Miles had been when Miles was pulled
by the police from an animal cage, raving that two men
were trying to kill him. Miles had struggled with the police,
Scowcroft said, had become verbally abusive, had accused
Scowcroft of trying to murder him.

Scowcroft was sure Miles was seriously deranged. He
inquired whether there was a history of mental illness
while Miles squirmed in his chair and Goldstein shot him
ugly looks to keep him quiet.

Goldstein wanted to know why Scowcroft hadn't pressed
charges. The landlord sighed wistfully, indicated huge
stacks of papers on his desk, assumed a conspiratorial air.
Surely Goldstein could appreciate the plight of over-
worked municipal servants, couldn't he? Who had time to

go to court? Goldstein grunted noncommittally, wrote something on the pad.

Scowcroft rose and checked his watch. He made a joke about how much work he had to do. No one laughed but Goldstein took the hint and got up, his raincoat crackling around him like a storm of static electricity. Miles rose to his feet slowly, trying to irritate Scowcroft with his lack of speed, but the landlord didn't seem to notice. Miles was puzzled by Goldstein's failure to challenge Scowcroft's lies.

The landlord extended his hand, but Goldstein wasn't finished. He asked Scowcroft if any of his acquaintances drove a black Ford Torino. Puzzled, Scowcroft shook his head. For the first time he showed nervousness. He apologized that he couldn't be of more assistance and Goldstein said impassively, "A black Torino followed us here."

From Miles' point of view Scowcroft betrayed himself then, his features going slack, recomposing themselves too late, rat eyes receding down a tunnel. His tiny teeth gleamed in the light. He tried to laugh but he failed.

"Why would you be followed?" he said.

Minutes later they were standing on the central plaza, near the seal pools. The plaza was ringed with the monkey house, the camel ride and the cages of big cats. The snow leopards were being fed. They snarled as they ate. Overhead and several hundred yards away, tourists rode the tram toward "Wild Asia." Goldstein glanced back at Scowcroft's window, troubled for the first time. He said, "He was lying."

Now it was Miles who remained confidently silent while the arson inspector mulled over disturbing impressions. Finally Goldstein said, "To the Grand Concourse Hotel."

"Where?"

Goldstein explained it all on the way over. "It's an aban-

132

doned hotel near Yankee Stadium. The City stores real-estate records there for the Bronx, because its main office is overcrowded. I want to double-check some information. For instance, how do you know Scowcroft is the landlord of the building that Carlos died in?"

"The Latin Kings told me."

"And how do *they* know?"

Miles paused. "Ah, ha. So we find the deed and check the owner of record." Goldstein braked for a light. They were on a wide and well-traveled thoroughfare called Westchester Avenue, lined with brick storefronts which crowded up along the sidewalks. The side streets, only fleetingly visible, gaped like craters.

Goldstein said, "I took the liberty before coming today of checking arson statistics for your neighborhood. Up fifty percent in the last five months. Could be a hot summer. Could be something else. I found several other buildings I'd like to check too. Landlords. What the hell."

The light turned green and they passed under the El and back into the sunlight. The sun baked Miles's arm on the windowsill. Goldstein said, "Five months. Isn't that the length of time you've been here?"

"You'll even start to like me. You don't think you will, but you will," Goldstein had said only a day before. Now the memory jolted Miles like a slap. Suddenly he wasn't sure *what* Goldstein thought about Scowcroft or why they were *really* going to the hotel. Gruffly, to hide his fear that he was heading into some kind of trap, he said, *"Nine* months." Neither of them spoke again until they reached their destination.

The Grand Concourse Hotel lay in resplendent abandonment near the Bronx's newly completed County Courthouse, a gleaming glass-and-marble structure whose

133

white facades beckoned their neighborhood back from decay. Older apartment buildings squatted on side streets, one or two blocks away. The flags of rebuilt Yankee Stadium lay limp above the towers and Miles scanned the stands from afar. Empty.

Goldstein issued a nostalgic sigh. He was a walking lament for glories past. He crossed the street to the hotel with a reverent sadness, glancing up at the gaping windows and missing letters on the marquee. A scribbled note on the streaked glass doors read, "Records . . . Around the Corner and in the Basement," but Goldstein pushed forward anyway, up a series of wide, sweeping steps to a dimly lit lobby, which smelled of dust and urine. At a far corner a young City employee with a transistor radio sat at a wooden desk which had probably come from the courthouse they'd torn down to make way for the new one. He watched them with one eye as if to let them know that maybe he'd let them stay and maybe he wouldn't.

Goldstein considered the old mosaics, dusty carpets, bank of stilled elevators, the stairway rising majestically into the empty hulk. He said, "When my sister and I were kids my father used to bring us here before games for autographs. Used to find Yankees here. My sister got Gehrig the day he hit the four home runs. Only Yankee ever to do it. 1932. Nice guy, Gehrig. Walked like this."

Goldstein assumed that slightly bowlegged gait which characterizes stocky athletes, dropped the pose after a moment and walked around dreamily. "New York," he said. Miles could imagine the little Goldstein brother and sister and the big Yankee. The voice of the kid across the lobby came to them.

"Hey, you guys. This building is closed."

Goldstein snapped out of his reverie, but when they left he lowered his shoulders as if leaving the hospital room of a sick friend.

134

The hall of records resembled a thousand other record halls in a thousand other cities in its impersonal mix of gray steel, formica and linoleum under sallow bright lights. Rows of metal shelves were filled with huge loose-leaf binders. Behind a counter at the front of the room, four potbellied men sat in swivel chairs smoking cigars. One of them grinned when he saw them.

"*Ed Goldstein,*" the man cried with pleasure, jumping up and hurrying over. Miles was startled. He'd never thought of Goldstein as having a first name. Ed? Ed what? Ed*ward?* Ed*mund?* "Glad to see you!" the man said. "My little girl really loved that doll! Poor kid. Only four years old and appendicitis. Thanks."

Goldstein said, "She's okay then?"

"Yeah. Operation went without a hitch, kept her home from nursery school. She liked that." He smiled. "But what a nice thing to do. You don't even know her. You must love kids."

Obviously embarrassed, Goldstein shrugged. The man noticed Miles for the first time. "Who's this, Ed? Got a partner?"

Dryly, Goldstein nodded. "Of sorts."

The big man's warmth was suddenly directed at Miles. "Glad to know you. I'm Frank Swidler. Anything you need . . ." He swept his arm around the room, exhibiting his personal domain, and said to Goldstein, "Bring 'im around for dinner sometime. Wife always asks me what you're like. Bachelors," he said. He looked at Miles. "You don't know what you're missing. You married?"

Uncomfortable with the question, Miles shook his head, but Swidler didn't seem to notice his mood. He slapped Goldstein on the back. "What can I do for you?"

Goldstein began rummaging through his pockets. "Got six addresses to check," he said. He extracted a tattered sheet of paper and unfolded it.

Swidler's mood changed. He looked nervously at the clock. He said, "We close in forty-five minutes. Can we do it tomorrow? The boss here's a real bastard."

Goldstein tore the paper carefully in two. "We'll split them," he said. "Three apiece. Why don't you show Miles how to do it?"

Miles figured that Goldstein was palming him off on Swidler to keep Swidler from worrying about the time, and at least for the moment the tactic seemed to work. Swidler looked doubtful but said, "Glad to." He looked like the type of person who could lose himself in helping people. His big hand was on Miles's shoulder and his shiny face filled with pride. Clutching the sheet Goldstein had given him, Swidler led Miles toward the rear of the room.

"Every piece of property in the Bronx has a number and all numbers are recorded in the stacks," he said, indicating the rows stretching in all directions. "If Goldstein wants to know who six landlords are, first thing we do is find the numbers of the properties."

Miles nodded, thinking that anyone who went to law school knew this but that he was going to have to pretend ignorance. "Okay," he said. "How do you find the numbers?"

Swidler hitched up his belt as if he'd expected the question. "Follow me." He led Miles to a back corner where a series of street maps was suspended from a long metal rack and began looking through the maps one by one, sliding them along the rack.

"First we find the map of the overall *section* of the Bronx we want," he said. "In this case, Southeast. *Here.*" He scanned the map. "Then we check the street index to find the coordinates of the *address* we want. Understand?"

"Yes."

Swidler beamed. "Good. Now we locate the specific address we're interested in . . . 143-24 113 Street . . . *here.*"

136

He indicated a tiny square in the sea of numbered boxes on the map. Swidler wrote down some numbers, then scanned the shelves. A minute later he pulled a mammoth loose-leaf binder out of its berth and began thumbing pages. He said, "How come Ed is interested in these buildings anyway? What's the story?"

Miles said, "Arson."

Swidler paused a moment. "I see. *Here,*" he said, bending over eagerly. Miles strained to see. Swidler said, "See how the number on the page corresponds to the number on the map? That means this part of the book deals with our building. All buying and selling is recorded here by date. We start with the most recent. Let's see. This building was sold . . . *how do you like that!* Just two days ago! To a finance company. Harlan Trust. Ever hear of it?"

Miles was gripped by excitement. He said, "I thought someone named Scowcroft owned that building."

"He did but he sold it. See? Under this heading, recipient, it says Harlan Trust, and over *here,* seller, William H. Scowcroft."

Miles scanned the page eagerly, the blood pounding in his chest. Why hadn't Scowcroft told them? "Why would someone buy a building that just burned down?" Miles said.

Swidler laughed. "Who knows? It's cheaper. Someone wants the land. Come on. We got two more buildings to check. Office closes in thirty minutes and Goldstein will be mad if we don't finish."

Ten minutes later, hunched over another loose-leaf binder, he said, "I'll be damned. This one was sold too."

Five minutes after that he said, "Three in a row."

"*Six* in a row," Goldstein said when he joined them.

"Six fires. Six sales," Miles said in bewilderment. Swidler's earlier statement surfaced at the back of his mind, "*Someone wants the land,*" and mirroring Miles's thoughts, Swidler said, "But six *different people* bought the buildings."

"That doesn't mean anything," Goldstein said impatiently. "Come on, Frank. I need to see the deeds."

"CLOSING TIME," someone yelled from the front. The few people scattered among the stacks began trickling toward the door. The lights blinked an electronic order to exit. Swidler looked uncomfortable, caught between loyalties. Goldstein put his hands on his hips. "The deeds."

Swidler looked at his watch nervously. "You don't know the boss," he said. "This guy loves to make out bad reports." He looked around. "What the hell. You sent the doll, right? Fuck him." He went to the front of the room and started arguing with a fat man waiting there. After a moment the fat man threw up his arms, tossed the key to Swidler, spun on his heel and stomped out. Swidler returned, mopping his brow. He held up the keys and grinned. "That bastard," he said. "He's going to check with the arson bureau to see if you work there. I told him it was official business."

After shutting the lights off in the outer office he took them into an adjacent room filled with microfilm machines under protective vinyl coverings. The atmosphere was morguelike, ominously still. Swidler slid open a cabinet and removed boxes of microfilm while Goldstein uncovered a machine. Miles imagined the pleasant-faced man entering from the outer office. After all, he'd already tracked Miles down twice.

Swidler said, "Found what you want," then laughed nervously. "Boy, voices sound weird in here when everybody's gone."

Goldstein put the film on the machine, talked as he scanned the rolls. "We know all six buildings were bought by different people but that doesn't necessarily mean one person isn't coordinating the purchases, which is unlikely but conceivable. So we check it out. Lots of property owners don't want people to know what they own, for lots of reasons—taxes, alimony, whatever. And there are lots of different ways of disguising ownership. Sometimes one name is in the book and another's on the deed. Other times a secret legal agreement specifies the real owner. What I'd like to know is why all these buildings were sold so soon after being burned. Coincidence? Maybe. Something more? Probably not but conceivable."

Fifteen minutes later he switched off the machine, dissatisfied. The names on the deeds had matched those in the books.

Goldstein said, "I'll have to find those landlords."

"Your glass is empty," Miles told Elena, and poured. The wine made a soft burbling sound. He felt buoyed by the unexpected find at the records office and what looked like a strengthening alliance with Goldstein. And about Elena. The rich aroma of the meal wafted up to him, *pollo cazuela,* she had called it, a tart and succulent Caribbean chicken garnished with ham and sausage and served with cheese dumplings she called *fritadas con llapingachos.* He patted his stomach, said, "Aaaaah."

The room seemed warm despite the air conditioning. Elena shifted, inclined her head in appreciation. He was charmed by the gesture and wanted to kiss her. She rose, put a steadying hand to her forehead, then smiled.

"Dessert," she said.

She moved on colt legs into the kitchen. Miles heard dishes clattering. He wondered if he should help but decided she would prefer him not to. After a moment she emerged with a white cream cake covered with fruit. A record dropped automatically on the stereo—"Appalachian Spring."

She'd changed tonight. Every feature seemed sharper; the eyes luminously large, her mouth a soft O, her skin that entrancing golden color, but even more so.

They discussed apartments, neighbors, music for a long

139

time. The cake was delicious. After a while Miles said, "I haven't had a home-cooked meal in months," which made him think of Paula. He grew sad, looked around the room hoping the feeling would pass. The shelves were covered with little mementos: glass figurines, seashells, wicker baskets, books, a photograph he had not seen before. Her husband. Miles stared at the thick features, wide lips, friendly eyes and short, powerful forehead. Elena had mentioned a scar but he couldn't see it.

In his fascination he forgot she was there, but then he heard her low voice from across the table. "What was *your* marriage like?"

He was surprised not only that she would ask, but that he felt like answering. He hadn't talked about Paula since the fire, maybe because anyone who asked had always spoken to Goldstein first.

She said, "You don't have to answer if you don't want to," but he shook his head to indicate that he was quiet only because he was thinking how to begin.

Then he said, "I met her in Buffalo. In school. She was an arts major. A waitress." He paused, sketching her in his mind. "Tall, very slim. Soft brown eyes." He looked at Elena, whose eyes seemed soft themselves. "Classic Irish face, beautiful to me. Small features, mouth, upturned nose. She used to press her lips together when she was mad." He laughed. "Like this. Long legs. My friends gave her the best-legs-of-Buffalo award.

"We were different kinds of people. I think I'm a little too stiff. A good lawyer. She used to tease me about it. I didn't know anything about art or music. I'd always studied . . . well . . . I called them more practical things at the time. Math. History. She introduced me to her world. Concerts. Museums.

"First time, I asked her out on an impulse. Normally I didn't do things like that, not in a restaurant, in front of a table. I was too shy. She was our waitress. But I liked her. I had to ask her."

He felt like rambling but Elena didn't seem to mind. Her eyes were boring into his. Slightly shaken he said, "There are so many things. She was a teacher. Liked to camp. Had a temper. A baseball fan. Nothing sounds special but it all is. I wish I could explain *how* special. What can you say in five minutes?

"I'll tell you a story. One time she came back from the beauty parlor, pulled one of those women's magazines from her pocketbook. It had some kind of 'average person test' in it, you know? Rate yourself? She started reading off the criteria. Average male sleeps with so many women before marriage. 'Hey,' she said, 'that's you!' Average person watches so many hours of TV a day. 'That's you too!' Average person sleeps so many hours, drives the car so much each week, likes to eat in restaurants so many times a month. Each time it was me. She thought it was real funny. When she was finished she said, 'If you're so average I must be madly in love with a lot of people.' "

He hung his head and his voice cracked. "Jesus Christ. I killed her."

In his mind it was the night of the fire. The blaze shot across the room, crackling. The flame parted to reveal Paula on the bed. The fire pulled itself up the curtain as the door opened and his daughter ran in, terror on her face, arms outstretched. "Daddy!" The image switched to hours before. A boy had asked her to go to the movies. First date. Could she go? Miles shook his head no. Too early. Plenty of time later. Back to Louise screaming as the firemen pulled him away. Why wasn't he fighting them off? Running to her? A wall of flame shot up between them . . .

He broke away, breathing heavily. Elena's face was horrified. She left the table and walked across the room.

At once the air of intimacy was gone, replaced by a cold discomfort. The room seemed to be spinning. He would

141

have liked to have been somewhere else, and she must have felt the same way. Looking out the window, she said, "I haven't been down there in months."

Despite his mood he was surprised. She never talked about the outside with any sense of longing, but now she said, "I wonder what it's like. I've forgotten." She paused. "Isn't that something? I can't smell it or feel it. Those people down there might as well be dolls. *You* go outside every day. I'm tired of staying here."

He was amazed that she would allow herself the dissatisfaction in front of him. "You could go outside," he said weakly.

She didn't answer. Miles said, "You could see a doctor about it."

"A doctor?"

"Yes."

"A *psychiatrist?*" She laughed. "What would *he* do? Hold my hand? Tell me about my mother?"

"Do you have a better idea? It's only five flights." He stopped. A strange idea began to take hold. He liked it, cast about for a means of suggesting it. "Why don't we go outside? Both of us. Now."

She didn't say anything but her fingers started drumming on the windowsill.

He said, "You've been in here for months. We could be outside in five minutes."

"Five minutes, huh?" she said, trying for sarcasm but failing.

"That's right. I'll come with you."

"No."

He was drunk and as excited as she was vulnerable. "You *want* to go. I can see it."

"*I can't.*" Her voice was strident but there was a weakening in her face.

He said, "Sure you can. I'll help."

142

Her fingers drummed more rapidly. Laughing uneasily to herself, she said, "He'll help me walk down the stairs." She flushed with embarrassment at her fear of the simple journey. After a moment, in a little voice she said, "Don't be angry with me."

Her vulnerability charmed him but made him all the more determined to, as he saw it, help her. He said, "I'm not angry. I just think we should try."

No answer.

"We'll both go."

Long pause. Fright on her face.

"What do you think? Okay?"

Silence.

"*Okay?*"

Finally, very, very slightly, she nodded.

"Good." He took her hand, waited a moment to allow her to compose herself, then led her to the door. Her grip tightened as he turned the knob and she broke into rapid conversation.

"When I was a girl my father decided to teach me to swim. My mother was afraid of the water, and she'd told him not to, but she was away that day. At least that was what my father thought."

Miles opened the door and Elena shifted her hand to his forearm, the gesture of a child about to cross a busy street with an adult. They moved slowly into the hallway and he shut the door behind them. Her eyes were big, as if everything were magnified, and her voice grew louder as she tried to distract herself.

"We were fifty yards from shore when my mother came running onto the beach, screaming and waving her arms frantically. She'd gotten home early. Miguel was with her. My father smiled. That was the first time it occurred to me that he didn't like her."

One flight down. As they rounded the landing, a door

143

jerked open and an eye peered out through the crack. Elena started to let go but Miles tightened his grip to reassure her. The door closed. They moved down the next flight.

"My mother was independently wealthy and Miguel worked for her. He had almost reached us in the water. My father was holding me up and told Miguel not to touch me. . . . The walls!" She stopped.

Miles said, "What's the matter?"

"Far . . . away." A light sheen broke out on her forehead and her breathing became labored. He guided her along the bannister. She said, "Miguel tried to grab . . . me. My father pushed him away." They reached the next landing and she fumbled with the top button of her blouse. Miles was baffled, amazed. This was a perfectly innocent stairway.

He put an arm around her. "Do you want to go back?"

She shook her head. "Let me catch my breath."   ‧

"You're sure?"

She swallowed and squeezed his hand. They began walking again. She said, "They . . . started . . . to . . . fight. . . . I was in . . . the . . . water . . ." Her face grew chillingly blank and she was trembling, yet continued to allow Miles to lead her.

There was one more flight to go. The steps stretched before them like an endless accordion. Below, the street became visible through the front door; a little bit of sidewalk and the flash of passing cars. Elena stiffened and transferred her weight onto him. Sweat was pouring down her face.

Then she glanced ahead and her features became distorted with fear. Five teenagers with baseball bats and mitts had appeared in the doorway, blocking out the street light. Elena's fingers grew clawlike, digging into Miles's hand until he thought she was going to draw blood. She

144

began shaking uncontrollably. He had never seen a human being so terrified in his life. Her forehead was bathed in sweat, her pupils and nostrils dilated, her mouth twisted horribly. The boys stared at her. She buried her face in his neck, saying "I can't" over and over.

After a moment the boys moved slowly up the stairs, pulling away as they passed. There was a burst of their laughter from a landing above, the slam of a door, then silence.

Miles stroked her head to reassure her. The street was only twenty feet away but he knew he had to get her back to the apartment.

Then she collapsed in his arms. He said, "Elena," but she didn't answer. Gently but urgently, he carried her back up the stairs. The sixth floor seemed far away, and when they reached it the apartment was waiting like a comfortable bed after an arduous journey. It seemed as if they'd been gone for a long time. He helped her onto the couch. Without looking at him she said, "I think I'm going to be sick," then, "No, I'm not."

She lay on her arm, staring up at the ceiling. Miles felt responsible. He wanted to know why she had reacted so strongly to the boys but didn't dare ask. He desperately wanted to make her feel better. He started to get up for a cold compress but her fingers locked on his wrist. He sat down again, began to stroke her forehead. After a long time she spoke.

"I . . . told you . . . that I stayed . . . here . . . after Esteban died. I was still . . . going out then . . . to the market, the movies, for walks. That day I'd already gone to the . . . store but I'd forgotten soap. . . . I had to go back. It was rainy. Everyone was inside. I had to pass an empty lot and I didn't see the boys."

Miles stiffened, a chilling premonition sweeping through him.

145

She said, "Four or five of them, the same age as the boys downstairs. In an empty lot. They laughed at me and wouldn't let me by. Then they grabbed me and pushed me into a car. They stuffed something in my mouth. There was a broken light on the ceiling. Two of them climbed in, held me down."

She began to tremble. Miles touched her shoulder. "You don't have to talk about it."

"They smelled like grease and their legs were pale. They came in one after the other. They burned. Hurt." She grimaced as if feeling it now. "One kept laughing, another slapped me, asked if I liked it."

She began crying. Her arms went around his neck and he was seized with a sense of protectiveness and outrage and helplessness. He wanted to kill the boys. He pressed his body against hers, stroked her head, felt the tears on his neck. He wished he could think of something to say to make her feel better.

After a while he kissed her on the forehead. She stiffened slightly but then clung to him more tightly. He kissed her again, and then again, very lightly. Her head came up. He kissed the line of the jaw, the cheek, touched her lips with his own, rimming her mouth gently. She was silk. Her fingers slid down his neck and traced little lines on his face. Trembling, she returned his kisses.

He was seized with passion. Their heat was rising through their clothing. He rubbed his hands against her neck. She brought his hand to her mouth, kissed it, and bit it gently. She sucked on his finger.

The room had gone still except for their breathing. Slowly, they began unbuttoning each other's clothes. Her body was exquisite: copper, the breasts small, rising, the legs supine, long, the thighs smooth electricity, the arms curling, the hair fragrant. When he put his hand between her thighs it basked in radiant heat. She touched him,

146

moaned when he entered her, and then they were caught in each other's eyes almost until the end when he dropped onto her perfectly flat belly and they rose and fell in unison, Elena uttering little sounds, her back arching slowly, higher with each thrust, until they came together.

They remained embraced, lying in the dark, their legs tangled, her eyes closed, his open. She looked like an exhausted child, traces of fright still on her youthful face. He watched her for a long time. After a while he thought about moving into the bedroom but decided not to disturb her sleep. She snuggled close. When morning came she was still locked in his arms.

NINE

It was two days later. The phone kept ringing but nobody answered. Miles shifted stance in the hot booth, anxiously scanned his street for Goldstein's car and checked his watch. Yesterday had been a series of frustrating interviews with owners of burned buildings, but Goldstein had assured him that he would arrive this morning by nine. For the first time, quite disconcertingly, the fire marshal was late.

The phone rang again and an out-of-breath voice said, "Arson Bureau. McCully. Sorry."

Miles identified himself. "Bradshaw, huh?" said the officer. "Goldstein left a message for you. Said he'd be working alone today, double-checking stories. Said you didn't have a phone or he would have called. Said you'd understand."

Miles understood, all right. Goldstein had planned all along to work by himself today but had lied to keep him from "warning" possible co-conspirators. As usual, Goldstein wasn't trusting anyone.

He thanked the officer and hung up, irritated by the change in plans and surprised to find himself disappointed because he'd expected better from the marshal. Now, he collected his thoughts, and made two decisions. He called the telephone company to order a phone for his apartment. It was time to get in touch with people again. Then he dialed his office to tell his delighted supervisor he could work today. "We have thirty people in the waiting room and it's only nine-forty. Get in here, Miles."

Miles went upstairs, told Elena what had happened, changed in his apartment and went back to kiss her goodbye. Although they'd spent the last two nights together, he had been careful both times to be back home by the time Goldstein showed up, not wanting to sully the more joyful aspects of his life with the inspector's presence. And joyful was the perfect word for it, he thought now. Miles was continually amazed that Elena, so aloof at their first meeting, had become so loving, supportive, so giving and needing of warmth; so much, in fact, what he needed. He was beginning to feel whole again. To hell with Goldstein. So what if the marshal hadn't shown up. In the end everything would work out.

It was a beautiful morning. A flock of pigeons flew in and out of the sun, lazily circling a rooftop several blocks away. He rounded a corner five blocks from his office and approached the low-income project he always passed on the way to work. Ahead, above the wooden slat fence, a bulldozer roared across the lot amid the clanging of heavy machinery. Miles moved up until he stood directly across the street from the barbed-wire gate.

The site was bustling with activity. The only other movement on the otherwise deserted street was a couple of workers with containers of coffee leaving a small candy store to his rear. Work must just have started for the day.

He stood there, wondering when the project might be completed, when a dark shape at the edge of his vision, a black Torino, pulled up and stopped before the gate. He backed off a foot or two, trying to shake off the uneasiness caused by the sight of the car. After all, the license plates were New Jersey, not New York, and there were probably hundreds of black Torinos in the city. It would be ridiculous to become frightened every time he saw one.

Still, he kept an eye on the car. A short, stocky man emerged from the driver's seat and surveyed the site. Viewed from the rear he might have been Oriental, with his jet-black hair and compact body. Heart beating faster, Miles dodged behind a parked car and waited, feeling as if he were indulging in childish games, but wondering whether he should call the police.

The driver strode through the gate and a man Miles imagined was a foreman ran up to greet him. Soon the driver began gesturing, obviously giving instructions, and then the foreman moved off. The driver turned, revealing his face.

It *was* the pleasant-faced man.

The blood began pounding in Miles's fingers and toes. What was the Filipino doing here? *Call Goldstein,* he told himself, and looked around for a phone booth, but there was none on the street.

Hoping the candy store might have a phone, Miles waited until the pleasant-faced man had disappeared into the building, then walked into the shop, a tiny, boxlike vantage point which smelled of newsprint and vibrated from the machinery across the street. He occupied one of several threadbare stools at the counter, spotted the phone between the front window and the comic books, and dug into his pockets for change. He had none.

A voice said, "Want breakfast?"

Miles looked up to see a bleary-eyed, unshaven Hispanic holding a huge transistor radio in a doorway behind the counter. His apron was splattered with red and orange stains and he looked happy to see a customer. He said, "Special on eggs today."

"Just coffee, thanks."

The counterman grunted his disappointment, poured, and changed a dollar. He put the radio on a shelf and turned it up full volume. Latin music blasted Miles back toward the phone as the counterman snapped his fingers, turned away as if to isolate himself in a fantasy world, and danced behind the counter.

The noise was deafening. Holding a finger in one ear, Miles dialed the arson bureau and was connected to an officer who said Goldstein wasn't there and couldn't be reached because he didn't have a radio car today. Miles asked that Goldstein call him as soon as possible and read off the number of the phone.

He went back to the counter. Across the street the bull-dozer was pushing a pile of earth from one end of the lot to the other. The Spaniard spread a *Daily News* on the counter. He talked to himself as he read. "Look at this— they killed a girl in Central Park. Look at this—Arabs are raising the price of oil. The President's getting aid for the Bronx. Aid. Ha."

Thirty minutes later the pleasant-faced man still hadn't come out of the building. The bulldozer moved the earth back to where it had been originally.

A piercing whistle sounded across the street and men poured out of the site toward the candy store. Miles looked around wildly. It was too late to leave. He pulled a magazine from a rack and buried his face in it as the door opened and men pushed in, ordering cold drinks. Two of them occupied adjacent stools, glanced at him and lost interest.

"Working *hard* today?" one asked the other. They both found something funny in the question and laughed. The friend said, "Yeah, I got a *strain* from lifting heavy stuff," but neither seemed particularly tired. Several minutes later a whistle called them back and the store emptied. The bulldozer fired up again. The stools began to vibrate.

As Miles ordered more coffee, the phone rang. He leaped for it. A raspy Latin voice spoke before he could say anything. "My wife had a dream last night about Vermont so I want to put twenty dollars on Vermont Dream, first at Belmont." A pause. "Okay? Guillermo?"

The counterman grabbed the receiver as Miles's heart sank. A bookie! Of all the luck! The phone would be busy all day.

Miserably Miles finished his coffee, watching as three trucks rolled up to the site and were admitted, the first two ordinary flatbeds hauling pipes, the third an oddly stubby semitrailer, moving very slowly, as if the driver was afraid of damaging a valuable cargo. Miles wondered what was inside.

One by one the flatbeds backed up to the building and were unloaded by workers who carried the pipes into the project. Then the semi moved into place and the men clustered around the back, struggling to remove something heavy. The pleasant-faced man appeared in the doorway and walked over to the truck. Miles experienced a short stab in his chest, worried that he could be seen at this distance, but the pleasant-faced man had other interests at the moment. He moved up to the truck to supervise the unloading, then accompanied the workers, whose bodies hid the cargo, into the project.

The door closed behind them.

Miles let out a deep breath. The bulldozer chugged across his line of vision, moving the pile of earth to a third location. The phone rang. For the counterman. He realized that hours might pass before Goldstein called. Suppose the pleasant-faced man left before then? What would he do?

When he knew the answer he ran the four blocks to his office, and he burst in panting. Twenty people in the waiting room gave him ugly looks. Marcus appeared in the doorway of his cubicle. "Well, well. Could it be *Miles Bradshaw?* Two hours late? What could have delayed him?"

Normally Miles might have been embarrassed, but now he grabbed the supervisor's arm and pushed him back into the office, babbling, "I need your car. It's an emergency. A woman is having a baby. Hurry up, the keys!"

Marcus, responding more to the pressure than the logic, pulled out the keys. He sputtered, "Wait a minute," but Miles grabbed them and raced out the door. Marcus cried after him, *"What about all these people!"*

The Torino was still there when he returned, and the counterman said, *"Jesucristo.* You again." Miles ordered a grilled cheese sandwich to placate him, bought some magazines and settled down to read.

Hours passed. He wondered if Goldstein got bored on stakeouts. At five the whistle sent the workers scurrying to their cars. Soon the street was empty except for the Torino. And Miles, who had parked around the corner, nervously wondered whether the pleasant-faced man had left without taking the car.

But then the Filipino emerged from the project. Miles's pulse quickened. He had never trailed anyone before and

153

a more prudent voice in his mind warned of serious trouble if he tried to do so. *Call Goldstein and bring him back tomorrow. Let him take care of the Filipino.*

But suppose the man didn't return here tomorrow? While the Filipino was locking the gate Miles sneaked out of the candy store and into the car. When the Torino pulled away from the curb Miles counted twenty and followed, playing cat and mouse through a mazelike series of side streets, holding back on long stretches, rushing to catch up at corners, all the while feeling conspicuous. When they reached Westchester Avenue, he felt safer—he would be less noticeable in traffic. A red light separated them but he caught up again. "CROSS BRONX EXPRESSWAY" a passing sign read. They headed south toward the George Washington Bridge.

So it was going to be a long drive, maybe to Manhattan or New Jersey. Miles, guessing Jersey because of the Torino's license, glanced at the gas gauge and hit the dashboard in frustration. The gauge registered near empty. He was infuriated by his thoughtlessness and by visions of running out of gas two hundred feet above the Hudson River while the pleasant-faced man got away.

Soon the bridge loomed ahead and they began the climb to the suspension decks, but then the Torino veered under the "RIVERSIDE DRIVE" sign and descended onto Manhattan's West Side Highway. Miles followed, one woeful eye on the gauge.

The stream of cars headed downtown made it difficult to keep the Torino in sight. Traffic slowed for a stalled car, crawled for a hundred yards and then quickened again.

The gas gauge dropped to empty, twitching like a dying fish. The Torino's right blinker signaled a turn at the exit for the 79th Street Boat Basin. Miles started to signal and then thought, *He'll see me,* but there was no way he could avoid letting the pleasant-faced man know he was behind as both cars took the circular exit to street level.

The Torino halted at the top of the ramp, then plunged down another ramp past a "Parking Lot" sign into what looked to Miles like an underground facility.

Heart pounding, he thought, *Wasn't this what Goldstein had tried to do to the pleasant-faced man? Trap him in a parking lot with one entrance?*

The engine was idling badly and could stop at any second. The streets at Miles' left led off toward busy Riverside Drive. To his right the masts of the marina rose above the stone guardrail. If the Oriental's destination was the boat-yard, Miles could park here, watch over the wall and keep track of where he went. The boats and docks of the marina were laid out below.

But suppose there was *more* than one exit down there? Suppose the Filipino was even now disappearing down a tunnel or a subway entrance, only to resurface when Miles wasn't expecting him?

A car came up the ramp and honked for him to move.

He touched the accelerator, began the slow descent into the dark. The walls of the ramp closed in on him. He smelled stagnant water and prayed he wouldn't run out of gas. The black Torino was in the lot, fifty feet away, partially obscured behind a girder, and the pleasant-faced man, getting out, turned toward Miles's car. Miles went cold.

In the instant it took to scan the garage, Miles saw two exits: a ramp returning to the street and a door across the lot leading toward the marina.

Hoping he couldn't be seen in the dark and assuming the man would use the door, Miles rolled up the ramp to the top of the circular drive, where he pulled over and got out. He stood at the wall and waited.

Directly below, the pleasant-faced man hurried across a

155

walkway to the marina gate, which was opened by a boy in a sailor hat. He moved down a ramp and along the docks toward the big boats and deeper water. He reached the most mammoth boat in the marina, mounted the ramp to the towering sailboat and disappeared.

Miles exhaled. He waited to see if the Oriental would reappear, then climbed over the wall and ran down a small hill to the path. He wanted to question the watchman at the gate, not knowing what he was going to ask but thinking he might learn something of importance.

A sign on the fence said "NO ADMITTANCE" and the teenager with the sailor hat wore mirror sunglasses which reflected Miles, smiling uncertainly. The boy didn't smile back. Miles said, "Nice night." The boy didn't answer. Miles had the feeling he was a snob. *Try small talk,* Miles thought.

"Some marina."

"I suppose."

"A lot of boats."

"Uh huh."

"Any chance of being allowed inside?"

The boy jerked his finger at the sign. Miles pretended to catch sight of the big sailboat for the first time; he pointed. "What a ship!"

The boy glanced back and said, showing off, "Sparkman and Stephens. Custom made, two hundred feet."

Miles whistled admiringly. "Owner must be rich."

The sunglasses moved up and down as did Miles's reflection. "A Korean. Billionaire. Maybe you've heard of him. Trench. He's in magazines sometimes. You read magazines?"

Searching his memory, Miles said, "I never heard of him."

"Wot Chow Trench. Owns factories or something."

"I see." Miles tried to seem disinterested but could

hardly restrain his questions. Why was the Filipino here? Was there any connection between the boat and the construction site? Could the billionaire be involved in the Carlos Perez death? Was that . . . how would Goldstein say it . . . conceivable?

Calm down, he told himself. For all he knew the Filipino might not even *know* the owner of the boat. He might have come to visit a sailor, a cabin boy, a cook. He could be here on an errand totally unrelated to the Perez boy. Miles cleared his throat.

"I guess he gets a lot of visitors."

"Who does?"

"Trench. That was his name, right? The owner of the boat?"

The boy said, "What do you mean, *visitors?*"

And Miles, imagining the eyes behind the sunglasses, wished he could see them. A tremor ran through his bowels. He said, "I don't know. A rich man like that comes to town. I bet lots of famous people come to see him."

The boy nodded distastefully, as if he were a butler dealing with an autograph hunter. Neither of them spoke for several moments, and then Miles said, "Take the man who just arrived here . . ."

"*Who?*"

"I . . . I couldn't help seeing that he went to the yacht."

"*Why are you asking these questions?*"

Miles hesitated, starting to sweat. "I was just curious. I noticed—"

"You didn't *notice* anything. You can't even *see* the deck of that ship from here. You were *watching* from up *there.* You're a reporter!"

There was a small black phone next to the boy and Miles was afraid he was going to call the ship. He said, "Yes."

"*What paper?*"

"The *Post.*"

157

"The *Post*, huh? The guy from the *Post* was here when the boat came in. You got an ID?"

The light on the phone went on and the boy reached for it. Miles thought, *Get out of here.* He spun on his heel and walked off, feeling the eyes on his back. *That was stupid. You have to think next time.*

The boy watched him ascend the ramp. Would he tell the pleasant-faced man what had happened? Miles felt incompetent, ridiculous. He had to reach Goldstein before the Filipino left the marina. Thirty minutes had elapsed since their arrival here and Miles needed to find a phone.

He jumped into the car. Two blocks away he found a booth under a streetlamp and dialed the arson bureau. Goldstein still wasn't there and the officer who answered wasn't permitted to give out home numbers. He offered to try to reach Goldstein if Miles would stay on the line.

Miles drummed his fingers against the glass. The booth was stifling. He opened the door. The light went out. The line clicked to life. Goldstein wasn't answering his phone at home, the officer said. Did Miles want to leave a message?

Miles said he'd already left one, hung up and headed for the car. There was a gas station on 79th Street where he could fill up his tank. By the time he got back to the marina the black Torino was gone.

He went straight back to the construction site, hoping the Torino might be there, but the street was empty, the candy store dark. A long, thin cloud hung above the unfinished building like a stiletto, then drifted to the east where the sky was faintly red from a fire.

He felt frustrated, angry and depressed. He had held answers in his hand today but had not known how to understand them. Not only had the pleasant-faced man disappeared but perhaps he even knew that Miles had followed him. There was no point in trying to reach Goldstein again tonight. Miles had no evidence to back up his story.

A car in need of a muffler roared by. Miles wrapped his hands around the wire gate and stared like a boy at a knothole. Two dark loping shapes left the shadow of the building. Dobermans materialized in the darkness. A low snarl reached his ears.

Startled, he moved back. One of the dogs slid directly up to the fence, ears pricked straight, bared teeth fluorescently wolfish in the moonlight. Its tongue hung from its mouth and its breathing was steady and audible. It seemed to dare him to climb over the fence.

He shivered. For the life of him he couldn't figure out what the pleasant-faced man had been doing for eight hours in that building today. Why had he been the last to leave the site? What was the machinery which had been taken from the covered truck? Also, and, as Goldstein would say, *conceivably*, Miles wondered whether any of this was related to the death of Carlos Perez or the attack on him at the zoo. And, looking at the sign on the fence, another question occurred to him. Why, unlike the other low-income projects he had ever seen, was there no mention of government funding?

What the hell was in that building?

"I won't do it," Eduardo said.

Carlos' friend shook his head vigorously and glanced around as if to see if he was being observed. He said, "I don't have anything to do with things like that. I'm no criminal. Go away."

The junior high school across the street was disgorging a steady parade of raucous humanity, and they were on a

159

street corner where Miles had parked fifteen minutes earlier to air a desperate idea.

The boy said, "First you showed up interested in Carlos. Then you brought a cop. Now you want me to tell you who can break into a housing project. Leave me alone."

Miles bent over the boy, the friendly lawyer trying for trust. "I'm doing this for Carlos," he said.

Eduardo made a face. "Yeah, Carlos. What did Carlos have to do with a building under construction?"

Miles shook his head. "To tell you the truth, I don't know, but I think it's important that I get in there."

Eduardo said, "Then let Goldstein get a warrant."

Miles shifted uneasily, not wanting to tell the boy that he was leaving Goldstein out of this because he didn't want to lead the arson inspector on a wild-goose chase, not wanting to admit to himself that he didn't completely trust Goldstein.

Eduardo said, "Everybody knows people who break into buildings. Ask someone else to help you."

"I'm asking you."

"*I'm* going home."

He didn't move though, probably knowing Miles would stop him. A group of girls in halter tops sashayed by, giving Eduardo the eye, but the boy ignored them. Stubbornly Miles put his hands on his hips. "If you don't help I'll wait for you every day. How will *that* look to the Kings?"

Eduardo groaned. A trapped look appeared in his eyes. He glanced about as if the Kings were watching now, tightened his lips, looked at the ground and shuddered. He let his breath out slowly. He said, "This last time I'll help. Promise you'll leave me alone after this."

Miles nodded, afraid that if he spoke the boy might change his mind. Eduardo lowered his voice. "I have a friend, Paco, who knows people who might help you." He paused. "You're not going to steal anything, are you?"

"Of course not. I just want to look around."

160

Eduardo said, "I don't want to have anything to do with stealing. I'll talk to Paco. He'll want money. I don't want to know who he gets to do it, okay? You know Rosado's Spanish Grocery on Fox Street?"

"I can find it."

"Tomorrow at four-thirty. If Paco doesn't want to come, I'll tell you, but I don't want to talk to you here again. That's the best I can do. Remember, leave me alone after this."

Paco did come, though, a small boy with a pudding face covered with blackheads. Brown piercing eyes looked out from the ravaged skin, and the handshake was childlike, the voice high but firm. "Twenty dollars before we talk," he said.

Miles, pulling out his billfold, could scarcely imagine how this child would be able to help him. Paco stuffed the money in his dungarees, listened to Miles's needs and assured him that although he *personally* never broke into buildings he might be able to find people who would "do a job" for the right amount of cash.

"How much?"

"For me or for them?"

Miles sighed. "For you."

The eyes lit up. Miles wondered what the boy would spend it on—bubble gum? Paco thrust his hand into his pocket, fingering the money. He looked up appraisingly. "Another twenty."

Wearily, Miles handed it over. Paco smiled. "Tomorrow night."

It was getting dark fast outside the Spanish grocery. The nearest streetlamp was broken and the next one down the block flickered. The air smelled of garbage, oil and

161

dog excrement. Nearby, two cats in heat were howling at each other.

Miles had a hundred dollars in his pocket to pay whoever showed up, but he had no idea whether that was too much or too little. He had been waiting more than an hour and was starting to worry that Paco had tricked him.

A pair of headlights rounded the corner, slowed and stopped. Several shadowy figures were visible inside the dilapidated Chevrolet. One, a broad-shouldered teenager, opened the back door and got out. Miles looked up into the bland oval face of an idiot. From the back seat a voice called to him.

"Miles Bradshaw?"

He had an urge to deny it. "Yes."

"Get in."

He did so, crouching and feeling the idiot at his back. The door closed. The smell of marijuana was overpowering. There was the hiss of a match being struck beside him and he turned to see, in its flare, Rodriguez' grinning face.

He grabbed for the door. Rodriguez barked "Stop!" and hands gripped him from all directions, the idiot's powerful fist locking on his forearm, another King going for his knees. He recognized one of the kids from the meth clinic. Rodriguez grabbed his other arm in a painful vise.

Miles felt his blood rushing. He wanted to cry out but stopped himself. Last time he'd met Rodriguez the gang leader had gone for his knife, restraining himself at the last minute only because Goldstein had been there.

Goldstein wasn't here now.

The King in the front seat smiled blandly. The driver's eyes met Miles' in the rearview mirror and Rodriguez said, "Watch the road." Miles remembered with terror the story of the half-wit on the tenement floor.

Rodriguez said, "So you want to do some business."

The words filled the car as if bridging a great gulf. Miles could scarcely believe he heard them correctly. "What?"

Rodriguez mimicked him. "What? W-h-a-t?" The King in the front seat laughed and the idiot grinned uncertainly. Rodriguez leaned over, spraying saliva as he talked. "Paco said you wanted to get into that construction site. He said you'd pay."

Miles nodded, unsure if Rodriguez was playing with him, and the gang leader growled, "Say it!"

"Yes."

His throat felt like rubber. Rodriguez loosened his grip and appraised him with a shrewdness which made Miles wonder whether all this intimidation was designed to get the price up. The car left the side street and shot onto busy Westchester Avenue. If the Kings were planning to hurt him, Miles asked himself, would they travel in such a public place?

Rodriguez said, "How much will you pay?"

Miles hesitated. Paco hadn't mentioned specific figures. "I don't know."

"Tell me an amount."

Miles shrugged. "Fifty dollars."

There was a dumfounded silence, then Rodriguez exploded in ugly laughter. "F-i-f-t-y d-o-l-l-a-r-s!" He was astounded, enraged. He couldn't believe what he'd heard. He pressed his face close and hissed, "Three hundred dollars! That's what you'll pay," and Miles, surprised, sputtered, "Three hundred? You're only kids and . . ."

He didn't know where the knives had come from but they were out, the King in front glaring behind a long stiletto, a poised switchblade in the idiot's hand, the gang leader pressing a sharp point against Miles' cheek. He heard the snarl in his ear.

"You think you're getting cheap bums to work for you? We're professionals! For fifty dollars you get winos who

163

screw up and get everyone in trouble! Why are you insulting us?"

"I'm . . . sorry."

" 'I'm sorry,' he says. *'I'm sorry'!*"

The driver was watching in the rearview mirror again. Miles said, "R-really."

Rodriguez seemed to reconsider, perhaps because he didn't want to lose the money. He eased up on the knife. "That's better. I accept your apology." To the boy in the front seat, "Ricardo, put that away." The stiletto disappeared behind the seat, but Miles waited until both of Ricardo's hands were visible again before breathing easier. Rodriguez grinned and slapped Miles on the arm. "Don't worry! I have a hot temper!" He rubbed his hands and held one out. "Three hundred dollars."

Miles swallowed. "I only have a hundred on me."

Rodriguez peered at him, trying to determine the truth of this statement. He tapped a finger on his knee. "You got credit cards?"

"Yes."

"Gimme one."

Miles pulled out a Visa and Rodriguez examined it. "Give us one day with this, then report it stolen. We'll only spend three hundred dollars. You can trust us."

Miles said hesitantly, "I can get the cash tomorrow," but Rodriguez' voice hardened. "We'll take the card."

Miles didn't like that. Was some bizarre point of honor involved here or was Rodriguez outright lying? Either way he wasn't going to get the card back. Rodriguez eased against the back seat, satisfied with the way the evening was going. They were almost at the construction site.

Miles said, "I'm a little surprised to see you here."

"Why?"

Miles chose his words carefully. "You and I argued at the meth clinic."

Rodriguez waved away the memory. "That was one

thing. This is another. Pay me and I work for you. I'm an in-de-pen-dent." He paused. "Let me ask *you* something. Paco said you weren't going to take anything tonight."

"That's right."

Rodriguez lifted his hands in a gesture of incomprehension, then said, "But you won't stop *us,* will you?"

Miles felt a twitch in his neck. "From what?"

"Taking some plumbing. Some tools."

Miles sat forward and shook his head vigorously. "I told Paco no one should take anything."

Rodriguez rubbed his cheek thoughtfully but a little too dramatically, so that Miles anticipated another demand for money, sensing Rodriguez had known the instructions all along. Rodriguez said, "If you want us not to take anything you have to pay more."

"*How* much more?"

Rodriguez considered. "*Two* days with the credit card. Double."

"That's robbery!"

Rodriguez grinned this time. "Decide."

He started to clean his fingernails with the knife, and there was something in his eyes which made up Miles's mind. They pulled up across the street from the construction site and three or four more Kings materialized out of the shadows of the candy store in sleeveless denim jackets with gang insignias. The smallest marched up to Rodriguez like a lieutenant about to issue a report. Rodriguez poked him in the chest proudly. "This is Jesús. My war counselor." Inwardly, Miles groaned. Rodriguez said, "Wha'd you find, Jesús?"

The war counselor, who had quick, darting eyes and couldn't stop shuffling, said, "Pretty strange for a construction site. Three dogs in there instead of one. The locks on the gate look normal but there's a camera above the door. Like at the supermarket."

Rodriguez said, "Shut up about the supermarket."

Jesús looked at the ground, embarrassed. Rodriguez tapped him on the shoulder like a father reassuring an errant son, and Jesús smiled, forgiven. "I saw it with the binoculars," he said. Miles gaped in amazement at the boy's thoroughness. "Cops go by every twenty-five minutes. There's a phone line out of the building. We'll have to cut it. Someone might be inside."

Miles was having second thoughts now, but Rodriguez' eyes were glowing dangerously. The gang leader beckoned everyone into the shadows and gave instructions.

"Three teams. Cutters and pistols. Jesús will take the phone line and I'll give the signal with the lighter."

Four of the boys melted down the block. Another produced a long-handled wire cutter and a second pulled from his jacket a shiny blue pistol and a tube which he screwed onto the bore. Miles felt an increasing turmoil in his stomach.

Rodriguez, seeing him eye the gun, said, "Silencers. A guy brings 'em up from Carolina. Very expensive. We've come a long way from when my brother ran this club. In those days they just used chains or antennas, knives. Then the South Gaylords got zip guns, so we got zip guns. Then a pistol or two. Now we buy the guns." Miles must have looked as uncomfortable as he felt because Rodriguez grew contemptuous. "How'd you *think* we were going to take care of the dogs? Or didn't you think about it at all? People like you make me sick."

He fell silent, waiting, Miles realized, for the police to pass. As if on cue, a pair of headlights appeared at the end of the block, moved to the site and stopped. A searchlight stabbed out of the darkness, illuminating the bulldozer, the trucks, the periphery of the fence. It halted, probing, then reversed direction.

The light was extinguished and the car began to roll away. Miles was seized with the urge to run. What was he doing here, a lawyer teamed up with a street gang, paying kids to shoot dogs and break into buildings. He could be arrested, jailed, disbarred, and for what? Suddenly the construction site seemed absolutely normal to him.

Too late. Rodriguez was moving into the street, tiny flame flickering from his raised hand.

Jesús shimmied up a telephone pole with a strap as shadowy teams of two raced, cutters and pistols in hand, toward the lot. Miles was amazed at the full-scale assault. They *were* professionals.

The phone line dropped away, sparking, into the lot as two dogs charged the gate, barking, to blunt the attack. The kids with the cutters stood back as the gunmen crouched, aimed and fired. A series of soft "pffts" followed and a dog howled, twisted in the air and dropped. The other Doberman backed behind the bulldozer. There came the smack of bullets on steel. The barking grew more frantic.

Two of the kids with cutters went to work at opposite ends of the gate, snipping wire so that the gunmen, who still had the dog pinned behind the bulldozer, could get in. The third kid with cutters perched on his gunman's shoulders, slicing a hole above the wooden fence. When they were all finished, the two cutters at the gate retreated back to the shadows like sappers who had mined a dam, and the cutter at the fence cupped his hands to lift his partner through the gap. All three gunmen advanced into the lot, two heading for the bulldozer and the Doberman, the third racing for the building. He reached the door and fired at the camera and it exploded. The gunman kicked the door open and disappeared inside.

Rodriguez pulled a reluctant Miles across the street. The Doberman at the bulldozer squealed as if it had been hit and began running in circles. The gunmen, enjoying themselves now that the dog appeared less dangerous,

167

began closing on it, firing. The animal squealed again as a third shape shot around the building on the Kings' blind side. Rodriguez screamed a warning, but he was too late. One of the gunmen whirled, but the dog, launching into the air, hit him in the shoulder and knocked him to the ground. The boy screamed, an awful rising sound which became a gagging as the animal reached his throat.

When the other gunman turned to help, the wounded Doberman charged. Rodriguez yelled again. The gunman fired in time and the dog crumpled to the ground.

The gunman turned back to his partner and the animal rolling in the dust as Rodriguez ran up, grabbed the gun and fired three times. The boy screeched. The dog snarled and broke away to leap at Rodriguez, who kept firing. The dog hit him. They fell. Then the dog was still.

Rodriguez scrambled out from under the body. A dark stain was seeping into the earth beside the boy who was moaning, "Rodriguez, you shot me." Blood drenched the neck, the mouth, the shirt. Loose pieces of flesh flapped at his chin and the bone was visible. The dog's teeth had raked the jacket. Rodriguez took off his jacket and laid it on the boy's chest. He said, "Get him in the car." He glared at Miles as if the lawyer were to blame but said nothing.

The King who had kicked in the door to the building ran up. "There was a guard. Old guy. I tied him up." He looked at the boy on the ground. "Oh, God."

The injured boy started to cough brutally. Blood oozed from his mouth. They picked him up and left as quickly as they had come, melting into the darkness, leaving Miles among the dead dogs, the blood, the phone line trailing on the ground nearby. Somewhere behind him the Chevy roared off. The moon went behind clouds.

Miles was alone.

He stood there swaying slightly in shock and horror, struggling with the reality and responsibility of what had just occurred. *"Cops go by every twenty-five minutes,"* Jesús had said. Only fifteen were left, ten if he wanted to be safe. *Think about the dogs later.*

He reached the building in seconds and slipped inside. Someone was moaning on the ground a few feet away, bound, gagged and facing in the other direction. He wanted to make sure the man wasn't seriously hurt but couldn't let himself be seen. He turned, eyes adjusting to the darkness.

Then he caught his breath.

The building had no floors in its center for at least 150, 160 feet up, the floors looking as if someone had removed their centers with an oddly shaped cookie cutter. He was reminded, gaping at it, of the Hyatt Regency in Atlanta, where a cavernous multistoried lobby astounded visitors. Steel crossbeams were visible in the dimly lit area above in which a high tower telescoped upward, like a monstrous conning tower. He'd never seen anything like it, a pole in a high steel frame resting on a wide platform which in itself was ten feet off the ground. The tower was anchored by cables which ran from periodic points to corners of the building's foundation and walls.

What the hell was it? Fascinated, Miles stepped forward, sank into something soft and jumped back, frightened. His hands encountered mud. *In here? But it was dry in here.* And as his vision adjusted better to the lighting he could see the outlines of a huge pit filled with mud by the tower.

He stood there trying to figure it all out, and when he looked at his watch again four minutes had elapsed. He skirted the pit, scrambled past what looked like large gasoline engines and shot up a steel ladder to the deck of the platform. The numerous dials and levers there gave no hint as to their function and it was too dark to make out whatever directions there might have been. He wished he had thought to bring a flashlight. This was so frustrating,

169

so tantalizing. He probed at the machinery, felt with his hands, sniffed, found nothing.

The police were due back in three minutes. Reluctantly he turned to leave. The guard was still moaning when he passed. The dogs lay inert under the cold moon, puddles of blood and urine staining the earth at their flanks. A rat scurried away from one of their bellies.

He slipped through the fence even as the headlights began to light the corner, ran across the street and hid in an alley. *Like a criminal.* The police rolled up. The searchlight shot out, traveled along the fence, stopped on the holes, traveled again and illuminated the dead dogs. Officers got out of the car and drew guns.

Miles moved off, his mind in turmoil. Nothing about the building made any sense, not the huge crossbeams, the tower, the strange machinery, heavy security precautions, the pit filled with mud. Obviously, from what he had seen, little work had been done on the outside for some time. So why did the workmen come back day after day?

Why?

He slipped through the streets, watching for police and using the alleys as if he'd been doing it for years. There was no way he could tell Goldstein what he had done tonight, not after breaking so many laws. And yet there was so much more he felt he needed to know about the project. Somehow, he felt, there was a relationship between what he had seen tonight and the death of Carlos Perez, although he couldn't begin to guess what it was.

He was going to have to find out alone.

He was going to have to get in there during the day.

TEN

Stretching above the Jersey Palisades and threatening to push out over the river and blacken Manhattan with storm, the squall line was an ugly rolling cloud which threw lightning against the distant cliffs and sent thunder rumbling across the Hudson. The wind was rising and the water becoming choppy. Lines of steady gray rain fell to the Jersey shore, and overhead came the footsteps of sailors battening down the ship.

Hanging up the phone in his cabin, and watching the storm through the porthole, Wot Chow Trench allowed himself his first smile in what seemed to him like days. He strolled to the sprawling plastic model in the corner, extracted three red plastic buildings from a box nearby and

171

scanned the miniature city at his waist. He scooped away three black buildings and replaced them with the red. He put the black in an ashtray and applied a cigarette lighter to them one by one. They smoldered, blazed and melted.

When all that remained of the buildings was a thick black pool, Trench went to a liquor cabinet, slid open a teak panel, selected a bottle of red wine, uncorked it and stopped it up again. Then he left the cabin, rapidly making his way through the descending passageways until he came to a door guarded by two sailors who stiffened at his approach. Noting the reaction with approval, Trench said, "How is he?"

The first sailor looked at him and shrugged. "DT's. Want us to go in with you?"

Trench declined the offer with a shake of his head, holding up the wine as if it were an explanation. The sailor nodded, relaxed, and turned the knob. The slowly opening door revealed a cabin in shambles, with a long figure sprawled amid the shattered glass, broken furniture and shredded curtains and bedding. The room smelled of urine. Scratch marks covered the porthole as if the occupant had been trying to smash his way out, and the wasted middle-aged alcoholic on the floor fastened his pale-blue eyes on Trench without moving his head. The brittle chest rose and fell slowly. The breathing was hoarse.

Trench closed the door, stepped calmly over the debris and made his way to a tattered single bed. The eyes stayed on him all the time but the head still didn't move. Trench wrinkled his nose at the smell, held out the bottle and said, "Wine."

The ruby liquid caught the light and played with it. The breathing quickened and the eyes lit up but the man looked away. Trench uncorked the wine, brought it to his nose and sniffed. The hands began to tremble. The voice, when it came, was dry and ravaged. "I don't want it."

172

Trench kept the bottle extended. Several moments later the head swung slowly around and the body began to stir as if a thousand tiny parts were mobilizing on their own, producing a bizarre twitching progress across the floor. "Take it away."

But the hand reached out to take the bottle and the prisoner dragged himself back into a corner where he drank with long, noisy swallows. Then he wiped his mouth and looked away.

And Trench, inclining his head in disgusted fascination, said, "Tell me again how you're going to make me rich."

All his plans would be ruined if it rained, Miles told himself. He scowled at the darkening southern sky and realized it was probably pouring in Manhattan. Maybe the storm would veer away. *If it rains they'll stop work.*

He was dressed in an old work shirt, coveralls and construction boots he'd bought at a Salvation Army outlet. A hard hat lay on the counter beside his untouched coffee, under the incredulous stare of the candy store owner. There was a tightness in his stomach which wouldn't go away. If the pleasant-faced man didn't arrive at the site in ten minutes and if an impending work break occurred on schedule, Miles planned to accompany the workers back to the construction project. He hoped to make his way into the building, hide behind the piles of pipes or lumber he'd seen the night before and observe the machinery in action.

Unfortunately, the hard hat's shade of yellow was lighter than the hats in the site, but it was too late to do anything about that. At least he'd remembered to dirty the clothing.

It wasn't the safest plan imaginable, but it was the best he could think of, considering his determination to get into the site.

With a pang he realized that he should have anticipated, the night before, Elena's furious opposition to his idea, coming as it did after his story about Trench's yacht, the boat basin, and the Latin Kings' assault on the construction site. She had eyed him then with a hollow flatness, which, in hindsight, he recognized as building anger, and at the part about the dead Dobermans her face had become white and pinched. He'd been mid-sentence describing the plan for getting into the place when she'd interrupted.

"Why do *you* have to do this?"

He'd been too caught up in what he was saying to see how mad she was. "I told you. It's the best way to deal with Goldstein." She had fallen sullenly silent while he told her about buying the secondhand clothing as well as the pocketknife he had with him now, which he realized was pretty pathetic "protection." Then a second interruption.

"How do you know the pleasant-faced man won't arrive while you're inside?"

It was a question he had uncomfortably considered. "I'll only stay for ten minutes."

"That's no answer."

Undeterred, Miles said, "I'll get out."

For a moment she looked like the old sarcastic Elena. "You think this is all a big game, don't you? You're enjoying it."

"That's not it at all."

"Sure," she insisted, speaking very slowly, "a little adventure. A fantasy for the out-of-shape lawyer, breaking into construction sites, shooting dogs. Disguises."

Miles said, "Stop it."

She lapsed into silence again, getting herself under control, and her voice, when she spoke again, was coldly reasonable. "What about the *other* man who attacked you at the zoo? Suppose *he's* there?"

"He wasn't there today. Listen," he said, in his most measured, logical lawyer's voice, "I think the risks of this thing are justified by the benefits." But rather than easing her fears he seemed only to exacerbate them.

She looked like a mime artist mocking a pompous judge. "The *risks* and the *benefits!*" she said, agitated. "Know what the *risks* are? The risks are that you'll get your throat cut and land up roasting in a fire; *those* are the risks." She shook her head in disgust. "And what are the *benefits*, or are there even any benefits at all? You don't even know what the machinery you saw *was*. You don't know if it has anything to do with Carlos Perez. Listen to the crazy things you've been talking about—buildings without ceilings, a billionaire's yacht . . ."

He cried, "You don't believe me!"

"Oh, I believe you all right. That's why I think you're crazy for going in there alone, a little guy like you, stumbling around, no idea of what you might find. If there *are* connections here, a lot more is involved than the death of a twelve-year-old boy. Maybe *he* saw something he wasn't supposed to."

Miles, admitting to himself that she had a point, nevertheless said stubbornly, "I'm going in there tomorrow."

They stared at each other, he in obstinance, she in anger, and suddenly she started to shout. "Stay out of it! You've done as much as you can! You're not a detective! You're a lawyer! Look at you—paying kids to shoot dogs!"

"I didn't know they'd shoot them!"

"Of course you didn't! You didn't even know enough to *think* about it."

"Elena—"

"You have an obsession with a boy you didn't know and a need to hurt yourself."

"*Elena—*"

"It's dangerous in there and you're going to get hurt!"

"Elena, shut up! If I'm supposed to be so worried about getting hurt maybe I should move away from *here!*"

He regretted the words as soon as they were out. Elena

175

went mute, her face chalk white. He was up in an instant, arm encircling her shoulder. "I'm sorry. I didn't mean it," and when she finally met his stricken gaze her face had crumpled and her voice was low and miserable.

"I just don't want to see you get hurt."

The whistle blew across the street and the workers poured into the store. When the break was over he tried inconspicuously to melt into the crowd of returning workmen. Nearing the barbed-wire gate, he felt a growing uneasiness in his stomach. Would the workers recognize a new face? He pulled his hard hat lower. Suppose someone started talking to him? What would he do? He could imagine the scene: an innocent question about the job and his inadequate reply resulting in a look of curiosity turning to alarm. A watchman or laborer on break, he couldn't decide which, lounged against a post at the entrance and surveyed those who passed. Miles realized with a jolt that although he'd remembered to dirty his clothes, his body was still clean.

The holes left in the fence by the Latin Kings had been repaired and the dead Dobermans were gone, the blood-stained earth of last night now parched, as if the dogs had never been there at all. There was something eerie in the complete lack of evidence of last night's attack. Workers began peeling away from the group and heading for their respective jobs, stripping Miles of cover until only five or six men remained around him.

The camera above the building's entrance was sweeping back and forth, probably picking him up as he approached. He lowered his head and prayed that whoever was watching wasn't counting workers or looking too closely. Talking about entering the site had been easy. Doing it was something else.

But he reached the door and passed inside to be struck immediately by the roar of machinery reverberating through the multistoried cavern in which he stood, dwarfed and awed. Light streamed in through the upper windows, and additional illumination was provided by a lengthy series of electric bulbs strung between the tower, a gasoline generator and a couple of mammoth engines beside a catwalk piled high with pipes. The tower itself was manned by four hard-hatted workers, one of whom occupied a monkey walk twenty feet up and directed the raising of more pipe out of the ground. Even though Miles had already been here it was an astounding sight.

As the workers beside him moved off, he took it all in at a glance: the steaming mud pit, the men carrying pipe and the scattered piles of lumber or steel which might provide cover. One such pile was blocking off a corner of the foundation as if it were the base of a triangle and the walls were sides. Slowly, he edged toward it, all the while conscious of the workers nearby, certain that someone was going to see him. But he reached the pile, dropped behind it and peered out.

At first he could make little sense of all the activity before him, but Miles soon decided that three separate operations were taking place here. The men on the tower were maneuvering a massive traveling block and hydraulic jaw to raise a sixty-foot section of pipe out of the ground. When the block stopped, the men clustered around the base of the pipe, then struggled away with a heavy metal object they deposited on the platform. The object looked like a pair of huge mandibles or a cluster of steel pinecones and had obviously been detached from the pipe. The man on the monkey walk then gave a signal and the tongs carried the pipe into a slip twenty feet up. The worker locked the pipe in place and the traveling block swung back for another trip.

Meanwhile, a second crew was carrying pipes from a catwalk beside the tower to another one forty feet away. Obviously they were making room for something, but Miles had no idea what it was. At the foot of the first catwalk a third crew was rolling an electric console into position and hooking it up by wire to a tremendous wheel-backed roll of cable. Miles watched in perplexed fascination as one worker took a seat behind the console to begin testing while the other two struggled to loop the heavy cable around one pulley at the base of the tower and another fifty feet up. After a while, two more workers appeared with what looked like a particularly shiny twenty-five-foot length of pipe, but which, after watching the delicate way it was handled, Miles decided was another piece of valuable equipment. The new "pipe" was going to be attached to the cable and raised into the air.

Although Miles was still burning with curiosity, he realized that forty-five minutes had elapsed since his arrival and that he should leave. His next move, after reaching the street, would be to visit a construction company, describe what he had seen and get an explanation, but when he dared raise his head again it seemed as if more workers had appeared on the site and the door was farther away. All of Elena's warnings flooded into his mind. It looked like getting out of here wasn't going to be as easy as getting in.

The foreman again began to swing in his direction and Miles dropped to the earth. Gingerly, he peeked above the pile again. The foreman was looking toward the door, where a short, stocky figure was dark against the entrance. Miles experienced a heart-stopping premonition, and the pleasant-faced man stepped forward.

Miles was trapped.

He sank down for an instant, the blood rushing back to his heart, and controlled the urge to bolt. In his mind he

178

saw himself tied up and killed in a fire like Carlos Perez, perhaps stabbed and dragged to another building to be burned. Could that have been what happened to the boy?

The figure at the door slowly looked in all directions, as if sensing an unfriendly presence. The crashing din seemed to grow louder, the space in which he was hiding to shrink, so that the slightest movement would be seen. Miles didn't care about the machinery anymore, he didn't care about the pleasant-faced man or even Carlos Perez' killer. He only wanted to leave.

When he calmed down enough to look above the pile again, he saw that the pleasant-faced man had joined the foreman by the tower and was watching with keen proprietary interest as the shiny silver pipe was hoisted into the air and steadied above the platform. The foreman cupped his hands to yell instructions, but his voice was lost amid the noise.

All backs were turned. Miles began trudging toward the door. His knees felt weak, his chest was pounding, and he was sweating all over. When he heard no shout of warning and felt no restraining hand on his shoulder, he had the wild thought that maybe he *would* get out, but as he reached the door it began to open in his face. Panic-stricken, Miles spun on his heel and made his way *back* toward the pleasant-faced man. The Filipino, several feet away from the catwalk, was facing away from him. With each step the powerful rhythm of the machinery seemed to grow louder, merging into one crashing cacophony which overpowered Miles's thoughts, breaking them into magnified and disconnected images: the mud shooting into the pit, the back of the pleasant-faced man's head, the huge swaying tongs.

Mechanically, he reached the catwalk and bent to join the stream of laborers carrying pipes. The pleasant-faced man was less than three feet away. Miles imagined he

179

could smell the after shave and *could* see the little black hairs and dots of sweat on the bull-like neck, the bulge of muscle under the suit, the thick, powerful hands at the sides and the slight swelling of a pocket where the knife probably lay.

A voice next to him yelled, "COME ON, YOU ASS-HOLES! BIG BONUS IF WE LOG IT UP BY THREE!" The foreman, a barrel-chested, flat-featured Slav, had moved close, looking as if he wanted that bonus pretty badly. Miles turned the words "*log it up*" over in his mind. A worker at the catwalk broke toward the door but the foreman grabbed his wrist. Although they shouted at the top of their lungs, Miles had to strain to hear over the thundering machinery.

"WHERE THE FUCK YOU THINK YOU'RE GOING!"

"THE CAN, MAN!"

"FORGET IT! WE DON'T BREAK UNTIL THE LOGGING'S FINISHED!"

The worker flashed a look of sullen anger. "FUCK THE LOGGING! WE'LL FINISH ON TIME! I WISH THE MACHINE WOULD BREAK!" But he turned back to work. The worker who was carrying the other end of Miles' pipe pulled away, and Miles, his load heavy on a shoulder unaccustomed to physical labor, followed, the words "*I wish the machine would break*" sticking in his mind, although he wasn't thinking clearly enough to do anything with them. After a while, he was surprised to find the professional part of his mind battering down panic and actually considering how to distract the foreman and disable the machinery.

The platform and tower were too far away and within the pleasant-faced man's line of vision, the console too well guarded. The generator, two feet away from the pile of pipes, was another story.

Miles, who had lived in Manhattan and hadn't even

owned a car since he was a teenager in Queens, remembered only sketchy information about generators and was limited to envisioning basic kinds of sabotage, like letting out the gas or water, a notion he rejected because it involved conspicuously crawling under the machine. Opening the gas tank and throwing dirt in seemed like a better idea until he remembered how hot the generator must be and how it would feel to touch it. Besides, he didn't know where the gas tank was. While lifting another pipe he scanned the big machine—the metal cylinders which baffled him, the knobs he didn't understand, the thick lengths of rubber tubing running along the side over a wide shallow pan.

It was on this tubing that his thoughts rested as he began the walk with the pipe to the second catwalk. The generator's tubing was obviously carrying oil, gas or water and if punctured would leak until the engine stopped and distracted the foreman. Miles could then slip away.

The choice was frighteningly clear. He could either take a chance on slicing a tube or wait until a work break, which might not occur for hours, or until the pleasant-faced man turned around.

Miles reached the catwalk, waited until the other worker had started back toward the generator and then followed, glancing around to make sure no one was watching. He casually extracted the knife from his pocket, hid it in his hands and opened it as he moved. He'd need one swift, powerful and miraculously unobserved jab to slice open a hole large enough for his purposes.

He reached the catwalk, bent, ostensibly to lift his end of a pipe, and shot out his arm with a strong gutting motion, feeling the blade dig into the rubber. Liquid sprayed onto his wrist, and then his hand slammed into searing hot metal. He pulled away, stifling a cry of pain and not wanting to look at the burn.

He smelled gasoline. So *that* was the hose he had

opened. He stood up, dizzy and vaguely aware, through clouds of pain, that his partner was eyeing him with suspicion. Miles hefted his end of the pipe and began the journey back to the other catwalk. The skin on his hand was peeling and the flesh raw, but as if that wasn't bad enough, envisioning the gasoline dripping out of the fuel line onto the ground, Miles realized that he'd made a serious mistake in his plan. The gasoline was actually spraying into the catch pan under the hose, which would fill up and then overflow onto the generator. If the fuel came in contact with a spark, or even if it simply touched the hotter metal of the exhaust manifold, it didn't take more than common sense to imagine the result.

Fire.

Even now the heat and gas were probably building toward ignition. Miles wanted to warn the workers away but knew he couldn't without endangering himself. Also, he realized that if he continued carrying the pipes, he might find himself less than twenty-four inches from the explosion when it occurred.

Slowly he began to walk back toward the engine, allowing himself twenty more feet before bolting. The foreman and the Filipino had their eyes on the tower. Ahead, two workers bent to lift pipes and moved off safely. Two other workers replaced them, again getting away.

Why the hell had he ever cut the hose in the first place? he thought, and at that moment the pleasant-faced man, who had kept his back to Miles for the last forty minutes, finally turned around.

Preoccupied with the machine, Miles didn't react quickly enough. Time seemed to stop. The eyes settled upon him, flickered with recognition, and then a huge flame leaped up and there was a hiss and a roar and everybody was screaming. The laborers threw the pipes from them and raced for the door. The men on the tower jumped off and began scrambling away. The hydraulic tongs opened and the silver pipe toppled over the side of the platform and caught a man on the shoulders, pinning him to the ground. His head jerked around. His mouth was open but Miles couldn't hear the screams over the thundering machinery.

The Filipino, whose normally pleasant features were twisted into a mask of rage, was pointing at him. Miles felt a blast of heat and the gasoline smell grew thick and smoky. Flames were reaching toward the skylight. The Filipino's mouth formed the word "You!"

Miles bolted for the door, where men in asbestos suits were running toward the blaze with fire-fighting equipment. He thought they were exceptionally well prepared to have appeared so quickly, but then he was past them, running for his life, the only factor in his favor that the pleasant-faced man's yells couldn't be heard in the din. The ground rumbled under his feet, as if there had been an explosion, but he didn't turn around.

He burst into the yard. The gate was slightly ajar, still guarded by the same workman who had been there earlier. Miles heard a voice behind him—"STOP HIM!"— and the workman moved quickly, his face looming close as the hands reached for him.

Wild with panic, Miles felt his fist smash the worker's jaw. The workman fell back. Feeling that he'd shattered his knuckles, Miles shot through the fence and across the street. There were footsteps behind him. He ran into an alley and across a lot to a busier street, another alley. Maybe he lost them because he knew the area. Maybe they gave up. Maybe they didn't want to go after him when other people were near.

Whatever the case, when he finally stopped and turned around, heaving, they were gone.

ELEVEN

THE SUBWAY let him off at 57th Street, and when he got outside and the sunlight hit him in the face he felt as if he had awakened from a dream. Except for the drive to the boat basin he had not been in Manhattan in months, and a sudden flood of sensations seized his attention and immobilized him, even though he had only fifteen minutes to reach an important appointment at a construction company.

The air was humid, the light opaque with an early hint of autumn, the smell of cement and exhaust. The streets were crawling with honking yellow taxicabs, the not-wide-enough sidewalks crammed with businessmen, dim-faced messengers and groups of giggling secretaries. There was even a three-card monty artist, out of place in this part of the city, squatting by a cardboard box before a hungry-eyed crowd, his quick hands shifting cards to a singsong, "Two black-ity jacks and a red. Find the red. Everybody wins."

This was all so different from the South Bronx that it was hard to imagine the two worlds could exist so closely together. Miles bought a cup of Italian ice from a pushcart vendor and shoved the sticky sweet contents into his mouth as he moved, afterward tossing the remains on an overflowing trash can with a "KEEP NEW YORK CLEAN" sign on it. His fingers were sticky and he licked them off, noticing that the ice had stained the bandage on his hand red.

"Scalded and severely bruised" had been the diagnosis, the doctor a stocky, elderly and gruff-spoken Jew whom Miles had located only three blocks from his apartment on a major thoroughfare in one of those private homes wedged, like a Charles Addams drawing, between an old church and a supermarket.

The inside of the three-room suite looked as if it had generally been left untouched since 1945, complete with grandfather clock, fireplace, and faded rosewood hat rack; the *Reader's Digest*s were new though. The waiting area was occupied by a Hispanic woman with lots of shopping bags and twins in Yankee tee shirts. The whole air of the place induced a feeling of trust, making Miles feel like a child again, visiting the family doctor. As it turned out, relaxing was a mistake.

"Your turn," the doctor growled when the twins left, motioning Miles through the suite onto an examining table where he could see himself reflected in ancient glass cabinets full of medicines. A rifle leaned against the windowsill.

"Twenty-two," the doctor explained, watching Miles eye

185

it. "I hate cats. Anyway, you never know who's going to show up. Addicts." He rinsed the wound and went to work. "You live around here?"

"Yes."

"*Where?*"

Miles told him. The doctor lowered bushy skeptical eyebrows. "*I* never saw you before. Who referred you to me?"

"Uh . . . the Yellow Pages."

The doctor seemed surprised and issued a gruff chuckle. In his irascible but not unlikable voice he demanded, "How'd you burn the hand?"

"On a stove." Miles realized he had answered too quickly. "Cooking." He tried to look sheepish, but the doctor's disbelieving expression returned.

"You punched the stove too? Is that how you hurt your knuckles?"

"The . . . wall," Miles stammered. He knew he wasn't fooling the doctor but didn't care as long as the hand was treated. "I got mad. I have a temper."

The doctor grunted. "Enough salve. I have to bandage you." He opened another drawer. "Damn. No more left. There are some in the back." He stomped into another room. Miles reclined on the examining table. Rather than intimidating him, the doctor's questions, delivered with a paternal gruffness, had made him feel he was being taken care of. Perhaps it was this sense of security or perhaps something inside him had changed with the visit to the construction site, but when his thoughts finally came to rest on the man with the pleasant face, Miles was surprised that for the first time he experienced a cold hatred. He even envisioned himself smashing the man to a pulp.

Just as it occurred to him that the doctor was taking an inordinate amount of time in the back room, the stocky white figure reappeared, arms full of packages of gauze which he dumped on the table. "The hand," the doctor demanded and, refusing to meet Miles's eyes, began to wrap it meticulously, or was it slowly? He burst into a rapid monologue.

"Bet you can't guess how old I am. *Eighty!* Been here thirty-seven years. Used to be a fair neighborhood; never great, but decent. Now people move in from all over the country because the welfare checks are better. From Nevada! Can you believe it? Or Cleveland." When the doorbell rang a little later he jerked up. "I'll answer that."

For the past several minutes Miles had been fighting off the feeling that there was something odd about the doctor's behavior, but watching the rapidly retreating back he was filled with a premonition of trouble too real to ignore. On a nervous hunch he got off the table, hurried to the back room and looked inside. Sure enough, a long, circular wire coiled away toward the rear of the building. While Miles had been daydreaming the doctor had called someone!

His hand was burning. There was no exit from the back room. Voices were coming from the outer office, and the rifle was still lying against the barred window. He reached for it. A sharp voice behind him said, "It isn't loaded."

Miles straightened and turned.

The first thing he saw was the gun; the second, the policeman holding it. He almost fainted with relief.

"With so few doctors in the neighborhood we go out of our way to protect the ones we have," the cop said after Miles had produced various ID's. "When the doctor calls we come running. Actually, you're one of the few people he's been wrong about. We've made several arrests here. Bank robber a month ago. Doctor figured you were talking strangely." When they left together a short while later the cop shook hands and said, "If you're a lawyer, with a salary like yours, why do you live *here?*"

The light changed to WALK and Miles ambled south along Sixth Avenue, keeping pace with the well-dressed pedestrians around him. Further badges of success were sweat-free faces. These people either took cabs everywhere or never walked more than two blocks from their offices.

The last time he had strolled down Sixth Avenue had been with his wife on a Sunday afternoon, window-shopping and enjoying the delicious sense of ownership created by the absence of crowds. They had even rented a hansom cab for a ride around Central Park. Remembering it all now, he felt a stab of guilt which quickly dissipated. He missed Paula but it was good to be back. You couldn't feel guilty forever.

The Fishman Construction Company occupied the fiftieth floor of a spanking-new steel-and-glass tower which featured a tremendous globe in the lobby and guards who prevented uninvited guests from going upstairs. The elevator doors opened to reveal a wide glass door with "FISHMAN" in gold lettering on it and a ravishing brunette at the reception desk. She smiled at him with wide brown eyes and said in a soft finishing-school voice, "You're the writer who called? Mr. Slattery, the vice president, will be with you in a moment."

He retreated across the plush carpet to occupy the corner of a deep sofa from where he scanned the plants and palms filling the reception room, as well as artists' conceptions of some grander Fishman projects: plazas, libraries and skyscraper condominiums. Sitting beyond a glass coffee table was a severe-looking pink-faced corporate type with a gray suit and a bulging briefcase. A lawyer, Miles guessed. They nodded at each other and then pinkface went back to his copy of *Engineering News*. Miles glanced through several other specialist publications but couldn't understand the technical jargon. He was uncomfortably aware that the receptionist hadn't stopped staring at him.

"MILES BRADSHAW," came a booming voice nearby. Startled, Miles looked up to see a ruddy-faced, white-haired giant marching in his direction, hand outstretched, making the room seem suddenly smaller. The well-pressed suit fit snugly on the wide shoulders but seemed somehow out of place, as if more appropriate garb would have been a western shirt and boots. The eyes were bright with hospitality and intelligence. His class ring cut into Miles's palm when they shook hands. "Jim Slattery," the vice president drawled. "My kid wants to be a writer. He's at Stanford, Just like Kesey!"

Miles nodded, wondering who Kesey was.

Slattery draped a heavy arm over Miles' shoulder and winked at the receptionist. "Dolores, I know that look. Think I can have Mr. Bradshaw for twenty minutes before you get started?" They both laughed and Slattery waved a greeting at the pink-faced attorney. "Werner's on the phone with Houston. Be out in a minute."

Slattery steered Miles through a labyrinth of deep-carpeted hallways decorated with more artists' concep-tions. "University of Miami gym," he said. "Won a prize for that one. Albuquerque. Office building. Shit, did we have union problems on that! Casino in Atlantic City. Ha! *No* union problems. You know anything about construc-tion?"

"Not really."

A slap on the back. "Course not! That's why you're here! Come on in! This is my office. What kind of book you writing anyway? Thriller? Love story? What?"

"Love story."

"Siddown."

The office was exactly what Miles would have envi-sioned: masculine, all dark woods and deep chairs the color of tobacco. Miles expected that were he to glance out the window he would see, instead of the cacophonous streets of New York, grazing cattle and a chuck wagon. Slattery dropped into a big swivel chair, opened a small refrigerator Miles hadn't even noticed, pulled out two Coors and a couple of frosted glasses and said, "What can I do for you?"

"Thanks for seeing me," Miles said. Slattery waved away the acknowledgment. "My book, as I told you, is a love story set in New York. One chapter takes place in a construction site. I want certain kinds of machinery there, but I want the details to be accurate." He paused. "When you build skyscrapers in New York—"

"Do plenty of that, by God!"

"Er . . . yes. Is there ever any reason to do any *drilling* on the sites?"

Slattery took a hefty draught of beer. "Sure," he said. "You have to know what's under the ground if you want to put a fifty-story building on it. Don't want the damn thing buckling. So we dig a little. Best rock in Manhattan is mica schist. Hard stuff. All the big skyscrapers are on that. We u⸱ ⸱ a machine called an auger to do the digging. You've probably seen them . . . look like big screws, just screwing down into the earth. Force up soil. If you don't like beer I have the hard stuff."

Miles said, "Excuse me?" He was repeating details in his mind so that he would remember them later as well as trying to recall if the big machine he'd seen at the low-income project had been forcing up soil. It hadn't.

Slattery said, "The beer. You haven't touched it."

Miles took a sip to be polite. "This is fine, thanks. Tell me, how big are the augers?"

"Twenty, thirty feet."

Miles frowned. "I needed something bigger," he said, and chose his next words carefully. "I thought I'd seen

190

something on TV. A really huge piece of machinery in a construction site. High."

Slattery considered. "Probably a crane," he said. "They're big mothers. Several stories."

Impatiently, Miles shook his head, then described what he had seen in the Bronx without mentioning where he had seen it.

Slattery said, "Fifteen stories?" He drained his glass, thought a while, slapped the desk and said, "Sounds to me like a telescope drilling rig. Gas or oil rig. Got 'em out in Utah, near my ranch, but not in New York. You must have been watching a western."

Miles, dumfounded, repeated, "Gas?"

"Sure, In Utah, Montana, they're not uncommon. You must have gotten your scenes mixed up."

Miles struggled to keep himself from looking as baffled as he felt. *Gas?* Suddenly the image came into his mind of the workers fleeing from the platform when he'd started the fire and of the exceptionally well-prepared fire fighters appearing at the scene immediately. And what had the foreman yelled before the blaze began? *"We have to log it up by three"*?

Slattery said, "Jesus, I can see the wheels turning in your head."

Miles tried to smile. "Is there an expression in construction, 'logging'?" he asked.

Slattery brushed his big hands through his hair. "Nosir," he said. "Never heard it."

Miles leaned forward. "And about the machine that takes soil samples. The auger?" Slattery nodded. "Do you ever use it *after* you've completed the outside of a building? Bring it inside, piece by piece, and reassemble it?"

Slattery gave him a cockeyed look. "You writing a science fiction book or what?"

Miles fell back in his chair. Another dead end. One last

191

question. "Have you ever heard of a low-income housing project that wasn't government funded?" he asked.

Slattery leaned back and put his hands behind his head and looked at the ceiling. "Hmmm. Never heard of it but . . . if the tax breaks were right and the land cheap . . . a public-relations effort . . . kind of wild but . . . hmmm." He snapped back. "Sorry," he said. "I'll have to store that one. Sure you don't want another drink?"

"No, thanks."

"Suit yourself. Any more questions?"

Miles sighed. "No, you've been very helpful." He wanted to be out on the street, alone, trying to make some sense out of a mass of conflicting information.

But Slattery leaned forward and popped open another beer. "My kid gets out of Stanford in two weeks," he said. "Summer school."

Miles sat down again. "Oh?"

"That's right. He's coming home for a month. Wants to write books, like you. I told him writing is a tough business. You agree?"

"Certainly," Miles said, fidgeting.

"Bet he'd like to meet a real writer. Maybe you could come down one evening, meet the kid, talk to him." Slattery eyed him hopefully.

"I'd, uh, be glad to."

"Good. *Good!*" To Miles's distress, the vice president leaned back expansively. "You know," he said, "when I was a kid in Utah, I wanted to be an actor. My father didn't like it. Said actors were fags. Said it was too hard a life. When Tommy told me he wanted to write I started to tell him forget it, go into construction, law, something solid. But I remembered my old man. I didn't want to do the same thing. Sometimes when I go to plays I think about what it would have been like. The stage. Know what I mean?"

Miles nodded and glanced at the door.

"Anyway," Slattery said, "you and the wife . . . you got a wife?"

Miles felt himself coloring. "No."

"Hell, just you then. Come out for a barbecue Western style. Got a nice place in Great Neck. On the water. Pool, everything. Half an hour on the Long Island Railroad. We'll pick you up at the station. Tommy'd love it. How about three weeks from now? The twenty-fifth?"

"Fine."

Slattery extended his hand. "Terrific. Normally in August I'm on the ranch, but this stupid Hartford job . . . what the hell . . . Everybody has problems. You got a card?"

"Sorry."

"Struggling writer, huh?"

Miles nodded.

Slattery reached for a leather-bound appointment book. "That's B-r-a-d-s-h-a-w, right? Give me your number."

Miles heard himself giving his old Manhattan address and telephone. A vision of Paula answering the phone came into his mind. Slattery banged the book shut and rose to escort Miles out of the office. Before they reached the reception room he nudged Miles and said, "That little honey Dolores likes you. Why don't you bring her along?"

Miles began ambling south when he got outside, thinking furiously, trying to dispel his confusion. He had described what he had seen in the Bronx to Slattery, and Slattery had told him that he couldn't have seen it, that what he had described belonged two thousand miles away, drilling for gas or oil. Impossible. Or was it? Or had he failed to describe some aspect of the machinery which would have placed it in New York? Or maybe Slattery had made an error, although he certainly seemed competent.

Double-check.

He was hungry anyway, he realized, and thirsty, and regretful that he hadn't taken Slattery up on the beer offer. After walking a while longer, he ducked under a green "Ireland Stone" sign into a raucous smoke-filled tavern with autographed pictures of prizefighters on the walls. The long wooden bar was draped with middle-aged regulars reading the *Post* or the *Daily News,* the booths in back crowded with younger people and echoing with laughter. Miles picked his way through the arguments on the floor and was lucky enough to find an empty stool. He shouted for a corned beef sandwich and ale at the cauliflower-eared bartender, who looked like an ex-fighter himself. The phone booth in back mercifully stifled but didn't eliminate the din pulsating through the glass. Miraculously, a Yellow Pages inside was only half torn and Miles ran his eye down the list of construction companies, then dialed five before finding an executive who was still in his office and willing to talk. Miles introduced himself as a writer again, apologized for calling so late, described what he had seen in the Bronx, pretending he had made it up, and asked if such machinery existed in New York.

The executive had the worst Brooklyn accent Miles had ever heard. Miles could envision him only in a leather jacket and dockman's cap. No machinery such as Miles described existed in the city, he said, and added that he had been in the construction business for seventeen years. He also asked the name of Miles's novel so that he could buy it when it came out.

Miles thought a moment. *"The Broken Heart."*

"Love story, huh?"

"Yeah."

"Gotcha. Good luck, buddy."

The corned beef was thick, greasy and delicious. Miles washed it down with a frosty dark ale, which, possibly because he hadn't eaten anything else today, lifted his spirits just a trifle. Two more drinks improved the situation even more, and after cooling off from the air conditioning and explaining to a dark Italian type next to him that he hadn't been following the pennant efforts of the Cincinnati Reds, he left a liberal tip, pushed off the stool and maneuvered out into the street. He turned east, toward Fifth Avenue.

By now he had decided that one more visit would be necessary today; to his old alma mater NYU and the geology department. He'd taken one geology course fifteen years ago but couldn't remember anything he had learned, although he thought his professor had been named Lawrence. To Miles, gas or oil under New York was not only inconceivable, it was laughable, but, as Goldstein would say, *make sure.*

The ales had mellowed his sense of urgency if not purpose. Fifth Avenue was much less crowded now that rush hour was over and walking was a pleasure. What Slattery had said about his son at Stanford had given rise to the idea that maybe it was summer-session finals week at NYU. Maybe the professors would be working late. It couldn't hurt to check. And anyway, the walk was pleasant.

When Miles got to 34th Street, past the expensive shops, he could see the sun dipping over the avenue like a huge, hot poker chip, and by the time he reached the teens, the streets were losing their cosmopolitan midtown flavor and acquiring more of a homey air, or at least homey for Manhattan. The buildings were shorter, the pedestrians slightly less hurried and more casually dressed. Many were walking dogs, carrying plastic scoops to keep New York clean and avoid fines if policemen were nearby. Fourteenth Street was glutted with late shoppers in search of cheaply made bargains. One or two artists at the foot of Fifth Avenue lounged on sun chairs, paintings laid out for sale.

This was Greenwich Village, the neighborhood where he had gone to school for four years. New York University lay across the expanse of Washington Square Park in scattered buildings, and the park itself was filled with street musicians with saxophones, a trumpet and about a dozen accompanists on soda bottles and beer cans improvising a Manhattan Latin. About a dozen doped-up men and women did modern dances on the edge of the fountain. A black kid sauntered by with a big transistor radio at his side. "Columbia Gold," he said. Miles shook his head and the kid moved off. A Frisbee pursued by a barking dog shot by his face, into the hands of a barefoot bearded expert in cutoffs. And a slightly heavy, curly-haired kid who looked Greek was staring at the musicians and muttering, "This is the coolest thing I've ever seen. All the fucked-up people are dancing."

Miles found the geology department at the end of a third-floor cinder-block hall two blocks away. He had guessed right about finals week. Three secretaries labored over typewriters and licked envelopes amid black file cabinets, frondy plants and piles of leaflets. A sign on a closed door with a shaft of light brightening the orange shag carpet announced the office of "DR. ROBERT S. LAWRENCE," Miles' old professor, now department head.

A stunning Asiatic secretary told Miles to sit while she checked with Dr. Lawrence, then told Miles the professor would see him momentarily. Miles waited on an ugly vinyl sofa in a corner and scanned a geology magazine for a while. It bored him. Through the doorway the minute hand of a large clock worked its way in jerks from marker to marker. A newspaper lying under some magazines caught his attention. He picked it up and absentmindedly began thumbing through it. An inside headline stopped him.

196

"You can go in now," the secretary said, waving an airy
hand at the door.

Rising from behind mounds of papers, Professor Lawrence was vaguely as Miles remembered him, a slightly
rotund sixty-year-old wearing loose-fitting, poorly coordi-
nated clothes and light-colored sunglasses which allowed a
view of kindly, competent eyes. The professor indicated a
vinyl chair and cleared away some papers so that they
could have an unobstructed view of each other and said,
"Finals time. So you were one of my students, eh? Can't
say I remember you. Must have been in one of those au-
ditorium classes."

Miles nodded. "Three, four hundred people."

"And now you're a writer. And you need some geologic
information."

Miles said, "Please."

Lawrence grinned. "Information which I undoubtedly
left out of my lectures."

Miles colored. "The truth is . . . well . . ."

"That you *forgot* the lectures?" He sighed theatrically
but there was a twinkle in his eye. "Years ago I took an
anthropology course. Only thing I could remember afterward was that the Hottentots had the biggest behinds.
Later I ran into the professor in a shop and told her. I
thought she was going to kill me with her umbrella."

197

Miles, charmed, said, "You aren't going to kill *me* with *your* umbrella, are you?"

"Unfortunately I left it home." Lawrence chuckled, then glanced at the uncorrected test papers. "How can I help you?"

This time feeling more adept as an actor, Miles said, "My book's a mystery. One chapter takes place in a construction site which I'd like to describe dramatically but accurately—huge machinery, lots of noise. The other day I saw a photograph of a telescope drilling rig in Utah." Dr. Lawrence nodded to show that he knew what a telescope rig was, and Miles said, "I thought it would be the perfect kind of machinery, in terms of size, to set the scene for the chapter. But frankly, I don't know enough about geology to know what such a rig might be doing in New York."

Dr. Lawrence pulled a pipe out of a drawer and leaned back. "Neither do I."

Miles' heart sank. "You don't?"

Lawrence produced matches and lit up. He blew a long stream of smoke toward the ceiling. "Not unless the drillers want to strike a gas main."

Miles didn't smile at the joke. "You mean there's *nothing* under New York to drill for? *Water? Gas or oil?*"

Lawrence gestured at one of the glossy photos, in striking blacks, reds and greens, of New York on the walls.

"Impossible. And I'll explain why. As you *undoubtedly remember* from my lectures, there are three basic kinds of rock. Igneous rock is formed by molten lava which solidifies. Metamorphic rock, slightly younger, is created when heat and pressure squeeze or chemically join existing rock. And sedimentary rock, the youngest type of formation, is formed by particles of existing rock washed into a riverbed or shallow sea and deposited, and over millions of years pressure cements them together.

"When we're talking about oil-bearing rock we're talking almost exclusively about sedimentary rock. Oh, it's not impossible to find gas or oil in a fissure in igneous or meta-morphic formations, but it happens very rarely, and then even more rarely, almost impossibly, in commercial quantities.

"And anyway, even if you *do* have sedimentary formations, you still need four major conditions for gas or oil to be present. You have to go back four hundred million years and have the right kind of plant or animal life die and decompose into hydrocarbons. They have to die in an area which will eventually form the right kind of rock, *source beds,* we call them, oftentimes shales or limestones. Then more porous sandstones or limestones are needed to become reservoir rock, rock which will hold the gas or oil, and finally you need a nonporous rock to trap the oil and keep it from flowing away."

Dr. Lawrence sighed. "In New York, you're defeated before you start. The rock isn't sedimentary. It's metamorphic. What part of the city does your book take place in?"

"The South Bronx."

"A mystery in the South Bronx, eh?" Lawrence pointed to the area on the satellite map. It was all green. "This land here is composed mainly of very old metamorphic rock called Fordheim gneiss. I'll show you some." He pulled out a rock from his desk drawer and placed it in Miles' hand. Miles examined its cool surface, banded in white and black.

Lawrence said, "What you're holding was formed five hundred million years ago when New York was a group of volcanic islands and swiftly flowing rivers.

"There are scattered hydrocarbons in the rock, all right, but they show up as graphite, which, in laymen's terms, is what gas or oil becomes if subjected to too much heat or pressure. Wait around another couple hundred million years and maybe you'll get lucky and the graphite will become diamonds." He grinned.

Miles shook his head stubbornly. "But hasn't oil or gas

been found off New Jersey? I keep reading about it in the paper. Is it so farfetched to find *more* of it here?"

Lawrence tapped the area of the map off the Jersey shore. "It *is* that farfetched," he said. "The rock they're finding gas in is a lot younger than New York rock, and besides, it's sedimentary. Take the Palisades. That rock is only one hundred eighty million years old. Workers found an entire dinosaur in it when they were building the George Washington Bridge." The finger on the map slid to midtown. "Here, just across the river in Manhattan, the rock is five hundred million years old. And the *reason* two kinds of rock with such differing ages can exist so closely together is . . . well . . . have you ever noticed how gouged out the rock looks in Central Park?"

Miles, remembering the clawed, stark outcroppings, nodded, and Lawrence said, "Glaciers did that. They were two hundred feet high in New York and they retreated only ten thousand years ago. Never made it to the Palisades. Swept everything away." He indicated several places on the map. "You can find the moraines, the points of farthermost progress, in Perth Amboy and Montauk. And also here, at Ronkonkoma. Ronkonkoma! Whenever I hear that name I imagine campers from Scarsdale running around with Indian feathers and rubber tomahawks."

He paused. "Of course, if you need some kind of rich natural resource in your book you could always put a silver mine in the metropolitan area. Jersey, to be precise."

Despite himself, Miles found that he was interested, and Lawrence began nodding vigorously. "West of the Palisades. South of Hoboken. Back around 1700 it used to be a mining area. Ever hear of the Schuyler family of New York?"

Miles nodded.

"Silver's how they got rich. Used to carry it out of the mine through a Dutch Reformed church so they wouldn't have to pay taxes."

Miles was silent.

Lawrence said, "I'm sure you'll think of a solution to your problem. I wish there were some way I could help."

I'm going to have to tell Goldstein everything, Miles thought. *About the gas, the construction site, the Kings . . . everything. Maybe he can figure out what's going on.*

Dr. Lawrence cleared his throat. "Is there anything else I can do?"

Miles said, shaking himself, "Sorry, no." He thought a moment and decided he'd better leave. "You've been very helpful."

TWELVE

ACROSS THE street from the line of crumbling tenements, near the entrance to an alley, the man with the pleasant face waited patiently for Miles to come home. Periodically, when a police car drove by, he stepped back into the shadows, but he had decided that these regularly passing patrols presented few obstacles to what he had been ordered to do.

The street was darkening, filling with the night sounds of the ghetto. Lai checked his watch and strolled to a phone booth, scanning the block all the while, dropped money in the slot and dialed. He'd broken the overhead light in case Miles came home while he was on the phone.

"Checking in," he said when Trench answered the direct

line. "Bradshaw isn't back yet." Fresh instructions came over the wire and Lai nodded as he memorized them.

When Trench was finished Lai said, "Sure I understand. It'll be a pleasure. Wait, I think I see him coming." He smiled. "Yeah. I do."

Whoever Rosemary was, Miles reflected, mounting the stairs to his apartment, she wasn't going to be too pleased when she saw what had been written about her all over the walls. "ROSEMARY SUCKS." The paint had dripped a lot before drying and Miles would have been furious at the vandalism, first sign that the building was going, if he hadn't been so exhausted and preoccupied.

Between the machinery he had seen at the housing project and his visits to Slattery and the professor, he had more than enough to think about. Right now he needed time to sort out the day's events and make some sense of the conflicting information he had been given.

He reached his own hallway, which was silent except for the ringing of a phone, and wearily inserted the key in the lock. As the door swung open the sound grew louder. A telephone beckoned him shrilly from the middle of the floor.

He reached it in time to hear a click on the other end.

He figured the superintendent had let the telephone people in this afternoon, but who could have been calling? Goldstein? Probably not. The marshal wouldn't have the number or even know Miles had a phone. Anyway, his number was supposed to be unlisted. He dialed the operator to make sure.

The operator didn't have any number yet.

Miles decided the call had either been a test or a mistake. He appraised the addition to his apartment; the phone, in its newness, looked pretty strange, accentuating the emptiness. He felt a surge of embarrassment and promised himself he'd buy furniture soon.

But for now the damn phone looked so out of place in the middle of the floor that he tried various other locations for it: by the sink, the rocking chair, in a corner and finally next to the rumpled mattress, where he left it.

That job done he returned to a more important problem, which was exactly how much to tell Goldstein about what he had been doing for the last few days. He wanted to keep his own illegalities from the marshal and decided to plan strategy while he ate. Rummaging through the cupboards, he came up with some string beans and an eggplant appetizer which could be eaten out of the can. He heated them together, left the pot on the stove for later cleaning, found a pen and paper, and transferred the plate to the counter by the sink, where he could write.

There was a noise outside on the fire escape. Probably kids, he figured.

He jotted down his thoughts as he chewed. Should he tell the inspector about breaking into the construction site two nights ago? Unavoidable, he decided, but he'd leave the Latin Kings out of the story. *Kings*, he wrote, *no*. If Goldstein ended up visiting the site, as Miles hoped he would, and found out about the Doberman killings and the attack on the guard, Miles would deny he had had anything to do with either. After all, there had been no witnesses.

But what about the *second* foray into the site, during which he'd started a fire, destroyed machinery, and injured at least two workmen, all before *lots* of witnesses, including the man with the pleasant face? Even if Goldstein became convinced of Miles' innocence in regard to the death of the Perez boy, Miles was still guilty of vandalism, assault and trespassing, all of which could be proved.

Miles wrote: *Don't go to the site, where you can be recognized.*

But the mild turmoil in his stomach did not go away. Should Goldstein pursue his investigation, Miles realized, the facts about the fire would eventually emerge, as would a description of the man who started it, and Goldstein would put the pieces together. By telling the arson inspector even part of what had happened today, Miles would be rendering himself vulnerable to a man who had sworn only a few days ago to put him in jail. And of all things to be guilty of, he thought, arson.

Maybe Elena was right. Maybe he was obsessed, but he had backed himself into a corner and the only alternative to dropping the investigation was to trust the fire marshal.

He considered what he had written. Simultaneously, there was a knock at the door.

Startled, Miles looked at his watch. Ten-thirty. A little late for a visit from Goldstein, the only person who ever came by. A neighbor? He called out, "Who's there?"

No answer. "Goldstein? Is that you?"

Shoe shadows were visible under the door. His bandaged hand was starting to itch. "Goldstein?"

The knocking came again, more insistent. Could the Filipino have found him? He glanced at the phone, wondered if he should call the police, wondered if that would be making a big deal out of nothing. He went to the door, cursing the landlord for not equipping his apartment with a peephole. His bowels were churning.

"Who is it?"

He started back for the phone.

The shadow under the door shifted. From outside, soft and nervous, came Elena's voice. "Can't anybody surprise a friend around here?"

When he flung open the door she was standing in the hallway, one hand on her hip, cigarette in her mouth, but the sheen on her forehead and the trembling butt made her a frightened parody of herself. He wanted to throw his arms around her in relief and amazement, but he just gaped.

She gave a sickly smile. "World record. Ten feet alone." Her eyes flickered nervously and settled on his bandage. She seemed eager to change the subject. "What happened to your hand?"

"A little accident. The doctor fixed it up."

She didn't believe him but at least she didn't challenge him. She was steadying an open magazine which she held out in one hand. "I found an article you'd be interested in," she said, voice tightening on the last word.

Miles said, "Are you all right?"

She nodded. He had the feeling she wasn't trusting her voice.

"Want to go back to your apartment?"

A stubborn shake of the head and a pale smile of triumph.

"Then you want to come in? Sit down?" She nodded. For the second time in the last half hour Miles felt a deep embarrassment at the pathetic condition of his living quarters.

He grasped her forearm and drew her in, one step at a time, to the chair by the window. When she sat down she said, "I feel so silly," but her face was flushed with pride and effort. Miles, recalling how terrifying a simple trip downstairs had been for her, was awed.

She said falteringly, "I tried to go out this afternoon but couldn't. But when I heard you come in I wanted to . . . see you. I've been thinking about what you said about moving away. You were right. It's dangerous for you to keep living here. People could be looking for you."

He blushed at the memory of his outburst and the obvious discomfort it had caused her. He said, "I didn't mean what I said. I was mad."

"You were still right."

206

"Forget it. I'm just glad you're here," and he thought, *Glad* wasn't the word for it. *Astounded* was more like it. Envisioning her struggling along the hallway between their apartments, he was filled with an almost choking appreciation of her concern. *Ten minutes,* she had said, *to go ten feet.*

He blurted out, "Maybe we can leave together," surprising himself, and, like an awkward schoolboy, felt the next hot blush. A vision of his wedding to Paula came to mind. Had he meant to propose? To ask her to live with him? He didn't know and his own words frightened him. Her look had become one he couldn't fathom and didn't want to. He picked up the magazine, *New York,* at an article by a writer named Salzberg, and began to read.

BEATING THE ULTIMATE PHOBIA: A CASE HISTORY

> One day nearly six years ago, Ellen and her husband, Fred, drove into the city to see an exhibition of abstract American art at the Metropolitan. They hadn't been there more than a couple of minutes when Ellen whispered to her husband in near frantic tones, "I have to leave." Ellen was having one of her attacks. By now she was sick to her stomach, weak in the knees, dizzy, and was gasping desperately for air. The walls, covered with bright paint-splotched canvases, began to spin slowly.

Miles looked up. The article was describing Elena on the stairs.

"Keep reading," she said. He lowered his gaze.

> Several of the twelve other people gathered in the large living room nod knowingly as Ellen's voice becomes almost inaudible. Most of them have had similar experiences, and hearing Ellen tell hers is like reliving their own. They are all agoraphobics, people with an irrational fear of open spaces. . . .

The article went on to describe the building of Ellen's fears from childhood until the art museum incident, after which, for six years, she had never left the house. Now she was involved with a self-help group for agoraphobics. The group leader said, " 'Phobics have fallen into a pattern of learned helplessness. They avoid any anxiety-provoking situation and become totally isolated.... We use the buddy system. If someone feels she is in a particularly difficult situation, she calls up her buddy.' "

Miles looked up. Elena, sensing he had finished, said, "Looks like you had the cure figured out. The buddy system." Her foot was moving more rapidly now and her hands were white on the armrests. She did not protest when he crossed the room, helped her up and began walking her to the door.

He said, "Enough for one day."

"Not bad for the first time, was it?"

He kissed her. They were halfway to her apartment when his phone started to ring again. At the sound his fingers loosened on her arm but he caught himself. She'd come ten long feet for him. He could stay with her back to her apartment.

"Whoever it is will call back," he said, hoping he was right.

She saw through his casual tone and squeezed his arm to show her appreciation. The ringing stopped as they reached her apartment. Miles steered her inside, watching her almost immediately perk up in the safe, familiar surroundings. But she looked tired.

He said, "I'll make coffee." Outside, from the hall, came the echo of slow, deliberate footsteps mounting the stairs, which reminded him that he had left his apartment open. Miles decided that if he was going to stay awhile he should lock his door, so as the footsteps grew louder, he went back to his apartment, turned the key in his lock and went back to Elena's. The back of a head rose above the railing, then a skinny birdlike neck and the familiar black raincoat belonging to Goldstein. It was eleven-fifteen.

Miles was seized with a surge of both trepidation and eagerness. He was afraid of having Goldstein discover him with Elena but was finally going to tell the marshal about the construction site and the yacht.

But when Miles saw the face, horribly changed, both emotions were wiped away instantly. Goldstein looked as if he had aged years in the last few days. The self-assurance was gone from the eyes; the lines seemed to have dug more deeply into the forehead. The cheeks were sunken, the posture more stooped. There was an upsetting bitter twist to the mouth, and even the usual gray pallor was drained from his face.

Each step that brought the inspector closer seemed to be preceded by some inner struggle, and when Goldstein reached Miles, he in no way acknowledged Elena's presence, but said, barely audible, "I have to talk to you."

He continued past them, toward Miles's apartment. Shocked, Miles looked at Elena, who waved him to go ahead without her. She said, "Come back after."

He backed out of the doorway and closed her in. Down the hall, the Spanish couple began screaming at each other.

Miles unlocked his door and the marshal trudged across the room to the mattress, dropped in a heap on his crackling raincoat and looked up, incomprehension and anger in his eyes. He said simply, "I'm not supposed to work on this case anymore."

The words fell stunningly between them. If it weren't for the fact that Miles was having trouble moving his mouth he would have started screaming in frustration. Goldstein ran his fingers through his hair. There was a singsong quality to his voice, as if he'd been repeating his words over and over to himself.

"Doesn't make sense. Boss calls me into his office. Too

much time on this case, he says. You're neglecting other work, he says. Bullshit. He's lying. But there's something in his face." Goldstein paused. "Thirty years. Never been called off a case." The hawklike jaw was buried in his bony palms. "All these incidents and no connections. But it's crazy. I know that guy. My father knew him, worked with him."

Miles wasn't sure what Goldstein was talking about until the marshal softened his voice. "He wouldn't take money," he said, but he sounded unconvinced.

After today's revelations, however, Miles was ready to accept plenty. Why not this too? The man with the pleasant face had already tried to kill him, hadn't he, so bribery wasn't that surprising. What *was* surprising was who had been bribed. The Filipino's reach was getting longer. As Goldstein sat in a depressed stupor, Miles reviewed questions and theories, with the inspector's new addition. He now believed that Carlos Perez' death had not been an isolated incident, but had been tied into something so massive it involved murder, scores of deliberately set fires and tremendous blocks of real estate changing hands. The instigator obviously had enough money to coordinate all these activities, bribe Goldstein's boss, and obtain and operate valuable construction machinery hidden in the shell of a building and attended by dozens of workers.

If, as Slattery had briefly led him to imagine today, there were oil under the city, that would account for all this secrecy, but the professor had ruled out oil, so where was the motivation?

Whatever it was, the scope of the emerging operation was incredible, mind boggling. He asked himself who might possibly have the kind of funding necessary to run such a project, and the answer came to him in the form of an image: the long, sleek yacht at the 79th Street Boat Basin, to which the pleasant-faced man had led him, and the words of the boy at the gate, *"Owner is a billionaire. Trench is his name."*

Goldstein abruptly strode to the window, looked down at the street and said, "I guess I owe you an apology." Miles flushed with joy at the much wished for words and Goldstein, probably embarrassed now as well as upset, took refuge in clinical analysis.

"I keep going over what I might have found to scare somebody. There's nothing specific, but maybe it's the pattern. I've talked to the owners of the buildings, to the people you introduced me to, and I haven't found anything concrete, no, but everybody's too nervous. A glance, a shake of the head—little things. Unless they're experts, people do something to give themselves away when they lie for the very reason that they're afraid they're going to reveal themselves. Look hard enough and you see it, but what do you do after you find it? I can't go to my boss's *boss* and say, 'Someone's eye twitched so I know he's guilty.' He'd understand what I meant, but he wouldn't be able to do anything about it. So what can we tell anyone? What have we found? And where do we even start?"

Morosely, the marshal shook his head. There was the crash of a dish on the other side of the wall. As bad as Goldstein's news was, in a way it was welcome. Suddenly the former antagonists were allies and Miles had been given the perfect opening for what he'd planned to say. Throat tense with excitement he said, "I'll *tell* you where we can start." The force of his voice caught Goldstein by surprise. Miles said, "We can start at a housing project. A few blocks from here. And at a yacht in Manhattan."

For the next twenty minutes he held Goldstein spellbound with his story of the incidents of the past few days, finishing with his conviction that everything was related. Why else would Goldstein have been ordered off the case by a supervisor who had always left him alone before?

211

While Miles spoke, the marshal paced back and forth, hands in his pockets, head up like a dog hearing a high-pitched whistle, eyes burning or going flat as his thoughts shifted in agitation. But, although there was sometimes doubt in Goldstein's expression, at no time did Miles detect disbelief.

When he was finished they sat in silence, Miles flushed with the effort of reliving the few days, Goldstein obviously turning the tale over in his mind. Neither of them moved for a while and then Miles, thirsty from talking, filled two glasses with cold water and brought one to the inspector.

Noticing Miles' bandage for the first time, Goldstein said, "Your hand."

Miles started to say he'd burned it on a stove but then, remembering that Goldstein would find out the truth if he went to the site, said, "I was chased out of the project and I hit someone."

Goldstein looked taken aback for a moment, then his expression changed to that of deep pleasure. "Why, *Counselor,*" he said, but the once dreaded word was, for the first time, spoken with warmth. "I didn't know you were the violent type." He grinned, then said, "Hmmm. The machine you saw was fifteen stories high?"

Miles nodded.

"And the workmen did no work? And Slattery and the professor told you that you couldn't possibly have seen the machinery?"

"That's right."

"But you did see it. You're positive."

"Yes."

Goldstein glanced at the hand again, brought out the pad and wrote something down. He said, "Are you sure you're telling me everything?"

Miles, remembering the Latin Kings as well as Goldstein's words about liars giving themselves away, tried to look nonchalant when he nodded, but Goldstein gave him a hard stare, then shrugged. He still seemed preoccupied over the disaster at his office. He said, "Why did you decide to tell me all this now?"

Miles had been ready for this question all along. "You didn't believe too much of what I said before. I'd hoped to come up with something more concrete."

Goldstein nodded. After a moment he said, "First we have to check the project's background, the plans submitted to the City. Find out if there's government funding. Blueprints. Talk to the real owner if we can find him. Second, inspect the site and the machinery. I think one person's been buying up land around here. I think he's starting the fires and I think he killed that boy." He paused. "And tried to kill you. I think you're right."

There was bitterness in his voice. Miles tried not to show the feeling of triumph Goldstein's words had given him. The marshal gave him a queer look, as if waiting for a response, then said, sidling toward the door, "I'm going back to the office to get a warrant. Wait here. I won't be long, but I don't want anyone to see you with me. They think I'm near the Throgs Neck Bridge on a bakery fire."

Miles agreed, his heart thudding at the vision of Goldstein stomping onto the construction site to confront the pleasant-faced man. How easy it all was for the marshal. Whereas Miles had been forced to risk his life for a five-minute glance at the machinery, Goldstein had only to obtain a warrant and walk in.

At the door Goldstein turned. "Give me your number, in case something happens." Miles read it off the phone and Goldstein gave him one last glance and left.

Miles went to the window and looked down at the street. Goldstein's battered Nova was parked at the end of a line of police cars, some of which were pulling out into the street as shifts changed.

The fire marshal emerged from the building, blending

with the night shadows, and trudged up the block without looking back, hands in his pockets. When he slid into his car Miles saw him briefly in the flare of the overhead light. Goldstein's headlights came on. The car eased into the street and disappeared around the corner.

Behind Miles, the phone began to ring.

He turned to answer it, but there was a tremendous crash at the door. The phone rang again. The door seemed to lean in toward Miles, who backed away, horrified. Two more powerful assaults rocked it on its hinges and then, with terrifying swiftness, it crashed open.

THIRTEEN

IN HIS worst nightmares it had always been like this: the crash of the door being kicked open, the blocked exit, the stiletto glinting in the light, the flat appraisal in the slanting black eyes. Miles might manage, in the more pleasant versions, to disarm his attacker, maybe even stab him in self-defense, but generally he would wake just before feeling the blade.

For an instant they were frozen together, staring, but then the phone stopped ringing and the silence brought Miles to life.

He hurled the telephone at the Filipino and leaped for the window, slamming it up into the frame. Already, in his mind, he was on the fire escape.

But someone else had gotten there first.

He spun from the oncoming hands, a cry of fear escaping him. Lai was still in the doorway and a short, broad-shouldered man with long arms came climbing through the window. The florid face was pitted, eyes small and closely set. They looked out at Miles like a butcher's measuring a pig for slaughter.

The phone played a recorded message that it was off the hook, startling all of them, and then Lai and his accomplice advanced, maneuvering Miles toward the kitchen. The second man found the radio and turned it on, raising the volume. Miles realized too late that he should have screamed for help. Backing away, he scanned the kitchen for a weapon, spotting only a bag of garbage which splattered the Filipino but didn't slow him, so Miles went for the knife drawer.

They reached him at the same time, pulling the blade from his hand and dropping him to his knees with dual blows to the solar plexus. The walls and floor came up in an arc, and he heard his head hit the floor. As bad as each blow was, it seemed only a prelude. He kept expecting to feel the stiletto.

He was hauled to his feet. Faces were going in and out of focus and the walls were spinning. They dragged him into the hallway and a door inched open and slammed shut. He watched his feet bumping and sliding on the stairs.

It occurred to him, as he watched three fat moons whirling in the sky, that he ought to be ashamed because he hadn't put up a good fight, and that whoever had been calling the apartment would get a busy signal now. Then he was being shoved into the back of a car. The engine thundered to life and the car started vibrating.

The Filipino was fitting something round and metallic onto his knuckles.

He yanked Miles up by the hair.

They're going to burn me, Miles thought, *like Carlos.*

There was a salt smell, a lapping sound, and increasing waves of pain. Instinctively he sought escape in sleep, but it eluded him and he knew that within minutes his body would be screaming.

Gently he ran his tongue around his mouth, stopping at the lower lip. He probed and found a hole, tender, flapping, sticky.

A voice said, "He's waking up."

He opened his eyes, squinting, and saw the Oriental above.

His first thought was that he was still in the car. He tried to lift his arms to ward off the expected blow, all the panic flooding back into him, but no one hit him. And he couldn't move at all. That jolted him into the present. His senses, foggy, began to take in elements of the scene.

Incredulous, he realized that he was alive.

He was in a plush leather chair, bound by straps.

The Oriental was someone he'd never seen before.

There was a powerful booming and throbbing in his head. The Oriental was studying him, checking the damages, the eyes chilling in their cold efficiency. The jaw was decisive, almost brutal. The faint whiff of ginger was discernible when the face came close. The lips were frozen in displeasure; the fingers, which pressed together, forming a web or a trap, were well manicured. The face seemed to be growing and shrinking. Miles had the cloudy impression, from his own mental state and the economy in the man's movements, of a rigidly disciplined body under well-tailored dress. There was an impatience in his demeanor, which suggested that he was accustomed to im-

217

mediate gratification, but the voice, when it came, was surprisingly soft and almost sympathetic.

"Can you hear me?"

Miles's thoughts were still clearing. He touched his lip with his tongue again and withdrew it in pain. He was in a spacious room dominated by an unnaturally large portrait of a woman whose dreamlike gaze bored into his own. The woman was harvesting rice under a blood-red sun. Portholes lining another wall indicated that he was on a boat. The furniture was polished mahogany, the crossbeamed ceiling low but not oppressive. The room was filled with sparkling glass cases of little seashells which would, at any other time, have intrigued Miles.

Now he just wanted to get out, but even if he could have escaped the straps, the door was blocked by the Filipino, a sailor in white ducks and an older man, silver-haired, with a pinkish paternal expression and the thick, drooping mustache of a stereotypical British colonel. He carried a black medical bag.

Everyone was looking at Miles and no one was saying anything.

It was one of those horrible frozen moments when the slightest signal is about to set a calamity in motion, and Miles was afraid that if he even spoke he might unleash whatever force was practically pulsating through the cabin, but his need to deal with his growing panic overcame his self-control and he said, turning back to the Oriental, "Who are you?"

The man waved a hand to dismiss the query, although he seemed pleased that it had been asked, that Miles had demonstrated a functioning mind. He leaned forward. His breath smelled of ginger. He said, very softly, "Whom are you working for?"

Miles started. "I . . . what?"

The voice was patient. The tone and inflection remained the same. "Whom are you working for?"

"Whom am I working for?"

The images which came to mind were comically absurd: Marcus, his supervisor at his office; Samantha; the complainants who daily filled the waiting room. Was *that* what he was being asked about? Impossible. If the situation weren't so chilling he'd laugh.

There was a glass filled with clear liquid on a metal tray fastened to the chair. The Oriental picked it up. "You can't talk with a dry throat." He held the glass while Miles swallowed water, then returned it to its place and wiped Miles's mouth with little pats of towel.

Again he bent forward. "Whom," he said, "are you working for?"

Miles still didn't know what to say, but the man obviously expected an answer. The drink had cleared his head and it struck him that he was probably at the 79th Street Boat Basin, on the yacht he had seen five days before. But who was the Oriental asking questions? The owner? Trench? Probably, since the Filipino looked so afraid of him. Miles was certain the interrogator was the Filipino's boss.

He was unsure whether, having a clearer picture of the situation, he felt better or worse. He swallowed and wiped his palms with his fingers under the straps. "I have a feeling you're not going to believe this but I really don't know what you're talking about," he said.

Trench glanced at the door. "Doctor," he said, and the man with the medical bag approached, bringing the odor of Old Spice. He placed his bag on the tray and slowly began laying out needles of varying lengths, a scalpel, a little bottle of alcohol, a hand mirror, a felt-tip pencil.

Miles said, watching him, "What's he doing that for? I told you I'm not working for anyone." No one said anything. "I mean I *am* working for someone, but it's not who you think." There was a rubber-lined forceps on the tray now, another liquid-filled vial, a long hypodermic. Miles

219

said, "That's the truth. I'm just a lawyer. You've made some kind of mistake."

Trench let him finish, nodding understandingly all the while, then spoke as if he hadn't heard any of it.

"You have two choices. You can talk to me now or talk to me later. I suggest now. You'll save yourself a great deal of pain, and I assure you that in the end you'll tell me anyway."

"Tell you *what?*"

"Your face looks terrible. Lai wasn't supposed to hurt you this badly, but you'd wounded his pride, gotten away from him twice. I'm quite angry at him for not following instructions." Trench lifted the hand mirror from the tray and thrust it in front of Miles's face. "See what you look like?"

Miles gagged. His flesh was swollen, blue-red, his lip split. The doctor lit a small Bunsen burner, lifted the scalpel and began rotating it in the flame. It turned black.

Trench said, "I'd like to tell you that at heart I'm peaceful, that I hate to hurt people. But the truth is that I very much enjoy inflicting pain on those who anger me. I have a difficult time stopping once I start. It's a fault. I admit it. But it relaxes me. I don't know why." He sighed. "I could peel you like an orange and no one would stop me. The hulls are soundproof. Other boat owners can't hear you. The crew is gone except for a watchman on deck. My men are reliable, but who needs witnesses?" He paused. "You're absolutely vulnerable. Wouldn't you rather we fix up that face? Let's try another question. Whom have you told about my site?"

Miles stiffened. This was a query which he understood, and the images of Elena and Goldstein appeared before him.

In that instant Miles remembered the marshal driving off to get a warrant just before Lai had burst into his apartment. He realized that Goldstein would return, if he had not done so already, find the place in shambles, guess what had happened, go to the construction site to look for Miles, and, finding no one there, try the boat.

He'd *have* to try the boat!

Hope soared within him but he tried to keep it from his face. He imagined the police crashing through the door, Goldstein in the lead, to release him from the chair and get him away from this madman. However, Goldstein would need time to reach the inevitable conclusions, marshal his forces and arrive. If Miles didn't keep quiet now, Trench might take him off the ship or move it.

Sweat dripped under his armpits. Trying to keep his tone level, he said, "I don't understand what you want." As if his answer had been a cue, the doctor lifted the pencil, probed Miles's forearm and drew a one-inch-long **H** on the skin. With alcohol-soaked cotton, he dabbed on the mark, then doused it with a cold spray.

To Trench he said, "Ready."

Trench replied, "In a moment. I want to talk to Mr. Bradshaw first. I feel like explaining a few things." He turned to Miles. "Pain is subjective, and I want you to be in the right frame of mind when we start inflicting it.

"There are two ways to regard the intentional infliction of pain: it is either benevolent or malicious. Imagine an operation where, say, a broken bone is rebroken. Benevolent pain. It hurts, but not as much as the original accident, even though the same bone is affected."

He began tapping a finger on the tray, his tone that of a professor lecturing a class. "Malicious pain is much, much worse. In a minute you'll see what I mean. You're becoming more frightened even as I speak; I can see it in your face. There's no relief, no cessation, no logical way of dealing with it. Each hurt, no matter how painful, is only a lower step on an ascending ladder. The human threshold of pain tolerance is enormous."

Trench looked at the doctor. "Go ahead."

221

So effective had his words been that Miles cried out even as the scalpel moved, and then it was slicing along the **H**, but there was no pain, only pressure. Somehow that was more horrifying than the hurt might have been. By showing his ability to deaden pain the doctor was enhancing his ability to inflict it.

Trench picked up the hypodermic. "The surface of your arm has been, as you've probably guessed, anesthetized. Soon the doctor will clamp back the skin. You still won't feel anything. Then he'll start probing. He's going to scrape the bone." Trench indicated the hypo. "Novocain. Just like the dentist uses. Any time you want the shot, start talking." He pointed at the doctor. "Pain," he said. He lifted the needle. "You decide."

The doctor was very gently clamping back the skin. There wasn't too much blood and Miles could see the inside of his arm. It reminded him of dissected frogs in high school. "I'm telling you . . ." he started to say, but Trench shut him up with a look. Bowels churning, he turned his eyes to the big picture on the wall.

Trench must have been looking at it too. "My mother. She taught me an important lesson. In Korea, 1950. I was sixteen. There was a Major Parks who was in charge of the village where we lived. Everyone liked him. He gave the kids candy."

For the first time, in an undertone, Trench began to speak more forcefully.

"We had terrible roads there. It was raining and the Chinese were coming. Our friend Parks knew it, but we didn't. He didn't tell us. He needed to keep the roads open for troops. Sound tactical decision—couldn't have refugees clogging up the only way in and out. He told us we were safe. The Chinese were miles away.

"My mother believed him. We could have gotten away. Parks expected reinforcements but they never came. Later

I found out. I tracked him down. But the Chinese took the village and my mother"—his eyes fastened on the rug —"died.

"And me. They hurt me badly. My father was fighting somewhere else. They killed him too. I got away, and I learned. Don't trust anyone, *anyone*. Make yourself strong."

He caught himself, then continued with icy calm.

"Why don't you save us both a lot of time? We'll fix your lip, give you money. Someone like you, a skilled man . . . working for me. . . . We already know you've broken into my construction site twice, once with the help of an armed force. You sabotaged my machinery, investigated people who manage my buildings, and questioned landlords who sold them to me. You've checked tax records on my properties. I want to know why."

He leaned forward. "And why, if my people have been looking for you, have they been unable to find you? Policemen, firemen, reporters, bartenders. You're a highly sought after man. A veritable army searches for you and you disappear. I can only conclude that you're remarkably lucky or extremely well trained. I want to know which.

"Think before you say anything. You can do yourself a great deal of good. This is the *last* time. Answer very carefully. *Whom are you working for?*"

Miles looked around the room slowly, breathing in short gasps. He said, enunciating each word, "Please, let's discuss—" but the rest was lost in a scream as the needle plunged into the explosed flesh. Miles felt as if his elbow was exploding, the splintered fragments tearing through his arm.

The needle, spotted with tiny blood rubies, glinted back into the light. Miles sagged against the straps.

Trench's voice was gentle, almost sympathetic. "I know it hurts. Surely you must have told *one* person about the

223

construction site. If you're a professional you've told a superior; if you're an amateur, a friend. Either way someone else knows what I'm doing. A single name and the pain stops. You think they'd keep quiet for you? Just one name. You don't have to tell it all at once."

Miles tried to concentrate on the vision of Goldstein coming through the door.

This time the needle plunged in farther, probing, scraping. Just as he thought he was about to faint the doctor pulled away.

Miles was heaving, panting for relief. To stop himself from telling Trench everything, he forced himself to think about the police. He moaned, fighting for time. "You don't understand. I'm a lawyer."

"A lawyer," Trench repeated.

Miles gasped. "Poverty lawyer."

"Where?"

"Carey Street."

Trench shook his head. "All the way."

The needle rammed into the soft flesh, deeper, deeper. It was picking him apart, blasting him apart, tearing severed nerve endings and shaving the bone. He couldn't bear it. He heard himself screeching, unearthly sounds.

The needle was withdrawn.

Miles was close to unconsciousness. Trench looked at him contemptuously. "You think that was painful? That was nothing—a taste, an acid test. Other people wouldn't have made a sound. It will get a lot worse. Whom are you working for? This time tell me the truth."

Miles threw up.

"Take him into the other room."

He was dimly aware of Lai and the sailor cleaning him up, bandaging his arm, lifting him out of the chair and dragging him down a narrow corridor to another wide

224

cabin which smelled of ammonia and was filled with glass cabinets, medical tinctures, rows of neatly arrayed knives and cutters, cotton swabs and an examination table. They strapped him onto the table.

An immense mirror stretched across the opposite wall reflected the image of a body bound to a bed in the corner. The head faced the wall. The back was crisscrossed by leather. Long legs hung over the side. There was something vaguely familiar about the figure.

Lai and the sailor finished securing Miles and left the room.

All was silent. For a moment Miles savored the quiet, the privacy, the ebbing pain. The throbbing that had extended up his shoulder to his jaw was lessening. He thought again about being rescued, losing himself in visions of police storming the boat, overwhelming the lookout and leading the Korean away in handcuffs. How much time had elapsed since Lai had broken into his apartment? An hour? Goldstein could be here at any moment.

Don't get carried away, he thought. The other prisoner's back was rising and falling slowly. Probably asleep. *Wake him up,* Miles told himself. No telling when Trench might come back. Maybe he could learn something. His lips felt swollen and puffy, but he managed a whisper. "Hey!"

No response. He raised his voice.

"Hey! Get up!"

Slowly, the head turned.

It was Goldstein.

Miles blinked. He told himself it was impossible, that he couldn't be seeing Goldstein, but the marshal wasn't disappearing. Half of his mind refused to believe what he was seeing, while the other half suffered a shock so profound that for a moment his body went numb. Then the throbbing and burning returned, much worse than before.

Goldstein's face was a mass of pounded flesh. The nose

225

looked broken, the eyes swollen, crimson, the chin pulpy, the cheeks scarred. The marshal opened his mouth and exposed broken or missing teeth. One of the ears was swollen by half its size.

All the hope that had sustained Miles during the session with Trench began draining away, leaving him clinging to some last shred of disbelief which Goldstein dispelled with a croaking whisper.

"Left your apartment . . . to go to the office. At a light . . . car in front wouldn't move. I got out . . . two men . . . big guys . . . opened the door. I used to be able to fight. Years ago. Now . . ." Goldstein indicated the wall with a slight movement of his head. "I don't think I even . . . hit them once. I heard them . . . beating you up. You okay?"

Miles shuddered at the image of the needle plunging into his arm. "Yeah, I guess. You don't look so good." Goldstein didn't answer, just closed his eyes to shut out the pain.

"You remember them?" Miles said.

"Who?"

"The guys who stopped you."

Goldstein's voice was permeated with self-disgust. "Yeah." They looked away from each other then, ashamed. Approaching footsteps grew loud in the hallway, paused and continued past. There was a click as the air conditioning started up, throwing cold air on Miles.

He found himself taking refuge in thoughts of Elena, her long brown arms and the way she tilted her head, the way she looked in the morning with the sunlight on her body. Then he imagined what it must have been like for her when Trench's men broke into his apartment. A nightmare of sounds: the crash of the door, the blaring radio, which she knew he never listened to, the scuffling against the wall, then finally just the music.

Elena, too frightened to run seventy yards to the police

226

station. And later, venturing out of the apartment, as she had done earlier today, to stand in his doorway, agape at the splattered garbage, the overturned chair, the knife Trench's men had wrenched from him. He saw her shutting off the radio, staring at the beeping phone.

The images stopped then, like a film freezing on one important shot.

The phone!

Elena would call the police!

Sure! She knew everything Goldstein knew; about the site, the yacht, everything!

The police could *still come.*

Goldstein was talking to him. ". . . asking questions about you. I said you were a lawyer, but they didn't believe me. They said you were working for some rival."

Miles, who had been about to interrupt, was sidetracked. "A rival?"

"Yeah. They said you'd sabotaged a well."

Miles's bandaged hand began to burn.

"At the construction site. They said you'd started a fire."

Miles's heart pounded. "A well? You sure they said that?"

"Absolutely. You blew up a pump, they said. An engine. Stopped the whole operation, hurt some of their men. I said, 'What the fuck, a well?' I didn't know anything about a well."

Miles thought back to the construction site, to cutting the pump hose, and to the explosion he'd heard as he was running away. Almost afraid to hear the answer, he asked, "An oil well?"

"Yes."

"An oil well! In the Bronx!" He shook his head in wonder, in disbelief—but so many crazy things were happening—in acceptance too. "The goddamn Bronx! *That's* why he wants the land!"

More slowly he said, "But I don't understand it. It's not supposed to be there, oil. I checked."

"With the professor."

"That's right."

"Trench wanted to know who else you talked to."

"You *told* him about the professor?"

"No, about the site. He knew about it anyway so there wasn't any point in denying it." His mind seemed to drift away. "Oil," he mused. "You realize what it means? It's fantastic. A dream. This city used to be great. And now it's a dump and it can be great again. The highways and the buildings. Hotels. The parks clean again. We can fix it up, make it like new, make it like when I was a kid. A big present. A city like this, that I love, should be beautiful. A queen. Even the Bronx. It used to be different."

He remembered where he was and stopped. "That doctor. He's the worst."

Goldstein's hands were wedged under his body. Miles felt a wave of nausea. Neither of them said anything for some moments and then Goldstein said, "*Did* you blow up the engine?"

Miles felt a flush of pride. "Damn right I did."

"Serves 'em right. Goddamn good," Goldstein said, although he seemed, in some childish way, hurt. He said petulantly, "How come you didn't tell me about it before?"

Miles's flush became one of embarrassment. "I didn't think you'd understand. After all, me—starting a fire?"

Goldstein agreed. "Sure, I suppose you're right." There was an element of surrender in the voice which gave Miles the impression that some subtle role reversal had just taken place and that for the first time he was the stronger one.

A fit of coughing wasted Goldstein on the bed, arching his back against the straps and pushing his face into the mattress. Then he muttered, "They were so sure of themselves I thought . . . maybe I was wrong. Maybe you *were* working for someone else. Maybe you had told other people."

"Christ, Goldstein, you know damn well whom I told, you and El—"

The force of a sudden thought shut Miles' mouth. He stared at himself in the mirror, at the dawning understanding in his face.

"You know something?" he said. "Why they're leaving us alone? You know why they put us together?" Goldstein was watching him intently. "They *want* us to talk, that's why. They're listening!"

The same look of frightened comprehension came into Goldstein's eyes and Miles said furiously, "Sure. They figured we wouldn't be thinking clearly. They'd beaten us up pretty badly and our minds were cloudy. They figured we'd be so glad to see each other we'd slip up, tell each other what they wanted to know. If we knew it. Shit."

It was so obvious that neither of them said another word. The room seemed suddenly hotter. All the test tubes, the doorknobs, the picture frames, which moments before had been innocent trappings, now became suspect. They looked for wires, Their breathing sounded loud in their ears.

The door opened and Trench entered, followed by Lai and the doctor; shuffling reluctantly behind them, pushed along by the sailor, was an emaciated man with a scraggly beard.

Trench tapped his fingers against each other in annoyance and said, "Your powers of intuition are excellent, Mr. Bradshaw. You're to be commended." His face assumed the already familiar look of false sympathy, dispelling any sense of triumph Miles retained.

"Unfortunately, your cleverness won't do you any good. You're probably pleased with yourself for not mentioning

Elena's name a moment ago, and yet I already know it. She called her local precinct out of concern for you and reached one of our friends who asked her to wait. That's what she's doing, waiting. Two of my men have gone to get her and what will happen to her depends on you."

He paused to let the implications of his words sink in, and Miles, whose body had jerked involuntarily at the mention of her name, went wide-eyed as the full impact rammed home. He opened his mouth but no sound emerged. His visions of police rescue vanished, to be replaced by images of Elena in his apartment, Elena dragged into the street, Elena tied to the chair in the next room while the doctor bent close, instruments twitching like insect appendages.

He did start to scream then, savaging his wrists on the straps, but only for a moment, because, as if someone had pressed a switch in his mind, he quieted, horrified by his surging emotions. *Jesus,* he thought, *I'm losing control,* and he didn't even want to look at Trench now, so great was his dread, but the Korean must have known about the whole process, must have done this all before, because the soft voice coaxed him back.

"One more surprise," Trench said, stepping forward casually and fixing Goldstein with his eyes. "Lai, untie him."

Miles said, "Don't hurt him. He doesn't know anything. Really."

Slowly, Goldstein stood up and Trench threw him a towel.

"Wipe the makeup off your face."

There was a long pause during which time was suspended; Trench watching, the marshal looking at the floor, Lai smiling expectantly at Miles. Then Goldstein, with infinite slowness, applied the towel to his face. The pulpy part of the nose was wiped away. It might never have existed. The cauliflower ear assumed normal proportions and stained the terry cloth yellow. Unable to look him in the face, Goldstein averted his eyes, showing Miles his profile. His voice was choked with humiliation. "They traced me through the car. Offered me money. I said no. They found my sister. She's on vacation. They have someone watching her. She doesn't know."

Miles heard the words but they didn't register, as he watched the "scars" and "broken teeth" wiped clean, the mangled flesh restored with the application of a cloth. Too much was happening at once. An abyss had opened before him and he was tumbling in; the marshal's words came at him from far away.

"You or my sister," Goldstein said, swinging toward him, supreme misery and supplication twisting his features. "I had to do it. I don't have anyone else. And thirty years with the department! Trench is burning buildings! I'd never help him for money! Miles? Please say something!"

But Miles, reeling, was remembering Goldstein's last visit to the apartment, thinking, *He was never ordered off the case. He never went to get a warrant. He signaled Lai to break in. And when he was angry it wasn't at the arson bureau, it was at Trench.*

Goldstein said, "I had to file a report. Write that we didn't find anything. Blame the kid, Carlos, for the fire. The bureau won't send another investigator." He sighed. "I have no illusions about what will happen to me, but my sister . . . They'll leave her alone. No point hurting her. And I know you didn't start the fires. Either of them. I know that now."

Docile, the marshal allowed the sailor to lead him from the room. Miles felt an urge to call him back, to make him feel better, but he couldn't bring himself to do it.

Then Goldstein was gone. For the first time there was a real smile on Trench's face, and the Korean seemed less human, more like some mystical intelligence, some primal overwhelming force. Miles felt stripped, powerless, out-maneuvered. He even experienced, to his dismay, vague stirrings of admiration. He had a bizarre recollection of an article he had read as a child called "The Ant Lion." The ant lion was an insect which dug sand pits and waited at the bottom for an ant to begin sliding into the trap toward his waiting jaws. The ant would struggle madly, slipping; there was nothing to hold on to and in the end it would be devoured.

"Oil," Miles said, reaching like a drowning swimmer for a buoy. "It's impossible. I checked."

Trench waved away the protest, his face normal again. "Oh, it's possible all right. There's the scientist who found it." He pointed to the man in the corner. "Funny, the whole country dying for oil and an ocean of it beneath your feet. No one believed him. He's an alcoholic. Now he's a guest here like you. We still need his expertise. Every once in a while he gets unruly and I show him what happens to other people who behave badly."

Judging by the look on the scientist's face, he shared Miles' feelings toward Trench.

Trench drew Miles' attention again. "So you see, mine is no haphazard operation. The major problems were solved long ago. The minor ones, like you or," he said, frowning, "Goldstein, are taken care of as they arise. Goldstein didn't do everything we asked of him. He didn't tell us about Elena. Couldn't bring himself to go that far." His fingers began tapping together again. "Resistance."

The doctor rolled a steel machine the size of a large portable television toward the table. It was covered with dials and was topped by two loops of cable.

Trench said, "I've always considered electroshock to be vastly underrated in popular fiction as a means of persuasion. I like simplicity."

The doctor began unrolling the cables, checking that

the wires weren't tangled. Lai stepp~
open the stiletto, and began slitting M...
worked smoothly, meeting Miles' eyes once or
an amused glance, careful not to damage the straps.

"A universe of pain," Trench said. "Unstoppable, unfor.
gettable, unescapable pain. Not a single part of your body
or mind is spared. Applied to the genitals, the shocks burn
them off. To the ears and they shatter your teeth and
hearing. To your stomach and they can rip the muscles
from your back and thighs. That's how powerful the
spasms are. But we won't start out full force. We'll build
up to it."

A rising scream that could have been only from Goldstein came through the wall, changed to a gurgle, and was
cut off as swiftly as it had erupted. Miles was left trembling, afraid to speak. Trench's expression was impassive.
The doctor paused briefly, satisfying himself that there
would be no more interruption, then took a sponge from
the sink and started wetting down Miles's naked body.

Trench said, "Water conducts electricity. Be reasonable.
A man like you would tell us what we need to know once
we started on your girl friend. But time is a problem. I
don't want to wait."

The doctor turned on the machine, which made a faint
humming noise. He handed the cables to Trench, who
stepped forward and held them a foot from Miles's head.

"Whom have you told about my oil well?"

Miles, still hearing in his mind that awful scream, could
only whisper, "You killed Goldstein."

Trench lowered the cables, touching the chest. Miles
leaped from the table, straining against his bonds, engulfed by oceans of pain, sparks, convulsions. His hands
felt as if they were being pulled off. He was gagging, close
to swallowing his tongue.

He fell back against the table.

233

.....ter a second application of the cables, the scientist started whimpering. Trench said, "Lock him up next door." The sailor led him out.

After the third time Miles started to cry. He imagined Goldstein dead in the next room, Elena in the Korean's grasp, and himself, a pathetic white collar out of his depth from the moment he'd started his investigation. He was drained of resistance. He saw his wife and daughter, dead because of his carelessness; Carlos Perez, whom he'd been unable to rescue or even clear with the police; and again, Goldstein, Elena, himself, soon to be a mangled corpse.

The cables were lowered yet again, the current increased. His body was almost ripping through the straps. He shrieked, grasping for a footing amid the chaos of convulsions. His body felt as if it were being torn apart.

The pain stopped.

Trench had not yet touched his head.

Miles gasped, "Not . . . again. Please." He smelled his own urine.

Trench leaned over and said, "You're working for someone. Whom?"

Miles was sobbing. "The aid office. I'm a lawyer. Nothing . . . more. Saw the boy die."

"What boy?"

"Carlos. In the window. From my apartment."

Trench appraised him. "What do *you* care about Carlos? Why did you start investigating?"

The cables inched closer and Miles spoke rapidly. "Had a daughter. Burned up. I did it."

Trench pulled back and tapped his fingers together. He said, "You know what we're going to do? Blindfold you. You won't know where we're going to apply the cables. Sometimes I'll tell you so you can concentrate on that part of your body, but sometimes I'll be lying. Anytime you want me to stop, tell the truth."

234

Shudders rippled through Miles's whole body. "*Am* telling the truth."

"Who helped you break into the site?"

Miles gulped air. "The Kings."

"Kings?"

"Latin . . . Kings."

Trench recoiled, startled, but after a moment actually grinned and turned to Lai. "Imagine that," he said. "The Latin Kings."

Lai's expression wasn't as benevolent. "Rodriguez," he said. "I'll take care of him."

"No, no point in that. After all, Rodriguez had no idea he was breaking into our project. He doesn't know you're connected with that building. To him you're only the man who pays him to burn tenements. He doesn't even know I exist so he can't be blamed for what he did." Trench looked amused. "A little healthy free enterprise," he said. "And the boy's only fifteen." The friendly light went out of his eyes. "We need a few more buildings. But afterward, when he knows whose property he destroyed . . ."

Trench looked down at Miles. "Give them a few dollars —they'll burn anything. You paid them, of course. How much?"

"Six . . . hundred . . . dollars."

Appalled by the smallness of the sum, Trench issued a sound of disgust. He went across the cabin, returned and fastened a strip of cloth around Miles's eyes. "Think about your ears. We're going to touch your ears with the cables. Your teeth will shatter."

"I DON'T WORK FOR ANYONE! I TOLD YOU!"

Trench said, "Yes, well, I'm starting to believe you. I just don't want to stop."

There was a tremendous explosion in Miles's head, as if he'd been slammed by a board. Whimpering, he tasted blood.

"The stomach."

"What do you want me to say? I'll say it! Tell me what to say!"

"No, maybe not the stomach. Maybe the penis."

Another voice said, "Get away from the table."

Miles moaned. How could he get away from the table? He was *strapped* to the table. There was another explosion which he heard but did not feel. And now a thud and the sound of glass breaking. Someone said, "Shit. She shot me." Miles smelled smoke.

His eyes were closed under the blindfold, trying to make it all disappear. It struck him that the first voice had been a woman's, her tone halting, terrified, but somehow, despite his pain and confusion, familiar.

He opened his eyes. The blindfold kept everything dark.

No, it was impossible.

Elena?

FOURTEEN

NINETY MINUTES before the electric cables were applied to Miles's body, fifty minutes before his forearm was anesthetized for persuasive surgery, and only two minutes before Lai broke down his door, Elena was thinking that she had no more cookies in her apartment. The last of the almond squares, little sugar-coated patties that Miles gobbled by the dozen, were warming in the oven while coffee perked on the stove. Elena would have to add sweets to the shopping list before the delivery boy came tomorrow.

She had just heard Goldstein leave and assumed that she would hear Miles's knock momentarily. She finished setting a place for him and went over to the window. The arson inspector was trudging to his car.

Looking down at the street, which had been barred to her for months, she was gripped by excitement. She had left her apartment today! Only ten feet to Miles's door and it had taken ages to get there, but as far as she was concerned she might as well have walked a tightrope between skyscrapers, so great was her sense of pride. Envisioning the delivery boy pedaling his basketed bike up the street tomorrow, she dared to imagine a time when he wouldn't have to come at all and she could go to the store by herself.

That would be something.

The image was almost enough to make her laugh. After all, here she was, "tough" Elena, taking pride in a ten-foot journey. Amazing to think that she had once roamed the island of Puerto Rico at will, albeit with a bodyguard, and even those intimidating avenues below until that day when . . . well . . .

She let the curtain drop and surveyed the apartment that had been for almost a whole year her entire world: the stark expensive furniture, the polished silverware, the stereo and magazines. Tonight, however, there was a hint of ridicule in her self-appraisal.

She had taken the first step!

She went to the stove and lowered the flame under the coffee. Today had been full of such new sensations: pride and jealousy when she heard Miles's phone ringing—because he had begun his return to that world that was still denied to her. She batted down that petty envy, which, combined with concern for his safety and disgust at her self-imposed confinement, had helped her leave the apartment today.

There was a noise on the fire escape.

She went to the sofa, picked up the agoraphobia article and began thumbing the pages. It was reassuring to know there were other people like her and she felt a kinship with the phobics described in the piece. She wondered if Miles would take her to the group's meeting and decided he would—one of his finest qualities was his concern for other people. When he talked about clients he was unable to help, she always detected the frustration he tried to ignore or joke away. And his quest to find the murderer of a boy he never knew, putting up with that cadaverous Goldstein. For that she loved him, for the way he gave her strength and needed her support, for his pain and his gentle intensity.

Even if he *hadn't* been the only person she'd met in months she would still feel the same way about him, she told herself, and whenever she found the courage to leave this cozy prison she'd created, they would be able to go somewhere safer together.

Glancing at the wall adjoining his apartment, she heard a tremendous crash from next door.

Her knee jerked. Her first thought was that a large piece of furniture had fallen, perhaps injuring him, but as she rose in concern, she recalled that there wasn't any furniture in his apartment except the rocking chair.

From outside, on the fire escape, came another scraping sound.

Wanting to check what it was this time, she pulled back the curtain from the window and wiped the haze off the pane.

Someone was climbing through Miles's window.

She banged on the glass, yelled "Hey!" and "Stop!" which of course did no good. Then the man was inside. She took two steps back and the radio went on next door, loud.

Miles never listened to the radio.

She thought, *They're killing him.*

Instinctively, she leaped across the room and yanked open the door. She began to charge into the hallway but stopped suddenly, froze, as if she had hit an invisible barrier.

The whole hallway was wavering, shifting. Only minutes

before it had been peaceful, but now it was dancing, like the time she'd tried to leave the apartment months before. The thunderous sounds from next door were getting louder; the crescendo of musical instruments, scrapings. Something hit the wall.

She felt nauseous, her windpipe was closing, her legs refused to move.

The radio next door was blaring a waltz.

It got louder now, like some crazy echo chamber. The bannister was undulating. She backed into her apartment, slamming the door. There was a booming, staccato run of strings from the other side of the wall and then a siren, the *police,* but it was fading, going elsewhere. Any other person could have had the cops here.

She thought she heard Miles cry out over the music.

She began weaving, uttering little groans, circling in the living room like a rodent in a cage, fists clenched. And her mind—that brilliant mind of which she was so proud, that sarcastic, clever mind that absorbed articles and followed the news and thought up witty sayings for Miles, Miles who was being beaten to a pulp ten feet away, maybe stabbed—that terrific mind was reduced, loathsomely, to fielding some dim obsessive repetition, two words over and over, like a broken record timed to the roaring of her heart, "Have to, have to." And then a series of images broke in on her: the beach in Puerto Rico, Miles' phone ringing, her husband in the casket, her mother screaming at her for going into the water, the hallway outside dancing crazily, the glass-littered lot near the grocery and the boys with Levi jackets, Miles being attacked. Her hands hammered on the wall between their apartments to the booming, crashing music.

The waltz.

It stopped. The cultured tones of the radio announcer came on. Otherwise, there was silence from Miles' apartment.

She stepped back from the wall. Her hands were raw from striking the plaster and her cheeks were wet with her tears.

Outside, a siren cut the night and faded.

Across the room, a light breeze played at the curtain.

An overturned coffee table lay between her and the door. The little silver dolphin ashtray was upside down, the dolphin's head buried in the blue-carpet sea.

She felt, without knowing, that the attackers had left Miles' apartment.

And if they were gone, they'd finished what they had come to do.

She was exhausted, drained by a sleep-preventing weariness. How much time had elapsed since she'd heard that first crash. Five minutes? Enough time for someone else to have run to the police station? For a normal person to have called for help?

She saw her husband, Esteban, laid out in the casket at the church, that pasty white makeup on his face, the lipstick grotesque, the countenance cold, distant. Then the face grew longer and lighter and it was Miles' face. And instead of the silk cushions under the head there was the hard wooden floor of that pathetically sparse apartment, whose emptiness, whose yearning to be filled up, had surprised her when she had finally seen it for the first time an hour and a half ago. And the floor was red, stained, and Miles, unlike Esteban, who had been laid out so formal and stiff, was splayed out, twisted. And unlike the eyes in the casket, which had been closed so discreetly, Miles' were open, fastened on the wall between the two apartments, because hadn't he known during the attack that she could hear the whole thing?

She started to weep.

Several moments later, amid the numbing shock, horror and grief, came the need to go to him, the terror over what he might look like. Perhaps, somehow, he was still alive, although she grasped at the hope not so much because she believed it but because she needed a defense against her deepening despondency, which was going to get a lot worse before it bottomed out. Crushing guilt and loneliness were crowding in. With Miles' death she would cross the line into an abysmal world of desolation far worse than anything she had ever imagined.

The radio next door began broadcasting "The Afternoon of a Faun." Leaving the apartment, now that the reverberations of the fight had ceased, seemed absurdly simple, and she was at Miles' door without thinking about how she had gotten there.

Her mouth dropped open.

He was gone.

From the doorway, she could survey the entire apartment, and Miles wasn't there. Garbage was strewn everywhere and was dripping down the walls. The rocking chair was overturned, the phone off the hook. A cutlery drawer hung open, and a knife lay on the floor. No blood anywhere.

She checked the fire escape, then slowly opened the closets, pushed back the shower curtain, and even looked under the sink, expecting at each moment, through some horrible oversight, that the body would spill out before her.

She turned off the radio, then stood in the middle of the room, pivoting.

Her earlier strains of foolish hope were fusing into something stronger. Could he actually be alive? Strange, but part of her fought the idea, wanting to prevent a worse disappointment. No, he wasn't alive, because hadn't they tried to kill him twice already? They must have taken the body somewhere to dispose of it.

But why would they do that? And if he were already dead, why wasn't there any blood?

242

She grabbed the phone as if it were a lifeline and called the police station down the block.

Two rings. "Forty-First Precinct. Sergeant Pearson."

She began babbling. "There's been an attack. My friend. Someone climbed through the window. A crash but I thought it was furniture."

The cop said, "Slow down, hold it," and finally, when she was quiet, began to question her. She envisioned an efficient young policeman, maybe twenty-five, asking in a baritone, "When did it happen? And the address? How many assailants? You didn't *see* the assault. You heard it. Uh huh. And your friend was gone when you went to check? His name?"

He inhaled noticeably when she answered. "Miles *Bradshaw?*"

She remembered that Miles had visited the police station several days before. "You know him?"

"No." Quickly. Then awkwardly, "You're in his apartment now? Stay there. Someone will be right over."

She went to the window to wait. After what seemed like a very long time she looked at the clock. Four minutes had elapsed.

Still, the goddamn police station was only seventy yards away, and she'd reported a kidnapping and attempted murder, hadn't she? So where were all those cops who spent so much time double-parking below? Why weren't four or five of New York's finest tearing up the sidewalk right now?

She called back and got Pearson again. He sounded more frightened than she did. "Christ, lady, I just hung up with you."

"You said someone would be right over."

"Calm down. Even in emergencies it takes a couple of minutes. They'll be there soon, I promise."

Across the street, a cab pulled up to a tenement and an

old woman struggled out. Elena's hands were white on the receiver. "How soon?"

"You gotta understand. First one who comes back I'll send over."

The cab pulled off. Elena cried, hyperventilating, "*You* understand!" and slammed down the receiver. She picked up the phone and dialed.

"Sergeant Pearson."

"It's me again. I'm sorry I yelled."

"Perfectly all right, miss."

She tried to keep her tone steady. "Maybe I didn't explain myself correctly. You can *save* him. One man went in through the fire escape. I know where they took him!"

"Lady, I . . . *Where* did they take him?"

"A building. Under construction, four blocks away. He's there, I know it!"

Pearson paused. "If you know where he is then . . . well . . . First one back. It's a priority call."

She was almost crying. *"Isn't there one extra man in the whole station?"*

"The other phone is ringing. Hold on a sec—"

She hung up. She was shaking from the effort. She called again.

"Pearson. Forty-First Precinct."

Slam. Back to the window to wait for the cops. Another car was cruising up the street. It paused at the corner, rear lights glowing, then disappeared.

The police were nowhere in sight.

A second chance and she was botching it.

She exhaled deeply and steadied herself on the windowsill. Eight months, she thought. I haven't been outside in eight months and I'm scared.

But she remembered the awful guilt and sense of loss when she'd been certain Miles was dead. Now even the apartment seemed to be mocking her. Her gun was in the

244

next apartment. She considered calling Sergeant Pearson again.

She reached for the phone.

The cabby arrived before the police, which surprised her. The taxi company had been easier to call because deep down she'd believed the cops would beat the driver to the door, but suddenly there he was, a portly, grandfatherly black, unlit cigar stub in his mouth, white stubble coating his cheeks, forehead damp from the five-flight climb. Even though it was hot, he wore an old cardigan.

Elena picked up her purse. The gun weighed down the bag.

She said, "Can you help me down the stairs, please?"

Her voice was strangled, but fortunately, the cabby was too preoccupied to notice. Taking her arm, he said good-naturedly, "Know what tomorrow is? My thirtieth wedding anniversary. *Thirty years!* Ain't that somethin'?" Elena was unsteady on the stairs but the cabby was a rock. "We're going dancing," he said. "Not that disco stuff. I see it on TV. Uh uh! I love dancing but not that kind. Rhumba, tango. Me an' my wife won a prize in 1947 at the Apollo. She was something then."

They reached the doorway. Elena was panting, concentrating on Miles. The night air was alive with the sounds of television shows. A couple of scrawny-looking mutts sulked by, casting defiant glances at her.

The cab was double-parked fifteen feet away, hazard lights blinking. As they walked, the driver said, "The bones get old but it's the rhythm that's important. People just stop doing things at a certain age. What a waste. You listening?"

But Elena was thinking how Miles had divided her future into two possibilities. The first she had been daydreaming about just a short time before. Nothing she could imagine would be worse than the second.

In a small, thin voice that didn't seem to come from her, she said, "We're going only four blocks away."

The site, when they glided to a halt before it, was still, black under the white-yellow moon. The half-finished building, monolithic, loomed before them on a street deserted not only of people but of cars as well. There was no black Torino. Miles had told her about it and she'd been sure she was going to find it here.

She was drowning. The driver opened the glass partition between them. "You sure this is the right address?" he said. "Doesn't seem to be anybody here. Maybe we should call wherever you're going, get directions."

Elena nodded dumbly, half listening. Her eyes scanned the brick facades, searching for a light or movement as she strained to hear the slightest sound, thinking, *Where else could they have taken him?*

She racked her brain trying to recall whether Miles had told her about seeing the Filipino anywhere else.

Of course. The boat.

She'd forgotten what it was like to travel on a highway, and the speed and lights flooded her with forgotten impressions that she fought to keep from overwhelming her. They were heading south on the Cross Bronx Expressway, past an endless traffic jam crawling out of Manhattan. She traced the outlines of the gun, remembering the trips, at her mother's insistence, to the target range in Puerto Rico. "Know how to protect yourself," her mother had always said, and Elena had won her medals firing at cardboard targets.

She wished the driver would start talking again, but he had fallen silent and was watching her suspiciously in the rearview mirror. The meter kept making little *snap* noises as it turned over.

Every few minutes she started to feel dizzy, closed her eyes and squeezed them, expelling thoughts.

"GEORGE WASHINGTON BRIDGE" said a sign.

Elena asked, "Can't we go a little faster?"

"Miss," said the driver, watching the mirror, "you don't look well. Pardon me, but maybe you should go home."

Elena cried, pointing to a sign and leaning forward, "The boat basin!"

"Stop here."

They were atop the circular drive overlooking the marina, which hadn't changed since she had visited it with her husband months ago. The dark docks and berths were vague outlines against the night river, the silver moonlight stretched across the Hudson from the Palisades, pointing out Manhattan.

A party was in progress out by the docks. Bright lights reflected festively in the dark water, disco music throbbing, people coming and going through the main gate.

And all the way in the back, where Miles had said it would be, impaled by that shaft of moonlight, the long, sleek shadow, masted and dark except for three little circles of light, portholes on Trench's ship.

Three little lights. And Miles.

Her mouth was dry, her throat burning. The pocketbook on her lap weighed a million pounds. Reluctantly she tore her gaze from the waterfront, directing it instead

247

down the ramp which led to the underground parking lot, a dark square entrance with tile walls dully reflecting the cab's headlights.

She pointed.

"Down there," she said.

The black Torino was there, all right, parked close to the door which led to the waterfront, Jersey plates, just as Miles had said. Now there was only the matter of getting a message to Sergeant Pearson. For all her need to take a personal role in helping Miles, she knew the police could do a better job. She had already rejected the idea of wasting more time finding a phone booth, so now the driver was the key.

The meter read $18.50, but she gave him $35, noted the cabby's widening eyes with satisfaction and drew the gun from her purse. She was careful not to point it or even to place her finger near the trigger. She only wanted him to see it. He froze.

She tried to keep her voice calm. "A friend of mine is in the marina. In trouble. That probably sounds crazy, but it's true." She saw the fear in his face. "Call the police, the Forty-First Precinct in the Bronx. Sergeant Pearson. He knows what this is about. Tell him I'm sorry I didn't wait. He'll know what you mean. Please. Tell him the boat he wants belongs to a man named Trench."

The driver, whose breathing was audible, didn't take his eyes off the gun.

Elena said, "Will you do that? Please?"

Slowly, a nod.

"And you'll remember? Sergeant P-e-a-r-s-o-n? And Trench owns the boat?"

"Yes."

Elena said, "Tell him I couldn't wait. I went to the boat.

248

Tell him I have a gun. That will make him send people faster. Do you want more money?"

The driver said, "I'll call."

"Thank you. You have change for the phone? Thank you."

She got out of the cab.

The brake lights flared, went out.

Twenty seconds later she was alone in the lot.

As she moved she concentrated on the doorway leading to the riverfront and then on the marina gate. She didn't look to either side, although she was conscious of passersby. Behind the wire mesh a pimply teenager stared out at her with the look of awe adolescents reserve for hot numbers like Elena. The walkway was alive with music from a houseboat. Trying to appear confident, she said, "Party time."

Her voice sounded frightened to her but the boy opened the gate. She passed into the marina and along the docks until she stood at the foot of the ramp to Trench's ship.

Close up, the boat looked even larger than it had from the shore, but it was just as lifeless. No sounds, no lights except from the portholes.

She stepped on the ramp.

A voice said, "Sorry, miss. You can't come on board."

The man who confronted her from the deck had an Irish face and small, amused eyes which probably had been following her progress all along. A cigarette glowed in his fleshy, violent lips. And, although the voice had been polite, Elena had the feeling that the speaker was uncomfortable using that tone.

He was the man who had been on Miles' fire escape.

She thought, *Pull out the gun,* but her hand wouldn't move.

The man sauntered one step down the ramp, hand casually gliding along the hemp railing. His posture conveyed his intention to keep her off the deck, but the way he glanced at the houseboat indicated that he wasn't completely unsociable.

He said, flicking one red ash into the Hudson, "Good party?"

Like the gate boy, he was assuming she was one of the revelers. She followed his gaze back to the boat. A burst of hearty male laughter came across the water.

She said, "I guess. Good music. After a while it's a little too crowded. You need some quiet."

"Not me. Big parties, that's what I like. It's quiet enough when you sleep." He chuckled at his own joke. Her hand still wouldn't move into the bag. *Say something*, she thought, and his bored look gave her a gambit.

"Too bad you got duty tonight. Looks like everyone else is off the ship."

He took a drag on the cigarette and nodded. "Yeah. Out partying. Boss is here though."

"Oh?"

"Yeah."

One large hand slide back and forth on the rope, an unconscious caress. He had a clipped Irish accent, and when he took another half step down toward her she saw he wore a leisure suit, well fitted on the sinewy frame.

He said, "I never seen you before in the marina. Just come for the party, huh?" He gave a little sashay of the hip to accentuate the word "party."

"Yes, just for that."

"Parties. Right." He was staring at her now, his eyes traveling downward. He smiled and leaned against the guard rope. "Whaddaya do when you aren't going to parties?"

She tossed her head but felt herself blushing. "Why do you think I do anything else?"

He laughed. "Hey, you ever been to the Caribbean?"

She almost dropped the purse. "I grew up there."

"I knew it! Dominican Republic, right? I worked there."

"No. Puerto Rico."

He slumped. "Oh. You look familiar, but I never been in Puerto Rico."

She didn't think he'd seen her from the fire escape but maybe he had.

He took another step forward, the hand starting to move back and forth on the hemp again. One more foot and she'd never get the gun out. He said, "I never forget a face."

Four blocks away, one eye on his double-parked Checker cab, William Swann was waiting impatiently in front of a phone booth occupied by some obnoxious Park Avenue type—hoity-toity hat, cigarette holder, fingernails as long as toothpicks and a French poodle. Swann hated poodles, worthless little runts. This one was no exception. When it wasn't pissing on the phone booth it was barking at him.

Swann kept glancing back in the direction of the marina, wondering what the woman with the gun was doing. The woman in the booth had already put one extra dime in the slot and showed no signs of ending her conversation. He waved impatiently for her to get out.

She waved back.

In twenty-two years of driving a cab, William Swann had encountered plenty of nuts, and when he had picked up Elena Moreno tonight he'd known right away he had one on his hands. Everything about her—the way she spoke, the fright she'd shown going down the stairs, the way she'd directed him to an empty construction site and then to the marina—had convinced him she was wacko. He'd tried to loosen her up by talking about his upcoming anniversary, but she'd been tight as a drum. When she'd pulled that pistol out of her purse he'd thought he was going to shit in his pants. A friend of hers was in trouble, she'd said. Yeah, and he was Shaft. Still, he'd better call the police, because she might hurt someone.

The woman in the booth hung up, flashing him an offended look.

Swann rushed into the booth. When he was finally connected to Sergeant Pearson he laid the whole story on him in less than sixty seconds. When he was finished Pearson said, in a voice of hushed awe, "Jesus Fucking Christ" and hung up.

Swann shrugged. At least Elena had been telling the truth about knowing the cop. For a moment he wondered if she had been telling the truth about the boat, too, but that was ridiculous. He dipped his finger into the coin return—after all, you never knew what was in there, and one time he'd found a dollar fifty—then got into his cab and headed for Broadway. Always customers on Broadway.

He hoped Elena Moreno wouldn't hurt anyone in the marina.

Sergeant Pearson, meanwhile, was dialing the boat.

"Another couple of minutes and I'll remember where I saw you," Irish face said. "What's your name, anyway?"

"Elena."

"Elena what?" He smiled because she wasn't answering. "Well, well, well. Let's play a game. Let's guess Elena's name." He started to move closer, but a phone at the top of the ramp rang. He turned to answer it.

Now that he'd distanced himself she found she could move her hand. She opened her bag while he said, "Pearson? What's up?" He was quiet a moment and turned to her just as she pulled out the gun.

A muscle on his neck jumped.

Slowly, he dropped the phone in its cradle. He said, "Now I remember."

Looking from the guard to the phone, Elena whispered, "Sergeant Pearson!"

Neither of them spoke for a moment, then Elena said, "Where's Miles?"

The guard looked at the gun. "Who?"

"Miles Bradshaw."

"I don't know any Miles Bradshaw."

"I saw you climb through his window."

No response.

"I can shoot you and look myself."

"*You're* not going to use that." He glared at her contemptuously, but whatever he saw in her eyes made him falter. After a moment he said, "Lai'll kill me."

"One of us will."

A moment later they were threading their way through the upper hallway, Elena's gun trained on the V-shaped back. The shutters at each doorway were dark. The guard said halfheartedly, "The crew will never let you down there."

"There isn't any crew. You said so. Where's the stairway?"

She had decided that Miles was in one of the lighted cabins below, and although the guard led her to the stairway, his surly sluggishness was getting to the point where she thought he might turn on her. Worse, the boat had more than two levels. They descended one flight and to Elena's dismay more stairs stretched toward the hull. For the first time she stopped, unsure of what to do, but then the lights dimmed and a scream came from below.

The guard turned and, trying not to show how shaken

253

she was, she waved him ahead, not trusting her voice, trying to keep the gun steady. He kept stopping and she had to touch him with the pistol before he would move, but they reached the bottom deck.

Another scream. Miles' pleading voice came from a door to the right. *"What do you want me to say? I'll say it! Tell me what to say!"*

Elena leveled the gun. The guard was eyeing it.

She said, "Open the door and get in fast." He hesitated, but must have sensed her finger tightening on the trigger. When he turned the knob she pushed him into the room and stood in the doorway.

She looked, blinked, looked again.

A naked body, clothes cut away, partially obscured from view by a man's back, was strapped to a table. The man turned and straightened. He was an Oriental holding two cables in his hands; the cables were attached to a steel machine. She wondered if he were the pleasant-faced man Miles had described. He didn't look too pleasant.

The man on the table was blindfolded but she recognized him—Miles.

The Oriental was staring, baffled, as were three men against a far wall—a sailor, a mustached man with a medical bag, and another Oriental.

To the man with the cables, Elena said, "Get away from the table."

He was about to comply when the Irishman lunged. Elena automatically squeezed the trigger, wincing at the explosion. The guard stopped, a startled expression growing on his face. His legs dipped, his heels rose slowly and he covered his stomach with his hand. He said disbelievingly, "Shit. She shot me."

Miles knew that Trench had gone away because he couldn't smell the ginger anymore, and then there was

254

another odor, smoke, *cordite*, and then . . . perfume? A hand touched his chest, tugging at the straps, untying them. Fingers groped at the blindfold. His senses were clogged with pain.

The blindfold was lifted from his eyes. Elena stood above him.

He told himself that Elena couldn't be there, that she was supposed to be arriving here with Trench's men, that she couldn't be holding a gun, and, certainly, that she couldn't have left her apartment, alone.

The moaning distracted him. The Irishman who had climbed into his apartment was kneeling on the floor, fist against his stomach. Blood spurted from between the fingers and dribbled down one side of his mouth.

Miles looked down at his own stomach, saw fiery red points from the cables.

Elena said, "Miles?"

He tested his wrist, his fingers. They ached but they moved.

More to herself than to him, Elena said, "I never shot anybody before."

Slowly, Miles started to piece together small realities. Trench and his men were backed against the other side of the room, eyeing Elena and the gun. He remembered Trench saying that two of his men had gone for Elena, so where were they? And how had Elena reached him?

He tried to sit up, groaned, fell back. He was on fire.

Trench, using his soft voice, addressed Elena. "Can the doctor look at Sweeney? That's a bad stomach wound."

The groaning Irishman was only a few feet away. Miles wanted to tell her not to do it but he couldn't talk yet.

Eyes wide, Elena nodded.

Miles sat up.

His head, arms and stomach exploded in pain. The room rocked gently.

255

Elena touched his shoulder. Her fingers were trembling. "We have to leave," she said.

She was right, of course, but he couldn't make his limbs respond. Groggily aware of the doctor and of his abused, throbbing body, Miles envisioned what Trench would do if he somehow managed to turn the tables. He summoned enough strength to grip the edge of the table and inch his way to the floor. He stood up, almost fell, grabbing the table for support.

The doctor, kneeling by the wounded guard, said, "This is very bad." There was a little pool on the carpet.

Elena said, "I only wanted to shoot the leg, not the stomach. He moved too fast."

She seemed mesmerized, as if for the first time she was realizing where she was. Whatever magical force had brought her to this cabin was fading and she was reverting to the old Elena. He thought, *She's apologizing to them. This is crazy.*

He reached out and reassured her with a touch. She leaned against him.

Lai and the sailor began inching apart. Miles looked from Elena's crumpling face to the gun. Gently but swiftly he took the revolver from her hand. He could speak now. "Don't do it."

They moved back together. He was wobbly, but he knew they had better leave quickly.

Trench asked Elena, "What happened to the men who went to find you?"

"Find me?" Then, watching Trench's face, she said, "Sergeant Pearson?"

"Yes."

Elena whispered, "I called a cab."

Now it was Miles who looked incredulous, but the Korean said, "They'll be back any minute. They left some time ago."

The voice was too confident, and although the words unnerved Miles, he came to the startling realization that the situation which had existed five minutes before in this cabin was now completely reversed. Even if only for the moment, he was in total control, and with that thought came the memory of himself strapped to the table, of the doctor cutting his forearm, of Trench telling him, "I don't want to stop." The urge to pull the trigger was accompanied by the savagely joyous image of Trench falling to the floor in agony. It took all of Miles's professional training to control himself. Killing Trench now would defeat his purpose: to clear his own name with the police, unmask the real murderers of Carlos Perez and expose the Korean's operation. He had to keep himself from wasting revenge on immediate gratification.

To the sailor he said, "Get undressed."

As the man complied, Miles decided that he had better give Elena little tasks to keep her functional. He could move the fingers on the bandaged hand and, transferring the gun from hand to hand, put on the sailor's outfit with Elena's help. Pain punctuated each movement. The uniform fit loosely and he patted the pockets. As hoped for, he heard the jangle of keys and felt a billfold which Elena took out. Lots of money.

To Trench and the others he said, "Pockets inside out. On the floor."

More keys fell to the ground, along with Lai's stiletto, a pocketknife, a watch on a chain. He prayed he would be able to walk.

Now to get them into the corridor, quickly, because Trench's men were returning. Putting on the sailor suit had given him an idea. "Drop your pants. To your ankles," he ordered them.

They looked at him as if he were mad.

"Do it!"

The harsh, forceful tone was new even to Miles, and slowly Trench began loosening his belt. Lai too. The doctor hesitated and Miles fired into the medicine case, shattering glass. The doctor grabbed his belt. Miles smiled.

"Come here," he said to Trench. The Korean shuffled across the room, tanned muscular legs comical, his trousers bunched around his shoes. Miles pressed the gun against the throbbing temple.

The doctor, pointing at the gasping guard on the floor, said, "What about Sweeney?"

"Nothing I can do." Miles' regret was genuine. "Elena?" He was picturing her, almost catatonic, on the stairway of their building. If that were to happen now, they'd never escape.

She said, "I'm fine," but she sounded terrible.

Holding the gun against Trench's skull, Miles ordered the others into the hall, and like a clown safari they obeyed. Miles followed with Trench and Elena.

He knew the anemic was in one of the adjacent cabins because of Trench's earlier remark, and the anemic would be able to tell him all about the oil. He picked a door and knocked. From within, a petulant voice cried, "Go away!"

He instructed Elena to pull the thick chain of at least a dozen keys from his pocket, then to try the lock.

The first didn't open the door, nor did the second.

Trench had said his men would be here any minute.

She fumbled with the chain. Trying to mask his nervousness, Miles said to Trench, "I'm taking you to the police."

"By all means."

Miles' eyes narrowed, but at that moment came the click of tumblers in the lock. Elena pushed the door open to reveal the anemic, scowling on a bed. His expression grew puzzled. He looked from Miles to the gun to Trench.

The anemic looked at Trench's legs.

He stood up and, like a child, pointed.

Miles said, "We're leaving. Do you want to come?"

Instead of answering, the anemic moved toward the door, fascinated by the whole scene. He said, "I saw them giving you the cables; they really hurt you." He looked at Trench. "This isn't one of his games?"

Miles said, "Hurry. His men will be coming in a couple of minutes."

But the anemic just stared, then broke into great big belly laughs, pointing at their legs, at the trousers bunched about their ankles. He slapped his head, howling like a madman. He fell against the doorway, roaring, and Elena began to smile. Even Miles grinned.

The scientist gasped, "I cannot tell you, sir, how many forms of rescue I have conjured up in my . . . my . . . many months here. I've imagined the Coast Guard boarding this ship, the Marines storming it. I've prayed for a collision which would cast me into the waves. Or the Port Authority conducting an inspection and stumbling on this poor prisoner in the hold, but . . . never, NEVER in my wildest fantasies . . ." He stopped to catch his breath. There was an empty wine bottle on a table. "NEVER did I foresee such a . . . a vaudevillian scene. Grotesque comedy! The infamous Wot Chow Trench with his pants around his knees! It almost makes it all worthwhile. Yes, almost, *almost!*"

Miles said, "We have to go now."

The anemic quieted. "Of course. Others will be coming." He moved into the hall, behind Miles, who ordered Trench's men into the little prison cabin, saying, "If you get out while I'm still on board I shoot him, then you," and told Elena to lock them in.

Then he said to Trench, "Pick up your pants. I want to see Goldstein."

For the first time there was fear in Trench's eyes. He said, "Mr. Goldstein left a while ago."

"You're lying."

"He had to hand in a report. Last one. At his office."

Miles pushed Trench down the corridor and shoved a door open. The cabin was empty. He tried the next one, looked in and retched violently.

Goldstein was tangled up on the floor, head thrown back in death, eyes bulging, a dark-purple line stretching across his Adam's apple. There were brown stains on the head and shoulders and ropes around the wrists.

Whatever last measure of compassion or control Miles might have retained toward Trench disappeared, to be replaced by an inhuman rage, not only for what had happened to the marshal, but for Carlos, Elena, the torture. Before Miles had time to think, he'd pushed the Korean away, leveled the gun between the slanting black eyes, and pulled the trigger twice.

There were two resounding clicks.

The gun was out of ammunition.

The enormity of that revelation stunned them for an instant. Then, with a yell of "No bullets," the Korean hurled himself at Miles, who stepped inside and smashed the gun, full force, into Trench's face. Trench retreated, shielding himself with his arms. Miles advanced on the Korean, whipping his head, neck, shoulders. There was the crack of something breaking. Trench's shirt was drenched with blood, and although he had fallen to his knees, Miles kept hitting him.

He felt hands on his shoulders, pulling him away. Elena was calling his name. "They're breaking out!"

The door behind was shuddering, crashing, cracking. He looked down. Trench was unconscious, breathing fitfully.

Miles straightened, shaky as Elena. The anemic was staring down at Trench emotionlessly.

The three of them raced to the stairwell and up toward

the deck, their footsteps loud in the empty boat. At any minute Trench's men would be after them.

They crashed onto the deck.

But there were voices ahead. "Hey! Where is everybody?" Miles pulled Elena and the anemic back into a corridor, into a room, and they stood against the door, not breathing, until the voices passed. They went out again.

The night was calm, unreal after the scenes below, and the marina was alive with party sounds. They raced along the docks, out of the gate and into the underground lot, then, their footsteps echoing, up a stairway to a circular concrete courtyard bathed in moonlight and covered with graffiti.

Elena was out of breath and Miles had to pull her along, wincing in pain with each step. The anemic needed no urging.

A small forested area provided cover until they reached Riverside Drive. If only they could find a cab . . .

The street was deserted.

He turned, peered back at the park. They waited another half minute, catching their breath, but only a van passed. They ran up to the next street, West End Avenue, which was busier, but there were no free taxis.

Miles was frantic, almost too exhausted to move, but Broadway was only one block away and Broadway was always crowded, even at night.

They were almost there when, looking behind, Miles saw the four figures burst out of the darkness of the park.

FIFTEEN

A VERY small room. Peeling plaster. Brown water-marked walls.

Elena, eyes closed, was in bed beside Miles; the anemic slumped in a chair by the dirty window, an empty bourbon bottle between his legs.

Miles, who was just waking up, didn't remember where he was. Morning light, slanting in through the barred window, warmed his face, and he heard the sounds of a radio outside and an airplane above. He had a feeling he'd been asleep a long time. Although he was drowsy, he felt refreshed.

Slowly, everything came back to him.

All of it—the last-minute arrival of the cab last night;

262

Trench's men watching, helpless; the drive to the police station; and the strange, resulting midnight journey across Manhattan, which had brought them, after several stops, to this hotel.

But right now all those memories were eclipsed by the fantastic explanation the anemic had given him in the cab: how it was possible that oil was under New York.

"Oil!" he'd cried as they bumped along Broadway toward the police station. "They said it was impossible here, but they were wrong! The great East Texas oil field, one of the biggest in North America, wasn't supposed to be there either. A wildcatter brought it in. Hundred thousand barrels a day, but that's nothing compared to what they'll pull out of New York!"

He smiled gleefully, breathing hard, and waved at the streets flowing by. "Look at it out there, and imagine what it was like four hundred million years ago. A vast shallow sea teeming with prehistoric life; microscopic plants and animals, armor-plated fish the size of locomotives. Imagine a series of swiftly flowing rivers feeding that sea, depositing sediments which would turn it into a swamp. Towering trees and ferns, mammoth insects, all dying, becoming part of the land, and the scene alternating every few million years: first the swamp, then the sea, but always the sediments being deposited, one over the other, breaking down the dead plants and animals into carbon, into oil.

"It's the same way oil formed everywhere, but in New York something additional occurred two hundred and fifty million years ago to hide it: an accepted and fantastic geologic event that changed the face of North America and sealed the oil in a tomb three miles deep."

He paused dramatically, enjoying the sight of Miles and Elena hanging on every word, and was suddenly distracted by a neon sign, "LIQUOR." He said, touching his throat,

"Can't we stop for a moment?" and Miles groaned but told the driver to pull over. They bought a bottle of bourbon which the anemic opened as soon as they moved back into traffic. He lowered the level by one-fourth. The air in the cab was becoming rancid.

"So sorry," he shouted happily, holding the bottle to his chest. His voice became hushed. "Some of what I'll tell you now is fact and some is speculation. But events have borne me out.

"Fact. Two hundred and fifty million years ago there occurred, all up and down the East Coast, a mammoth geologic collision called the Appalachian Revolution. A crash of continents. It's true. Part of Nova Scotia was once attached to Europe, and areas in Carolina may have been part of Africa."

Noting the puzzlement on their faces, he balled one hand into a fist and held it up for explanation.

"The earth is like an apple. The continents, our very thin crust, are the skin. The interior is the earth's molten core. The continents float, so slowly that you could never see the movement, but it exists nonetheless.

"Two hundred and fifty million years ago when the collision occurred way out in the Atlantic, the African or European continental plate was driven down into the molten zone underneath the North American plate. The rock heated and swelled. It buckled. It was uplifted. That shove produced the Appalachian Mountains. Oh, it happened slowly, over millions of years, so that the rock could bend, and it resulted in large areas of land being pushed up to one hundred and fifty miles from east to west. In South Carolina, rocks of the east side of the Blue Ridge Plateau moved westward at least forty miles.

"Now the speculation. I'm guessing that a few million years before all this started, lying out to sea, maybe fifty miles from where New York is today, was a large area of metamorphic non-oil-bearing rock. And in layman's terms, when the Appalachian Revolution occurred, the rock was pushed west along the other land masses until it rolled over New York and covered it up. All nature's trickery to conceal her bounty. No one suspected. Exxon, Shell, all the giants with their headquarters literally floating on a subterranean sea, sending their geologists to the jungles of Asia, the Alaskan tundra, the faults and crevices of the Atlantic, and all the while the treasure they sought was under their feet, hidden.

"Until now."

They were stalled in honking traffic on a side street. The scientist treated himself to another draught, smacked his lips and said, "There you have it! And I found it! I cannot tell you, sir, how delightful it is to be off that boat! Look at the streets, the restaurants! I can smell them! Ah, French cuisine! I must see a play! *Cars!* It's all so free and beautiful!"

Still concentrating on the man's story, Miles asked, "How did you know the oil was there if no one else did?"

The alcoholic jerked back from the window, a sly look of pride growing on his face. He nodded in appreciation of a good question, and sipped the bourbon. He melodramatically swept a hand about the cramped cab. "Allow me to introduce myself," he said. "Dr. John Ciccone. Scientist, seismologist, oil finder *extraordinaire!*"

He grinned. Miles smiled back to encourage him.

Dr. Ciccone said, "A seismologist, as you probably know, finds oil with the use of a seismograph, a machine that measures shock waves under the ground. The waves, which we create artificially, shoot into the earth, hit rock, and bounce back. Based on the speed of the rebound we can guess, and the key word is *guess,* what lies below—the kind of rock and the nature of the formation.

"Two years ago I was working near Calgary, Canada.

265

Oil fields there have metamorphic rock on top, sedimentary underneath. Just like Montana, where we have found gas, or, as we now know, New York. Only difference in Calgary is that the metamorphic rock moved from west to east."

He held up the bottle and let the traffic and neon lights play off the glass. "I had a wife. She died." A pause. "But that's another story. I lost the job, drifted east. Levine Carlton Labs in New York was running tests to see what lies beneath the metropolitan area—an academic study. We don't know much about the subsurface rock here, but most people assume since it's metamorphic on top and metamorphic up and down the coast, it's metamorphic all the way down."

He looked ruefully at the bottle, seeming sorry he had not bought another. "You have no idea, sir, how I dreamed about getting off that ship. The absence of people to talk to was awful, of children, women." He gave an embarrassed smile. "In all fairness, Trench did take care of women. At least he had a little compassion. But you want more than . . . well . . ." He looked at Elena. "You know."

"You were talking about metamorphic rock," Miles said.

"Ah, yes. Metamorphic rock. Actually, the rest of the story is simple. I'm a drunk. Yes, I admit it, but in my rare sober moments, few that they are, but they exist anyway . . . this little mind"—he tapped his forehead—"is second to none. When I saw those seismograph readings I thought, *Ah, ha! Just like Calgary!*"

A smile at the memory lit up his face. "But as I've already told you, we can only guess what lies under the ground, and the sad fact is that certain oil-bearing sedimentary rock and certain non-oil-bearing metamorphic rock, *the kind of rock most geologists always assumed was under New York,* gave similar readings! How you interpret the

266

results depends on your own reference points. Sure it was a one-in-a-million shot, but I'm a gambler, a wildcatter, and I was coming from a place where I'd seen something like this. So what if a city was on top of the ground? What was important was what was underneath. I told those scientists, 'Hey! That's a trapped Paleozoic basic with potential down there.'" He winked at Miles. "Oil rock. They disagreed, said the rock was Grenville, metamorphic. They said I was crazy."

He shrugged. "I lost that job too. Drifted to the Far East. Even the sots can still find work in Asia. I kept the readings with me. Met this engineer in Korea. Trench is a big industrialist there, and we got to talking, and—"

"Twenty-Eighth Precinct," the cabby interrupted.

He was careful when he got off the creaking concave bed not to awaken Elena or Ciccone. The threadbare carpet was scratchy against his stocking feet. There was a single bedside table with a phone book but no phone.

The room smelled of Lysol.

For twenty dollars a night Miles didn't really expect more. They'd decided not to waste money on two rooms.

Clomping footsteps passed in the hallway. Probably a prostitute heading for the street. Plenty of them here when they checked in last night.

Or had it been last night? With a start Miles spotted the Burger King bag in the wastebasket and the extra bourbon bottle on the floor. Had Elena and Ciccone gone out? How long had he been asleep?

In the narrow street below, cabs, trucks and pedestrians jostled for space. The owner of a camera store was unlocking a steel grille that had protected his display window all night. Beside him, a black cutout nude silhouette and the words "GIRLS, TOPLESS."

One of the people below looked up and Miles involuntarily moved back two steps, surprised by his reaction. When he looked again the man was sauntering away, but the crowd below filled him with uneasiness. Trench's words kept running through his mind: *A veritable army searches for you. . . . Policemen, firemen, reporters, bartenders. . . ."* Elena had told him about the phone call to Sergeant Pearson, and hadn't Trench, on the boat, seemed almost eager to be taken to the police?

That's why he had changed his mind yesterday evening at the police station at the last minute. When Elena had started to open the door he'd pulled her back. He needed time to think. They'd sat in the cab, watching cops hurrying in and out, as Miles searched face after face, wondering which might belong to Trench's people.

The result had been another destination, a new apartment building on the East Side, with a marble foyer, gilded glass and a doorman who cast disapproving glances at Ciccone's paper bag and Miles in the oversize sailor suit. Twelve stories up they found an old law associate whose welcome smile had faded at the door and become, as Miles told his story, a look of tolerant and sympathetic concern. Out of the blue, at 11:30 p.m., Bradshaw had shown up with a drunk and a strange girl, babbling about oil and torture. Not a believable combination. The stylish wife had never stopped casting horrified glances at the upholstery. Frustrated and in pain, Miles had finally started shouting, "Don't you understand how important this is! I'm telling the truth!" which made everything worse.

The friend had wanted to believe Miles, had even lent him clothing and money despite disapproving looks from his wife, but the tale had sounded as absurd to him as it would have, a scant two weeks before, to Miles.

Small compensation. They'd left.

Then, alone in a way only possible in crowded, impersonal New York, they had bungled a call to *The New York Times,* where a reporter hadn't believed them, and another to CBS, where some bitch of an operator wouldn't even put them through.

Finally, in despair and exhaustion, they'd found the hotel.

He'd slept for twenty-four hours straight, they told him. Ciccone was red-eyed but sober and Elena wanted a toothbrush and comb, a healthy sign, Miles thought. She even joked about the agoraphobia, although her voice, which was strong, still wasn't back to normal. "I'm like one of those amnesiacs who gets hit over the head and gets better."

Miles thought he might call the *Daily News* first today and try to find a sympathetic reporter. Ciccone, who'd been sitting quietly, interrupted his thoughts. "I hope you hurt Trench badly," he said. "He used to bring businessmen to my cabin. Wanted me to tell how I found the deposit. They were arranging some kind of joint venture, Trench and the oil companies. Trench acquires the land and leases it out. Everyone shares profits." He mimicked the Korean. " 'Tell them about the oil, Dr. Ciccone. Maybe we'll open a bottle of wine.' "

Embarrassed, Ciccone went to the closet where two more bottles of bourbon glinted on the top shelf. He picked one up, cradled it in his hand, then put it back.

He said, "I used to imagine myself smashing in his skull with an ashtray, a crowbar, anything. Fantasizing was how I passed the time. Or blowing up his precious well while he watched. It would only take fifteen minutes and wouldn't even require explosives."

"How?" asked Elena.

Ciccone exhibited a vengeful leer, glanced at the bottles

again but closed the closet door. He said, "Most people think a well can't blow out unless it's struck oil, but that's a fallacy. Let me show you what I mean. Imagine two pipes, a thin one and one which is much fatter and hollow inside. The thin pipe, the drill pipe, does the actual drilling. The fat pipe is the *drill casing,* which protects the drill pipe. In between there's empty space, and in that space, pressure can build up, which you can use to do a lot of damage."

His eyes twinkled. "Trench's rig goes down about fifteen thousand feet. Six thousand pounds of pressure per square inch down there. The well, I happen to know, goes through gas pockets and an artesian formation, a highly pressurized underground river. All that gas and water is always ready to shoot out of the hole.

"Obviously, you need something to counterbalance it. Miles, you say you've been to the rig, so you must have seen the mud pit, right?"

Miles nodded.

"Actually that's not pure mud. Barium sulfate is added to make it heavier, and it's pumped into the well and circulated, partially to transport drill cuttings to the surface and partially to keep the water and gas from blowing out. It keeps them down. The mud steams when the drill's in operation because it goes down all the way. Temperature's three hundred degrees down there." Ciccone leaned forward. "Someone wanting to wreck the well would need to get to the controls, stop sending down mud and circulate water instead. Water's lighter. As soon as the balance changed, everything would start shooting out of the hole. A lot of damage. You'd have to speed up the circulation process, but that could be done with another lever."

Miles whistled. "It *is* simple."

"Yes, but I'm not finished yet. Like all wells, Trench's is equipped with a *blowout preventer,* which is, if you can picture this, an eight-ton steel fist poised around the drill casing just above the ground. If a blowout starts, it's sup-

270

posed to close automatically, sealing the hole. A saboteur would have to disable the preventer, maybe by slicing some wiring. Then nothing could stop the blowout."

Miles saw it all, that mud blowing into the faces of Trench's workers, the men scattering in panic, the whole rig roaring and shaking. He said, rubbing his jaw, "But how do you reach the controls? The site is crawling with people."

Ciccone smiled shyly. "I *said* it was only a fantasy."

Impatiently lighting a cigarette Elena said, "Why don't we talk about something practical?"

That brought Miles back to the present. "How much money do we have?"

"Thirty, forty dollars. Enough for one more night."

"We should call the newspapers, the TV and radio stations. Someone has to believe us. If only we had proof. Pictures. And Trench said he was paying off journalists."

"Not all of them," Ciccone said.

"Yeah, but how do we know which ones?"

Elena stabbed out the butt. "Let's forget about the well and go away. You don't even want to go outside. I saw you at the window. And Carlos. You didn't even know him!"

"Are you going to start that again?"

"Yes. He was a stranger! You think he cared about you?"

"You sound like Trench."

"Maybe he's right! He's too smart for us. An organization! You've done all you can. He'll kill us if we stay. We can borrow money and leave. How about your boss? He lent you his car, didn't he?"

"My *boss?*"

She paused. "What's the matter?"

Miles touched his forehead with his fingers. "Oh, God," he said. He looked around dumbly. "I told Trench about my boss. And Slattery. And the professor." He looked up at Elena. "And I've been sleeping for twenty-four hours."

The cleaning lady was outside with her cart and radio

when he pushed out of the room and the desk clerk
wanted money for another night before he'd let Miles
leave. No time to argue. Miles paid, ran into the street and
found a phone booth on a crowded corner. He dialed his
office, and when Samantha answered in her normal bored
voice, he was flooded with relief, but only for a moment.
Marcus came on the line.

"Miles, where are you?"

Only one sentence, yet something was wrong with his
voice. The cadence was too quick, too nervous. "In Manhattan," Miles said. "In trouble. You might be too. Can
you get out of the office for a couple of days?"

A pause, then, "What . . . are . . . you talking about?"
Slow, precise, a total switch in tone. What the hell was
going on?

"Miles? You there?"

"Yeah. Sure." But the voice had been different *again,*
this time containing a note of urgency. Miles realized what
had been wrong with Marcus a moment before.

He had been afraid even as he answered the phone.

So they'd found the supervisor. Miles had an image of
Lai listening on an extension.

"Tell me where you are," Marcus said. "I'll meet you
and we'll talk."

Miles made a quick decision. "In the Village, Twelfth
and University. A place called Bradley's. I'll wait for you."

The voice was hollow with relief. "Okay."

They hung up. Miles immediately dialed the Forty-First
Precinct and yelled that a robbery was in progress at the
poverty office. He hoped Trench would keep Marcus
there and send someone else to Bradley's.

He fell against the booth, heart hammering, trying to
calm himself for the next call.

"Sorry," the sexy secretary at Slattery's office said, "but
Mr. Slattery is in Connecticut until tomorrow. I can't give

272

out the number but I can take a message. Oh, is this Mr. Bradshaw?" the voice lilted. "I remember you. Remember me?"

"Yes, I—"

"You left so quickly the other day we didn't have a chance to talk."

Miles cut her off. "This is urgent. I have to reach him before he comes back to New York. Can you get permission to give me the number?"

"He could call you," she suggested.

"Impossible. I'm moving around."

"Then can I tell him what this is in reference to, Mr. Bradshaw?"

What could he say? She'd never believe the truth. He was dragging more and more people into trouble. "Tell him," he said, his mind working furiously, "the book I'm working on isn't really a novel. It's true. By talking to me the other day he might have gotten himself into trouble."

Lame story, he thought, full of holes, but as long as it kept the construction man in Connecticut, Miles didn't care.

"Trouble?"

"Tell him I'll call him in Connecticut. This afternoon. I'll get back to you for the number."

The professor wasn't in and the woman who answered his phone sounded worried. "He should have been here by now. Who is this?"

"A former student, Miles Bradshaw. It's important that I reach him."

The woman sounded frantic. "Three years I've been his secretary and only twice in all that time has he been late, and both times he called to let me know."

Miles imagined the professor, throat cut like Goldstein.

273

He tried to push the image from his mind. Maybe he was being paranoid, he told himself, and the professor and Marcus were perfectly all right. Maybe the professor had blown a tire somewhere far from a phone. Maybe Marcus had been preoccupied with a family or office problem, and Lai hadn't been there at all. Maybe, but Miles doubted it.

No point in further alarming the secretary. "I'll call back later."

The day clerk didn't look up when he passed. The cleaning cart was still in front of the room and the maid was emptying the wastebaskets. Her radio told him, ". . . the wrap-up of major local stories. Two die in apartment fire in Queens, subway strikers are back on the job after a two-day walkout, and police seek a Bronx attorney in the knife slaying of a city arson inspector."

Ten minutes later, searching through a *Times,* Miles said, "Maybe that's why Marcus sounded so strange. Trench believed me. His people weren't there at all. It was the police."

"Waiting," said Ciccone, gloomily working his way through a *Daily News,* a bottle of bourbon beside him.

Miles' eyes raced along the columns. "There has to be a story about Goldstein here somewhere."

Elena was turning the pages of the *Post.* She said, "Why even look? I'll tell you what we'll find. Trench will have arranged for witnesses, fingerprints, everything."

"Arson Walk Tomorrow" read a headline in Miles' paper, jarring his memory. Another story about the congressman in New York for the National Arson Subcommittee.

"You don't seriously think you're going to take the story to reporters now, do you?" Elena said. "Let's get out. Go to Puerto Rico. We can talk to my mother. She's not that bad. Or Florida. Anywhere. You pick."

Miles didn't answer. Ciccone was fuzzy but coherent. "I think reporters are a bad idea, too. Don't identify yourself and they won't believe you. Identify yourself and they'll go after you for murder. Forget the locals. Try the federal level. Maybe the FBI."

Miles said, "I found the story."

He read them the piece. One "witness" had seen the knifing in the Bronx; another, the body dumped in Manhattan. A complete description of the killer had been given to homicide detectives. Fingerprints and bits of clothing, as well as a wallet, which police guessed must have fallen from the assailant's pocket, had established the identity of the suspect, a former subject of two Goldstein investigations. The suspect was not named.

Elena said, "A wallet, huh?" Miles silently reread the story, wondering who the "witnesses" were. Lai? The doctor? Someone he'd never seen? Were the homicide detectives working for Trench, too?

After a while he said, "One thing I can't figure out. Doesn't Trench realize I'll tell the whole story if I go to trial?"

Ciccone glanced up from the bottle and snorted. "Another nice fantasy. That you would ever reach trial. The distraught attorney is arrested and found hanging in his cell. A fight breaks out in the exercise yard and you end up with a knife in your back. Et cetera, et cetera, et cetera. Trench knows what he's doing."

For a time, they all nursed private thoughts. Then Miles stood up, a weird smile on his face. He said thoughtfully, "You know, in a crazy way I owe that bastard a favor. I was all dead inside and he woke me up. Brought us together. Nothing's making me go back to before, to hiding. If we left, where would we go? Between Trench and the police we'd always be running. Somehow there's a way to beat him here."

He was amazed at his calmness. Perhaps all this calamity

had pushed him into some realm where he could view the situation logically and, at least for the moment, without fear. He placed his hands on Elena's shoulders. "Maybe you were right in the beginning. I shouldn't have gotten involved. Now it's too late." He looked at Ciccone for support. He said, "If we couldn't hurt Trench, he wouldn't be looking for us."

"Brave words in a little room," said Elena.

Another long silence, then the scientist put down the bottle and went to the window. "You're right about not running. But as I said before, a federal agency is safer. The FBI."

Elena laughed bitterly. "Great idea. The FBI turns Miles over to the police while they check his story. By the time they find out he's right, Miles is dead."

"They wouldn't necessarily give him to the local authorities. They'd probably take him into protective custody."

"Probably, but suppose they didn't?"

Ciccone was growing irritated. "Can you think of a better idea?"

And Miles, who had been listening to them and looking at the paper, said, "I can."

It took a long time to reach South Carolina Congressman Peter C. Macklinburg. Miles first had to call Washington, then the Waldorf-Astoria and then an aide named Ruth, but finally the big, booming southern voice came on the line.

"Macklinburg here! I understand you got quite a story for me! Something the subcommittee can sink its teeth into! Ruth is one tough person to convince!"

"Yes, sir," Miles said, pitching all his professionalism into his voice. "I'm a city attorney here in the Bronx."

"Gotcha!"

276

"And it's come to my attention, and I can cite names and records, that a large arson ring is systematically destroying vast tracts of Bronx real estate in order to acquire property. Over a full square mile of tenements is affected. Millions of dollars of property is being burned down."

He had decided not to mention the oil but to get the congressman interested in the arson and let things proceed from there. Macklinburg paused briefly, then said, "My God!"

"It's been going on for several months."

"And you haven't notified the police?"

"No, sir. I have reason to believe that local officials may be cooperating. That's why I'd like to remain anonymous as far as anyone else is concerned. I'm afraid for my job."

"Of course. Rest assured." The voice was getting excited. "And you have *names?* Why this is . . . incredible. Just what I've been looking for. You must come and talk to me in person!"

Miles flashed a smile and thumbs-up signal to Ciccone and Elena, who were watching. He said, "At your convenience."

"Then right now. No. Let me see." Macklinburg excused himself for a moment and returned. "I have a luncheon in half an hour. Then a press conference. What about five o'clock? Suite 605. South lobby elevators."

"Yes, sir. And sir?"

"This is damned amazing."

"As I said before, I don't want the authorities to know who I am, so I'd appreciate it if you could limit the meeting to just ourselves. No police. No arson people. No law enforcement officials of any kind."

Macklinburg agreed. "And you'll bring the records?"

"I don't have the records, sir, but I know where to find them."

"Good enough. Five o'clock then, Mr. . . . ah . . ."

"Dickey."

South Carolina Congressman Peter Macklinburg, head of the congressional subcommittee on arson and possible Vice-Presidential nominee, very slowly placed the receiver in its cradle and unconsciously dried his palms on his trousers. He had known, ever since his recent visit to Trench's yacht in the Mediterranean, exactly how big a goddamn fool he had been for accepting the Korean's cash gifts over the last few years, but the bitter knowledge had come too late. Trench had wanted him to altogether prevent the subcommittee from looking into arson in New York, but that would have been too risky, so Macklinburg had steered the investigation to Brooklyn, ignoring protests by Bronx congressmen.

He had thought, until five minutes ago, that he had weathered the storm, but now, dear God, someone had found out about the burnings. And how close were they to finding out about the oil, too?

His immediate inclination was to call Trench, but if he did that, he had few illusions as to what the wily Korean might do to Mr. Dickey.

On the other hand, if he didn't notify Trench, he was afraid of what Mr. Dickey's disclosures might do to Peter C. Macklinburg.

He wasn't a bad person, just, on occasion, a weak one, and he tried to convince himself to meet with Dickey, tell him in private that he would take care of everything, and shut the man up.

But suppose Dickey eventually went to the papers?

Again he slid the palms back and forth over his knees. Why couldn't Dickey have called anyone, *anyone* else? Why him?

At least he agreed with Dickey about keeping the police away from this afternoon's meeting.

Macklinburg told his aide to leave the room and then he called Trench. He asked the Korean not to hurt Mr. Dickey.

"He believed me!" Miles shouted, emerging into the sunlight. "Five o'clock at the Waldorf. I can convince him!"

He danced a jig in the street.

Ciccone, grinning, said, "They televise congressional hearings, don't they? The important ones? I can just see Trench squirming under the lights. And the Arabs. Their faces when the oil starts coming out of the ground."

They triumphantly congratulated one another. After a moment Elena said, "What about Goldstein?"

Miles sobered and put an arm around her shoulder. "Once Trench has been arrested and the facts about the oil are known, then I'll turn myself in to the FBI. They'll be ready to believe me. The congressman will back me up." She didn't respond. He said, "I know it's chancy, but at least we're in a better position than we were ten minutes ago. This phone call is the first good thing that's happened since we got off the boat. I'm starved. Let's celebrate." He looked at the Times Square clock. "I want to be at the Waldorf early, three-thirty."

Elena and Ciccone shot him inquiring glances.

Miles said, "To make sure Macklinburg keeps his word about not calling the police. I don't want to take any chances." He told them that he would go alone, watching Elena for her reaction.

She said, "I'll be fine," but she looked away.

The lobby of the Waldorf-Astoria was smaller than Miles had expected, but more lush, Empire style, guarded by two porcelain lions. The high ceiling was supported by four fat black marble columns. Potted palms prevented an overall view of the room. A blue settee occupied a central location and was topped by the gold-leaf Waldorf clock, which chimed a quarter to the hour and which was crowned by a gold-leaf statue of Liberty. "WELCOME CHRISTIAN SCIENTISTS," read lettering on a board by the bellhop desk. "MEATCUTTERS OF AMERICA." "TRANSCENDENTAL ALUMNI."

Miles bought a newspaper from the purple-clad bell captain and, after strolling about the lobby, seated himself on the settee so that he faced a chandeliered lobby which led to the Park Avenue entrance. From here he also had a good view of the elevator bank. He opened the paper. An hour and ten minutes until his appointment.

Elena and Ciccone were waiting in a coffee shop across Park Avenue. He had the telephone number there in case something went wrong. Miles alternately glanced around the lobby and searched for more stories about Goldstein.

He played with the idea of telling Macklinburg his real name and rejected it. He would tell the congressman that Dickey was a false identity and that he preferred to remain anonymous. Surely the congressman would be sympathetic to a frightened informer.

He reminded himself to phone Slattery in Connecticut, as well as the professor.

Fifteen minutes passed and no uniformed policemen entered the lobby, nor anyone who looked like a plainclothesman. He would avoid discussing oil and explain, logically and coolly, how his own interest in arson had been aroused when he had witnessed the death of Carlos Perez and had been heightened by peculiarities in real-estate records.

He had a list of landlords with him.

Ten more minutes. No police.

Uncomfortably, he realized that someone was spying on him from beside the lions, a man in black, gold wire-rimmed glasses. Hotel man, he figured, and wondered if he should leave and return at five, but the prospect of walking into the meeting blind made him too uncomfortable.

The man looked away.

By four-twenty he was starting over the *Post* for the second time.

At four-thirty Trench appeared in the hallway.

He knew it was Trench only because Lai and Ravenel were there too. The stocky Korean was swathed in bandages, his face and head obscured. His bulky shoulder suggested padding under the jacket. His step was as brisk and determined as ever, however, hinting of anger.

Miles registered a moment's pleasure that he had hurt Trench so badly, but the emotion passed instantly. He was directly in the path of the advancing trio, his face shielded by the *Post*.

He wanted to bolt but knew that was impossible. They would see him the moment he stood up and all they would have to do was yell for the police. Miles saw himself being pursued through the lobby, tackled on the street, dragged into a precinct house yelling about oil. They would throw him into a cramped cage like the detention area at Fort Apache, maybe into one of those five-by-five offices where Trench himself, or Trench's cops, or Trench's fire inspectors, or Trench's congressman for God's sake, because didn't the Korean have the whole goddamn world on his payroll, could work him over while Trench said things like "I don't want to stop." And this time would be much worse than last time, as hard as that was to imagine, because Trench would be seeking revenge for the beating. This time would make the boat look like playland. Miles tried to keep the paper from trembling. For what seemed like an eternity he didn't move, praying that Trench and the drones would go upstairs.

Cautiously, he inched the paper away from his eyes.

Trench and Lai were gone.

Ravenel was still there, looking at the lions.

A real sightseer, that Ravenel, and now the sailor decided he wanted to look over the glass case of crystal nearby, the potted palms, the . . . uh oh . . . the clock.

Ravenel had spotted that gold-leaf Statue of Liberty three feet above Miles' head and he was drifting over. No hurry. Ten feet and closing. No way he could reach the settee without seeing who was crouching behind the newspaper. Miles's heart was pounding like one of the machines in the construction site.

The shoes, polished and black, came into view below the paper, and stopped. Had Ravenel seen him? Was the sailor standing there, joy and amazement stretching across the face? What the hell was he doing?

Miles tensed for the dash.

But another pair of shoes appeared, smaller, and Miles was close enough to hear Lai's annoyed whisper. "Trench is furious. What are you doing down here? Bradshaw could come early."

Yeah, Miles thought, *early,* and fought off the hysterical urge to laugh. The shoes moved away.

He counted to fifty and peeked out at the lobby.

The man with the wire rims was watching him again, but Lai and Ravenel had gone.

He exited quickly through the Lexington Avenue door and found a phone from where he called Elena and Ciccone to tell them to avoid Park Avenue, as he had done, to avoid being spotted from above.

He was shocked by what had happened in the lobby, but he wasn't surprised.

282

And then in the middle of the street, cars honking at him to get out of the way, he realized to whom he could turn for help, who couldn't possibly be reporting to Trench. At that moment he decided what he had to do and who could help him do it; who, without a doubt, would *have* to help him do it; who had as much to lose as he did.

It was, he knew, his very last chance.

And Trench had shown him where to find it.

SIXTEEN

"YOU'RE CRAZY," Rodriguez said.

The president of the Latin Kings drew his boots across the top of his desk and dropped them to the floor. The ceiling fan circulated slowly. The meth clinic office smelled of wood, smoke and cheap, pungent after shave. Rodriguez was wearing a black tee shirt which bulged at the biceps and tapered along the lean, muscular torso. His crowned denim jacket was draped over the back of the brown swivel chair and he rocked back and forth, chewing gum.

Two more Kings watched from the doorway.

Rodriguez said, "You want to go *back* into the construction site after what you've told me?"

Miles was outwardly calm but his chest was constricted

with fear. By prearrangement with Elena and Ciccone, he had done all the talking during their surprise visit, telling Rodriguez, after preliminary banter, about the oil, the secret well, the Korean who, by means of arson, was acquiring land. He outlined to him about how he wanted to sabotage the well and get proof of its existence for the papers.

"Trench has been paying arsonists a few dollars to burn properties that'll be worth millions," he had said. "And making fools out of the people working for him."

Rodriguez' eyes had narrowed at that, which was good, but Miles had the feeling, when he lied about not knowing who the arsonists were, that Rodriguez didn't believe him. That was very bad. Rodriguez had glanced at the doorway at that point and one of the Kings had gone off. Miles figured he was collecting troops and once again remembered Freddy the half-wit.

Flight was out of the question. The main chance for safety lay in an alliance with the Kings, but Miles was unsure whether Rodriguez, after realizing the precariousness of his own position, would see the logic of joining forces or just lose his temper.

Touchy bastard, Miles thought. *Has to be treated with the right mixture of deference and strength.*

His major regret was that he had allowed Ciccone and Elena to convince him, after a long argument, that they should accompany him here. He didn't like the way Rodriguez was looking at Elena, and he was afraid the other Kings would come back before he had a chance to finish what he wanted to say.

He hadn't even reached the tricky part yet.

He felt the sweat on his back but willed himself to concentrate on Rodriguez, who still might be won over if Miles could keep him interested with a carefully planned series of disclosures.

Casually, as if he had no idea that word of his presence was spreading below, he said, "It'll be much more dangerous to go in this time. They might have extra guards, guns."

Rodriguez nodded, feigning interest, killing time. "You sound like you want me to keep the Kings out," he said. "Why should I help you?"

Here goes, Miles thought. "Three reasons. First, they killed your friend Carlos Perez."

That jarred him. Rodriguez leaned back, reached behind the chair and came up with a package of cigarettes which turned out to be empty. He crumpled it up and threw it at a wastebasket. It missed. One of the Kings picked it up.

Rodriguez demanded, "How do you know?"

"I saw the fire, remember?"

"You *saw* them kill him?"

"He was tied up. Who else would have done it? Remember you told me the name of the landlord? When I went to see him someone tried to kill *me*. And then later, when Goldstein and I found out the burned buildings were being sold, they tried again." He paused. "Maybe Carlos saw something. Maybe he went into the site to steal plumbing and they caught him."

Rodriguez said, visibly disquieted, "And Goldstein. That cop. Where's he?"

Miles told him. "The police are blaming me for the murder."

One of the Kings at the door said something about hearing the Goldstein story on the radio. *Shock number two*, Miles thought. Keep him off balance and maybe I can finish and convince him.

Rodriguez said, "They're looking for *you?*"

"Trench arranged it."

"You? That's crazy! You, kill a guy?" Rodriguez started to laugh.

286

Miles said, "I don't need your fucking levity."

Rodriguez shut up. For a moment Miles thought he might have overstepped his bounds, but the King looked away, shifting uncomfortably in his chair.

After a minute he said, "Carlos wasn't a member." But he was obviously turning over everything in his mind. "You said three reasons. That's two."

This was going to be the most dangerous part. Miles watched the face carefully. He said, "They're after you too."

The eyes slowly met his own. The office was utterly silent. There were footsteps coming closer in the hall. Miles said, "They know you helped me break into the site."

"And *how* do they know that?"

"Because I told them."

When Rodriguez stood up his shoulders seemed much more powerful, more taut. A vein was throbbing on his forehead. Miles guessed four or five Kings were in the doorway, but he didn't dare look. Rodriguez' pupils seemed to have grown smaller. He didn't seem like a fifteen-year-old anymore.

He came around the side of the desk, boots scraping. Rodriguez looked closely into his face. His thumbs were hooked in his belt and his breath smelled of smoke and sugar. He repeated, much too quietly, "You told them."

Miles knew if he looked away, even for an instant, Rodriguez would lose control. Instead he slowly began unbuttoning his shirt, the angry Kings watching. Miles's chest was covered with ugly prominent welts which he pointed to, one by one. "They did this to me," he said. He described what had happened: the electroshock, the doctor, Trench's relentless interrogation, and Goldstein's betrayal and death.

Rodriguez' expression remained icy at first, but as the tale progressed the look changed to reluctant interest, doubt, disgust, maybe even, for an instant, sympathy.

Miles concluded, "Maybe it's wrong that I told them about you, but you've never felt anything like that machine. I held out a long time. *I protected you.* And I'm *not* a member, but now they know. I heard Trench say so. He was standing next to me."

Rodriguez was leaning on the desk, looking at the floor, cheeks sucked in. Miles risked a glance at the door. Sure enough, the troops were standing around uncertainly, big guys, watching Rodriguez to follow his cue. Ciccone was trying to steady his hands in his lap. Elena reached over and squeezed Miles' arm. Her touch was cold.

Rodriguez was quiet for a long time. He pushed himself off the desk after a while, looked at the ceiling, the walls. He paced the room, fell into his chair, drummed his knuckles on the desk. The Kings at the door muttered in Spanish but Miles didn't turn around. His heart was thudding like crazy.

Rodriguez said, "This guy Trench. If he's so smart and he moves so fast, how come he hasn't come after me yet?"

And Miles, praying he had been right about why Rodriguez had sent for reinforcements, knowing the boy wouldn't take another shock, calmly said, "He needs you to burn more buildings."

Rodriguez' face fell. He muttered, his answer flooding Miles with relief, "Yeah, I guessed you knew about that."

He looked at the Kings in the doorway.

Miles started talking again to keep Rodriguez from giving any orders. "The man who does the killings is the same one who pays for the fires. A short Oriental. Lai is his name. Real friendly face. He runs the construction site. After you take care of the last fire, then he'll come for you."

"Yeah, yeah," Rodriguez acknowledged the truth of what Miles was saying. He was quiet a moment longer, the turmoil evident on his face. Then suddenly he was up, pointing, all the anger spilling out. "You had to tell them! That half-wit, Freddy! We can do it to you too!" He swept his arm about, including Ciccone and Elena in the gesture. "All of you!" The other Kings moved into the room.

The exit was blocked. Rodriguez ranted, "Who asked you to come in the first place? Carlos shouldn'ta gone in there! You Anglo bastard! You don't even know what you're dealing with! A billionaire. Yeah, a billionaire. What the fuck do we do with a billionaire?"

He fell back in the chair, trembling with rage, looking at the other Kings as if he'd forgotten they were there or couldn't decide what to do with them. It would go either way any second.

Fighting off his fear, Miles forcefully pressed home his arguments.

"Kill us and what happens to you? Only Dr. Ciccone knows how to sabotage that well, and I'll take the pictures and get to the papers. I know where to go. They'll believe us. Between us we can do it. Separately we won't."

He sat down. The Kings had surrounded his chair, their shirts at eye level.

Rodriguez' pupils went back to normal size. His breathing grew steady. He looked slowly around the office. Still hesitant to commit himself, he said, "Three reasons. What's the third?"

And Miles answered, "Sixty thousand dollars."

Ten minutes later, after Miles had explained that he would turn over his wife's insurance policy if the Kings would get him into the site, after Rodriguez had sent the drones back to the door, after Miles had congratulated himself for letting the cash be the clinching argument, Rodriguez asked, "How do I know you're telling the truth?" He folded his powerful arms across his chest. "About the money, the oil, all of it. And the guy . . . the guy who you say wants to kill me."

289

Miles stood up. For the moment he had won. He said, "I'll show you the records. They're public. And we'll go to the construction site. You'll see Lai there and you'll know."

They were careful to approach the site from the rear, jolting along cobblestone streets in the same ancient Chevy in which Miles had ridden before. He sat in back with Rodriguez. The driver was a forgettable-looking King who had an endless supply of reefers that Miles declined but Rodriguez didn't.

They had already visited the real-estate office.

Elena and Ciccone were back at the clinic with other Kings, an arrangement Miles didn't like but had not protested.

Once this had been a busy factory area. The few apartment buildings Miles saw were abandoned. They passed an out-of-place-looking ice cream truck dispensing wares to school-age children. The windows were rolled down and the air was cool but not chilly.

After a while they halted before a vacant tenement and got out. The driver took a bag of food and a pair of expensive-looking binoculars from the trunk. He handed the latter to Rodriguez and they moved up the cracked brick stoop. One or two boards blocked the doorway. They ducked under, and then they were inside.

Rat droppings and sandwich wrappers left by other visitors littered the hallway. The floor was coated with dust but was otherwise sound. Miles tried to imagine, as they mounted the steps, what had caused the tenants to leave. Fire? Crime? Had the heating failed in the winter? Good buildings like this were the first to be abandoned.

A flash of color on the third landing caught his eye and he stepped into an apartment, then blinked in surprise. Dozens of brightly colored papier-mâché balls and broken

290

toys filled a corner, near a pile of filthy blankets. There was a makeshift bed with some empty wine bottles beside it. Miles looked into a large cardboard box under the window and recoiled. A dog lay inside, neck broken.

From the doorway Rodriguez said, "Bums."

Miles pictured some derelict up here alone at night, those warm summer evenings, doing God knows what with the toys and the paper. The image, frighteningly incomprehensible, made him shudder.

Rodriguez called him back to the stairway.

On the fifth floor he discovered what had emptied the building: fire. Two blackened apartments had had their windows broken and smelled of charred plaster and wood and rainwater. Rodriguez watched him sideways as he inspected the premises. He realized the Kings had started the blaze. For what, fifty dollars? Miles forced himself to remain calm. He couldn't afford to antagonize Rodriguez.

But when they reached the roof he forgot about his anger and understood the wisdom of coming here. They were a block and a half from the construction site with a generally unobstructed view. It was windy but the sun was strong. They crouched by the rampart, gravel warm on their knees. Rodriguez slipped the binoculars over his neck. The bulldozer roar rose from below and workers scurried, antlike, about the lot. Miles looked down on rubble yards and stripped cars.

Rodriguez raised the field glasses. "Now we'll see," he said.

He scanned the site slowly. Thirty minutes passed. The driver retreated to a corner, slumped against the wall and pulled a ham sandwich from the bag.

Miles said, "Sometimes Lai stays in the building all day."

Rodriguez grunted. Miles couldn't find the black Torino below but perhaps it was hidden by a building. The driver finished a Coke and shattered the bottle against the chimney, Rodriguez spinning at the sound. Green shards of glass glittered in the sun.

The driver apologized.

After an hour Rodriguez, growing irritated at the wait, mumbled, "No one's working. They're just moving dirt." He tried a sandwich and snapped at the driver. "This is fat. I hate fat." Sheepishly, the driver offered half of his share and Rodriguez took a bite. Grudgingly, "That's better." Miles worried that he might decide to leave.

The glasses went up again. Miles asked if he could take over but Rodriguez shook his head. The driver napped. Forty-five minutes dragged by, an hour, an hour and a half. Rodriguez continued to hold the binoculars firmly in place, amazing Miles with the strength of his arms, which must have been aching badly. The breeze picked up. By nightfall it would be cold. A group of kids on bicycles shot by below like a marauding pack.

Then Rodriguez said, "I see him."

It was Lai, all right. He had come out of the building and, framed in that big binocular **O** was summoning workers, who moments later disappeared inside with him.

All Rodriguez said, "You were right."

He turned and his friend followed. Miles wanted to pick up the trash they had left behind but felt self-conscious about it. Downstairs, on the third landing, they were halted by a weird childlike guttural singing from the apartment with the papier-maché. Inside, on the blankets, legs in lotus position and dead dog on his lap, a huge derelict sat rocking, cooing a giant's lament in a sea of bright crumpled paper.

"Used to be a pretty nice building," Rodriguez said when they got outside. "Okay, we'll do it. After we get the money."

The home office of the American Insurance Company, fifteen stories above Manhattan, featured Hellenic statues, a fountain in the reception area, and a "policy executive" named Miss Chang, a petite woman with an unnerving expectant smile and bright businesslike manner.

After guiding Miles into her small, comfortable office, she said, poring over a manila folder on her desk, "Your agent told us you were coming. We've been looking for you for months but we had no address. Once the arson people concluded their investigation and we had the death certificates, the money was yours. Actually it's been collecting interest, so it will be more than the face value of the policy. Just sign the loss-of-policy statement and we'll fix you right up."

Miles tried to keep himself from appearing as nervous as he felt. He had not liked the idea of venturing into Manhattan, or even out on the street, when the police were looking for him. Last night he'd slept at the meth clinic with Elena, their bedroom an old factory area they'd swept clean. Ciccone had been next door. This morning he'd called the insurance agent, surprising the man by demanding the face value of Paula's policy. The agent had told him it would take two weeks to get the money because it would be necessary to write the home office for a check.

Rodriguez wanted the money now so Miles decided to come to the home office himself. In return for this risky appearance, Rodriguez, who was waiting outside, had called his "war counselor" this morning and ordered him to spend the day on the roof across from the construction site, watching and planning.

An inquisitive smile spread across Miss Chang's face. She said, closing the folder, "I must confess I wondered why you wanted the money immediately, especially after such a long time." She blushed. "Personal curiosity. People

293

are so different. If you don't want to answer, please say so."

"I don't want to answer."

"I see." The smile disappeared. "If you'll please wait here." She left the office with an offended glide.

Miles glanced at the "Saleswoman of 1974" award, the photos of the husband and little girl, and he couldn't help but think about Paula and his own daughter. It hurt him deeply to be using the insurance money. The old series of images crowded in, strong as ever: the Carson show, the cigarette smoldering on the mattress, the smoke under the bathroom door, the flaming curtain falling over his daughter's head, the firemen pulling him out the bathroom window.

He shook himself. Miss Chang was standing in front of him, a rectangular blue piece of paper in her hand.

"Sixty-five thousand with interest," she said.

The bank was full of uniformed guards and TV cameras, the teller a willowy, balding man with a clipped nasal voice. "Am I to understand, sir, that you want to *cash* this check?"

"That's right."

Rodriguez was standing by Miles's side. The teller eyed him suspiciously. "But it's for sixty-five thousand dollars and you don't have an account with us, sir."

Rodriguez snapped, "What's the problem?"

Miles wished he would go away.

He smiled, all politeness, and laid his wallet on the counter. "Yes, but my insurance company has an account here. Your bank's letterhead is on the check. Here are my driver's license and credit cards. You can call American, ask for a Miss Chang. She'll verify who I am."

Rodriguez and the teller watched each other. The teller licked his lips. "Could you wait here a moment?"

"Of course," Miles said. He thought, *run.*

The teller shimmied off. Rodriguez hissed "Faggot" after him. Miles watched the man make his way across the lobby to a series of desks occupied by bank officers. The teller cupped his hand when he spoke to a woman at one of the desks. She looked guardedly at Miles and nodded.

Rodriguez appeared to be casing the place. A guard observed him from the door.

The teller returned. "Follow me, please."

Miles motioned Rodriguez to stay where he was. The woman across the lobby listened to his explanation, called Miss Chang, talked a little and listened a lot. Miles suffered a whole series of police-capture visions, watching Rodriguez wander around conspicuously.

Finally the woman hung up. She was quite sympathetic now. "Please excuse our precautions. Miss Chang explained everything. You want the entire sixty-five thousand?"

Miles shook his head, instituting the part of his plan of which Rodriguez was ignorant. "Just forty-five. I'd like to start an account with the rest."

The woman beamed. "Excellent. Just fill out these papers. I'll get the passbook and the money."

She left.

Fifteen minutes went by.

Twenty-five.

Forty. Had she lied about the phone call?

She returned, gave him the book and placed neat rows of bills in the attaché case he'd brought. Miles thanked her and walked back to Rodriguez, who was smiling wolfishly. He gave the King the case.

"Forty-five thousand dollars," he said.

The smile faded. "Forty-five? You said sixty."

"That's right. Twenty after. An extra five with interest now."

It was his no-nonsense voice. Rodriguez looked unde-
cided for a moment, then his expression changed to
grudging respect.

His mood improved when he laid the case on a glass-
topped table and opened it.

"Forty-five thousand dollars," he whispered, looking at
the bills.

He surprised Miles by counting out the five thousand in
interest, returning to the teller, and starting an account
for himself. He grinned as they left the bank. "Ever tell
anyone about that money and you're dead."

Elena and Ciccone were waiting in Rodriguez' office
when Miles returned. He recounted the day's events.
Jesús, the war counselor, ambled in. He had a cold and
was sniffling in a way that made him look about eleven
years old. He and Rodriguez went into a corner where
they gleefully counted money, periodically tossing packets
into the air and laughing.

Rodriguez snapped the attaché case shut when he was
finished counting and said, "Jesús will tell us what he saw."
He looked expectantly at Elena.

She looked back, confused.

It took about a minute, then Rodriguez said, "Well?"

"Well what?" Elena replied.

Rodriguez and Jesús glanced at each other. They were
growing irritated. To Miles, Rodriguez said, "Isn't she
going to leave?"

Miles thought he must be missing something. "Leave?"
he repeated dully. "Why should she leave?"

"Whaddaya mean why? There's work. We don't want
girls here."

Miles looked at Rodriguez as if he were from another
planet. Elena chortled dangerously, hands on her hips.

Her tone was getting edgy. She said, "I don't believe this. You want me to go because you don't conduct business in front of women?"

"Yeah."

"That's the stupidest thing I ever heard."

Rodriguez jerked. The pale-blue eyes grew flinty and the lips formed a thin line. Nobody talked to him like that. Unsure how to ease an increasingly volatile situation, Miles said softly, "Elena?"

She impaled him with a look. "Don't tell me you're going to ask me to go, too! I got you off that boat and I have as much right to be here as . . . no . . . more than you!" She glared at Rodriguez. "I'm not going."

She sat down haughtily. For a moment Rodriguez was too astounded to respond. He stood absolutely still, mouth slack, hands at his sides in shock. Then the fingers curled and he began to move toward Elena while Miles, afraid he might hit her, was getting up, thinking bitterly, *Such a stupid way to end it. A fight over this.*

Rodriguez said quietly, "Get out."

Slowly, she shook her head.

Miles winced, expecting the explosion, but Rodriguez surprised him. He went behind the desk, sat down, put his feet up and pulled a *Sgt. Rock* comic from a drawer. He looked at Miles as if to say, "She's your problem, not mine."

He began to read.

He mouthed the words silently.

Jesús sat down also. If the president was calm so was his war counselor. Periodic sniffles broke the silence. The room seemed like a funeral parlor. If Miles hadn't known the dangerous tempers of the antagonists he would have burst out laughing.

He told himself, frustrated, that he needed this boy and could not afford to antagonize him. For all Rodriguez'

297

forced blandness, he was seething inside and Miles didn't know how long Rodriguez could maintain control.

On the other hand, he was afraid if he tried to reason with Elena she might explode.

She said to Rodriguez, glancing from his face to the comic book, "Having trouble pronouncing the big words?"

Rodriguez' mouth kept moving as if he had not heard.

She leaned over the desk, on her elbows. Her voice was honeyed ice. "You can sit there all afternoon."

Jesús blew his nose on a ratty-looking tissue. He wiped his face on his sleeve. Ciccone, looking from Rodriguez to Elena, said, "Elena, perhaps it would be more practical, considering the circumstances, if you left us alone this one time."

Instead, she said something in Spanish, and Rodriguez jerked again, glanced at her murderously and shot something back in the same tongue. When she responded he turned purple and started to get up.

He stopped himself, took a deep breath. He went back to reading.

But Elena was incensed now and the Spanish came shooting out. Rodriguez calmly turned a page. She pounded on the desk. He didn't look up. She started on Miles, pointing; at Ciccone, Jesús, all of them. She was rabid, white-faced in fury.

There was no response from Rodriguez but his ears were red. Her hand was on the door. She showed her teeth. She threw up her hands.

She slammed the door behind her.

Rodriguez looked up a moment later, smiling. "To business," he said.

Jesús had drawn a map. The four men clustered around it while the war counselor outlined his plan. The voice was nasal, the eyes watery. Once again, the reasoning awed Miles. Jesús was a little Napoleon.

"This is the whole Forty-First Precinct." The boy indicated a bloblike shape encompassing most of the paper. "Over here"—he pointed to a small box—"the construction site. I waited until five o'clock, closing time. Sixteen, seventeen men went in when the workers came out. Uniformed guards. Private service. Most of them went into the building. They had guns." He looked at each of them. "And Dobermans. Maybe six." He glanced at Rodriguez. "You were right yesterday. We can't go in at night. They'd be ready. I'd *rather* go in at night . . . we couldn't be seen from the street . . . but . . ."

He looked uncomfortable. Miles blanched. "But during the day, all those workers?"

Jesús shrugged unhappily. "Rodriguez says we gotta go in. If we gotta go in at least the workers won't be armed. It'll be easier."

Ciccone was looking ill. "But there are so many of them."

Rodriguez snapped, "You got a better idea? You're the guys who got us in trouble."

Miles grimaced, feeling icy barbs in his chest just listening to this.

Jesús said, "I figure we go in daytime, maybe lunchtime, when the workers are all together, standing around. Just before they leave the site. We use three cars. Boom! Through the gate, right after the police patrol passes. One or two guys in the candy store across the street. One guy to cut the phone wire. Five guys to keep guns on the workers while the others go in the building."

Miles, envisioning the Chevy's crashing through the gate, the Kings leaping out, the potential battle with the workers, asked himself if he had done the right thing convincing Rodriguez to commit himself to the attack.

299

Rodriguez pointed at the comic book on the desk and said, with a halfhearted smile, "Just like Sergeant Rock."

Jesús grinned. He looked ten now. "Or the Dirty Dozen."

Rodriguez said, "Or the Dirty Three Dozen."

When they laughed some of the tension eased. Jesús rapped the desk. "Now we get to the cops," he said. "See this X? It's Fort Apache. And this," he said, pointing to a little mark on the other side of the map, "is a bank. South Bronx Community Savings and Loan. On a side street. Real tiny. We get Denise or Esmeralda to call the Fort, yell there's a robbery at the bank. The cops freak out and send all their cars. We get a couple of Kings, guys with licenses, to pretend an accident. Block off both ends of the street. Two accidents. Maybe we could wreck a junk or maybe a traffic jam. The cops can't get out if someone calls about the construction raid."

Miles gaped. "That's brilliant."

Jesús glowed like a seventh grader who's just won the spelling bee.

Miles said, "I would never have thought of these things: extra police cars, a lunchtime assault. What a mind!"

"And no one wears King jackets," Jesús said.

Rodriguez basked in the admiration, too, the enmity of several moments before forgotten. "That's why *I* made him war counselor," he said.

Jesús sneezed again. The sleeve was getting dirtier. He redirected them to the desk. "One last problem, the police patrol that passes the site. Today it went by five minutes to noon, then again at twelve-forty. If that's a daily schedule just maybe we'll have enough time. If not we have to delay the patrol. Snatch a purse or something." To Ciccone, Jesús said, "You sure you know how to fuck up that machinery in there?"

Ciccone was green. "Most assuredly, sir. It will be my . . . uh . . . pleasure."

And to Miles, "And if we don't do it they'll be coming after us for the other attack?"

"That's right."

Jesús sighed. Rodriguez said, looking at each of them in turn, "Imagine what they'll look like when we come through those gates." He threw up his hands like a kid at a birthday party. "Sur-PRISE!"

Rodriguez had three lieutenants who had to be informed of the plan before they told the troops. Miles and Rodriguez drove off to gather them.

Guillermo, the first, lived in a surprisingly well furnished apartment, with pictures of Puerto Rico on the walls, a smiling patrician father, silver-haired, and everyone respectful and well behaved. The mother insisted they stay for dinner and they agreed, Rodriguez bafflingly polite and deferential to the father. They talked about baseball for forty minutes. Finally they excused themselves. The three of them wedged into the front seat of the Chevy.

"Twenty years ago Guillermo's father was president of the Kings," Rodriguez said.

The second lieutenant was Pablo, a corpulent, waddling boy in a dirty Kings jacket whose parents were apparently in the latter rounds of a battle when they arrived. Two smelly dogs and a dirty little girl sat by a TV whose picture was rolling. There were bags of garbage in the kitchen and the screaming was nonstop. Pablo seemed eager to get out. When they left Miles said, trying to come up with conversation, "Some fight your parents were having."

Pablo picked at a food particle between his teeth with an index finger. "Who says they're my parents?"

Alphonso, the third lieutenant, had come on the first construction raid, Rodriguez said, and had no family. They tried the pinball palace first, then a park where boys without shirts were shooting baskets, a park where boys with shirts were shooting up, a park where no one was doing anything, and finally a formica and linoleum Asian and Cuban restaurant where a single harried waiter did both the cooking and serving. The room was filled with Spanish chatter and the pungent smells of beans, rice and steaming meats. Rodriguez waved away the waiter. Alphonso, a handsome, intelligent-looking kid, was in the back with a raven-haired beauty. When he saw them he stood up and threw money on the table. The girl looked up at him adoringly.

He said, "Later."

"And so," Rodriguez concluded two hours later, "that's why you've been picked for this."

This time he was addressing the entire assault crew, twenty-five Kings, upstairs at the meth clinic, in a cavernous old factory room which magnified his voice. Miles' and Elena's sleeping bags had been pushed into a corner. The Kings, ranging in size, shape and disposition, some smoking, some lounging against the wall in a sort of universal tough-guy pose, some sprawled or sitting on the floor, were rapt.

If Miles had ever had any doubts about why Rodriguez was leader of the Latin Kings, they had evaporated during the masterful presentation. Miles had rejected the patriotic appeal, but Rodriguez had laid it on thick. The neighborhood was being raped. All their friends were in trouble: the little storekeepers, their parents, their girl friends. He'd brought up the sixty thousand dollars early, hooking them with equal shares. The Kings were in great danger, he said, all because of "that guy." He pointed to Miles, who squirmed under the group stare and thanked Rodriguez under his breath. "That guy" had convinced them to assault a construction site a few nights ago and now it turned out that a big gang owned the site and would be seeking revenge. The Kings had to strike back first. Jesús had one of his usual foolproof plans.

They'd be on the site for only fifteen minutes, he said. With good planning they'd get out untouched to enjoy twenty-four-hundred-dollar shares.

He added a word about the gang that ran the site. Fortunately, the Kings had not offended "the mob" or "the syndicate." The enemy was powerful but isolated, and if the attack succeeded, the police might never know. The other gang wouldn't want to call attention to itself.

He finished up. "Twenty years ago the Kings were started to protect the neighborhoods." The minions nodded agreement. "Your fathers, my father, they didn't like the Anglos beating up their fathers and mothers. So we formed to protect ourselves, and we got respect."

Miles looked at the ceiling. *I don't believe this.*

"Well, now, it's just like then, except maybe it's a little more dangerous. But remember the Mighty Devils? When Pablo Mendez ran the Kings? The big assault on 256th Street? Six, seven guys landed up in the hospital from that. Yeah, one guy got killed." They were silent, remembering the story. "But those fucking Mighty Devils, they never came back after that. We hurt them and they ran. Our big brothers got hurt in that fight. Now we gotta do it."

Rodriguez fell silent and hooked his thumbs in his belt and sauntered into the human cul-de-sac. Any questions? He stared malevolently at the troops. Miles held his breath. Rodriguez' eyes swept the floor once, twice . . .

Someone stepped into the open.

Miles thought, *That one. He didn't look happy during the talk.*

He was maybe six feet tall, older than most of them, maybe as old as twenty. He wore the traditional summer denim jacket but his hair was longer than most. A narrow, suspicious face. He said, looking at Miles with disgust, "Maybe this guy did get us in trouble, but maybe there's another way out. Why are we attacking the construction site? Why not find the headquarters and go there?"

There was a rumble of discussion. The Kings swung toward Rodriguez. Miles pictured the Latin Kings storming the yacht. Not a bad idea except that it wouldn't get him any proof of the oil well.

Rodriguez came up with the same answer.

The tall King shifted uneasily and peered at Miles again. He said, "Then maybe if we give them that guy they leave us alone. Fighting not needed then."

This time Miles sucked in his breath, aware that half the troops were watching him now. He heard Rodriguez' voice, angry at being challenged, yet appraising. "Yeah, I thought of that too, but I couldn't be sure it would work. Anyway, he still owes us twenty thousand."

Miles looked at him. The face, which was turning back to the Kings, was the familiar cold mask. Rodriguez glanced around again. "No more questions? Good. Tomorrow, at twelve, we go in."

SEVENTEEN

AT EXACTLY 11:45 the next morning, a black limousine moved slowly up to Wot Chow Trench's construction site and honked once to attract attention.

Two workers ran into the building immediately. Others quickly unlocked the gate. By the time the car had rolled to a halt, Lai was in the yard to open the back door.

"Mr. Trench," he said, "what a pleasant surprise." He was already starting to sweat because he couldn't think of a reason for the visit. He still hadn't found Miles Bradshaw, but Trench had generally chastised him for that over the phone.

Trench got out of the car. He was heavily bandaged about the chest and shoulders but the head wrappings had been removed. Stitches crisscrossed the face.

A ruddy, barrel-chested man emerged behind him wearing a green-and-blue-plaid jacket, loafers, sunglasses and a digital watch.

Trench said, "This is Mr. Frank Duerr of the Bay Oil Company. The company has been doing some heavy bidding on the site. Mr. Duerr wanted to have a look around."

"Glad to meet you." Lai's smile faded when Ravenel got out of the car, gave a feline stretch, and acknowledged the Filipino with a mocking curl of the lip.

They strolled about the yard, Trench with one hand on Duerr's elbow, the other indicating sights. He bobbed and smiled charmingly, without being subservient, although the heavy stitching lent a grotesqueness to his features. To Lai, however, he still had the same menacing air. From long experience, Lai knew the Korean could turn in an instant from gracious host to deadly inquisitor, and Trench's expressions, no matter how amiable, were masks.

Trench raised his voice over the bulldozer. "My own men. I flew them in for this."

Duerr drank it all in while Lai wondered if the oilman had been told about the burnings. He and Ravenel were trailing Trench by three feet, but, uncomfortable this close to the sailor, Lai edged away.

They neared the building. Trench turned. "How far down are we?"

Lai addressed them both, knowing the answer was for Duerr's benefit because Trench received daily reports. "Fifteen thousand feet. Where we struck the other well. Could be any time."

"Excellent. Excellent." Beaming with the frightening new face, Trench opened the door and the four of them moved inside. The roar of the machinery hit them.

Duerr looked up, awed. "I heard about this but I had to see it."

"I brought it in piece by piece," Trench explained.

"Quite a job but no one ever suspected. We considered using the building itself as a derrick, hoisting the drill from the ceiling. It might have been less expensive, but we decided the traditional way would have structural advantages. Stress."

Four workers in steel hats dotted the rig. Others carried pipes. Strong light streamed in through the skylight and upper windows, motes of dust gold in the beams. The place smelled of wood and steel.

While the oilman was totally engrossed in the view, Trench took a step back and nodded to Ravenel. The sailor took his boss's place, touched Duerr on the shoulder, and began talking.

Trench stepped up to Lai, who started to sweat again.

Ravenel moved off with Duerr, circling the rig.

Trench dropped his smile. "Where's Bradshaw?"

Lai felt the barb move from his groin to his belly but kept his voice steady. "I'm offering ten thousand. He won't run, Mr. Trench, not him. Sooner or later . . ."

Trench said, "I'll have to sell early if you don't find him."

Lai flinched. The Korean's reasonable voice belied a bad mood that might easily worsen if Trench weren't diverted. Casting about frantically for a distraction, Lai's eyes settled on a long steel box resting several yards away against the foundation, partially hidden behind a pile of pipes. "May I show you something?" he said, simultaneously beginning to lead Trench toward the box, which, when opened, revealed a pile of stacked weapons.

"M-16's," Lai said, knowing how much Trench loved to talk about security precautions. He saw the features change to what he hoped was an expression of interest. It was hard to tell with the scars. "I didn't want to risk the guards carrying them when they come in at five and have someone pass by. I thought we'd keep them here. Also"—

he touched a smaller metal box on the wall—"a separate link-up with an apartment five blocks away. Ten men always there. Just hit the button."

Trench said, "I want Bradshaw."

They moved back toward the rig, passing Ravenel and Duerr. Lai was irritated that the sailor got the easy jobs while he got all the problems. He cursed Miles Bradshaw under his breath. No one had ever given him as much trouble as this amateur.

"I'd love that bastard to sneak in here one more time," he said.

The lead Chevy took out the gate at forty miles an hour, veering in from the street, snapping chains, and smashing open the wide, swinging doors. Caught in barbed wire and splintering two-by-fours, it spun into the yard and sent up an arc of gravel.

Miles dug his nails into the back seat, pressed himself into the upholstery, wished he could close his eyes but didn't dare. The car straightened, tossing off debris, and headed for the building. Rodriguez shouted directions from the front seat. Ciccone, in a drunken daze, sat next to Miles.

Two others cars followed, turning right and left, and skidded to a halt. Kings, armed with .45's, .32's and Saturday night specials, jumped out. The arsenal had been emptied for the assault. Three boys from each car herded the workers, who were too stunned to resist, toward a corner spot not visible from the street. The others ran to join Rodriguez at the building. Less than thirty seconds had elapsed since the Kings had crashed the gate. A stolen camera hung from Miles's neck. Rodriguez had tried to charge him for it on the way here.

Sledgehammers and tire irons were in the trunks. The

Kings would smash the machinery after Ciccone set off the blowout.

If Ciccone set off the blowout.

He'd been barely coherent when they'd come to wake him this morning, two empty bottles beside the sleeping bag, his pants wet with urine. He had pleaded with them. "Don't want to go!"

Rodriguez had hit him, dragged him about the room until his legs had begun to function feebly, then poured coffee down his throat and cold water over his head. Ciccone had sputtered all the while. "I'll tell Miles how to do it! Don't make me go!"

Now the scientist stood, tense and ready, outside the doorway of the construction site. Rodriguez had gone ahead with eight Kings to prepare the way, leaving a guard to make sure Ciccone and Miles didn't run.

Rodriguez appeared in the doorway. "Let's go!"

He pulled the scientist inside.

The rig was just as Miles remembered it except that there were no workers on the platform.

At the foot of the platform, four Kings held pistols on a small circle of milling workmen, whose hands were on their heads, fear on their weather-beaten faces. Other boys searched among the machinery and the piles of wood and pipes for roustabouts who might have hidden themselves.

Miles readied the camera, moving forward, spotted Trench among the prisoners, and froze. After a moment his automatic fear reaction changed to joy as the implications of having the Korean in his power sank in. The wrappings had come off the face and Trench, badly scarred, looked like an Oriental Frankenstein. Lai was at his side. Only Ravenel was missing.

Miles composed himself and started taking pictures.

He snapped the prisoners, and Ciccone cutting wires on the blowout preventer and fumbling with the controls while Rodriguez harangued him, as well as the rig from various angles to prove it was inside the building. A photo of the Kings holding guns on Trench's men, especially with an oil well in the background, would grab the attention of any reporter, and plenty of reporters were going to get the pictures.

Miles felt the stirrings of triumph even though the operation wasn't finished yet. Everything was going so unbelievably smoothly. He got pictures of the mud pit and the huge curving floors above. Then, through the lens, he detected a movement behind the platform.

He adjusted the focus.

Miles had grown so confident in the last few moments that the sight of Ravenel running in a crouch in that wide glass field didn't seem real at first. For an instant he watched, captivated. Ravenel was moving out from behind a pile of pipes toward a steel box in a corner, and of course he was real, and had a gun, besides. By the time Miles had moved the camera away from his face, Ravenel had seen him. Miles' warning shout was drowned out by the machinery. Ravenel's arm came up, there was a flash of light at the fist, and something struck the camera.

Miles turned, dodging and flailing his arms to catch attention. The pounding of the machinery seemed to grow louder. He reached the platform and Rodriguez glanced down to where he was pointing, spun, gripped his shoulder and started to topple, his gun falling to the ground. He grabbed the railing with one hand.

Miles leaped up the ladder to help. Something whined by his head and slapped against the steel. As he pulled Rodriguez to the ground he saw Ravenel had a rifle. Miles hit the dirt behind a pile of pipes, pulling Rodriguez to safety. He peeked out just as the head of one of the King guards snapped back, the mouth opened, the red flower burst on the forehead, and then everyone was running:

310

the Kings for protection behind the rig, the workers and
Trench toward Ravenel, who began giving out more rifles.
The rain of bullets began. Two Kings ran ten feet toward
the door and fell, their legs tangling. A crimson stain was
spreading across Rodriguez' jacket. Ciccone, still on the
rig, was flat on his stomach, hands over his ears. A couple
of Kings pitifully returned fire. The Kings were being
flanked.

Only fifteen minutes to disable the machinery, Ciccone had
said. How much time had elapsed since the scientist had
finished, or had he finished at all? And where the hell
had the rifles come from? Why hadn't Jesús known about
them? A boy to Miles' right looked over the top of the
pipes, flew backward and landed on his stomach. Miles
turned him over. Part of the face was shot away. Another
boy grabbed him, screaming in Spanish. Miles pushed him
away, took the gun and turned. A worker stood atop the
pipes; his rifle bucked. The boy beside Miles was still. The
rifle swung toward Miles.

Miles shot the worker.

But the Kings were dropping their guns, raising hands
and emerging from hiding places, the workers surround-
ing them, prodding them into a bloody, helpless circle
dwarfed by the rig. Miles had no choice. He dropped the
gun and joined them.

Lai scurried up the ladder, hauled Ciccone to his feet,
hit him brutally in the face. He frantically began working
the levers, trying to reverse whatever the scientist had
done.

Ravenel sauntered into the circle, grinned, moved up to
Miles, started to ram the rifle butt into his stomach,
stopped an inch away, laughed and turned.

Then Trench appeared.

He moved into the circle, pushing through his men,
agitation barely restrained, his posture slightly less regal

than usual, although his presence was just as commanding. The stitching on the face accentuated the rage and triumph which brutalized the features. This was his moment; the last important obstacle was about to be removed. For an instant he halted, gently touched his face. To Miles, even though the machinery was still operating, the air seemed still. The roaring which had been in his ears diminished. He was clearheaded and calm.

Trench's eyes were grinding him to ashes.

He took a deep breath, realizing he would never see Elena again, and briefly relived moments they had shared, even the escape from the yacht. Then sadness turned to concern when he looked at Rodriguez, who was on the ground, one hand pressing against his chest. Sweat soaked his forehead and he winced periodically. The Kings looked like a bunch of little boys, totally unthreatening, and yet Miles was glad he'd tried to get into the site. If not for Ravenel, he told himself . . . well . . . he'd come damn close to succeeding.

Trench took two steps toward him.

He stopped and cocked his head.

It took a moment and then the others heard it too, a distant rumbling, like a muffled jet engine.

The rig was trembling.

Mud started shooting out of the top.

Gray steaming mud! Ciccone had done it! With a roar the mud plummeted to earth, pelting them, burning, and they began to scatter, but Trench held them together, barking commands. Amid the steaming shower the group moved off, rifles unsteady but still restraining the Kings.

Trench pointed under the platform and gave an order to Ravenel, who, with two workers, rushed to the blowout preventer, grabbed a steel wheel at its side, and, oblivious to the falling mud, began straining to turn it.

"Close it!" Trench yelled, watching the rig as if he expected it to blow apart any second.

312

One of the other workers rushed up to Trench and began gesturing, pointing at the blowout preventer and yelling "Don't do it!" and ". . . pressure once it's started." Trench pushed him away imperiously and waved at Ravenel to keep going.

But suddenly the steel pipe *below the preventer* was splitting open and an arc of steaming water and mud was spraying out. Ravenel and the workers were rolling in the scalding bath, screeching, covering their faces. The workers and the Kings had all hit the dirt or were running away, all except Trench, who was coming at Miles, eyes never wavering.

At that moment the well struck oil.

It was in a hurry to get out after four hundred million years, and it raced up the pipe at two hundred miles an hour, six thousand pounds of pressure per square inch behind it, and it crashed to the surface with a black roar and swept Lai off the platform and must have touched a sparking wire that Ciccone had cut because suddenly Lai was a flaming torch, writhing in the air.

Miles was slammed to earth by the blast. The center of the building was a tower of flame.

The skylight had shattered. Glass fell and fire swept it back into the air. The heat was scorching, the air too thick to breathe. The lower windows blew in, shards slicing at the men. A galelike wind rushed in to feed the blaze. Someone ran by in the wrong direction, toward the fire, blood streaming between his fingers. Kings and workmen were trying to get the door open against the wind, and Miles started to run to help, but something plowed into his shoulder. The earth came up, hard. He rolled over.

Trench was standing above him, a two-by-four in one hand, the firelight doing terrible things to the scars on his face. The club came down just as Miles rolled away and scrambled to his feet. There was an explosion behind them, but neither looked.

313

They circled each other. Trench jerked the club and Miles leaped away, realizing too late that the Korean had feinted. This time the blow caught him on the collarbone. Fighting off excruciating pain, he grabbed the Korean. They fell to the ground, gouging and kicking. Miles drove a fist into the stitched face, heard a grunt, and then Trench was throttling his neck, choking him. He couldn't loosen the hold and he couldn't get away. His shoulder was on fire. Trench was growing hazy. He shoved his fingers into the black eyes and, when Trench tried to protect his face, rolled sideways, pushed himself to his feet, and the Korean got up too, and they were very close to the fire.

The two-by-four lay at Miles' feet. He threw it blindly, saw it hit Trench in the chest. The arms went up in a cartwheel. A powerful gust of wind swept in, caught the flailing body as if it were a parachute, and heaved it toward the flame.

The Korean's scream was drowned out by the machinery. For an instant he was a glowing silhouette. Then he was gone.

Miles gaped at where Trench had been. Smoke billowed from the rig, which was groaning, shimmering in the scorched air. Cinders flew overhead. Coughing, he turned to run.

Something heavy struck his head.

He stood there, swaying, expecting a further blow, trying to focus. His collarbone was in agonizing pain and his head was pounding.

He managed to stumble forward but fell.

People were running into the building. Too big to be Kings, so they must be Trench's men.

No way to stop this fire. The whole sky will be lit up tonight. Maybe, he thought, *I've won.*

He collapsed. Everything was black.

EIGHTEEN

ONE MONTH later in a tastefully decorated Washington, D.C., office, New York City Congressman Lester Mazer prepared himself for what he judged was going to be the most important performance of his career. Ten minutes from now, when the hearing began downstairs, he would emerge into national prominence as the new chairman of the congressional subcommittee on arson in the United States. His picture would be on every television set in the country.

A month ago, Mazer had been a one-term nobody with a less-than-even chance for re-election, particularly since he'd been unable to get the subcommittee to look into arson in his own Bronx district. All that had changed one

315

afternoon when New York City firemen, arriving to combat a sudden blaze in a construction site, had found, astoundingly, an oil well and one of Mazer's star witnesses: Miles Bradshaw.

The former chairman of the subcommittee, Peter Macklinburg, had resigned, and was currently under investigation for alleged ties with a dead Korean businessman and a cartel of oil companies.

Mazer surveyed the files on his desk. There were reports from oil-fire fighter Red Adair, whose men had needed a week to quell the massive blaze, which had lit up the sky for days. There were reports which speculated that the Bruckner Field, as they were calling the new find, would eventually offset twenty-five percent of U.S. foreign oil imports by supplying two million barrels a day. One report dealt with new job possibilities in New York, another with testimony to be given against oil companies which had conspired to keep the field secret until oil prices rose. There were proposals for a pipeline to New England, proposals for revitalization of the West Side docks so that they could feed tankers, proposals for new construction projects and proposals for the return of the land to former owners.

The only certainty in this morass of charges, suggestions and countersuggestions was that Mazer would be in the spotlight for some time. Maybe even the vice-presidency was within reach.

Thank heaven, he thought, *for Miles Bradshaw.*

He left the office and descended in the VIP elevator. Cameras started clicking as soon as he entered the hearing room. Newspaper headlines on the packed tables proclaimed, "Bare Plot to Steal Billions," "Bay Oil Knew About Oil a Year Ago," "Bradshaw to Testify Today."

He banged the gavel. In front of him, in the first row of seats, sat Bradshaw, his wife, Elena, and the seismologist

Ciccone, clad in a new white suit with the bulge of a flask in the breast pocket. And behind them, at least two dozen teenage gangsters in denim jackets.

"I would like to thank Miles Bradshaw for taking time out from his Bronx practice to come here today," said Mazer, "as well as Elena Bradshaw and Dr. John Ciccone, and the representatives from the . . . er . . . Latin Kings . . ." And the newsmen wrote and the cameras whirled, and behind Miles, who was grinning like a happy fool and holding Elena's hand under the table, behind Ciccone, who could have used a nip from the flask, Rodriguez shifted uncomfortably in his seat and looked at his watch. Jesús, beside him, asked, "What's the matter?"

"Nothing. We gotta be back tonight."

"Tonight?" How come?"

Rodriguez delved into his pocket and extracted, as the congressman began asking Elena questions, a book of matches. He opened the book and struck a match, glancing around to see if anyone was watching him. He held the tiny flame between himself and Jesús.

"We got things to do," he said.